KILLING VOICE

He hunched low, darting into an alley, dark and safe in the lee of a dripping overhang. He didn't want to go back out into the light again. Tonight The Voice had indicated deep shadows, a soft amber glow. And he must go where The Voice directed. He had gone to The Temple and prayed on it and he knew his course to be true.

. . . soft amber glow . . .

What could The Voice have meant by that?

He shivered under the windbreaker. He was cold and wet and longed for his quiet apartment, the warm, familiar decor. He ached to get on with it, to get this done. But those who spoke to him had their own timetable, and it was not his place to question. Patience was a virtue. His mother had always said so.

Suddenly, he had a good feeling despite the miserable weather, the glaring, alien surroundings. Tonight was going to be special. Smiling, listening, the man turned from the dark alley.

Time to go hunting . . .

ALSO BY BRUCE ELLIOT

Still Life

DEATH RITES

Bruce Elliot

AN ONYX BOOK

ONYX
Published by New American Library, a division of
Penguin Putnam Inc., 375 Hudson Street,
New York, New York 10014, U.S.A.
Penguin Books Ltd, 80 Strand,
London WC2R 0RL, England
Penguin Books Australia Ltd, Ringwood,
Victoria, Australia
Penguin Books Canada Ltd, 10 Alcorn Avenue,
Toronto, Ontario, Canada M4V 3B2
Penguin Books (N.Z.) Ltd, 182–190 Wairau Road,
Auckland 10, New Zealand

Penguin Books Ltd, Registered Offices:
Harmondsworth, Middlesex, England

First published by Onyx, an imprint of New American Library,
a division of Penguin Putnam Inc.

First Printing, February 2002
10 9 8 7 6 5 4 3 2 1

 REGISTERED TRADEMARK—MARCA REGISTRADA

Printed in the United States of America

PUBLISHER'S NOTE
This is a work of fiction. Names, characters, places, and incidents either are
the product of the author's imagination or are used fictitiously, and any resem-
blance to actual persons, living or dead, business establishments, events, or
locales is entirely coincidental.

For my daughter, Robin
. . . love rites

1

Benson had drunk himself to sleep again.

It was becoming a habit. Not good, and he knew it.

But on those lucky nights he could fall to sleep while Liz was still talking, drift right off in the middle of her conversation, and make it all the way through to three, sometimes four in the morning.

Of course, she was still there when he woke up. Right there in the same place, picking up the thread of conversation like she'd never stopped . . . from brushing his teeth, to picking his tie, to the drive into the office. Liz had always been a tenacious wife. Even more so now she was dead.

Still the booze worked. Even if he had to pay for it the next day in the squad room. Or the same night. Like right now, when the bedside phone jarred them both awake, and he had to reach across Liz there next to him, trying to ignore her disapproval (she'd always hated his job, and apparently still did), grapple for the receiver, and fight his way back up to reality.

"Benson."

"Top o' the morning. The captain wants to buy you a cup of coffee." Amanda Blaine, his partner of four years. And he knew what the coffee catch phrase meant.

"Shit. Are we on call this week?"

"Oh, man, you *do* have a hangover. We got a movie star this time."

"What time is it?"

"It's Sally Struthers time."

"She's a TV star."

"I just said that."

"You said movie star."

"Whatever. Lieutenant Scott would like to know why you don't answer your friggin' cell phone. That's a quote."

"It's"—Benson looked around the clothes-strewn bedroom—"here somewhere. Why didn't he use my home number like you?"

"Because you keep changing it, and some of us you don't inform."

"Lot of fans out there who love me, Mandy."

"Yeah, me too. Some so much they'd like to kill me. You know where Reservoir and Twenty-third is in Silverlake?"

"Yeah, give me ten."

Amanda yawned in the receiver. "Drive safe. She won't get any deader."

The chief wants to buy you a cup of coffee.
It always meant the same thing: get up and go to work immediately, no matter what the hour.

Benson came down Reservoir Road in Silverlake, a stable community not far from L.A. proper but, like so many Southern California communities, cut off from the rest of the world by virtue of its ubiquitous canyons and arroyos. Lost momentarily amid its narrow mountain roads (sometimes with barely room for two cars going opposite ways), it was easy to imagine you were in another world, a world walled away behind tall acacias, drooping palms, and lush ground cover. Until you came around a bend with a break in the foliage, and there spread below you was sprawling Los Angeles and its signature skein of haze.

Benson had nearly bought a house in Silverlake in the late eighties in an attempt to get away from that smoggy skein of haze. That was back in the days of the live Liz, back in another life.

Just before he could close the deal, Liz had had one of her spells. Had it right in front of the owners, right in front of the real estate agent, and the deal, within five minutes, had gone south. So they'd moved to the little house in the valley that Benson had never much liked but which he now occupied. Alone.

Silverlake was nice, though. Had a small-town feeling about it in some ways. Only Benson could never figure out why they called it Silver *Lake*. There was no lake. It was a city reservoir, surrounded by houses on hills and a jogging path. The road he was driving his Mustang over now was even called Reservoir.

"It has water in it," Liz had said, when it was still a possibility. "It's bigger than a pond. It's a lake."

"A lake has trees and bushes and some attempt at landscaping, natural or otherwise," Benson had argued. "This has a cement sidewalk around a cement basin, and not a very pretty one at that. Besides, you can't swim in it."

Liz had sighed out the side window, not in the mood. He'd taken her to Tahoe once—a tourist trap—so he thought he knew lakes. "You're right, Touch," she'd replied with standard Liz sarcasm, "they should have named it 'Silver Basin.' That would have drawn a lot more potential buyers."

"Look," he'd sighed, "I'm only saying—"

"Or 'Lake Culvert'—that would have been pretty. Or how about, 'Lake Titty-Condom?' That has a nice ring."

As always, he'd let it go, stopped while he was behind. You didn't argue with Liz when she was in one of her manic moods, the cost was too high. In this case, the cost of a home. So shortly after that debacle, they'd settled on the valley house, a common tract with no canyons or arroyos and no water at all besides the neighborhood pool for the kids. Kids he and Liz would never have. And soon after, she'd moved out. Into her little Hollywood walk-up to be alone with her painting. She never called and the times he visited, drawn by the aching pain of her absence, he always regretted it. And soon after that she was dead. Murdered. Never to argue with him again. Except as a ghost.

It amazed Benson how much he still missed the live arguing.

The victim, Sally Struthers, lived in an off-orange stucco house with dark green tile roof, the opposite of what you usually saw in L.A.—opposite but tasteful: one of those houses built in the forties on a steep canyon hill riotous with plants and a glaring white cement staircase that went up and up, then turned sharply and went up some more to a veranda with lots more riotous vegetation, this time in pots lining the black railings.

Benson had to block a driveway to park on the hill. He left his keys inside and signaled to a uniformed cop eating a doughnut by the curb. "Move it if you have to, huh?" The patrol cop nodded around a mouthful.

Benson hit the first flight of stairs as another detective was coming down trailing steam: Ditko, tall and rangy, lateral thinker, good man to have at your back.

"What've we got, Steve?" Benson asked.

Benson—not quite awake—wasn't wearing his shield pouch, and Ditko tapped his chest to remind him. Ditko wore his own badge on a necklace. "DB. Young woman. Place is a mess."

Benson paused to clip on his badge. "Sally Struthers?"

"It's not the actress. Somebody screwed that up."

Benson grimaced. "Great." Sniffed. "That coffee smells good."

"Starbucks. Rancho Avenue."

"I came up Reservoir. 7-Eleven."

"Yeah."

Benson was winded by the time he reached the landing, another thing to feel guilty about. He didn't exercise anymore. Didn't jog, didn't walk, didn't watch TV. Didn't sleep. Drank, though.

Amanda was in the foyer taking notes. She looked great this morning; green suit, matching shoes, this great black belt with a big round buckle. Hair done.

"Wow," from Benson, getting her attention, and Amanda looked up, not happily.

"Dressed to go downtown when I got the call."

"On Sunday morning?"

"It's Saturday, Touch."

"Is it? Is her name really Sally Struthers?"

Amanda put the pad in her purse, still watching him—that jaundiced look he knew too well—and joined him. "It isn't the actress."

"I know."

They went down a white narrow hall lined neatly with small tastefully framed David Hockney prints: lots of empty blue swimming pools against eggshell walls; something lonely about it, something sad. The bedroom, mostly obscured for the moment by suit backs, was a mess, like Ditko had said.

The body sprawled naked against a far corner of the bedroom. Sid Mathers, the chief ME, moved aside to do something, and Touch could see that, although her mouth was clamped tight, the victim's eyes were open wide, bulging. Her face was gray. Her chest was punctuated with a series of dark purple stab wounds.

Mathers was at the woman's vulva with plastic-covered hands and absorbent tissue and a little plastic bag beside his bigger black satchel. Benson blinked as a photographer lit up and began taking the scene, his assistant moving the light around, stepping over mountains of debris: lamps, books, tables, like a tornado had hit the room.

When the men were through, Benson stepped past two crime-scene guys and hunkered down beside the ME.

"Hi, Touch. Name's Sally Struthers. She isn't the actress."

"I know," Benson said. "Where's your assistant, Sid?"

"Flu. Some guys have all the luck." Mathers tilted his head and paused in his swabbing. "Condition of vulva and pubic hair suggest recent sexual activity. Looks like semen in there. Lividity would put the death about ten, twelve hours old. Don't ask about the chest wounds."

"Why?"

"Because I don't know what made them. Knife, I'd guess, but what kind? Weird."

Benson leaned over the corpse, peered at the purple inch-wide openings. There was blood, but not as much as one would have thought.

Mathers finished what he was doing, snapped off the plastic gloves. "Not a typical sort of blade—tell you that. Awful wide. Like a damn bayonet or something. Anyway, I'm not convinced that's what killed her."

Benson turned to him in surprise.

Mathers indicated the dried blood pooled beneath the body. "We need the results from tox to be sure, but those kinds of chest wounds would, ordinarily, give up gallons of blood. I'd say the heart had already stopped beating by the time the stabbing started."

Benson looked back at the corpse. "Overkill?"

Mathers shrugged. "You can see from her skin tone she appears to have suffered asphyxiation. But there are no ligature marks, no thumb bruises, nothing around her neck. So that lets out plastic bags and the like." Mathers shook his head. "I don't know. It's a weird one."

"Who's doing the cut?" Benson asked him.

"Think I'll handle this one."

Benson brightened. "Great. By this afternoon, right?"

"Fuck you."

"Tonight then."

"Tonight is Kenny's Little League."

"Come on, Sid."

"Yeah, yeah, by tonight."

Benson used the ME's shoulder to stand. He turned as Amanda came up. "Who called it in?"

"Neighbor," Amanda told him, checking her notebook. "Got her prints all over the doorknobs, inside and out, plus the telephone."

"Nice of her," Benson grunted.

"Got something weird under her nails," Mathers said from the floor.

Benson looked down. "I wish you'd quit using that word 'weird.' Weird how?"

"Weird. Not skin. Fiber I'd say, but not clothing. Not carpet, not drapes, nothing from around here. And have a look at her face."

Benson bent close. She was twenty, maybe twenty-one. Blond. Big bosom. But plain. Or maybe it was just the lack of makeup.

Mathers pointed. "See those lines, kinda crisscrossing, faint but red?"

"What are they?"

"I thought scratches at first, but when I took a swab nothing came up. Just very light upper epidermal marks."

"Made by what?" Benson wanted to know.

Mathers shrugged. "They're fading too fast to find out. Like a slap. No other marks on the body except the stab wounds."

Benson stood, turned to the photographer. "I want good close shots of her face, several."

The man nodded. "I got 'em. All angles."

"Good. And every inch of the room. Every over-turned table and book."

"Yes, sir."

Benson turned back to the body. "No other marks, Sid? You're sure?"

"Oh, light bruises, but not like punches. More like she fell against her own furniture. Not hard enough to do real damage. Skull's untouched."

Benson muttered to himself, "Her own furniture." Then he turned as Steve Ditko came back into the room, joined them in the pit. "Windows?" Benson asked him.

Ditko shook his head. "Locked. Same with the back door. No cellar door. No side doors. Front door wasn't jimmied. Looks like she let him in."

"Or he got her key," Amanda told them. "Or some key."

Ditko shrugged.

Benson kept glancing around the hurricane of a room.

"Sherlock Holmes," a nearby patrol cop summarized.

Benson shouldered past him irritably. "Don't think he's available."

Outside on the steep sidewalk near green trash bags, Amanda asked, "So are we going to handle this now that it's not high profile, or is it the Silverlake Division's?"

Benson shrugged. "I don't know. Scotty will tell us. I just work here. You had breakfast?"

"Yes. I was on my way downtown, remember? They have a sale on dress heels at the Beverly Center this morning. Only now I have to work. Guy couldn't wait to kill her on a workday."

"Life's unjust. How about Denny's? Take my car."

"Christ, Touch, you *always* say goddamn Denny's and I always say no!"

"Boy"—Benson genuflected at the door to his Mustang—"must have been some shoe sale."

Amanda slid into the passenger side next to him. "So. Got any ideas how she died?"

Benson didn't start the car right away.

He stared out the front windshield thoughtfully. "Mandy, how old you think she was?"

Amanda pursed her lips. "Oh, twenty, thereabout."

Benson gazed out the window at thin air.

"Hey!"

He turned to her. Smiled. "You look nice. Nice suit."

"Thanks, you look like shit. What's going on?"

Benson turned back, gave the neighborhood the once-over. Nice neighborhood. Nice morning. "I don't know. I was just thinking . . ." He drifted again.

"Thinking what? You know how she got it?"

"I was just thinking . . ." He shook his head, throwing it off. "Oh, fuck it. You're right. Let's go eat someplace you like this time. Where would you like to go, Amanda Blaine, in your new green suit?"

His partner assessed him patiently. "Are you getting weird on me? This one get to you—is that it?"

Benson looked into her pretty detective eyes. "You know how old I am, Mandy?"

She rolled the pretty eyes. "I get it. This is going to be the she-could-have-been-my-daughter thing, right? The I'm-getting-too-old-for-this-shit speech? Christ, Touch, not today, huh? I just missed the best sale of the year."

Benson didn't smile. He was staring back at the house they'd just left.

"Touch? Hey!" She leaned toward him. "You had a drink before you came this morning, didn't you?"

Benson said nothing.

"Should I be worried about you?" She jabbed his shoulder hard. "Hey!"

He rubbed absently at the shoulder without turning to her. "Did I ever tell you Liz and I almost bought a house out here?"

"Yeah, you told me that." Amanda studied him another moment. "You sure you're all right?"

He gazed at the house a moment longer, snapped out of it again, and turned over the engine quickly. "Yeah, hell, sure, fine. You want to interview the neighbor, or me?"

"I already checked. She's at her doctor. Won't be back for an hour."

He nodded. "Good. That gives us time to eat. Did you say Denny's is okay?"

Amanda sat back with a sigh, shaking her head. "Yeah, Denny's is swell."

2

"Traditionally speaking, of course," Professor Ivers espoused, striding before the ancient blackboard, "the throne of Egypt was held by men alone. Even the lovely Nefertiti, though she may have claimed great renown as a wife, never ruled in her own right."

Before Iver, UCLA Ancient Studies, class of thirty-two, heads down, scribbled furiously on spiral pads to keep up.

Kurstin Mallon, six rows back on the left, scribbled too—though hardly what the other students scribbled—and looked up often, though not at Professor Ivers.

Ivers said, "of course," a lot, as though he owned the words and their meaning. And he didn't *speak* to the students, he *espoused*. A dictionary definition of *espouse* rose in Kurtzy's computerlike brain: *to make one's own; adopt or embrace, as a cause.* It fit Ivers's inflated tone to a tee. Kurstin smirked self-amusement, went on scribbling.

". . . rising in terraces to the cliffs at Deir el Bhri is a complex of colonnaded shrines marking the temple of one of Egypt's most celebrated rulers. Who might that be? Mr. Blackshear?"

Kurstin looked up expectantly. A hard question, and Blackshear never knew anything.

Two rows from front, Lawrence Blackshear looked up hopelessly from his spiral pad, began a thoughtful if feigned tapping of pen against chin, as if he might have some actual clue. "Deir el Bhri . . ."

Professor Ivers paced, hands behind his back, eyes on the floor, chin out, everything—from his neatly trimmed Vandyke to his charcoal jacket with leather elbow patches—was impeccably imperious. "Come, come, Mr. Blackshear, regent to her stepson Thutmose III, she usurped the reins of government even before the prince reached maturity. I believe this was covered in the syllabus."

Blackshear, roundly cowed, withered valiantly. "Not Nefertiti . . ."

Ivers sighed ennui. "Most assuredly not Nefertiti, as I believe we just established."

Blackshear shrank deeper into despair. "Well . . ."

"Miss Holister?"

Kurstin smiled to herself. Kim Holister wouldn't know either, but she was always better at faking it than Blackshear, especially in one of her bright sweaters. Ivers liked girls in bright sweaters.

"Uh, I believe Thutmose reclaimed his throne after her death, is that correct, Professor Ivers?"

"Indeed, Miss Holister, but we're still looking for a name."

No one was scribbling now, except Kurstin, and she was barely looking at her pad at all.

One aisle over, Susan Thornquist wondered how this could be. How could shy, silent Kurtzy write and not look down at what she was writing? Everyone knew she was brilliant, by far the smartest girl in *this* class, the only one who seemed to really understand the material—but she wasn't psychic, was she? Sue stared at her until Kurstin looked up, caught her eye, and blushed. Brilliant or not, people seldom paid Kurtzy much attention. With no makeup and no sweaters, she had a way of blending in with the desks and walls. But she had noticed Sue's attention of late. Looking for some help with her homework perhaps? That was probably it. Certainly not an attempt at genuine friendship. Kurstin couldn't remember the last genuine friendship she'd shared. Still, she smiled politely at Sue, then resumed her scribbling.

". . . one of Egypt's more somber relics lies in a red granite quarry near the town of Aswan," Professor Ivers explained, having apparently given up on Miss Holister and already announced the answer to his question, which Kurtzy knew was Queen Hatshepsut. "It is an immense unfinished statue of Osiris. And mighty Osiris was what? Mr. Billingsly?"

Kurtzy felt rising impatience. Did Ivers *have* to abuse The struggling students this way? It didn't seem fair. Still, Billingsly might know. He'd been quick and incisive with questions about the Third Dynasty. Kurtzy let the answer billow large in her mind, as if she could will it across the room to the grappling Billingsly.

From the corner of her eye she detected Sue Thornquist watching again.

But watching what? A wan, undistinguished face obscured by oversized owl glasses? Dishwater blond hair pulled back in a hardly becoming ponytail? Nothing to be envious of.

Yet nothing to be ashamed of, maybe. It wasn't a bad face, Kurtzy told herself. Good bone structure, in profile maybe almost pretty. No blemishes at least, which some of the girls were covering with pancake. A natural wholesomeness. Okay, maybe even a natural beauty, if she ever really admitted it, ever really half tried.

Maybe Thornquist felt a distant kinship, having made the most of her own natural beauty, maybe that was it. An opposite beauty, of course, dark and vivid and carefully attended. Guys noticed her. Maybe even more than Sue knew. Or cared.

"Miss Thornquist?"

Kurstin blinked from her reverie: Ivers had Sue on the rack.

She glanced over. Sue sat rigidly at her desk, face blank, pale, then red. Dark eyes empty. No clue. No clue at all.

Kurtzy felt herself bristle. *Damn* that Ivers! Damn his snotty superiority!

"We were discussing the fall of Egypt's great and long-lived empire, Miss Thornquist. Lord Byron's famous poem, penned upon seeing the relic in question."

All eyes turned to Sue.

She faltered valiantly. "The relic . . ." Then she stalled.

Ivers waited like a circling shark.

". . . that would be . . . Osiris?"

"Are you asking or answering, Miss Thornquist?"

Sue withered in humiliation, made a stab at it. "Answering?"

Ivers smiled venom. "Incorrectly. Osiris was several minutes ago. We are presently discussing another ancient deity. Would you care to venture a guess? Educated, we can only pray."

Sue closed her eyes, as though summoning answers from the dark. She remained alone there.

"Shelley." Kurtzy blurted across from her. Sue opened astonished eyes.

Professor Ivers adjusted his attention by movement of pupils only. "Beg pardon, Miss Mallon?"

All eyes on Kurtzy now.

She looked up from her scribbling—not notes, but a pencil portrait of hunky Jason Richards four rows down. She met Ivers's stony challenge with guarded confidence. She had the answers. She always had the answers. More answers than Ivers. Did she have the courage, though, to cross him, to risk a grade for a girl she couldn't really yet call friend?

"The statue in question is Ramses II." Kurtzy spoke softly, barely audibly.

"Didn't quite catch that, Miss Mallon. Bit more volume if you will, so the whole class can hear."

Kurtzy swallowed. "The statue is Ramses II. The poet was Shelley, I believe, not Lord Byron."

Ivers's icy smile held a moment, then seemed to fade slightly. He turned quickly to his desk, riffled pages. In a moment he cleared his throat, brightened disingenuously. "Ah . . ."

All eyes fixed on the professor now.

"Ah . . . yes. Quite right, Miss Mallon. Well!" He slapped the book shut. "It seems someone in class has been doing her homework at least."

Kurtzy sighed inward relief.

The ice returned to Ivers's eyes. Damn. He wasn't going to let her off easy.

"Perhaps Miss Mallon would grace us with a recitation of said poem."

Sue watched, face apprehensive, as Kurtzy removed her glasses from the bridge of her nose, placed them atop her portrait, and glanced briefly at Jason Richards's Byronic face. He was looking right at her. She felt her knees give. Ivers was one thing . . . but to actually have the attention of Jason Richards . . .

" 'On the sand, Half sunk, a shattered visage lies . . . And on the pedestal these words appear: My name is Ozymandias, king of kings: look on my works, ye Mighty, and despair!' "

Ivers lifted a sculped brow. "Very nice, Miss Mallon." And the bell rang.

Kurtzy tucked her portrait safely into the back of her notebook. Had—in the ensuing rush of student bodies pushing for the door—Jason's eyes lingered a moment on hers?

Just a moment?

"Hey."

Kurtzy turned in the echo-distorted hallway, thinking for one mad moment that it might be a jealous Jana Ransom. Everybody knew she and Jason were heavy.

Of course it wasn't. Silly.

Sue Thornquist caught up to her. "Hey, thanks for saving my ass."

Kurtzy shrugged demurely. Would saying "you're welcome" be improper, imply Sue was stupid? God, she was never any good at social protocol, never any good at all. So she said nothing at all. Which probably came off as snotty. Like Ivers. Great!

But Sue didn't seem offended. Fell right into step beside her. The first time someone had walked school halls with Kurtzy since she could remember. Maybe ever.

"How did you do that, anyway?"

"Do? What?" Had she stepped on someone's foot?

"Sit through Ivers's lecture and not take notes? I scribble till my hand falls off and I still can't keep up with him. Fatuous prick."

Kurtzy tried to turn her reflexive laugh into a sneeze. It didn't work.

Sue grinned, played to it. "Self-inflated asswipe."

Kurtzy sputtered laughter, craning around them in horror. No one was looking.

Now Sue was chuckling. "You are one mopey chick, Mallon."

Kurtzy stiffened. Here it came. She had humiliated Sue in class and now she was—

"But you've got a nice smile. When you use it. Why don't you?"

Kurtzy gripped her books. Was this a trick question? Her mind raced. She could quote school text verbatim, but in the hallways all questions were potential tricks.

"So. Do you always chatter away like this?"

Don't say anything. It's best if you don't risk screwing it up. "When there's something worth chattering about," someone said that turned out to be her. *Idiot!*

But cute, dark-eyed Sue was laughing. "And the owl glasses—you always wear those too?"

"Only to see with."

Sue elbowed her. Hard but friendly. "Well, they're pretty bad, girlfriend."

Kurtzy shrugged. "Dorothy Parker did all right with them."

Thornquist blinked. "Who?"

Kurtzy turned to her. Sue had no idea. But she was still smiling. A nice smile. And had somebody just called her "girlfriend"?

"Anyway, thanks for rescuing my butt. Where you headed?"

"Headed?"

"You have another class right now?"

"No. I was going to Residence Life to sort out a problem with my room and—"

"How about a drink? I'm buying."

Was this really happening? "At the student union you mean?"

Sue's laugh was loud now. Harsh. But still somehow without malice. High and sharp and wondrously unabashed. "I said *drink*, Kurtzy. The nerds go to the union. I was thinking of His Pants."

"Off campus?"

"Doesn't your mommy let you go off campus?"

Kurtzy looked at her blankly. "She's dead."

Now why had she said that? Why tell that to a perfect stranger, someone just trying to be friendly. It was curt. Embarrassing. Thornquist would hate her now.

But Sue was still smiling. "Then she won't mind, I guess."

Kurtzy glanced askance at her, searching for hidden meaning in the dark, bright eyes, finding none. Then, to her astonishment, Kurtzy laughed.

In a moment, both girls were laughing. Walking down the university hall together laughing out loud.

And no one seemed to notice.

His Pants was crowded. Some townies, mostly students.

Loud students. Nice-looking students. The beautiful people.

Sue ordered beer for them, pulling out a realistic-looking fake ID. In the middle of the day, thought Kurtzy, who'd never had a beer before, never wanted one particularly. She took a tentative sip, found it bitter and smelly as piss. With a pleasant aftertaste.

"So who were you drawing?" Thornquist gulped.

"What do you mean?"

"Come on! In class. Is it your boyfriend?"

"No, I was just—"

"Can I see it?"

"It's nothing, really."

"Jesus, does a person always have to pry stuff out of you? Let me have a look!"

"It isn't good."

"Oh. Okay, then I really don't feel I can associate with you any longer."

Kurtzy couldn't not smile. She sighed, fumbled in her notebook, and drew out the sketch. Hesitated. Made a face and slid it across the scarred oak.

Sue said nothing for nearly a minute. But her mouth

parted slightly. "Jesus. You're good. This is . . . you're really good."

"No." But Kurtzy's heart swelled.

"Don't tell me. My parents crammed art lessons down my throat for ten years before they croaked. Wow. It's Jason Richards, isn't it? Are you dating him?"

Kurtzy faltered. Was Sue making fun of her? "No. Of course not. He's going with Jana Ransom."

"Oh, yeah. Ransom. The pedigree with the boobs."

"She seems nice."

Thornquist snorted. "We were at summer camp together once in high school. Want to know something about Miss Pom Pom?"

Sue leaned toward Kurtzy confidently.

"Jana girl's got a bed-wetting problem."

Kurtzy sat in disbelief.

"Hey, swear to God! She had to take pills for it, the whole nine yards. And sometimes the old pills didn't work. Ask Kim Saunders. She bunked below her. Watch out, leaky roof!"

Kurtzy smiled hazily, beer on an empty stomach probably. Was this going to be a real friendship?

Sue handed back the portrait. "You should give it to Jason."

Kurtzy actually blushed at the idea.

"No kidding. He's actually pretty bright outside of asshole Ivers's class. Bright enough to see that kind of talent. Who isn't?"

Kurtzy tucked the portrait away. "No, I . . ."

"Why not. You're hot for him, aren't you?"

Kurtzy looked wistful. "As you said, 'Who isn't?' "

Sue watched her a moment, then leaned across and

touched her wrist. So unexpected a move, so rare in her life, Kurtzy nearly jerked away, which would have spoiled it. "Hey. He's just a guy. And Ransom is just a girl. No better than you." Her eyes roamed Kurtzy's pale face a moment. "And no prettier, really."

She reached out, pulled a stray curl from the wan little face. Kurtzy was so glad she remembered not to flinch. "Not that you couldn't use some pointers. You allergic or something?"

Kurtzy actually didn't get it for a second. "To makeup? No. I just—"

Sue sat back so quickly Kurtzy felt her heart jump. "Hey! I'm about to be brilliant!"

A makeover, Kurtzy thought with rising panic. She's going to offer to give me a makeover . . .

"My roommate's moving off campus next week. Three more days and I'm free of the stuck-up bitch! What do you say?"

This *had* to be a rib. It had all come to this moment when the joke would at last be revealed. "A-are you asking me to move in with you, Sue?"

"It's Dykstra Hall. Coziest little dorm on campus."

"Well, I probably do need to move, but . . ."

"Why not? We could gab all night and never get any homework done." She flashed a smile. "I'm dark, you're light. You're brilliant, I'm an ignoramus. A marriage made in heaven!"

This was real. Really happening. Right now. She'd made a friend.

Head swimming ever so slightly, Kurtzy felt herself nodding. Then laughing.

Both of them laughing again.

A day that seemed created for laughter.

3

The first time Charlie visited The Temple he was eight years old.

It changed his life. Changed the course of his life.

He sat quietly within The Temple's warm glow and let it cast its magic over him. Its reverence. It was here he encountered the Ancient Ones in their dark and shadowed places. It was here he was taught their single driving message. Which was, of course, the path of his journey, the map for the rest of his life.

At home that night he watched Nephthys dance for the first time.

Charlie sat on the lumpy cushions of his sprung green sofa and, under billowing fireplace glow, watched the goddess dance. Watched her swoop and spin and draw him inexorably into her world, draw his preadolescent mind into hers, into a place where he was held spellbound in the warmth and security of her embrace.

The goddess danced and danced until the worn phonograph record jumped with pops and skips, and still she danced for him, ivory skin a sheen of sweet-smelling sweat, flashing eyes and golden hair holding him steadfast, mesmerized. *This is your destiny,* the goddess told him, and never uttered a word.

Then—the dance at last finished—the shimmering Nephthys of the cascading tresses and trembling bosom padded to Charlie's sofa, offered him her hand, and led him into the next room of the old house. A small house with thin, faded walls.

Outside in the dark, a passerby would have heard her groans.

There was a long black space after the fire.

A blank spot, during which Charlie never saw The Temple again, never saw the goddess Nephthys dance for him.

It was as if his memory, wrapped in his personality, went away and hid somewhere.

He recalled little about the fire, except for the obvious things it did to him, to his face. He vaguely remembered that—now the goddess was gone, the Ancient Ones seemingly abandoned him—he was sent away to spend a portion of his life living with his aunt and uncle in a little town not far from Blaine, Missouri, which was not far from St. Louis. But he didn't remember much else.

An occasional unpleasant flash—the kids at school staring at his waxy face, then looking quickly away . . . secrets whispered, giggles behind his back, fists pounding him on the playground blacktop, the repugnant wince of the teacher every time he came near to turn in a paper . . .

Little else.

He recalled time in a hospital, the antiseptic reek, his body swathed in bandages from head to foot, half conscious on drugs, half afire from a pain so intense it was nearly exquisite. More clearly he recalled his ascent, during which he rose from his own ashes like a phoenix, thus proving his royal origins (at least to himself, though the doctors concluded possible brain damage). Then, for a few months in St. Louis, further recovery in a different kind of hospital, a funny kind of hospital that didn't have the antiseptic smell of the burn unit, smelled only of flowers, so many flowers in so many bright colors it was nearly suffocating.

Most of the time in that place he spent walking. In the garden. In the halls. In his little room. Walked and thought about The Temple and the dancing goddess but mostly just breathed—in and out, in and out, suffocating flowers or no—amazed that he was still alive, that he had lived and the goddess had died.

Then there was some time afterward working. Working in a cold place, an icehouse it was called, where he lifted heavy, translucent blocks all day, and hauled big pallets of brown sacks that left his skinny back slightly bent and his skinny arms ropy with muscle. There was a dog at the icehouse that belonged to the owner, a nice little black dog that liked everyone and that Charlie petted at lunchtime outside on the loading dock under the warm sun. But somebody killed the dog—Charlie didn't know who—and shortly afterward, Charlie was fired from the job and sent back to live with his aunt and uncle.

One night he ran away from there. He couldn't remember why. They were perfectly nice people. His aunt even looked a bit like the goddess Nephthys. But he ran away. Hopped a freight. Went two whole nights without eating or drinking. All the way to the end of the line.

The end of the line was California. Los Angeles. *Home.*

The sun was warm here, a kingdom built on sand, like his beloved Egypt, yet everything verdant as the Nile, the trees filled with fruit and singing birds, the sky forever blue. Truly a home for royalty. And that alone would have assured his stay.

What really did it, though—what really made Charlie know he was at last home again—was the day he found The Temple again.

Just seeing it brought back a torrent of memories.

Walking its sacred halls reminded him again why he was here on Earth.

His purpose. Who he was.

It was The Temple that reawakened his memory. It was The Voice that put him in motion.

He heard it shortly after he arrived, shortly after he took the little run-down apartment and got himself a job, some money to live on. The Voice spoke to him every week, like clockwork, and he listened, entranced. And always did as The Voice instructed.

What choice did he have? He was home again. This was his destiny. And when it was fulfilled he would be complete. He had The Temple, he had a place to live, he had a job. All he needed was a wife.

There were certain caveats, however.

The Voice was sometimes confusing.

Oh, its directives were clear. There was nothing vague about its commandments, no doubt in Charlie's mind that he was The Chosen One. But the thing was, The Voice didn't always get it right. Or maybe it was Charlie who wasn't getting it quite right. Maybe he was the one doing something wrong. Or maybe the whole thing was some kind of test for him, devised by the Ancient Ones.

It was all very confusing sometimes. The only thing for certain was that The Voice was always there. Dependable. Every week. That much was clear and bright as the rising sun.

Finding his destined wife—that wasn't so clear.

4

Amanda finally reached Benson on his cell phone. "Where the hell are you?"

"I'm home. What time is it?"

"It's three in the afternoon. Jesus, Touch, are you sleeping?"

"What's going on?"

A metallic sigh in the receiver. "We were supposed to be in Noland's office an hour ago to discuss the Sally Struthers thing."

Benson pushed up on his green sofa and reached for what was left of a warm bottle of Budweiser, knocking it over and ruining Jennifer Lopez's face on the cover of *Newsweek*. "Oh, yeah. Is he pissed?"

"Are you sick?"

"No. Is he pissed?"

"I covered for you. As usual."

"As usual. Like always. My sweet partner. I've been thinking. Will you marry me?"

"Okay. But there's that problem."

"Your husband? We'll work something out. Did Noland think it was Sally Struthers the actress? Did he make his frog face?"

"Why are you at home if you're not sick? You sound like you've been boozing."

"You are fucking uncanny. How do women do that? Just a little beer. I was wrestling with this thing. And I fell asleep. Wrestling with this thing."

"The Sally Struthers thing?"

"What to wear. I'm going to go, Mandy. I've decided to go. I've never been, and I think I should go because it would be good for me . . . get me—you know—out of myself. I think I never went before because I was afraid of what to say . . . What if somebody recognized me and I didn't know them sort of thing. But I've conquered my fear and I'm damn well going to go and not be a chickenshit about this thing. I've decided."

"Great."

"So will you go with me?"

"This is the high school reunion thing?"

"You're in Beverly Hills, aren't you? You're outside, right? Know how I know that? How my agile cop's mind has deduced that from clear over here on the phone?"

"You can hear traffic?"

"I can hear that little ping-ping thing they have on crosswalks there for blind people."

"What is my husband going to think if I'm your date to your high school reunion?"

"Tell him you're working. He doesn't give a shit anyway."

Silence.

"Shit. Mandy, I didn't mean it that way. I'm sorry. Christ, I am drunk. Let's just forget the whole thing, stupid idea anyway, stupid high school reunion. What the fuck am I going to say to those people? Hi, remember me, Amiel Benson? I married Lizzie Holcraft, the manic depressive. She got more manic and made my life hell, and by the way, she was murdered because I wasn't around."

"Wear your blue suit."

"You think?"

"Can't go wrong with blue, highbrow or low-. I'll wear the green number. We should go well together."

"We do go well together. Will you marry me?"

"After the reunion. Pick me up at eight."

"I think it starts at seven."

"Nothing starts at seven. And sober up."

"I can't. I'm scared."

"You're depressed. And it ain't about the reunion. We need to talk."

"You're a good friend to me, Mandy. Selfless. Caring . . ."

"I'm not getting my ass shot off on a bust 'cause you're drunk."

". . . selfless . . . caring . . ."

"The blue suit. And sober up."

There was lots of crepe paper in the Glendale High gymnasium. They certainly got that right. Even the flowers were made of crepe paper—black and gold, Glendale Cougar colors—and they were strung all over the ceiling and all over the walls and around the edges of the tables and the edges of the bandstand

and dangling in long streamers from the ceiling and
the basketball hoops and the big painted banner that
said:

1977 WELCOME COUGARS 2002

Benson wondered who in hell would commit to such
a task, much less so spiritedly. Some people, he supposed, just stayed spirited, just carried that high school
pluck right along with them into adult life.

Mary Kay Soppit certainly did. You could see it in
her bearing, in her carriage, in her every gesture,
which was exactly the same as when she addressed the
assembly during inner-city debate. She smiled a lot
then, smiled a lot now. She'd had no waist and no
chest then. Now she had both, mostly waist. Still had
the smile though. Benson had never had anything to
say to her, had studiously avoided the journalism
clique and hung with the jocks. But Mary Kay had
had a thing for him, and paranoid that she still might,
Benson spent the evening guiding Amanda expertly
around Mary Kay Soppit (or Comstock or whatever
her name was now) and several other men and women
in the crowded hall, which echoed with too much
Beach Boys music even though the Beach Boys had
pretty much broken up by 1976. Like the class had
broken up, gone its separate ways, leaving very little
but superficial prattle to say to each other, the men
all wondering if they'd done better than the other
guys, the women all wondering if they looked as old
as the rest.

Amanda, for one, looked great. Even better in the
green suit than she had the other day. Several years

younger than Benson's classmates and in great shape by virtue of her profession, she got looks from both sexes. Benson found himself proud to be dancing with her, content that those who didn't ask assumed he and Amanda were married, that he'd married a beautiful woman with a knockout bod and was doubtless a happy man.

Amanda smiled graciously at everyone and drank punch and brushed crepe from her face and danced with Touch and enjoyed herself, or seemed to. Anyway, Benson was a good dancer despite his size, and Amanda loved to dance. Her husband never danced with her.

"Wow," she said, holding him as the band slid into "In My Room."

Benson turned his head. "What?"

"By the punch bowl. I think she's looking at you."

Slim and pretty with a stunning orange strapless dress that shone like a flower amid conservative oaks. Whoever she was, she wasn't afraid to wear something as bright and daring as a high school girl. "No . . . I don't think so," Benson murmured. "I don't remember her."

"Too bad. Some dress. Some rack, for that matter. Listen, you dance divinely, Touch, but I really have to pee."

Benson motioned past the band. "Down the hall there past the pool, but you'll need a hall pass."

"A pass to piss. Ah, those were the days. Why don't you mix a little? I don't think the handsome rebel shtick is working. And, Touch? Lay off the booze. You stepped on my toe." She turned to go.

"The hell I did!"

"Almost. We need to talk."

"I'm not depressed, if that's what you're suggesting," he said but she was in the crowd and he was talking to himself.

Alone in the middle of the old gym floor about ten feet from the free throw line where he used to swoosh 'em and make the crowd cheer. *Only you're all alone now. A roomful of people and you're all alone . . .*

Guess what, he told himself. I was alone *then*.

He turned and his breath caught. Mary Kay Soppit was elbowing her way through the alumni, a *how-about-a-dance?* look on her constantly smiling face.

Benson turned again quickly. Where was the fucking punch bowl?

"Hi, stranger. Dance?"

It was the woman in the orange flowered strapless. Not as young this close up, but prettier, if anything. And somehow familiar.

"Unless your wife would mind—?"

"She wouldn't mind." Benson checked the ample bosom but she covered the name tag with her hand.

"Not so fast! Keep looking. It'll come to you, Amiel."

Benson floundered. "Well . . . no one's called me 'Amiel' since the eighth grade."

"Where you met the kid who could always outrun you." She extended a slim forearm. "Who sacrificed her life's fluid to be your blood brother . . . though the exact phrasing of that always eluded me."

Benson almost had it.

"Going to leave me hanging again, Amiel? Like that balmy summer, that starry, starry night?"

And the memory was there. Abruptly complete. "Michelle."

The woman in orange beamed, then forced a mock frown. "Just so you know, I'm not entirely prepared to forgive you for that long-ago night . . . those long-ago promises."

Benson held her hands marveling, all of it flooding back now. "Promised to take you to the sophomore ball. Stood you up." He shook his head. "I must have been a fool."

"Yes"—she smiled warmly, delightfully—"I always thought so."

Benson pulled her close, bussed her cheek. But even here the ghost haunted him. The girl he'd stood up Michelle Ransom for was Liz.

She caught it in his eyes, fast as ever. "Touch—?"

"Sorry. You just look so . . ."

She winked. "What contact lenses and a little lipstick can do, huh?"

"Mikki, dear Mikki. How can I ever apologize for the sophomore ball?"

Michelle glanced past him, lifted her arms. "Well, unless you'd rather deal with Mary Kay Soppit, who is headed decidedly this way, I suggest you ask me to dance." She came quickly into his arms. "I respectfully accept."

Benson held her, guided her swiftly to the middle of the gym floor. She was light as a feather, lighter even than Amanda. She smiled up at him, blond curls fanning. "Wow! No wonder they called you 'Touch.' Is this what I missed that night?"

"The 'Touch' was from football, actually."

"I remember. Do they still call you that?"

"Friends. Or associates."

"Which? Friends or associates?"

"Well, I have no friends, so . . ."

She laughed. A musical laugh, incongruously low and sexy. "And those wonderful different colored eyes. One green, one . . . is it blue or gray?"

"It's something to do with genes, less pigment or something. I'm defective."

"Only once. And after this dance, I may yet forgive you."

That great voice. Even as a kid. Totally distinct, husky. He should have recognized it immediately. All those youthful late-night hours, talking, about anything and everything, the most natural rapport he'd ever had with any woman, except maybe Mandy.

They'd stay up on her father's roof until dawn, gazing through her telescope at L.A. nights that actually contained stars as well as smog. Hot afternoons they'd scour the canyons with canteens and pretzels, looking for gopher snakes and scorpions and other creepy crawlies most girls wouldn't get near, much less touch. Weekends his parents would haul them to the drive-in to endure the latest triple-feature horror fest. Their parents were on the PTA. Everyone knew everyone back then, trusted everyone. Trusted him and Michelle to be alone together and away from prying eyes.

And never once had he taken advantage of it. Even kissed her. How had he let that happen?

He looked down. She was watching him. Reading his mind.

But then, she always could.

She had that old smile. Slightly lopsided, slightly sad. She tilted her head. "Dear Touch. Don't worry. You would have. Kissed me."

He made a wry sound. "But I didn't . . ."

She reached up and pecked his cheek. "Just wasn't enough time, Amiel. But we're not dead yet."

They swayed silently to the music. For a moment he thought it was something he'd said, that she'd grown pensive. Until he remembered that one thing he could never do was offend her. Never. In any way.

It wasn't pensiveness. But there was something about her now that hadn't been there before, some tenseness, a feeling of something unsaid. As if perhaps her light tone was a cover-up.

"She's very pretty, by the way," Michelle said against his chest. "Is she your wife?"

It actually took him a moment. "Amanda? She's my partner. I work for the LAPD. Homicide."

She raised an eyebrow. "You're a policeman? I always thought you'd end up in the natural sciences."

"Just a flatfoot. How about you? Did you pursue neurosurgery?"

She smiled. "I can't believe you remembered that."

"It's all you talked about, becoming a doctor, joining the Peace Corps?"

She snorted a laugh, but the smile faded. "Halcyon days." She looked wistful. "I was a paramedic for a while but I dropped out of medical school in my third year."

"You're kidding!" Though she obviously wasn't. "But why, Mikki?"

She tilted her chin at him, flashed that gorgeous smile. "No one calls me Mikki anymore."

"No. You're definitely a Michelle now."

And something passed between them, very old and very new. What had been, what might have been, what could be.

"I heard about Liz Holcraft, Touch. I'm so sorry."

And as if sensing his pain she immediately drew him close again. "It was terrible, wasn't it?"

Terrible enough that I may still be in love with her, he thought, but didn't tell her.

"Can you talk? Or . . . you don't have to . . ."

"I can talk." Benson shrugged. "Well, she was beautiful—you knew that. She was . . . *excruciatingly* intelligent. Being manic depressive the sex, of course, was great. And, well, the marriage went to shit as it naturally had to, and she moved out, into this little . . . apartment—I started to say hovel—to become a painter."

"A painter?"

"A painter, yes. And she couldn't pay the rent and wouldn't take money from me, so she advertised for a roommate. And the roommate turned out to be nuttier than Lizzie and . . . killed her."

"God. That's awful. I'm so sorry."

"I'll survive," he said shortly, not certain it was true. He realized suddenly the music had stopped and he was still holding Mikki—*Michelle*. He took her hand and led her back to the table. "Your turn."

"Well, I live in Pasadena now. I have a daughter in college who is devastating—beautiful, I mean—and smart enough not to waste it on Hollywood, and I have a dog with no pedigree and no back leg, and let's see . . . I have a degree in law and specialize in medical malpractice. And here comes your date, thank God, to save my dignity."

"Partner."

"Right." She gave him a quick glance. "Funny . . . looks more like your date." Michelle smiled as Amanda came up and said, "Hi. Michelle Ransom!" She extended her hand. "You can have him back now."

"Amanda Blaine. I hate your dress!"

"Thank you!" Michelle exclaimed, delighted. "How sweet! Sure you're not dating her, Touch? She's terrific."

"Terrific and married," Amanda said, and wiggled her cell phone at Benson with that face she always made.

Benson said, "Shit."

"Your husband?" Michelle asked innocently.

Amanda smiled. "Work. Sorry."

"Me too." She looked it. "Well. It was nice meeting you, Amanda."

Michelle stood on her toes again, kissed Benson lightly on the cheek. "I enjoyed the dance."

It became awkward.

Amanda looked from Michelle to Benson. "Touch—?"

"Huh?"

"Give her your card, Touch." She looked back at Michelle with vast patience. "He doesn't remember phone numbers, has to write everything down. An entire department, and they stick me with him."

"He's a good dancer, though."

"Yes. Weird, isn't it?"

Michelle scribbled on the back of his card and handed it back to Benson. She winked, the way she'd always winked as they said good-bye.

"Good to see you again, Michelle."

"Bet your bippy."

*   *   *

In the parking lot, Amanda said, "Please tell me your cell phone's got a dead battery."

Benson said nothing for a moment. "I left it at home."

"Jesus, Touch."

"We have to talk, I know. Am I in trouble?"

"I told Noland your cell phone had a dead battery. But I'm not the only one who's noticed the drinking."

"Okay, we'll talk."

Amanda looked at him as they marched to their cars. "Bet your bippy?"

Benson grinned. "Something we used to say as kids."

Amanda nodded. "She's beautiful, Touch. And smart."

"Thank you, Mother. What have we got?"

Amanda waited for him to unlock the Mustang's passenger door, threw her purse in the back, and slid in. "Santa Monica. The beach. Sally Struthers number two, it looks like."

"Crap," Benson said, climbing behind the wheel. "The beach. And I wore the blue suit."

5

"Her name was Allison Downey," the officer-on-the-scene read from his notebook. "Worked in the post office off Melrose. Was liked but shy, real mousy type, didn't date much. She leaves behind a sickly mother and no boyfriends we can find. That's about it."

She lay crumpled nude in the sand near a tall palm, not a hundred yards from the Santa Monica Pier. And there were always lots of people on the Santa Monica Pier.

"So how the hell did he kill her without being seen?" Captain Noland wanted to know. That Noland was here, attending the crime scene, was an indication that things were heating up. Next stop: mayor's office.

Sid Mathers, the chief ME, was just snapping off his plastic gloves, brushing sand from his brown slacks. Benson and Amanda watched him expectantly. "Well . . . we got us another Sally Struthers, it looks like. Same indications of asphyxiation, same unmarked, bruise-free body, victim recently engaged in intercourse. Willingly, I'd say. And, 'course, the stab wounds to the chest."

"How do you know that?" Noland stepped closer, wincing, but not from the corpse. He'd been called out of bed and put on the wrong shoes; sand was seeping into his loafers. "I mean how can you be sure it's the same as the Struthers girl? Lots of people get stabbed."

"Like I said, no bruising. No tearing of the labia, no roughhouse in that area." Mathers bent again and lifted the corpse's hand. "No blood or tissue under the nails, though there's a small piece of nail missing. And this again . . ."

Everyone but Benson stepped closer; Benson was doing something else.

Mathers held up a small plastic evidence bag. "Fiber."

Noland squinted. "Same stuff we found under Sally Struthers's nails? Stuff the lab still can't identify?"

Mathers nodded. "That and some other stuff. Looks organic."

"Skin?" Amanda, asked her arms wrapped about her, not dressed for the night chill.

"Not skin." Mathers took the bag back from the captain, held it to his Maglite, squinting. "I'd say wood fiber. Living."

Captain Noland made a face. "Living?"

"Fresh from the tree."

"Here's the tree," Benson called beside a tall palm, running his fingers over the bowl. Everyone stepped over. Bent, shone their lights. Noland turned to a uniform. "Cassidy, get that arc lamp over here!"

The white lamp glare showed several vivid runnels in the bark. Mathers studied them a moment, reached out with delicate fingers. "Ah." He smiled triumphantly. "My piece of missing fingernail."

Amanda stepped close, squinting. "Huh. She was trying to climb the tree, you think? Get away?"

A nearby uniform scoffed. "You don't climb one of those things, not unless you're a goddamn Samoan. Smooth as owl shit."

"Maybe she was sharpening her nails on them." A short uniform named Sydney smiled cutely. All eyes regarded him stonily. Sydney dropped the smile and turned away to scribble on his pad.

"Let's get the yellow tape up quick," Benson said from some distance away, "and I want a thirty-yard perimeter."

Noland gave him a sour look. He had never liked Benson, never liked the way everybody else did like him. Noland trudged smugly through the truculent sand to Benson's back. "Why the big perimeter, Detective?"

Benson swept his arm in a wide semicircle. "Look around. The sand outside where we're standing is relatively undisturbed, normal beach traffic. Right around the area where the victim was discovered it's all kicked up. She struggled. A lot. Tried to get away, I'd say."

Noland poked his fists on his hips with attitude. "You'd say that, huh? Well, the chief ME here says there was no struggle."

"No sexual struggle," Mathers corrected, coming to Benson's aid. "She could have tried to get away from him afterward. I'm only saying it doesn't look like rape."

Noland grunted, turned to Amanda, who stood barefoot, having come down here without shoes to navigate the sand. Noland stared at her long legs. Amanda endured it, as they all endured their captain's chauvinism, could do little else and keep their jobs.

Noland said, "So she has consensual sex, gets pissed, tries to leave, and he stabs and strangles her. Why both? And how? Where are the ligatures, the bruising? Even if he used ether she'd go for his face, his arms."

"He suffocated her first, then stabbed her," Mathers said. "Just like he did the Struthers girl. What we can't confirm is the type of knife. There isn't a blade on file that leaves that kind of wound. Also can't confirm if he drugged them first, until the tox report comes back."

Noland was cold and sandy and out of patience. "Okay, this is overkill, typical serial behavior. Why the hell else suffocate *and* stab her?" Noland winced again in his shoes. "Come on, people, let's get some answers. This is strike two! One more and we get a free enema from the DA's office!"

He turned back to Benson, who was still staring at the palm tree. "Let me know, Detective, if you find any coconuts with prints we can use up there." And when Benson still didn't turn, Noland added, "Or cell phone batteries."

Benson looked at him.

A crowd was gathering and ocean breezes were picking up.

Noland turned, grimacing at the sand. "Let's wrap it up, ladies," he said, speaking his signature departing comment. Then he trudged through the dunes back to his car.

Benson walked to the body, looked down at the blue face, the bulging eyes.

"Any of those funny red marks on her face this time?" he asked Mathers.

"Not by the time we got here, Touch." His cell phone burred. "Yeah, Mathers."

Benson kept looking back at the palm tree.

Mathers said to the phone, "Uh-huh. Where? You're kidding. Huh. All right. No, I'll be in later." He thumbed down the aerial.

He turned to Amanda and Touch. "Lab got an ID on the stuff under Sally Struthers's nails."

Benson looked up at him.

"Looks like cotton but it's not. Grows on a plant in the desert."

"California?"

"Nope. Farther east."

"Come on, Sid, what desert?"

Mathers smiled, enjoying this one. "Egyptian."

At home, later, Benson kicked off his shoes, turned on CNN twenty-four-hour news, poured himself a shot of Jim Beam, and sat in his green easy chair with all lights but the TV off.

After a moment he sat up, poured the drink back into the bottle, and reached for his coat jacket. He retrieved the card from his wallet and grabbed the phone. He sat there with his hand on the receiver for a moment, then lifted it and dialed.

"Hello?"

"Hi. Is this the most beautiful high school girl in Pasadena?"

"Why, how did you know?"

"We were always psychically linked, remember?"

"Ah!"

"For instance, I will now describe your present apparel. A long, but shamefully translucent nightgown. Blue. With matching panties, of course."

Silence.

"Hello? Michelle?"

"Uh . . . hold on a sec . . . *Mom! I think this is for you!*"

Oh, Christ.

"Hello?"

"This is beyond embarrassing."

"Touch, is that you? What's the matter?"

"Was that your daughter?"

"Yes, that was Jana. What happened?"

He could hear laughter in the background. "I'm sure she'll tell you all about it. I'm going to make myself comfortable in a very deep hole now."

"What on earth is going on?"

"I was describing her sleeping apparel. *'Translucent and shameless,'* I think were the terms. Only I thought it was you."

"Oh? Well. Just a minute . . ." There was a muffled movement like a hand over the receiver. Then Michelle returned. "Well, Jana doesn't seem to be around anymore. Please continue with your description."

"I will never live this down. Your daughter thinks I'm a letch."

"My very pretty, very precocious daughter will think

you're a delight. Anyway she's known all about you for years. You're the one that got away."

"You told her that?"

"She told me, actually. I think it was after the seventy-fifth time I was relating that time after school you and I drove down to Mexico and got into trouble with my father. 'Gee, Mom,' she informed me, 'he sounds great. I wish my boyfriend would run off with me to Mexico.' "

"Ouch. That's tougher than explaining about the pot-smoking thing."

"Ha! Kids today don't even think that's charming anymore. We've become the old farts. But enough about their generation. Let's talk about ours. How are you? You sound a trifle weary."

"You know, anyone else might find that a trifle offensive."

"But I'm not anyone else. I'm your best buddy, remember?"

"And my psychic link. Anybody else you happen to share this psychic thing with, by the way? I'm prepared to be very jealous."

"Then I'll never tell." Michelle made a settling sound on her end, as though drawing up her knees and getting in the mood. "So talk to me, Touch Benson. You are tired. And you had a very trying day. Close?"

"Close, but not exactly a psychic stretch. I am a cop."

"And a famous one from what I hear. What's it like being a big-city cop? Do you shoot at people a lot?"

"Every day."

"Even criminals?"

"Oh, funny! My childhood sweetheart is funny!"

Michelle's musical laughter. "I'm sorry. That was bad. But really, what are you working on these days that makes you sound so weary?"

Benson sighed. "Oh, it would really bore you, Michelle."

"No. No it wouldn't. I'd love to hear about your work. Love to hear everything about you."

He'd forgotten how funny she was, how easy to talk to. As if the twenty-five-year gap had never existed at all.

"So come on, talk! I'm a great listener, remember?" There was an insistence to her, though, he hadn't remembered . . . an impatience, as though time was an important commodity now. Perhaps it was.

"I remember. Okay. Well, we got this dead body over in West Hollywood, near Clark, the other day. It's a problem because she's—"

"The victim was a woman?"

"A young woman, yes. The room looked like a tornado hit it. She'd been suffocated, but there are no—it isn't immediately clear how. Suffocated, then stabbed. Then this call we got tonight, Santa Monica. The victim looked to be done the same way. Michelle? You there?"

"I'm here."

"Is this upsetting you?"

"Go on."

"Anyway, I already knew the first victim had died of suffocation because she's the one who wrecked the room, thrashing around. Same thing with the sand on the beach. He suffocates them first, then goes at them with the knife. Only we can't get a weapon lead because the

entrance wounds are weird. So . . . that's what I'm working on. Shall we talk about something else?"

"So it's a serial killer—is that what you're saying?"

"It's a little early to tell. Only two victims."

"But similar."

"Similar, yes. And neither victim appeared to have
resisted sex. But they also didn't appear to be prosti-
tutes, which means he must have known them. And
which makes it complicated." He shouldn't be telling
her this, technically. It was nice though, to get it off
his chest with an impartial ear. Maybe Michelle in-
stinctively knew that. Still . . . warning bells sounded.

"What did she look like, the second victim?"

"Like the first one. Young, dishwater blond, buxom.
Plain."

Silence from Michelle's end. He could hear her
breathing. Thinking about it?

Or had he finally upset her after all? She'd said she
could take it. He shouldn't have started this in the first
place. This really was confidential, old friend or not.

"Michelle—?"

"What did they look like?"

"I probably shouldn't even be discussing this with—"

"With who? Your best friend in the world? Come on!"

Benson sighed, torn. "Slightly morbid best friend, I
think. Where were we?"

"What they looked like in death, pathologically
speaking."

"Why on earth do you want to know that?"

"I was going to be a doctor, remember! Jesus,
Touch, don't you remember anything about me!"

He was slightly taken aback by her tone. Or maybe
he was just more tired than he thought. "I remember.

They were not exactly pleasant, if you must know. As I said, asphyxiated, but with no ligature marks, no bruising, no signs of struggling against someone."

A pause on her end for a moment. "Such an ugly word."

" 'Asphyxiated'? Yes. It is."

"An ugly way to die. Sad. Lonely."

Again the silence. "Mikki? I'd like to stop with the shop talk now, okay?"

A whispery sigh in the receiver. "I'm sorry. I'm being rude."

"It isn't that—"

"And a little tired myself I guess."

"My fault. I shouldn't have called so damn late."

"No, I'm glad you did. I was thinking about you. Don't be angry with me."

He felt a rush of the old warmth. "When was I ever?"

"I'm glad we ran into each other again, Touch. I've missed you. Missed us. I don't think I knew how much. That specialness between us. It didn't go away, did it?"

"No, it didn't. And to think I was dreading the class reunion. It was a special night for me, Mikki."

"Me too."

"Get some sleep now, okay?"

"I will. Sweet Touch. Hey!"

"What, honey?"

"Who's the fastest girl you know?"

He smiled. "Michelle Ransom."

"Bet your boots." And she hung up.

Just like old times.

6

Night and rain.

It could have been lovely against a bold, windswept plain, flanked by the sleeping sentinels of brooding monoliths, safe beneath the watchful eyes of the Ancient Ones.

Here in Studio City it just slowed traffic.

Like much of what was called modern, Charlie didn't understand Studio City, nor neighboring Sherman Oaks with its treacherous hills, hairpin turns, complicated canyons . . . couldn't imagine who would want to live here. And what was Ventura Boulevard but one unbroken strip mall, some fancier stores than Hollywood, sure, but who could afford the things in them? And who'd want to? Kitsch charading as art. Art Deco they called it, and it wasn't even truly that, not the real Deco of the thirties, which at least had some sense of geometric style, some harkening to the sacred lines of ancient times. Not like these hideous lamps, these faux tabletop radios pretending to be the streamlined Fadas of Karloff's day, James Whale's day. And just try and grab a cheap burger somewhere. The Daily Grill—sure, daily if you made a hundred grand a year. And now this rain.

Well, the ancients had to endure the rain, he supposed. And this is where The Voice had directed him. If Studio City was his destiny, then so be it.

Charlie turtled under his blue windbreaker, ducked beneath the flapping canopy out of the brunt of the downpour. And out of the dark, his back lit brightly now with gaudy store neon, leaving him feeling naked, exposed. A video store, one that sold only DVDs and high-end equipment. Digital. The entire nation was digital now, everything from TVs to cell phones, the whole world hooked together by a series of ones and zeros, marching to a digital beat. That was what the world had become. That was what the new century was all about: *connecting*. No matter to what, no matter to whom, no matter to what purpose—just get yourself connected to something, rush headlong and heedless into a doubtful future, lest you be left behind.

It was almost amusing. Considering that the key to all of it lay not in the future, but the past. Not that he expected others to comprehend it, he'd barely begun to understand it himself. All one continuous line, nothing really old, nothing truly new, certainly not digital technology. It was just another form of math. And the Ancient Ones understood the principles of that quite well, thank you.

And in their own way, both races—ancient and modern—sought the secrets of immortality. But modern man's crude attempts never surpassed the superficial: photography, motion pictures, and now digital recording. All so callow, so naive, capturing only outward, earthbound images.

The Ancient Ones captured the inner soul. The Divine Ones knew how to—

A cop was watching him.

In a patrol car across the rain-swept street. Or maybe not watching him, maybe just stopped at the light, but he was terribly exposed here under the glare from the video store.

Charlie hunched low and darted into a shadow-cloaked alley, dark and safe in the lee of a dripping overhang. He had a sudden burning urge to urinate. He looked around. He didn't relish going back out into the light again to find a gas station or restaurant, not tonight. Tonight The Voice had indicated deep shadows, a soft amber glow. And he must go where The Voice directed. He had gone to The Temple and prayed about it and he knew his course to be true.

Charlie looked up the reflective trench of alley, a hallway to blackness. Empty. Hunched against rust-stained stucco, he freed himself from his zipper, glanced over his shoulder, and arced a forceful loop, smiling as his glistening gold melded with neon-bloodied bricks. Pissing on Studio City. He chuckled along with the gutters.

. . . soft amber glow . . .

What could The Voice have meant by that?

He shivered under the windbreaker with his diminishing loop, shook, and zipped. He was cold and wet and longed for his quiet apartment, the warm, familiar decor. He ached to get on with it, to get this done. Yes the Ancients had their own timetable, it was not his place to question. Patience. A virtue. His mother had always said so. And really, he had a good feeling despite the miserable weather, the glaring, alien surroundings. Tonight would be special.

Charlie Grissom turned from the dark alley and went hunting.

" *'It never rains in Southern Callliforniaaaa . . .'* "

Rae Collins, not in good voice, rarely in good voice, really never in good voice and trying to sing while running between canopies, head down, coat pulled over her hair—which was frizzed out disastrously, wasting a painful night of curlers—turned as she caught up with Kurtzy and Sue Thornquist. "Who sang that, guys?"

"Maria Callas," from a caustic Sue.

Kurtzy ducked under a streaming cornice beside Sue. The light was yellow. They'd never make it. In a moment, Rae crammed herself awkwardly between them, apparently oblivious to Sue's put-down. And to the fact she really wasn't wanted here tonight.

"Very funny, Sue. Sue's a funny gal, huh, Kurtz?"

Kurtzy smiled, nodded politely.

Sue rolled her eyes. "Nobody says 'gal' anymore, Rae." She stuck a cigarette in her mouth wearily.

Rae Collins. The infinite source of aggravation. A hanger-on from high school days still trying doggedly to fit in somewhere the way she used to fit in with Sue. Trying way too hard to be part of the group. Only Sue didn't need a group now. She had Kurtzy.

Though it doubtless wasn't going to be a problem much longer, now that Rae had moved out, no longer wanted as a roommate.

Kurtzy squinted at the traffic light, the gelatin mirror of Ventura Boulevard. She was literally and figuratively caught in the middle here.

Kurstin didn't relate all that well to Rae Collins herself, although they were all in Ivers's class together. The poor girl was everything Sue privately railed about: an uninsightful, underread, underdeveloped bore. But she was a human being too. And Sue should have made arrangements with one roommate before selecting another. This way really wasn't kosher.

But a lot about Sue wasn't kosher. Maybe that was part of what made being with her so exciting. So poles apart from any lifestyle Kurtzy had ever known.

Befriending the dark-haired, flashing-eyed Thornquist had been an ongoing adventure of wild parties, kinetic road trips, whirlwind always-on-the-move excitement. Experiences always watched from afar in Kurtzy's old life. Watched and dreamed of.

She couldn't deny it was stimulating. If sometimes a little terrifying.

When you were with Sue, you were *alive*. On the other hand, when you were the recipient of Sue Thornquist's disapproval, you didn't need a wake-up call to recognize it. On the other other hand, when you were the object of her approval . . . well . . .

Kurtzy had not spent a great deal of life the object of any kind of affection. Now that she was, she was loath to let it go. And loath to criticize the source, even when criticism was likely due.

"—right over *there,* Sue. Are you *blind*?"

Kurtzy blinked back from the hypnotic patter of

rain. The two girls were hunched together for once, staring at something across the street.

"I don't see anything," Sue sighed irritably.

"Right *there* . . . by the fire hydrant."

Kurtzy followed their gaze. Was that a figure?

Sue squinted past billowing gray haze. An alley, across the way, someone standing in it, half in shadow. The upper half. The lower half was visible enough. A man, with something in his hand. That couldn't be his . . .

"Jesus," Sue breathed.

Kurtzy colored abruptly, turned quickly away.

Rae Collins gawked, unflinching. "Wow. I mean . . ."

Sue spat out smoke. "It's disgusting. Looks like a fucking elephant."

Kurtzy felt her arm tugged. "You okay, Kurtz? That creep scaring you?"

Kurtzy shook her head. "Of course not."

An explosion of lightning threw the alley into graphic chiaroscuro. The girls jumped, squealing with the attendant shock of thunder.

When they looked again, the alley was black, the figure gone.

Rae turned wide-eyed to the others. "Did you see . . . ?"

"I saw," from a smirking Sue.

"His face, I mean. His *face!* It was . . . *melted* or something! Kurtz?"

Kurtzy shuddered from a sudden chill. "I'm not certain . . ."

Sue rolled her eyes again, shook her head. "Probably the most formidably beautiful appendage of your entire lives, and you two look at his face." She threw up her hands histrionically. "I am saddled with schoolchildren."

Laughter from across the street, youthful laughter and whistling. "There's Jason," Rae said, jabbing Kurtzy's ribs.

Kurtzy turned so fast it sent a lance up her neck. Jason Richards was entering His Pants with a coterie of jock buddies. While his friends pushed and brayed, Jason moved with stately grace. A king in the company of jackals.

"Christ," Rae murmured reverently, "he's even beautiful wet."

Sue arced the remnants of her cigarette at the gutter. "Come on, *gals* . . . let's join the other members of his fiefdom."

Crossing the street, Rae indicated Sue's rain-plastered blouse. "Your nips are showing, Thornquist!"

Sue didn't break stride. "Gee, *really*? I hope no one notices!"

Almost darker here inside the bar than on the street. Everything orange-tinted from little amber ceiling spots, the little amber candleholders on the tables, everything warm and inviting and the opposite of the gusting reality beyond the door.

Rae hunched over Irish coffee, studying an oak framed photo of John Barrymore above their booth, sitting beside Sue nursing a rum and Coke and looking properly jaded. All of the frames lining the paneled walls held Barrymore photos from varying stages of his career, except those that displayed sketches, or facsimile blowups of sketches, anyway. Kurtzy could name every film if she had to. Right now she was preoccupied with the back of Jason Richards's head, three booths up.

It was warm in here, and Kurtzy's scotch—her second—was making her as mellow as the softly glowing lamps.

Rae tilted frizzy curls at a framed Barrymore. "So who is this guy, anyway?"

His hair is beautiful, Kurtzy thought, the lovely blond nape, the top all slicked back and spiky with rainwater. Even with his back to her, he was graceful, composed, not all awkward angles and elbows like his friends, not the constant chatter, the exaggerated, juvenile mannerisms. He didn't need them, was above them. In every way. Much as Barrymore had been above his peers. "He was an actor."

Rae turned to her. "Yeah? Movies?"

"He did film. Some. But a stage actor at heart. And an artist. A visual artist, I mean. The sketches are his. Himself in makeup."

"Yeah? Who's he supposed to be in this one?"

Kurtzy didn't have to look. "Othello."

Rae squinted upward. "Kind of a pointy nose. How come all the profiles?"

How could someone make it all the way to UCLA and not know Barrymore? "It was his trademark. 'The Great Profile.' "

"Huh." Rae shrugged, went back to her drink. "Not exactly handsome."

"Jesus, Rae," said an overpatient Sue, "it was the thirties! It was called glamor! You sound like you've never been out of your bedroom."

Kurtzy studied Jason. No, not handsome. Beautiful. A rare flower in a forest of dead wood. Only he wasn't coming over here to their table. He never had, in all the nights they'd been coming here. And abruptly, deep in her heart, Kurtzy knew he never would. And it made her chest below her wet blouse hurt terribly.

Even without Sue and Rae, even if she were alone here, Jason would never come. Because Jason couldn't *see* girls like her.

Kurtzy was invisible to him. Perhaps invisible to everyone. A ghost among the living, floating pale and unseen just outside, always outside. *Oh, Jason, see me! Take me from this place, this awful, empty plane . . . enfold me in your strong swimmer's arms and carry me away, toward the light! I'm dying. I'm evaporating right before you . . . a dying ghost you can't even see . . .*

Someone appeared beside Jason's booth, a girl. With hair of spun gold.

"Who's *that*?" Rae had been watching, voice now flat with envy.

Sue listed left, squinted. "Jesus, I've got to get glasses. Looks like Jana Ransom. Miss Glendale rich bitch. I hate her."

Kurtzy quietly watched Jana Ransom, from Ivers's class, in a kelly-green sweater that matched her eyes, matched her every effortless move, clinging smoothly, accentuating, but not vulgar, not like Kurtzy's matted blouse, which, by comparison, seemed cheap, crass. Desperate.

Jana laughed at something Jason said, slid into the booth next to him. Kurtzy felt an emptiness so visceral it left her breathless, hollowed out.

"So what movies did he make?"

Jana laughed harder now, punched Jason's shoulder playfully. He punched back, she punched harder, a little mock fight that ended with his left arm encircling, pulling her close.

"Kurtz?"

She turned lidded eyes to Rae. "Who? Oh . . . *Grand Hotel* with what's her name . . ."

"The Nazi," Sue filled in, "Garbo."

Jana's golden head rested against Jason's, two golden waterfalls blending, so you couldn't tell whose gold belonged to whom. Kurtzy was struck by how perfectly the couple fit together, like bright, disparate puzzle pieces suddenly joined to make a more beautifully perfect whole. And they will stay that way forever, she thought dreamily, be beautiful and perfect all the rest of their existence, the light from their golden bodies throwing back all shadows, guiding them toward the endless parade of happy days and nights that were theirs from the beginning. All of life, she realized with sudden swooping clarity, was one vast, interconnecting puzzle stretching to limitless horizons, into which you either fit perfectly, snugly, or not at all . . .

"A for-real Nazi?" Rae wanted to know.

Sue nodded, blew smoke. "Yeah. Married to Hitler. Gave him blow jobs."

Rae squinted suspiciously. "You're putting me on!"

"Would I do that?" Sue tapped Kurtzy's arm. "Hey. Remember that guy?"

Now some other girl was blocking the view, standing behind Jason and Jana, and Kurtzy could no longer see them. Couldn't see *them* and Jason couldn't see *her*. Made sense, really.

"The guy with the major unit. Peeing in the alley."

Kurtzy turned to her lazily. "What—?"

"He's watching you."

Kurtzy gazed sleepily at her. Blinked. "Me?"

Rae was craning at someone out in the bar. "Hey . . . she's right . . . It's the guy with the melted face."

Kurtzy turned again with effort; she really shouldn't have had that second drink. "I don't see anyone melting."

Rae picked up her purse. "He's gone now." She fished out bills. "I'd love to sit here and discuss noses and Nazis but I've got an oral tomorrow."

"Anyone we know?" Sue winked at Kurtzy.

Rae hesitated. Snapped her purse shut and turned to her former roommate. "You really are a complete asshole. You know that, Sue?"

Sue smiled obligingly, blew smoke. "Thought you'd never notice."

Rae pushed up with disgust, hesitated . . .

She looked suddenly at Kurstin, then Sue, then Kurstin. Her expression shifted. "Oh. Oh, I get it. Little slow tonight, but a light finally dawns. You're the new roommate," she said to Kurtzy.

Kurtzy came suddenly, dizzily awake, throat dry. "I . . ."

"Nice. Very nice. Well fuck you very much!" She pushed past Sue, nearly tripping. "And fuck you too, Thornquist!" Started out, turned back, and snatched her money back from the table. "And may the best lezzie win!" And stomped out.

Sue snorted, stubbed out her smoke. "Bitch."

Kurtzy frowned, having trouble focusing. "Lezzie?"

Sue waved her hand. "She's drunk. Forget her. Come on, let's blow this dump."

I couldn't get up right now if I wanted to, Kurtzy thought . . . and I don't want to.

Her eyes drifted automatically back to Jason's booth. "Think I'll stick around awhile. You go ahead."

Sue leaned toward her. "You pissed? About Rae?"

Kurtzy shook her head. "Just want to stick around awhile."

Sue followed her gaze, smiled. "Why don't you ask him to dance?"

Kurtzy gave her a stricken look.

"Why not? You're as cute as that Ransom chick."

Kurtzy smiled listlessly. "Sure I am. See you back at the dorm, Suze."

Sue patted her arm and was out of there.

All alone in the booth, Kurtzy suddenly was quite certain she could not get back to campus without falling down. But she had no money for a cab. And the bar would be closing in half an hour.

She started to push up, run after Sue . . .

. . . sank back holding her temple. "Oh . . . my head," she moaned to no one.

The booth shook as someone slid in across from her.

"Tomato juice and ginger ale's the cure for that!" The melted face smiled.

7

It was better outside in the cool rain.

But she threw up twice walking down the sidewalk anyway. Charlie held on to her gallantly as she retched. The generous downpour washed it away.

She didn't really remember how they got to his apartment.

But she remembered seeing the inside for the first time. "Wow."

Kurtzy stood in the doorway of Charlie's little two-room: just this small outer living room, a smaller bedroom, smaller still kitchen, bathroom door. And dark. Darker than His Pants, but filled with a similar amber glow, this time from slender tapers Charlie was busy lighting one by one, and the color of the wallpaper: limestone. Also the color of the ceiling. Also the color of the threadbare rug, and the molding around the door frames, the floors, all the old woodwork in the old West Hollywood apartment. Everything painted

that color, limestone. A burial vault, minus the sar-
cophagus. And that was just the start.

Charlie turned, candle in hand, and caught her staring at the wallpaper. "Do you like them? They're
called hieroglyphics."

"I know! Where on earth did you get them?"

Charlie beamed waxy pride. "I . . . sort of did them
myself. Not much of an artist, but they can be read."
He went to the nearest wall, pointed. "This section I
copied from a book on the New Kingdom. It's the
epitaph of an Egyptian military officer." He glanced
over his shoulder. "Are you cold? The rain . . . your
blouse . . ."

Kurtzy crossed her arms over her wet chest, eyes
on the wall. She actually felt better. "Go on."

Charlie's eyes lingered a moment on hers. He
flushed.

Him. Not her.

She was alone in a strange-looking man's apartment
and the man was blushing. More astonishing, he was
looking into her eyes for once, not at her breasts.

Was it Sue? Had being with Sue these past weeks
caused this . . . made her somehow more attractive?

Nor was she the least bit shy, the least bit embarrassed with this man. Not afraid. She was changing . . .
She *had* changed. This could actually be the start of
something.

Kurtzy nodded toward the wall, if only to get him
to stop gazing at her. "Go on—Charlie, is it?"

Charlie swallowed thickly, turned quickly back to
the wall. "What we have here is a reed leaf"—he
pointed to it—"followed by this jagged mark which
is the Egyptian sign for water"—pointing—"under

64   *Bruce Elliot*

which we have a goose, then the figure of the kneeling man, what is called a 'determinative man symbol,' in this case meaning *'my son,'* after which comes the picture of the folded cloth, then this religious-looking object which is actually a sandal strap, this red mouth sign above that, another water symbol beneath it, the face symbol next to that with a line below it which means *'upon,'* then a spindle and thread followed by this bird—a quail chick—then this thing up here which looks like a Christmas package, that's a determinative writing symbol—a book roll—which stands for *'Stela,'* next a mat over this last and final symbol for water."

He turned back to Kurtzy, little pig's eyes riveted to her face. He cleared his throat. "Egyptian hieroglyphics concerned themselves with beauty as well as basic practicality. In this way they could be read either vertically or horizontally. The trick is to not read them for their visual meaning. They were meant to be read phonetically, with assists from determinative and phonetic complements. They could not only form words and phrases, but"—he could not stop his eyes from devouring hers again— "emotion." He swallowed hard again. Face all red like that, he looked like a waxy Halloween pumpkin.

Kurtzy suppressed a giggle.

This is why people laugh at shy people. They're so silly. So self-involved. And she was one of them. *Had* been one of them.

Yet, somehow, in its own way, with this poor, melty-faced man, it was also endearing. He was like a puppy. A big, melty-faced puppy.

And she the master. She the one in control. For the first time in her life.

Not the kind of control someone like Jana Ransom

knew, of course. Not yet the smooth assurance of the beautiful people, with their wit and charm, their cars and yachts. Not on their level. But maybe not so far below them as she'd once thought.

And then she did the unthinkable.

The next time he turned to look at her, she unfolded her arms in front of him. Dropped them at her sides so her wet blouse was unobstructed. It brought a waxy flame to his face, an uncontrolled convulsion to his throat.

Kurtzy threw back her shoulders and addressed him confidently. The way Ivers might have addressed a lecture. The way Sue seduced boys on the quad. "Please continue, Charlie."

Charlie blinked numbly, looked up, turned quickly to the wall again. "The . . . uh . . . the entire passage, which conveys the pride of a doting Egyptian father to his son, reads, *'It is my . . .'* "

" *'My son who causes my name to live upon this stela,'* " Kurtzy finished for him. "Twelfth Dynasty."

Charlie froze, still facing the wall.

For a time there was only the sound of his breathing in the small room.

Finally he turned to her. "Who . . . *are* . . . you?"

Kurtzy extended her hand. "Kurstin Mallon, freshman, UCLA. Not pretty enough to be a Kurstin, so everyone calls me Kurtzy."

Charlie seemed staggered at her suggestion. "But . . . you're *beautiful!*"

There.

It had happened.

Someone had said it. And best of all, a man. *You are beautiful.*

And still her mind refused to cope with it.

But Charlie, clearly mesmerized by her beauty, was coming before her, seeming almost to *float* than walk. Knelt and took her hand. *"Nephthys,"* he whispered solemnly and bowed his head.

An extraordinary moment in any girl's life. An epiphany for Kurtzy's.

Confused, still slightly dizzy, she nonetheless let him kneel there awhile, let him kiss her hand—just once, tenderly—as she stared down at the top of his head. She pressed back another giggle. A wig. And a bad one. How clumsily guileless. How sweet.

When it became apparent Charlie wasn't going to stand again anytime soon, Kurtzy grew concerned. "Charlie? Hey. You can get up now. I'm not Nephthys."

Charlie remained bowed, head in his arm, still holding her hand. Then he did something truly remarkable, at least to Kurtzy, who had rarely been kissed at all. He bent lower and kissed her foot, the bare instep just above the sneaker tongue. It sent an unexpected jolt through her.

"Nephthys," Charlie repeated in breathless hush.

Kurtzy stared down at him. Nephthys, she thought, sister of Isis. Goddess of women. Her name meant *"Lady of the Castle."*

Only slightly embarrassed, she worked the toe of her sneaker under his chin, lifted the waxy head. "Charlie? Hey. I could use another drink . . ."

He finally stood, still bent at the waist, and began backing away, head down, arms extended, palms up like an Egyptian servant. It would have been comical if not so obviously sincere. He shuffled backward into the kitchen.

While he rattled around in there, she perused the living room, still wondering vaguely when she might wake up.

The furniture ranged from the incredible to the ludicrous. All of it was ancient Egyptian, none of it, of course, real. A cedar chest that was clearly handmade though not well, probably by Charlie; a hard-backed chair that at first looked dazzling until she realized it was covered in gold tin foil, ornamented with dimestore knickknacks. Lot of modern knockoffs you could buy at The Museum Company or even Kmart.

The shiny bladed dagger with the gold-encrusted hilt, however, looked real. She was examining it when he came back into the room. He handed her a slender glass of clear liquid. "Drink this," he said. He used that same reverential tone. Hushed. She could see where it could eventually become monotonous. But not yet. Not yet.

"This looks real," Kurtzy said, taking a sip.

"A ceremonial knife. It is real."

She studied the jeweled hilt. "Then it would cost a . . . It would be priceless."

Charlie nodded, milky eyes drinking her in like a man dying of thirst. "It is. I stole it."

"From where?"

"My mother."

"Your mother. And she stole it from—?"

"She didn't steal it. My mother was a goddess."

"I see. Like me?"

"No, not like you. But a goddess."

She nodded, smiled gently. He was certifiable. Why wasn't she afraid?

She held up the blade. "But where did she really get it?"

"Museum of Natural History, Hollywood."

"Is that where you're from?"

"No. I am from the Ancient Ones, even as you."

Uh-huh. Right. "Well, aside from the Ancient Ones, then."

"I was born in Glendale. Mother worked at the museum."

Kurtzy put down the dagger thoughtfully. "When she wasn't being a goddess . . ."

"What?" Charlie asked.

"I said, is that the bathroom? I'm feeling a little queasy."

He nodded, bowed. She weaved her way across the rug and closed the door behind her.

Charlie turned to the jackal statue of Anubis on the living room table: Cost Plus, $12.95. He closed his eyes, made a little half bow before it. "Thank you."

In a moment Kurtzy came out of the bathroom, draining the last of her drink. She got to the door before slumping against the jamb.

Charlie didn't even try to catch her. Just watched. Patiently.

"Charlie? I feel funny."

She slid to her knees. "Charlie—?"

When he was sure she was unconscious on the floor he lifted her—not easily because she was a buxom, robust goddess—and carried her, back straining, into the bedroom, laying her across the duvet with the Egyptian design. Set the incense to burning and drew the blinds tight. A single ceiling spot illuminated her goddess's body. He undressed himself, then her, hardly able to breathe when he removed her thong. He had never seen such abundant beauty. This was what all the waiting was about. The others were a mistake, but this time . . .

He knelt between her legs. Let the ceremony begin.

Wait! The sacred dagger! He looked around. Where had he put it? Back in the living room where she'd been admiring it.

Never mind, he could get it afterward. He adjusted her. Gods of the ancients, *look* at her!

Better than the others, better even than thinking about the dancing goddess before the fireplace.

Charlie rested a moment on her breast, listening to his pounding heart through hers. Home. Home at last. And soon to be with the gods themselves . . .

He cleansed her entire body with sandal soap and oil, even between her toes. He combed her wet hair, laid it about her head like a wreath, would have painted her delicate toe and fingernails but she'd already done that. Not exactly the ancient colors, but . . .

He took the sacred roll of binding cloth from the cedar chest and began the wrapping with her forehead.

Around, lift, around, lift . . . gently, reverently. She was so beautiful. And in a moment he'd know, know for sure. He was just covering her sacred eyebrows—*around, lift*—when he felt her stir. Charlie froze . . . looked down.

Kurtzy's blurry eyes watched him curiously, calmly. "What exactly are we doing, Charlie?"

He was completely motionless, holding the wrapping in both hands, as if waiting for her to pass out once more.

"Charlie?"

His eyes were all innocence. "Wrapping you, of course."

"Wrapping me. And then?" When he didn't answer immediately, she started to sit up. Why had she had that last drink? Had she let him undress her?

"I wait."

"Wait for what?"

"To see if you come back to life."

Kurtzy thought about it. "And when—*if*—I don't?"

"But you will! You are *she!*"

"Sure. Sure I am. But hypothetically, if I didn't survive being asphyxiated by ancient burial wrapping, what then?"

"Then I use the sacred knife to be sure."

Kurtzy's heart jumped. Dear God. "And if I'm still not dead?"

"Well, then I'd take you back." And he added quickly, "But it won't happen this time! You are *she!*"

"Back where? Take me back where?"

"Studio City!"

Kurtzy nodded slowly. It was some sort of kinky game, something he used to make up for his shyness and his scarred face. The pretend. Of course. She knew all about that. Had spent half her young life playing the pretend game. Still did. Most recently with Jason Richards. She was an expert at it.

After a minute, Charlie shifted his weight restively. "May I finish wrapping you now, Princess?"

Kurtzy, who seemed to have gone away for a moment, looked up into the waxy face.

All right, he was . . . different.

He's delusional! Get out of there!

Kurtzy pushed up.

He thought she was a goddess. She thought Jason Richards a god. Was there really such a difference?

Yes! Get out now before you become delusional yourself!

She sat musing calmly on the edge of the bed, looking down at his naked body. Crazy or not, nutcase or not, he wanted her, he worshiped her.

"I'm worshiped," she said it aloud.

"Yes." Charlie nodded attentively.

Kurtzy reached over and cupped the waxy face with her palm. Charlie closed his eyes, pressed her hand tighter. He purred.

"You'd do anything for me."

"Yes, Nephthys! Anything!"

The power bloomed in her loins. "You won't ever . . . need the sacred knife. Right, Charlie? Is that understood? I would be very displeased. Your princess would be extremely displeased."

Charlie bowed his head. "You are the one! The sacred one! Be my bride, sweet goddess of the ages! Say you will!"

Kurtzy chewed her lip a moment. She looked down at him again, still feeling a little drunk.

She shifted on the bed. "We'll have to talk about that, Charlie, we will. Right now why don't you reach over and blow out the candles?"

He lifted his eyes in obedience. "Why?"

Because in the dark I can pretend too . . . pretend your face is perfect and your hair golden and your figure graceful as a god's . . .

"Because we didn't quite finish what we started. And we want to get that part right, don't we?"

Charlie climbed over her, trembling, helpless. Her slave.

Kurtzy watched the dark apartment ceiling. She seemed to be living outside herself . . . watching all this from high above. Like a movie. A film in which she was the actor, cast and crew. But mostly the director. "Even if we have to practice a few times," she whispered to him. "Even if it takes a while . . ."

Charlie pinched out the candles. In the dark he whispered, "My timeless goddess!"

Kurtzy winced in quick pain . . . let out a slow breath. Smiled contentment. "Jason . . ."

"What?"

She pressed his mouth to her breast to muffle it.

She closed her eyes and began to pretend . . .

8

Michelle Ransom had a good session with her shrink for once. They could be pretty maddening.

She saw Dr. Otter once a week, had been doing so for nearly two months now, and he'd finally gotten around to interpreting the dreams. Not that she agreed with anything he said, but at least he was saying something now instead of grunting and nodding. And that seemed to indicate progress. Of a sort.

It was her daughter who had unwittingly put them together. Jana happened to mention noticing Otter's office near a hangout she and boyfriend, Jason, frequented. Michelle had driven by one day, caught Dr. Otter leaving the office into cool evening air, head encased in an old-fashioned fedora, small, compact body traversing the parking lot with a succinct efficiency she'd found somehow comforting. She'd made an appointment the next day.

He greeted her, doleful and immaculate, at his office door. "Ms. Ransom, I'm Dr. Otter."

Michelle had to bite her inner cheek hard not to laugh, and at that, she gave a short snort.

He *looked* like an otter.

The thick, flat, sleeked-back hair—as though he'd just emerged from a stream—the gray bushy mustache, the twinkling granny glasses. Extending his hand, he looked like he was begging for a mackerel. Not rambunctiously joyful like an otter, unfortunately. Rather cool, in fact.

Michelle put it down to professional detachment, de rigueur for analysts. Michelle would talk, Otter would listen. That's how it worked.

For the first few sessions it did work.

Michelle sat cool and contained before his burl-wood desk, eyes on the Goya print behind him, rambling on about this and that—rich, cold father, dead, cold mother . . . her first crush on a certain odd-eyed football player . . . the stockbroker who'd seen fit to leave her for his second cousin just weeks after she'd given birth to her only child, Jana.

Otter listened and jotted, nodded and listened.

Then during the third session he surprised her.

He put down his pad and asked her point-blank why she felt she needed to see a psychiatrist.

Michelle was taken aback. But much of her surprise and stammering were delayed.

Finally, in the middle of it, the tears came.

And she began to talk—at last—in earnest.

She began describing the dream. The recurring dream that had come to haunt her. The way it began, which was always with the mist. The lost feeling. And the dread.

And finally the woman. Fair of skin, gold of hair, winding shreds of cloth trailing the pale form as it approached Michelle out of the fog. And the thin, imploring reaching arms . . . summoning . . .

Otter listened raptly to every detail. A new Otter. An excited Otter.

Dreams! Something the Freudian-oriented analyst could sink his little Otter teeth into. From there on, every session revolved around Michelle's dreams. Each nuance, each *feeling,* each detail no matter how small or insignificant. Mustache twitching, eyes twinkling, cheeks rosy, Otter assured her they were making real progress.

Michelle was less elated. Try as she would, she could not understand how the continued reiterating of the same images, the same feelings of dread, the same reluctance to sleep, were having any beneficial significance in her case. She even tried hypnosis a few times but the dreams persisted.

Otter was unswerving. He wanted to talk dreams.

Michelle grew weary of it. Then rebellious.

She began entering his office intent on sidestepping the dream issue altogether. There must be more to her than that!

Agreeable if unmollified, Otter listened to her talk of things living . . . of high school reunions, and handsome jocks, and best friends in the eighth grade she'd secretly loved, and the boy who grew into the handsome police officer she might still conceivably love. How much she'd enjoyed dancing with him. Talking with him again. Just thinking about him.

She left out that one late-night elliptical phone call.

"And your dreams, Ms. Ransom? Is this policeman in your dreams?"

Michelle sagged. "Must we talk dreams today, Dr. Otter? I think I dread talking about them more than having them."

Otter shrugged. "It's your choice of course."

Michelle stood contritely. Crossed her arms and began pacing around the little office. She only paced when she talked about the dreams. That should have told her something. "It's always the same dream, Doctor, exactly the same. It really doesn't vary."

"When did you last have it?" Otter brightened.

"Right after the reunion, this time. I—I was having trouble sleeping. A friend called. We talked a few minutes. Then I fell asleep . . ."

Michelle drew distracted breath, arms folded tight, paced the doctor's Persian rug, the periphery of its scalloped border. "I'm walking along. Maybe day, maybe night, it's too misty to see. I feel . . . apprehensive. I seem to be lost. I can see the street signs clearly, but I still feel . . . I'm lost. Then I hear footsteps. Someone following me. I turn. A figure moves out of the fog toward me. A woman. She's pale, barely formed, ethereal. Like a goddess come to earth. I'm afraid of her, I don't know why. I try to run but my legs won't work. She comes toward me, hands outstretched. She wants . . ." Michelle stopped on the deep violet rug, looking down at the toes of her pumps.

"Yes?"

Michelle paced. "I feel . . . this woman in the dream . . . I feel she wants something from me."

"Yes?"

Michelle shook her head, began pacing again. "I don't know." She shook her head harder, lips a tight line. "I don't know."

"Does she speak?"

Michelle shut her eyes, picturing again the livid face, the pale flowing hair, the red misshapen mouth opening, opening . . .

"Hasten . . ."

She turned to the doctor who was craning toward her. "I remember now . . . she says, '*Hasten.*' "

Otter nodded encouragement. "Yes—?"

Michelle put a hand to her head. "But it's . . . it's more a shriek than a word, really . . . more . . . animal than human."

Otter sat back, eyes narrowed. He tapped his pencil tip atop his desk. "What do you think she means by that? 'Hasten'?"

Michelle thought about it. Finally threw up her hands and flopped back in her chair. "I have no idea." She blew out pent-up breath. "You tell me. You're the shrink." Too tired to mask her irritation.

Dr. Otter tapped the pencil rhythmically.

Michelle stared at the Goya.

Dr. Otter tapped.

Michelle looked at him. "You're not going to say anything, are you, Dr. Otter?"

"Pardon me?"

"I come in here every week and do all the talking, and you sit there and listen and say nothing and I go home and have that stupid nightmare all over again!"

Otter obliged her with a thin smile. "Psychotherapy is not an instant cure, Michelle, despite what the television shows portray."

"I don't think there are any shows on TV about psychiatrists. Just MDs."

Otter gestured apology. "I'm afraid I don't follow the TV plays much these days. Nor the tabloids. I find them depressing. Sorry."

Michelle crossed her legs, puffed out breath. "Don't be sorry. I'm just grateful to hear you talking. Do go on."

"What would you like me to say?"

"To say? Well, something analytical would be nice, but anything, really."

Otter almost formed a complete smile. "Earn my fee? All right." He stuck the pencil in a cup and leaned back in his chair. "Let's talk about two things. Let's talk about redundancy and inconsistency."

"My dreams are that boring, huh?"

"Redundancy isn't boring, Michelle. It's synonymous with 'recurring,' which is always significant where dreams are concerned. You also told me this dream woman could not be seen clearly, yet you described her as a goddess. That's an inconsistency."

Michelle thought about it. After a moment she looked up. "All I can say is she felt like a goddess to me. She had long blond hair."

"As in regal?"

Michelle's brows knitted. "No . . . not really. Just plain blond . . . dishwater, actually." She threw up her hands. "I don't know."

"Never mind. You also said you were lost in the mist, but that the streets signs could be clearly read. Also inconsistent. Can you remember the street signs now?"

Michelle touched a finger to her lips reflectively.

"Did I say that? When? I don't remember saying that."

"Trust me."

She looked back at the Goya. "Hmm." She brightened. "Highland. The street sign in the last dream was Highland."

"Ah! We have a location! You see, your dreams aren't without direction after all. Do you recall a cross street?"

Michelle shook her head. "No . . . but I just realized it was in Hollywood. I'm sure it was in Hollywood. I don't know why. What does that mean?"

"What do you think it means?"

"You're doing it again."

Otter let another little smile peep out. He was pulling over his appointment book. Her time was up.

It was the first time Michelle wished it wasn't.

9

.

Her therapy appointments were usually at one, which meant Michelle didn't arrive home in Pasadena until two-thirty or so. But today Dr. Otter had moved things up to fit his schedule and Michelle arrived in her big circular drive a little past noon. Early.

She parked the Lexus, strode gray flagstone walk to alabaster columns, fumbling for her key. The columns, the *Gone with the Wind* facade, had been the idea of Richard, her second husband. Richard had been in love with Vivian Leigh, had thought he'd found her in Michelle, minus the Southern accent, which was okay, he'd admitted, because Vivian had actually had a British accent. Michelle, though, had neither. Just occasional bouts of depression. The marriage lasted four years. She and Jana got the house.

Michelle twisted her key in the lock. Hesitated. Heart accelerating a little.

She could tell by the way it twisted that the door

was not locked. And she always locked the front door when leaving, always.

She opened up slowly, quietly, stepped inside, testing the air. Michelle seemed to know instantly she was not alone in the house.

She stood listening to her heart—feeling it, anyway—then turned to look at the phone in the hall.

But she didn't feel afraid, exactly. Just trepidation. No alarms sounded in her head. She simply sensed another presence. She shut the door softly and went quietly to the foot of the sweeping curve of staircase. Red carpet, just like Tara.

Michelle might have heard a soft moan from up there. Somewhere.

Better call the police, just to be sure.

And that made her think of Benson and that made her heart hurt a little with pleasure but also made her feel safer still. Ignoring inner voices, she climbed the stairs in silence.

Another soft sound on the landing, down toward the east end. Michelle watched herself a moment in the big oak framed hall mirror, found no fear in her reflection, and strode down the long hall past the bathroom, the ornate mahogany table with the Erte sculpture. Just even with Jana's bedroom when the moan came again. And she instantly knew.

Soft panic rose in her, laced with anger. Which was silly. Still, she nearly retraced her steps.

Jana's door was open a crack, emitting ocher noonday light. Michelle bit her lip, stepped to it.

Jason Richards, boyfriend and source of the moans, stood naked and golden under the glow of drawn shades, knees slightly bent before Jana's bed. Michelle's daughter, nude to the waist, sat facing him on the silk duvet Michelle had made up that very morning—Jana never remembering to do it herself. Her daughter proffered both breasts, a heavy globe in each hand, a soft niche for his eager member to traverse.

A surrogate to fucking? Michelle, watching in a strange, lazy calm, could only think how tan Jana's chest was, like the rest of her; she must sunbathe topless. And how taut and impossibly weightless her breasts. Michelle had given such firmness away, given it to Jana when birthing her. How lovely these children were, like fine porcelain in the wonderful light, innocent and bereft of all vulgarity, every golden line, cursive and luminous as art.

Michelle was beginning to turn from so much intimate spectacle, when her daughter spoke. "Does that feel *good*? Can you feel my *heart*?"

How anxious to please him she is, Michelle thought. *How unabashed.* Michelle, at that age, would have flushed scarlet at such perversion, had never performed such an act with either boyfriend or husband. Would she have kept them, if she had? Is this where she failed, in bed?

Jason whispered an urgent oath, a pleading command—Jana took him expertly in her mouth for the finish.

Michelle turned her face away to the hall. The long, empty hall, that had never looked so sterile until this moment.

Her baby daughter.

Algebra and housecleaning eluded Jana, but in this, her baby daughter was confident, flush with control. Michelle felt a wedge of jealousy.

Downstairs, Michelle stood about the foyer in an indecisive haze. She went to the door to open and shut it loudly—make a warning entrance racket—hesitated instead, hand on the knob. Finally came to sit on the white sofa instead, not sure why. She supposed to give them some time, some afterglow.

The knock nearly made her yelp.

Someone was making decisions for her; she moved quickly to the front door and opened it, face flushed. She found Touch Benson standing there under bright sun that hurt her eyes.

"Hi, Mikki."

"Touch!"

His own eyes went straight to her warm cheeks like a good detective. "Is this a bad time—?"

"No, of course not."

He was waiting for her to say something else.

"Come in. Please."

Benson stepped into the generous foyer.

"What a nice surprise!" Michelle said *louder* than necessary, shutting the big door even *louder*, flicking a glance upstairs. "Just in the neighborhood, or . . . ?"

"I could say I was working, but I'm really playing hooky to see you." He caught her glancing at the stairs again. "Sure this is all right?"

She beckoned him toward the sunken living room. "Of course. Actually you're lucky to find me here. I had an appointment moved around." She smiled. "We're both lucky. Drink?"

"Thanks. I'm fine." He swept an arm at the generous living room. "This is . . . impressive."

Michelle pointed to a baroque sofa far from the stairs, perched herself on an uncomfortable French

Provincial straight-back across from it. "Thanks for not saying 'gauche.' Richard—my ex—did the decorating, mostly. He was into Southern gothic, Civil War chic. Got his periods a little mixed up. I'm slowly trying to replace it."

Benson leaned back. "Your secret's safe. I'm no critic."

Michelle reached for a cigarette from a silver cup between them. "Oh, come. Some of Lizzie's influence must have rubbed off on you . . ."

Benson watched her. She was staring distractedly at the unlit cigarette. "Huh . . ."

"What is it?"

"That's funny. I quit smoking two months ago. Huh." She started replacing the cigarette, held it up for Benson who shook his head. Michelle sat back. "So, Detective, what do you deduce from that?"

"I don't know. You're nervous?" Before she could answer, he added, "I am. A little."

"Hi!" from the stairs. Jana and the Richards boy were marching down, Jana nearly hopping, a bit overly carefree. "You're home early, Mom!"

"So are *you*, kiddo."

Jana didn't let it faze her. "Lunch hour! We have to get back to class."

Michelle nodded ruefully at her radiant daughter. "Get enough to eat?"

And then, to let Jana off the hook, Michelle turned to Touch. "This is Detective Benson. Amiel, my daughter, Jana. And this is her friend, Jason Richards."

Jana waved, blond tresses swirling. She was stunning. Like her mother. If anything even more fiercely independent. The Richards kid would have his hands full.

"Touch and I were best friends in junior high."

Jana gave Touch the once-over. "I'll *bet*." She smiled her dazzling smile. "Are we under arrest?"

"Should you be?" Benson replied convivially. Jana's smile remained, but faltered. Michelle glanced at Benson, thought: *Smart cop, smart for a man with no kids.*

Jana, recovered, scooped up books. "Well, we have to scoot. Nice to meet you, Mr. Benson." She elbowed Jason.

Who jerked awake, then nodded obediently. "Nice to meet you, sir."

"Likewise."

And they were gone with thumping finality.

Michelle's gaze lingered on the front door. "They get away so fast . . ."

She snapped out of it, turned smiling to Benson. "I'm sorry. Did I sound rude before, about Liz?"

"Rude? How?"

She crossed her arms. "I don't know. Maybe it bothers you to talk about her?"

"Sometimes it does. Not right now."

"Sure you wouldn't like something to drink?"

"On duty. Your daughter sounds exactly like you. No wonder I thought she was you on the phone!"

Michelle laughed. "Poor kid! Jana hates her voice. Thinks it doesn't sound feminine."

"It's uniquely feminine. Like you."

Michelle felt herself color. Ridiculous that someone she'd known since she was twelve could make her blush. But there it was.

"Well"—she gestured at the air—"would you care to see the rest of my very gauche house?"

"I'm crazy for gauche."

She skipped the big kitchen, which she hadn't had time to clean, and led him straight upstairs. In the long hall, Michelle pointed out the Erte sculpture— her one source of pride—then showed him into the master bedroom.

"Very nice."

Michelle sighed at the big canopy bed, dark paneling, heavy buffets, and armoires. "All the warmth of a medieval refectory. Well, someday I'll get around to redecorating." Then, to her own surprise, she blurted, "How long can you stay?"

"Long as you want."

Michelle swallowed, abruptly nervous. "Then would you mind very much if I had a drink? There's a decanter and glasses on the bar, just left of the stairs."

"Sure." Benson went to get it for her.

Downstairs, he found the decanter, took down a glass . . . then another, and poured. He caught himself in the bar's mirror.

". . . *skyrockets in flight* . . ."

The old song lyrics went through his mind as he carried the glasses carefully up the red carpeted upstairs. ". . . *afternoon delight* . . ." Just before he reached the bedroom, a mental image flared: Amanda and he in the dark parking lot from the other night. *"She's beautiful, Touch. And smart."*

She was standing in the bedroom doorway when he rejoined her. Leaning against the jamb.

She accepted the drink, took a big gulp, nearly choking. She was different. The slope of her shoulders, weight of her hips; her whole bearing different. Something had happened. Just in the short space he'd been downstairs.

She stared at her glass a moment, then looked up at him. Tears rimmed her eyes.

"Mikki!"

He came to her, but she stopped him with her palm.

Finally her voice came, low and calm. "You were supposed to be the first . . ."

He watched her, surprised, started to say something but couldn't think of anything but her name. "Mikki."

She was staring past him into space, caught up in the memory. "The sophomore dance—I had it all planned. Daddy was out of town. We were going to come back to my house and make love. You were going to be my first."

Benson reached for her again. Again she stopped him.

"I know it was stupid. Skinny kid with braces and glasses and you coming into adolescence like testosterone gangbusters. It was just—it always felt so comfortable, so right with you." She looked at him now. "You're still the only guy I could ever really talk to, Touch."

"It wasn't stupid, Mikki. It isn't stupid now." He reached for her again, and when she stopped him this time he pushed her hand away, lips closing over hers.

Michelle stiffened. Whimpered. Finally dissolved to him.

He pulled her close, tasting her tongue, felt her hands start to go around him—

—and she was pushing away again. "No!"

"Michelle. . . ."

Shaking her head violently, pushing him back, pressing herself into the jamb. "I can't. I can't do this."

"Why?"

She pushed away into the hall, appeared to be looking for somewhere to run in her own house. Finally wrapped her arms about herself and fell back against the wall.

"Touch . . ."

He came to her, touched her arm gently. "I'm right here, honey."

"I'm so scared."

And she finally let him hold her.

10

They sat in the kitchen, at the side counter. Drinking coffee this time.

He had held her until she could allow herself to cry. And though she didn't cry long, it was fear racked. Enough to scare him.

He made the coffee himself while she was in the bathroom. She came out looking amazingly composed. Even lovely, except for the red-rimmed eyes.

So in control in fact he guessed she'd had some practice with it. He was afraid she wouldn't talk now.

But Michelle finally put down her cup, flicked a hand at her hair, took a deep breath, and let it come.

"Okay. Here we go." She cleared her throat. "First of all, I lied to you."

Benson waited.

"I did come to the reunion to see you. But I had ulterior motives."

He studied her face, wondering where in the world this could be going.

Michelle cleared her throat again. "That case you're working on. The first killing?"

"What about it?"

She licked her lips. "I knew about it. Read about it in the paper. Knew you were working the case."

He thought about his late night call, their conversation. "Okay . . ."

She searched his face a moment. "Uh . . . how do I put this?"

He gestured at the air. "Just put it. We were best friends, remember?"

For a moment he thought she was going to drift away again. "Touch . . . how . . . do you feel about psychics? I mean—not like us—real psychics."

He tried to look casual. "I've known a few."

She looked surprised. Not the answer she'd expected. "You're serious?"

"Sure. The department uses them occasionally. Usually last-ditch efforts, cases where we couldn't get a single foothold."

Michelle nodded. "I see." Seemed to consider that a moment. "Do they work?"

Benson sat back, searched for his memory in the ceiling. "We caught a killer with one of them, with her help, anyway. It wasn't a cinch, an overnight thing. But I think she helped, or might have helped." He looked back at her. "Do you think you're psychic, Mikki?"

She started to pick up her cup . . . changed her mind. Hand shaking? "No, I don't. I don't think I really believe such a thing is possible. I like to think myself open-minded, but when you start screwing with the space-time continuum, you lose me."

She took another moment, preparing herself maybe. Benson took a sip, giving her time.

"Look . . . this is going to sound really far out, I'm warning you."

"Michelle, I've heard it all."

"Maybe not. That girl . . . the first one that was killed in North Hollywood. . . . I saw her."

"Oh? Alive, you mean?"

"Alive. In a dream."

He didn't quite know the proper response to that so he just nodded. "Go on."

"I was in North Hollywood—in the dream—in exactly the area the dead girl was found. It was early-evening fog. She came at me out of the mist. Same hair, same build. Reaching out for me . . ." Hand definitely shaking now. Both hands.

"Take it easy. Same face?"

Michelle shook her head. "I couldn't see the face. But it was her. I *know* it was her!"

"Easy. Okay, it was her."

"And there's more. The girl you found on the beach. By the palm tree? I saw her too. Same hair, same build, same exact place there in Venice. I could describe it in detail. When I saw the pictures on TV, I . . . vomited. My dream was absolutely the same. *Identical!*"

Her eyes had that look again. Benson put a steadying hand on her wrist, squeezed. "Okay, it's all right. Michelle, listen—you're not the first person who's had dreams like this. Many witnesses, having observed a traumatic event, either in person, or even through the impersonal distance of a photograph, have—"

She was pulling away from him, stiffening.

"You don't get it. I saw them *before* they were murdered! *Weeks before!*" She looked at him quickly as if daring skepticism.

Benson didn't offer any. "All right."

She put her hand to her head, maybe to stop its shaking. "Damn it, I *knew* how this would sound!"

"Never mind that. What else?"

She was silent for a time. Then sighed, gestured dismissively. "Let's just forget this, huh? Shit." She cast about. "I need a cigarette."

"You quit. You were saying you don't believe in psychics."

She slumped. "I . . . don't know. I mean, how else can you explain it?" She turned to him levelly again. "You don't believe any of this, do you? Not really."

"I believe you had dreams, of course I do."

"Dreams, yes, but you think I got it confused, right? Out of order with the killings?"

"No, I think you've got the order right. That's why you're so upset. And I don't blame you."

She gazed at him a moment, eyes filling with relief, then sat back in her chair. "Christ. I've been going out of my mind!"

"I can imagine. How long has this been happening?"

"I don't know . . . months. It's been god-awful."

"And you've never told anyone?"

She hesitated. "Not exactly . . . You're the first."

He stretched, kissed her temple. "Well, I'm flattered. And here I was beginning to think you didn't trust my shifty, different-colored eyes."

Which brought a half smile. She searched him imploringly. "What am I going to do?"

Benson thought a moment, then said, "Have you thought about seeing a doctor?"

She went cold again, bundling up. "A psychiatrist? I knew you'd say that."

"It's a fair question."

Michelle made a resigned sound. "I suppose it is."

"And?"

"Even if I were delusional, which I'm not, that doesn't address this . . . *paranormal* thing. Those girls did die. And I did dream about them, in the exact places where they were found. How's a shrink going to explain that?"

Benson was thinking about it when his Rover chirped. "Shit. Excuse me. Won't be a sec—"

He fumbled it from his jacket. "Yeah. All right. Right." He put the plastic away.

"Hooky's over," Michelle intoned wistfully.

"I'm sorry. Goes with the territory. Anyway, now I have an official excuse to see you."

Her hand flinched toward him reflexively, face tight again. "Touch, please! I don't want this getting to the police. The papers. I'm not a . . ."

She looked away, not finishing, but he knew she was going to say "freak."

Benson thought of coming to her, but he'd already done that, hadn't he? He slid off the kitchen chair. "I'll call you tonight."

She made an impassive face. "I don't think that's such a good idea."

He sighed, started for the hall, turned back. "Michelle, I'm a cop. It's what I grew up to be. It doesn't have to interfere with us, change us."

She came to him then, hooked her arm in his, walked him to the hall. "I'm sorry, Touch. You know I wouldn't trust anyone else with this."

"Let me help you then."

"How?"

"By letting me see you, for starters. I can tell them you think you might have seen something. That's all they need to know."

"Will that work?"

"For a while. Also, I can check with the people we've used in the past."

"The psychics. Do *you* believe, Touch?"

"I believe in anything that will help stop a killer." He kissed her forehead. "Thank you."

Michelle snorted. "For what? The lovely view of my bedroom?"

"For telling me, trusting me. It means a lot. More than the bedroom." He lingered long enough for her to kiss him back but she didn't.

"I'll call you," he said from the door.

Michelle nodded, waved airily. Shut the door.

She stood staring at it for a long moment, then turned and climbed the long staircase.

She lay across the empty bed and closed her eyes, the shades pulled, the ocher light glowing behind them as it had in Jana's room just a short time earlier.

In the soft dark she played a short film of it happening another way.

In it, she was naked, golden as a Norse goddess, smiling up fiercely.

The big cop stood above her, encased and moaning in her uplifted breasts. "Do you *like* that?" she asked him huskily. "Can you feel my *heart*?"

11

It was truly disturbing.

Particularly when everything had seemed to be going so well.

Charlie Grissom sat alone in his small North Hollywood apartment of brick and Sheetrock, surrounded by the limestone and wood of the Ancient Ones, fingering the incredible jeweled dagger absently, tormented by a great weight of doubt.

The terrible truth was, he had been lied to. Lied to and falsely led by those whom he respected—indeed, depended on—above all others. The Ancient Ones.

They had led him step by step, inch by rain-swept inch to the beautiful blond girl called Kurtzy, but whom he, Charlie, knew to be Nephthys, sister of Isis. Even as he, Charlie—despite this modern incarnation—was truly Set, patron deity of Lower Egypt, brother of Osiris, enemy of Horus. In their good time, the Ancient Ones would tell him how it was he had been mistakenly reincarnated into this dreadful twenty-first century, just as they had always instructed him, chiefly through The Voice. And on that day there would be great rejoicing. A perfect wedding, a reuniting of Osiris and his lovely sister-bride Isis.

Except that now Charlie wasn't so sure the wedding would ever take place.

The Voice had spoken falsely.

There could be no other explanation. Why else guide his path to the blond, buxom college girl Kurstin Mallon, reveal unto him that she was indeed the sacred Nephthys, strengthen this belief through the perfect union of their bodies and spirits, then—just when his heart was soaring like the great hawks of Abu Simbel—confuse everything by sending him yet another message?

It made no sense. His bride had arrived. The Voice should have ceased. Yet it had not. It spoke to him still, demanded yet more searching, yet more killings. It made no sense at all.

The Ancient Ones had lied. Charlie was devastated.

He roamed the rooms of his small dwelling, lighting incense, intoning aloud like a priestess of Saqqara, begging, pleading for some message from above, some light unto his feet that he might understand. The killings of the earlier girls he could accept. It was not easy to discern his one true bride through a face swathed with ancient burial wrappings. This had been the test the Ancient Ones had given him, to insure his mettle was worthy, his faith unshakable. He had not relished the deaths, those innocent but unlucky girls, but he had proceeded with grim determination, obeying all that was asked of him. He had hoped, with the arrival of the Kurtz girl, that all that was behind him now. Yet only yesterday he had heard The Voice again. Demanding. Instructing. Another place to be sought, another girl to engage. And, unless this one was truly She, another death to endure. It made no sense.

Charlie sank miserably into the faded flea market sofa, consciously avoiding the boxwood Egyptian settee nearby. He was not a fool. He was not Charlie Grissom, even if his corporeal life had begun there. He was Set, bringer of storms, enemy of Horus, the dynastic god, brother of Osiris, Isis, and husband and brother of the lovely Nephthys whose corporeal self he had yet to discover.

Even his rebirth in this century was auspicious. Had he not been born of a mother well educated in Egyptian culture, whose very place of employment was steeped in the icons of the Ancients? Had not the Old Ones guided him from his childhood haunts, steered him from the mother he had adored to those strange people in Missouri, his baptism by fire? Then in a brilliant flash of insight shown him the way out of the hinterlands, to the deserts of the West Coast (so like the deserts of his ancient homeland) to this great city of Los Angeles—the one city in all the world save those that graced the mighty Nile—that housed The Temple, in whose sacred corridors and hidden depths he found solace and prayer? Could such an irrefutable chain of prophetic events be mere coincidence? They could not.

Why then had The Voice lied to him?

Charlie hung his head. Mysterious were the ways of the Old Ones. Perhaps . . .

Charlie lifted his eyes to the wall of hieroglyphics before him—a wall he had labored over meticulously for three back-breaking months. A sudden warmth rose unbidden in his thin chest.

The Ancients had never lied. Never. Perhaps it was Charlie himself who could not see, was not correctly interpreting their plan. Perhaps the last message, this last girl, was part of the test, to prove to Charlie, through one more false death, that the Kurtz girl was indeed his beloved bride, the goddess Nephthys, the Lady of the Castle! How else could he be sure?

Yes! A final test so there could be no mistake!

The blood surged in his temples.

Then dissipated.

Charlie faltered. There was yet a second possibility. The way to the True Kingdom was a difficult path, flanked by many cunning guises to fool and distract him from his goal. And which of all of the gods' creatures was the most cunning? Woman.

His mother had warned him.

The Kurtz girl. What if she were a ruse?

Charlie rose slowly from the faded chair, eyes dancing across the lovingly decorated wall, whose ancient idioms seemed to spell out a whole new message. The Kurtz girl a ruse, a fake. It was possible. And the Kurtz girl had stayed his hand before he could wrap her . . . had even taken the blessed ceremonial knife away from him!

The surging at his temples returned, expanded into a bright light that seemed to fill the room.

Think! Think!

The gods had not led him this careful if circuitous path to merely mock. They had to be sure, even as he, Charlie, had to be sure. Such was the importance of the wedding.

He looked down at the sacred blade in his hand. *Follow The Voice* . . .

Charlie nodded at the statue of Anubis atop the coffee table.

Yes. First the girl yesterday. Then—if it proved to be the case—the one who called herself Kurtzy. And on and on, a hundred victims if necessary, until the one true bride of Set was found. Such was his destiny.

Charlie rose from the faded sofa, grabbed his blue windbreaker, flush with the old resolve. So be it.

12

The dead girl on the beach, Allison Downey, had few friends at the post office where she worked and only one living relative, a sickly elderly mother. Upon hearing the news of her daughter's death, Mrs. Downey went into a deep, protracted faint. Benson phoned in an ambulance while Amanda attended the old woman on a lumpy couch in her Venice apartment. CPR had not been necessary, but the arriving ambulance crew confirmed that Mrs. Downey had been close to coma and she was rushed to St. Francis. The doctor there informed Detectives Benson and Blaine emphatically that Mrs. Downey, though awake now, would not be available for questioning for at least forty-eight hours. He didn't look like the kind of physician who could be intimidated by cops.

In the interim, Benson and Blaine split the canvassing of the remaining four acquaintances, one of whom was male. They were of little or no help in suggesting who Allison's killer might have been, and all four were given low priority suspicion.

The morning after his afternoon at Michelle Ransom's Pasadena home, Benson met with his partner at her cubicle, offering a box of doughnuts, all glazed. Amanda's favorites.

He set the white cardboard box atop her desk, and leaned against her partition while she finished a phone conversation. Amanda lifted the lid on the doughnut box, raised her brows, gave Benson a quick look, said, "All right, thanks," quickly to the receiver, and hung up.

She popped a doughnut into her mouth immediately, made an almost sexual sound of pleasure, and mouthed, cheeks full, "What are we doing?"

Benson said, "I don't know. Who was that?"

Amanda tried to answer—washed the doughnut down with coffee—and gulped. "The lab. Tox reports found cough syrup in the tummies of both victims."

Benson slouched as if waiting for the punch line. "Is that meaningful?"

"It is if you spike it with sodium dichloride and a few other things you can obtain over the counter. The killer drugged them." She tapped her computer screen, where the lab report was just coming up.

Benson bent over her shoulder, watching the screen. "Didn't drug them very much. According to this, that concoction can—depending on patient and dosage—either put you into a restful sleep or merely make you very drowsy."

Amanda munched. "So he wanted them semiawake? Wanted them to know they were being stabbed to death?"

Benson shook his head. "Suffocated first, remember? Then stabbed."

Amanda sighed, took another bite of doughnut. "It gets more and more bizarre. Guy has some weird fucking agenda going here."

Benson scooted over a chair, sat beside her studying the report. "He meets them—apparent strangers—talks them into going somewhere with him, maybe his place. He drugs them—lightly—waits until they're under, and suffocates them with some kind of esoteric material made only in Egypt. Kills them, presumably. Rapes them before or after. Then hacks them up with a knife."

"A weird knife, with a blade we can't match anywhere."

"A weird knife. What's he trying to say?"

Amanda reached for another doughnut. "I've been thinking. You know, maybe this guy's the exception to the usual signature killer. I mean, yeah, he stabs them, several times, but despite that, there doesn't seem to be the usual humiliation of the victim associated with serial killings. If anything, there's almost something reverential about the position of the bodies."

Benson gave her a dubious look.

"Okay, maybe not 'reverential' but not vulgar, not humiliating. And the sex isn't brutal, really. I almost get the feeling he doesn't hate them."

"He hates them enough to kill them."

Amanda sighed at the green computer screen. "I still say it's a fluke. There's a difference between killing and brutalizing. This looks less ritual than . . . what? Ceremonial?"

"As in cult?"

She shook her head. "No . . . I'm not getting that. Shit, I don't know." She reached into the box again. "Thanks for the doughnuts. But I still won't blow you." She held the box out and Benson shook his head.

Amanda repeated, "What are we doing?"

Benson shrugged. "We need a weapon."

Amanda nodded, chewing.

Benson looked very casual. "I phoned St. Francis. We have permission to interview Allison Downey's mother now from Dr. Kildare."

"Let's do it."

"Would you mind? I need to ask Sid Mathers a few questions."

Amanda swallowed. "Like what? What's the chief ME got that's new?"

"Just some follow-up. Do you mind?"

She watched him.

"Is there a problem?"

"No."

Benson nodded. "Thanks."

Amanda reached for another doughnut, thought better of it, closed the lid of the box. "So did you take my advice?"

"What advice?"

"You know, about Michelle Ransom. Ask her out?"

Benson fussed absently with his tie. "I called her. She wasn't particularly responsive. Mrs. Downey is in room 302."

"I know. What do you mean 'not responsive'?"

"You know."

Amanda reached for her purse, stood. "No, I don't. Like a brush-off, you mean?"

They walked past other detectives, out of the Homicide suite, toward the elevators. "I'm not sure. Women—who can figure them?"

At the elevators Amanda said, "You should try again. I think she really likes you."

"I haven't been thinking about it much, actually."

The doors slid open and Amanda stepped in. When Benson didn't, she said, "Hey."

He turned back to her.

"I thought you were going down to see Mathers, Touch. This is the elevator."

Benson nodded, hands in his pockets casually. "I am. Gotta make a couple of calls first."

He thought she was going to ask who, but the doors slid shut in her face.

Benson returned to his desk, flipped through his Rolodex, and dialed a private residence: Joe Sanguino, retired from the force now for six years.

As the line clicked and buzzed, Benson thought about the same thing he always thought when calling a retired cop: the high number of them who had put bullets through their heads after leaving the force. Was it just the action they missed so much, the esprit de corps unique to police work? Or simply their familiarity and easy access to firearms? No one had ever done a study.

Joe Sanguino had forgotten more about policing than Benson knew and would probably ever know. The number of cops, retired or not, Benson truly admired and respected he could count on one hand; Sanguino would be on the first finger.

"Yeah, Sanguino." Still answered the phone like he was a working cop.

"Been watching your house, Sanguino. There's a law against getting head from a teenager."

"Fuck you and the law, I'm a citizen now. I can get head from Airedales if I want. What's the matter, Benson? The latest serial killer too smart for you detective-grade flatfoots?"

Benson smiled; "Nah, I got him nailed. I'm just pulling Noland's putz."

Sanguino snorted into the receiver. "Sure you are. Speaking of putz pulling, how's that leggy partner, Amanda?"

"Those of us still in the employ of the LAPD maintain a veneer of professional decorum, unlike some useless retirees I could mention."

Another snort from Sanguino. " 'Veneer,' he says. 'Decorum.' College boy. Fucking RHD snot nose."

"This snot nose needs some tutoring. The not-over-the-phone variety."

"Jesus. Cloak-and-dagger shit. Okay, but I want lunch at Westlake Jack's—you buy."

"Cheap prick."

"At any price."

A transfer cop from narrow Brooklyn streets, Sanguino had chosen the wide, rolling hills of Thousand Oaks, forty minutes north of L.A., for his retirement. A New Yorker at heart, he had nonetheless fallen in with the easy southern California climate, the open ranges, a complacency that had strengthened with age. Like most Easterners, he dismissed L.A.'s purported vapid culture and arid wastes, while simultaneously soaking up a tan beside his suburban pool.

Benson pulled into the former RHD detective's

tract driveway, walked flagstones flanked by spiky yucca, and rapped on the door once. Sanguino's yard was yellow from lack of watering. Everything needed trimming.

When the door opened, Benson threw a bag of cheeseburgers in Sanguino's unshaven face. "Hey, fuck this! We said Westlake Jack's! I want *huevos rancheros.*"

Benson shouldered past the blocky Italian, took in the disheveled front room on his way to the kitchen. There was more gray in Joe Sanguino's hair these days—what he has left of it. "It's lunchtime. Get shaved for chrissake."

When Benson turned from the refrigerator, Sanguino was already munching a burger, bathrobe hanging loose, no sash. "This Mexican beer all you got?"

"It's good. Hey, ya can't get goddamn Rhinegold in this crummy state."

Benson uncapped a bottle, shoved newspapers aside, and sat at the littered table. "Christ, Joe, get a wife, huh? Or at least a maid."

"Look who's talking." Sanguino tossed him a burger, slippers slapping linoleum.

Benson ignored the burger, took a long pull. "Tell me about police psychics."

Sanguino groaned into a metal, fifties-style kitchen chair with yellow plastic cushions. "I knew this was a bullshit visit."

"You're the only cop I know who's worked with them."

"Why you want to get into that bullshit, Touch?"

"Because I lied to someone that I'd had experience."

"Why the lie? Oh, Christ, a woman."

"She was bordering on hysterics. I wanted to reassure her."

"They're always bordering on hysterics and you wanted to pork her. Okay. Here's the skivvy. The psychic stuff is all pretty much a big blank. Can we go to Westlake Jack's now?"

"It doesn't work?"

Sanguino shrugged, picking at greasy fries. "Depends on who you ask. It's the disparity in the approach that bothers me. Some of them *seem* to have successes, but I dunno. Dorothy Allison is considered the country's hotshot psychic sleuth at the moment, and she uses astrology, for chrissake. That gal Greta Alexander gets her information from her 'spirit guides.' Some use dowsing rods and pendulums and all that other archaic shit. Not what you'd call a state-of-the-art science. Of course, that's their big argument—science isn't working."

"But the department does use them. Lots of other states too."

"Only as a last resort. Look, I'm not saying I don't believe so-called clairvoyance is possible, but it's like flying saucers or God—who the hell can prove it?"

"Or disprove it."

"There you go. The fact is, the LAPD ran a battery of tests on these people back in 1991. It was reported in the *Journal of Police Science and Administration*. Didn't you read it?"

"Must have missed that."

"*You* were the one, huh? Anyhow, the results said that information generated by psychics was no better than chance would allow. I think that's a quote. I mean, use your common sense, Touch. If these people really possessed the powers they claim, wouldn't they have identified the Unabomber first, or found the remains of Jimmy Hoffa, shit like that?"

Benson nodded. "You don't buy it."

Sanguino held up his hands. "I'm an agnostic. But when I was on the New York force they had this case in Nutley, New Jersey. Department spent the whole goddamn afternoon digging up some drainage ditch this psychic Dorothy Allison claimed contained the body of a missing boy. It didn't. That kind of crap not only wastes valuable police time, but think how the kid's mother must've felt. I remember this one case where they called in the fire department to pump the water from a flooded basement in some abandoned building. They were looking for another little kid. Lots of man hours and money. The kid's remains were eventually found clear across town. Not only inaccurate and costly, but heart-wrenching. Ever hear of Peter Hurkos?"

"Identified the Boston Strangler."

"*Mistakenly* identified the Boston Strangler."

Benson took another thoughtful swig. "But there have been successes. I've read reports."

Joe Sanguino smiled. "Depends on how you define success. Look, the fact is, it's easy for a psychic to exaggerate their successes, even claim positive results in cases that were either failures or never even existed. A psychic is a human being like you or me. He or she can obtain all kinds of legit information they can later claim psychically *sent* to them. All they gotta do is brief themselves, same way we do: study newspaper files, area maps, whatever. Another thing. When they report this shit, they always seem to be dealing in vague generalities. Like say they claim they've supposedly perceived a name like 'John' or 'Joseph'—common names that don't really pin the psychic down. You know as a cop, social and psychological factors play a big role in influencing people to accept the accuracy of *any* information. A person's own belief system always has to be factored in. Oh, yeah, and then there's this 'retrofitting' technique."

"Which is?"

"After-the-fact matching. Example: psychic says, I see water and the number ten. Yeah, so? What the hell does that mean? It's a safe offering in almost any case. After all the facts are in, it would be pretty goddamn unusual if there weren't some stream or lake *somewhere* in the vicinity, right? And the number ten could be anything from a distance, to a highway, to the number of people in the search party, to a license plate number, *anything*. You get the idea." Sanguino took the beer from Benson's hand and tipped it back.

Benson stared at the littered kitchen. Littered like his brain. At length he said, "What about dreams?"

Sanguino shrugged. "Could be. I never had much experience with dreams."

Benson nodded, sighed.

Sanguino kept the beer. "So are you fucking her or what?"

"Does it matter?"

"If she's a witness, bet your little gold shield it matters."

Benson grunted. "Tell the truth, Joe, I don't know what the hell she is."

Sanguino smiled, took a pull. "Always the pussy-whipped schmuck. Them sexy different-colored eyes of yours get you in dutch. Better watch your butt, Touch. You still got lots of time in." He handed the empty bottle back to Benson, pushed away from the table, shuffled to the disastrous sink, and began rummaging through the mountain of dirty dishes under the wall phone. "Where'd I put that goddamn Rolodex?"

"That it?" Benson pointed at the litter atop the fridge.

"Oh, yeah. Little rascal." Sanguino snagged the Rolodex, flipped through it, pulled free a card. "Here. VICAP knows a lot more about this stuff than I do. They work directly with the local Psi Squad group."

"Whatever that is." Benson took the card, shook his head. "Noland would have my balls if I took this to the FBI without authorization. I really don't think my captain likes me, Joe."

"Well, you are an arrogant prick. But Noland can't nail you for playing golf with a feeb." Sanguino nodded at the card. "That's Bill Campbell, a straight shooter, likes cops. Or tolerates them, anyway. We go way back. Mention my name."

Joe Sanguino scratched his belly, belched luxuriously, and yawned. "Call from here if you like. I'm gonna take a shower."

"About time."

"Fuck you."

13

Sue Thornquist went through all of Kurtzy's drawers.

She looked through her closet, and under her bed, and through her cedar chest. Just as she did every day.

A lazy calm settled over her. The bright room faded . . . became the bright, deep green of the Angeles National Forest. Summer camp. Years ago. And only yesterday . . .

And Jana's golden tresses caught in the afternoon glow, the shards of light lancing the little forest path. Just Jana. Only Jana. Alone with that lovely goddess in a magical kingdom of towering redwoods, leaning pines.

Jana's soft hair against her fingers . . . her curious, but friendly smile, the clear blue eyes that so much appeared to beckon . . .

. . . . the brush of her red lips . . .

And the shock of anger that followed. The humiliation. The screaming. The accusation.

Please, Sue had begged . . . *It was a mistake,* she'd pleaded . . . *I'm sorry . . . don't tell . . .*

But Jana had told.

Told the camp supervisor, who'd told the team leaders, who'd talked to the other girls in the barracks, at least one of whom had told stories herself. Sue was out. Out for good.

Transferred by her mortified parents to a private school until after graduation.

And even there she couldn't stop thinking of her . . .

Until Kurtzy.

Kurtzy who hid herself behind owl-rimmed glasses, and slouched shoulders, and a straggly mane. But who was every bit Jana's equal . . . perhaps even more. She only needed drawing out . . . only needed keeping from danger, from idiots like Jason Richards.

Sue was stooped over the cedar chest when Kurtzy came in unexpectedly.

She straightened up casually, gave her new roommate a tight smile, brushed back her rich ebony locks casually. "Hi. Good day?"

Kurtzy frowned uncertainly, surveying the room. "You cleaned up."

"Somebody has to do it. God knows you're never here anymore."

Kurtzy hesitated, opened her mouth—perhaps to protest—

Sue swept away blithely, waving a hankie at the bedstead as though dusting. "So, where you been? Got a freshman hottie somewhere on the side?"

"I've just had a lot of studying to do is all." Kurtzy kept glancing around the dorm room distractedly.

"Ah, late nights in the library. All work and no

play." Sue flicked the hankie at her bedstead. "I thought maybe you and I could go out together tonight. It's Saturday. Maybe go to a movie or something."

"I really can't tonight, Sue. Maybe Rae—"

Sue shot daggers.

"—or Gail Hunnicut, or—"

Sue was wearing her petulant face. Kurtzy dreaded that face. "I don't want to go out with Gail Hunnicut, I want to go out with you."

Kurtzy pulled off her gray sweater, folded it, and placed it in her top bureau drawer. "I'm really sorry, Sue. Maybe next week?"

Sue eyed her coolly. She shrugged a smile, turned, and flopped on her bed. She picked up a movie magazine, slapped at the pages.

Kurtzy watched her briefly, then headed to the bathroom quietly.

"So who is it?"

Or almost to the bathroom. "Who is what?"

Sue slapped pages, posture relaxed, eyes still petulant. "It's always you timid little brainy types that have the lurid sex lives, right?"

Kurtzy stood rooted, three feet from the bathroom door. "What do you mean?"

" *'What do you mean?'* " in sarcastic singsong. "Whatever do you mean, Sue?" She slapped the page. "No makeup, hiding behind thick glasses and big sweaters that hide your big boobs."

Kurtzy closed her eyes. It could be such a good friendship sometimes, so much fun and lightheartedness sometimes. "Sue, please . . ."

" *'Sue, please!'* "

"Please don't. Why are you doing this? Have I done something?"

Sue tossed the magazine, scooped up another. Slapped pages.

Kurtzy sighed, went to the bathroom.

When she came out, Sue was sitting on the edge of the bed, smiling limply.

"Hey. I'm sorry. Okay?"

Kurtzy smiled. "Of course."

"It's just that I worry about you. I feel like . . . I dunno, a big sister, I guess. You're so . . . The thing is, I've been around the block a time or two. And the truth is, it's a pretty crummy block. Lots of assholes out there. Spend lots of money on you, promise you the moon, even take you to see their folks, if oh, you'll just suck their cocks."

Kurtzy colored. "It's not like that—" She bit her tongue, having fallen for it, and turned away.

"So there is someone."

Kurtzy grabbed her psych book, lay back on her bed, turned pages thoughtfully. Her cheeks burned. Even now she was using Sue's little theatrical tricks. But she couldn't make herself slap shut the book, toss it aside.

"Look, don't be like that. I'm sure he's very nice. I'm just trying to look out for you a little bit. Is that so wrong?"

Kurtzy stared unseeing at her book, heart conflicted. Why did it have to be like this? All her life looking for someone . . . someone to care for, someone to care about her. A friend. Or a lover. Now, in the space of just weeks, she had both! But it was too good to be real. Because the fact was, Sue was jealous. She didn't even know for sure about Charlie and she was *jealous*.

Kurtzy looked past the book a moment and the newly swept room. No . . . not jealous. Use the right word if you're going to talk about it. *Possessive*.

She sighed inwardly. Why hadn't she seen this side of Sue before? This *possessive* aspect of her personality? How had she missed it in all these weeks?

Or had she really seen it all along? Been actually flattered by it . . . Yes, even seduced by it.

A person in need of friends, in need of love, will leap at the first opportunity. In that, there was truth in what Sue said.

Kurtzy glanced over at her now. Her pretty, dark-haired roommate sitting dejectedly on her bed, head bowed, shoulders slumped, studying her hands absently.

Poor thing. She only had Kurtzy's best interests at heart. All right, she was a little overprotective. At least she *bothered* to be protective.

"Sue? Hey . . ."

Sue looked up hopefully.

"I don't want to fight. You're my friend. My best friend. I want it to stay that way."

"That's all I want, Kurtz."

Kurtzy put down the book. "I just need a little space, that's all. This is all kind of new for me, hard for me, in a way it wouldn't be for you. Can you understand that?"

Sue looked back at her hands, finally nodded slowly. "Is he someone I know?"

Kurtzy sighed. She wasn't going to give up. Then she smiled. "No. He's just a guy. But you . . . Sue, you don't have to be . . ."

Sue tucked her hands between her legs, sighed hugely. "Jealous?" She snorted a laugh, a mirthless one. "Because I'm dark and pretty and boys like me? That's what you think, right? That's what everyone thinks. Only it isn't that easy."

She looked up, eyes brimming. "I have insecurities too, Kurtz. Every bit as deep as yours. The truth is . . . behind the bravado, I'm pretty much a walking facade. People like me all right, in the beginning. Then they get to know me."

Kurtz pushed the book aside, came to her, sat with her. "No. I don't believe that."

Sue nodded rapidly. "It's true though. I don't make friends that readily. The only person I ever really got close to besides you was Jana Ransom. And that . . . well, that didn't work out. As I said, friendships rarely do." She looked into Kurtzy's eyes soulfully. "But when one does, like ours, I want to hold on to it. Maybe a little too tightly. I'm sorry."

Kurstin put her arm around her. She smiled. "Some pair we are."

She felt the tremble of Sue's faint laugh.

"I've had nothing all my life, Kurtz. Nothing. Poor white trash, that's my background. That's my future. Parents dead. Living with my psycho aunt." She looked up sharply. "Know what they left me, my parents? A log cabin. A fucking falling-down piece-of-shit cabin in the San Gabriel Mountains. In other words, squat. It isn't fair."

"No, it isn't." She glanced at her watch then, gave Sue's shoulders a squeeze, and stood. "I'm really sorry but I have to go."

Sue folded her arms. "To meet him? Kurtzy sighed, but her roommate held up her hands and said, "No, no, it's none of my business."

"I don't even know if it will come to anything, Suze . . . probably it won't."

Sue shook her head. "No, don't say that. You deserve for it to come to something. You're a good person, Kurtz. Thank you for putting up with me. I mean it."

Kurtzy bent and hugged her, ruffled the lustrous crown. "Knucklehead!"

There was only a light mist tonight.

But how the streets shone. So much rain for southern California. Messy. Inconvenient. But kind of fun.

Kurtzy crossed Cimarron Street, hopped the curb past gurgling water, and trotted the stone steps to Charlie's apartment.

Six long flights up through musty, mildew-smelling stairwells, a short turn down a dark, forbidding hallway, and she was there. Heart pounding. But not from exertion.

Not yet anyway. And she stifled a giggle, nearly embarrassing herself. Kurtzy Mallon, you must be the only girl in the world with a lover who's capable of embarrassing himself!

. . . *a lover* . . .

She hesitated, fist raised to knock. *I have a lover.*

No movie star maybe. But hers. Even now she

couldn't believe it, wouldn't believe it until she was inside the strange little painted temple again. In his bed again.

Kurtzy knocked.

No one answered.

Not with the third, fourth, or fifth knock.

She bit her lip, checked her watch. Had she gotten the wrong night?

She leaned to the door. *"Charlie?"*

But he wasn't there. He'd forgotten. *He's forgotten you . . .*

Oh, shut up! It was nothing of the kind! They'd just gotten their wires crossed was all. She'd said apartment, he'd said library—something like that. He wasn't exactly a paragon of organized thinking.

She found herself staring at the rusty knob. In a moment, she reached for it, turned it. The door gave way a crack. *"Charlie?"*

No, this wasn't right. She didn't know him well enough to let herself into his place, sit and wait for him. He might be hours. *And he might come back with someone else . . .*

She shook free of the thought, closed the door quickly—

—turned with a gasp. Was that a noise behind her?

She squinted at the dark hall. Nothing. Empty stained carpet and shadows. When they . . . if this ever came to anything, the first thing she'd do is find Charlie a less weird place to live.

For the moment, however, it was time to call it a night . . .

14

Benson held up the Rolodex card Joe Sanguino had given him.

From his third-floor desk phone at Parker Center, he dialed the Los Angeles branch of the FBI, one of fifty-six field offices and four hundred satellite or resident agencies they held in North America. He asked for Special Agent Bill Campbell.

Not a call Benson particularly relished. The control edge all federal agents held over local police inevitably led to some tension, though how much could depend on the attitude of the agent. Or the cop. Benson had known arrogant agents, indifferent ones, and those who—like himself—were merely trying to do their best work, taking leads and help from wherever, whomever they could get it.

Bill Campbell appeared to be of the latter variety, especially after Benson mentioned Joe Sanguino's name. "Yeah, how the hell is the old fart, anyway?"

"Retired," Benson told the receiver.

"Yeah, that's what I mean. Joe loved this shit."

"I know. He seems okay, though. Fatter, tanner."

"That's good. What can I do for you, Detective?"

"Need some info on police psychics from VICAP."

"You guys can access VICAP now."

"Yeah, I know," Benson said. "This is more in the way of personal advice. On the QT." When Campbell chuckled on the line, Benson asked, "What's funny?"

"Nothing. The words 'psychic' and 'QT' aren't often used in the same sentence."

"Joe says you play golf."

"Sure! What's your handicap?"

"What's a handicap?" Benson asked.

Campbell belonged to a private club in Long Beach. Not Beverly Hills ritzy but intimidating enough, especially if you hadn't played a round of golf since you were a kid.

"Must be nice to be a rich feeb," Benson goaded, pulling his rented caddy behind him, glancing over the lush, rolling course. Testing Campbell's sense of humor now could save them both time.

"Let me know when you meet one," Campbell replied good-naturedly.

Benson hooked the first shot straight into the rough. He winced painfully. "Should give you some idea what you're up against." He lowered his driver with disgust, backing away from his still upright tee.

Campbell grinned, placed his ball atop Benson's tee. "At least you don't have to bother replacing divots. Is this about the Mummy Killer?"

"Jesus," Benson sighed, "where the hell'd you get that?"

"That's what the ME called him—says he thinks the guy wraps them up like mummies! Catchy, heh?"

"Another stupid nickname for the *Times* to latch on to."

"Is the LAPD thinking of bringing in a psychic?" He slashed a rock-solid drive right down the middle. The little white ball seemed to ride the air forever.

"If we are, you don't know about it, okay?"

Campbell nodded, replacing his divot. "Message received."

They headed down the fairway, Benson almost feeling guilty about how pleasant this was. It had been a long time. He let it stay pleasant for a few more minutes across clean, brilliantly green lawn, then turned to Campbell. "I'll be blunt. I'm not exactly a metaphysical guy. I'd appreciate your private take on the subject."

Campbell squinted into the sun. He was tall, blond, good-looking enough to be with central casting but seemingly unaware of it, or indifferent. Open and easygoing—no wonder Sanguino liked him. "With psychics, it really comes down to deductive versus inductive."

"I'm listening."

Campbell plucked a crumpled aluminum can from the fairway, launched it toward the rough. "Kids . . ." He made a *snik* sound with his tongue. "The Violent Crime Analysis Program is basically computer-driven. They link similar patterns of crime from among all reported cases in the government's database. They analyze—that's what they *do*—all relevant details of a crime. Including offender info, suspect description, victimology, modus operandi, forensic, blah, blah, blah, including suspect behavior before, during, or after a crime. You know all this, right?"

"Go on."

"Once a case is entered into the database, it's compared continually against all other entries on the basis of certain aspects of the crime. The purpose is to detect signature aspects of homicide and similar patterns of MO, which in turn allows VICAP personnel to pinpoint any crime that might have been committed by the same offender, then notify the other agencies involved. Multiagency conferencing is great when a suspect has traveled all over hell and gone throughout the country. There's your ball, Detective."

Benson stopped long enough to hit himself out of the rough, then continued pace with Special Agent Campbell. "Still listening."

"The point is, even with all this high-tech computerized profiling, we still fail to solve crimes. Profiling merely points a finger, a place to begin. The best technology hasn't replaced the need for the trained senses of the human mind. When it does, you and I will be out of a job. What we do—guys like you and me—in essence, is deduce. What the psychic does is *induce*. The catch is, the two forms are not all that disparate."

Campbell lined up his next shot, bounced within yards of the green. "Both 'deductive' and 'inductive' incorporate reasoning. Induction just allows more room for the same flashes of inspiration and gut sense all good detectives use. Look, you must have solved or helped solve cases through pure insight, right? Some *feeling* you really couldn't back up by evidence or fact?"

"Sure. Hunches."

Campbell nodded. "Same way pilots, despite advanced instrumentation, still fly by the seat of their pants. Intuition is an accepted part of life, including police work."

"But we're not all psychic."

Campbell hesitated as Benson lined up his next shot. He looked like he was about to comment on Benson's last statement.

Benson looked up from his five iron. "What?"

Campbell smiled enigmatically, shook his head. "Nothing. Make your shot."

Benson hit the ball. It accidentally landed near the green.

Campbell chipped handsomely onto the green.

"What the hell is the Psi Squad?" Benson pursued.

"It's a group of civilian psychics the Bureau uses. They don't do readings and they aren't into a lot of mystical crap. And they don't charge for their efforts. Dorothy Allison is a Psi. Some members are actually working police officers and ex-police. All of them have supposedly been trained to utilize their inherent psi abilities. Remote viewing, stuff like that." Campbell lined up his putt.

"Remote viewing."

"The ability to utilize certain trained . . . *sensitivities* of the mind. The ability to see—in the mind's eye— beyond what we call the perceived barriers of space and time."

When Benson didn't respond, Campbell looked up with the enigmatic grin again. "Keeping up, Detective?"

"Trying."

Campbell laughed, made the putt; the ball rattled in the cup. "Now you're going to ask if I personally believe in this shit."

"You read my mind."

Campbell chuckled. He bent, held up the white golf ball for Benson to see. Closed his fingers over it, twisted his hand in the air, and opened it again to an empty palm. "Do you believe the ball disappeared?"

Benson grunted. "No."

"Doesn't really matter though, does it?"

"Meaning?"

"Meaning both the FBI and local law authorities have employed the use of psychics and will continue to do so, whether you or I personally believe it works or not. As to whether anybody can actually *prove* a psychic has aided in the solving of a crime . . . well, the Bureau's official posture is—"

"If it works, don't fuck with it?"

"Exactly. And if it's helpful, use it." Campbell produced the ball in his other hand, tossed it to Benson.

Benson caught it high, turned the label toward him. "What happened to the Titilus?"

Campbell beamed admiration. "Oh, you're *good*! We could *use* you!" and pulled the first ball—the Titilus—from his pocket.

Benson weighed the second ball thoughtfully, looked off at the trees a moment. "What about dreams?"

"What about them?"

"These so-called *visions* the psychics see—do they ever come to them in dreams?"

Campbell stuck the putter in his caddy thoughtfully. "Some of them do. There's been research that suggests this so-called seeing in the mind's eye can be done at any distance. Some psychics, purportedly, don't even have to be in the actual place a crime occurred. In some cases, certain information from months or even years before can be retrieved from the psychic and put to use. So they say."

Benson thought about it. He lined up his putt, hit the ball, watched it swing wide of the cup. Campbell winked at him.

"Bill, could a person be a psychic and not know it?"

Campbell stepped behind Benson's ball. "Well, the experts—for whatever their opinion is worth—say we all possess potential psychic ability. The key word here is 'potential.' You can't *create* it as such, but it can be nurtured, enhanced, like any other human skill. So they say." He looked up at Benson. "Someone you know?"

Benson chewed his lip. "Maybe."

"Friend?"

Benson snickered. "You guys *are* mind readers."

Bill Campbell smiled. "Poker players. Anyway, better find your Mummy guy soon or assholes like me will be breathing down your Kevlar."

Benson nodded, watched his ball rattle into the cup under Campbell's perfect putt. "Yeah."

Campbell rested the putter on his shoulder. "Maddeningly ambiguous, isn't it? Sorry. I wasn't much help to you, Detective."

Benson extended his hand. "It's Touch. And you

were helpful. I appreciate your candor. I'll return the favor someday."

Campbell shook hands, smiled, bent, and tossed Benson his ball. "You've already done that."

"I have? How?"

Campbell turned to the fairway. "By being a lousy golfer."

15

The depression hit Benson on the Hollywood Freeway, halfway back to Parker Center.

It was followed by a headache, which increased the depression. He wanted a drink. And drink was, of course, a depressant. He sat in the Mustang and fumed.

Traffic was stopped. When wasn't it in L.A.? All five lanes were bumper to bumper. People were leaning out their windows, craning ahead, trying to get a glimpse of the source of the holdup. People always did that—some sooner than others—but they always did it. Like it helped to know.

Benson sat behind the wheel and stared straight ahead into the rusted ass of a flatbed truck. It was always one of two things: an accident or roadwork. Or God forbid a combination of the two. Benson had suffered three hours straight on the 405 during one of those.

He ran a hand through his hair now, foot on the

brake, cheeks puffed. Too many hours in too much traffic. What the hell was he doing in this town? The smog never got better, the crime only got worse. What the hell was the point?

That's right. Think depressed and you'll get more depressed.

But he couldn't help it, the way a person will probe an aching tooth. *Am I getting too old for this job?* Probably. But too young for retirement, the kind that would pay anything anyway. And what was the alternative? Buck for detective three? Then captain? Noland would be no help there. Noland hated his guts. But Benson was well liked in other high places and Noland was hinting at hanging it up soon. It would be between Benson and Pete Saunders. Saunders was a good detective and wanted the captain's job and was a grade three already. Benson liked Saunders. So did the others. But Benson knew Amanda and the rest of the task force would be more comfortable around a boss with street smarts and dirty knuckles. Like Benson.

But being a captain . . . he just couldn't feature it.

Sitting behind a desk. Handing out orders. Loaded down with everyone else's paperwork *including* your own. Taking weekly shit from the AC, the Chief of Police, the DA, the fucking mayor. Heading up those lengthy goddamn quarterly homicide meetings with detectives from all over the damn city . . . reviewing suspect information and crime trends, keeping an eye on all the geographic boundaries, acting as liaison between outside agencies . . . Screw that.

Benson sighed wearily.

So here he sat, overqualified and fearful of moving up.

Joe Sanguino.

That was how he'd probably end up. And much as he loved Joe, the idea of spending his last days like that drove *real* depression through his gut. *"A man should be the best he can be."* Where had he read that? James Jones, *From Here to Eternity*?

Liz.

Those had been the best days.

The worst days too, unquestionably—she'd been certifiable—but the best days with Lizzie had been the best days of his life. Liz he had loved. At least the half of her that allowed herself to be loved. If he could have found a magic knife, cut out the other half, the crazy half . . .

Fuck this. Benson straightened behind the wheel.

He reached for the glove compartment and the magnetized roof flasher—he'd take the shoulder around this mess. He had the little door opened before remembering the battery in the flasher was dead. "Shit!"

He slapped the glove compartment door shut and it sprung back open. He slapped it shut and it sprung open again. He kicked it savagely and it stayed put.

That's brilliant, Detective. Take it out on the car. Dent the fucking dashboard.

Traffic surged ahead. Two whole feet.

Liz.

Married a manic depressive because *you're* a manic depressive, *that* it, Detective? A bi-polar? Scotty had been trying to get him to see the department shrink for months.

That got him thinking about Liz again, making love to her, and that got him thinking about Michelle Ransom. Michelle was bigger boned, with bigger breasts and hips. Liz had been a little thing. Oh, but how she could shake that thing.

He wanted a drink. And thinking about it made wanting it worse.

Horns honked ahead. The exhaust fumes were getting to him, increasing the headache. But if he rolled up the windows, turned on the air-conditioning, the Mustang would overheat standing still like this. He'd read somewhere you actually got more smog poisoning with the air conditioning *on*—the rolled-up windows trapped it or something. *Yeah. You read a lot. Try some books on mental well-being. Some chicken soup for the soul stuff.*

Screw the damn roof flasher!

Benson yanked the wheel hard and pulled onto the shoulder, feeling better the moment he was in motion again, air circulating the car. Two small rises, then a cluster of blinking red lights. Fucking roadwork. Why the hell don't they do it at night? In L.A. rush hour, all it takes is one closed lane to cause a major backup.

He gunned the Mustang to a few yards before the line of orange warning cones. Two cement trucks and a host of Day-Glo-vested workers toiled roadside. Benson slowed, hooked right, stopped again. He honked at the fender-to-fender traffic lane, trying to squeeze back in and get around the cement trucks. Nobody let him in. Benson leaned angrily on the horn.

A burly guy with a Marine cut and slitted eyes rolled down his window. "Hey, asshole! Who the fuck are *you?*" He glared from behind the wheel of an antique Caddy the size of a catamaran.

Benson leaned on his horn insistently.

The guy leaned out the Caddy's window. "Do that again and I'll come over there and stuff you up the tailpipe of that fuckin' 'stang!"

Benson leaned on the horn, raced the engine defiantly.

The Marine spat, shoved the Caddy in gear viciously, and hauled out of his car, face flaming. He strode toward Benson's Mustang.

Left his car running, Benson mused. *Apparently doesn't think this will take long.*

Marine Cut closed, sporting a tank top and tattooed biceps. He was bigger even than he'd appeared behind the wheel. Benson, in no mood, snapped off his engine, pushed open his door, adrenaline rising like sweet wine.

Marine Cut charged straight in, commando style. "Let's see what you *got*, asshole!" He came in fast with a muscled right and hidden tire iron. The muscular forearm declared *Semper Fi,* Benson noticed, as the iron came down.

Infuriated by sight of the iron, Benson no longer even considered going for his shield to stop this—guy pulls an iron on you, fuck him. He ducked under the descending metal easily, swiveled aside, let the Marine have it hard in the kidneys with his right—and again. The Marine went white-faced with surprise. The tire iron flew away, clanged, and slid under someone's car.

Benson waited.

Marine Cut, face tight with pain now, nevertheless

came back recklessly, fists flying like a windmill. Benson, adrenaline satisfied, held up a hand to stop it. It was over.

But the Marine didn't know it, or his pride wouldn't admit it. Maybe it was the crowd all around, watching from their cars. Benson let the guy's recklessness work against him, parried past the flying fists, hooked an arm under the tattoo, and let the momentum carry the Marine hard into the side of the Mustang. The big guy bounced once, denting the paneling.

The dent infuriated Benson for some reason. In a moment, he was all over the guy, raining jackhammer punches at the stupid razor cut, over and over—fury flooding him—still hammering after the guy had crumpled defeated against the front tire, curled protectively, a child trying to escape a bad dream.

Someone was yelling . . . *Hey, hey—he's had enough!* and Benson finally stopped, stepped back, nodding, saying, "Okay," to nobody, thinking to himself: *I'm breathing too hard. Got to get in shape.*

He turned at a *whooping* behind him. A black-and-white jerked up from the shoulder, spraying gravel. Two patrol uniforms leapt out, batons ready.

Benson showed them his shield, told them the guy was detaining an officer on duty.

The two cops—young kids pumped and scared behind crisp uniforms, shiny cap bills—lowered their batons, looked down at the battered Marine, then up at Benson's blood-spattered shirt. One of them said, "Jesus."

The other asked Benson if he wanted them to take the guy in. Benson shook his head, straightening his tie. "Just get him out of here. That's his car."

Back in the Mustang, starting the engine again, Benson was aware of gaping faces all around him, motorists and kids. For the first time he realized how it might have looked.

Screw it. He rolled over one of the orange cones, pulled onto the freeway, maneuvered around the cement trucks, and hit the gas. Open lanes ahead, wide and clear and free of traffic.

"All *right!*" he shouted into the wind.

But he didn't feel good about it.

He stopped off at his valley home to change the shirt, still feeling bad.

While there, having his second drink, his kitchen phone rang.

"What the hell are you doing?"

"What's up, Mandy?"

"What the hell are you doing?" Her tone was cold; he was in trouble. Noland?

"Trying to solve a—"

"Why aren't you answering your goddamn Rover?"

Shit. Benson pulled the cellular from his pocket, punched. Dead. "I just put new batteries in the goddamn thing. It must be screwed up." But *had* he put the new batteries in? He remembered *buying* them . . . or thought he did—

"Do you have a drink in your hand right now? Answer me, Touch."

Benson put the whiskey glass on the drainboard reflexively. "Listen, you're not my goddamn mother!"

"Are you having a *drink!* Answer the fucking question!"

She wasn't his superior. He didn't have to answer to her. "Listen, Amanda—"

"First you soften me up with a box of my favorite doughnuts. Then you lie about seeing the chief ME! Meanwhile I'm wasting my time on a worthless follow-up interview! Then you fucking disappear!"

"I didn't disappear. I told you, the Rover is—"

"Touch, we've got to talk." Her tone had changed.

"You keep saying that . . ."

"You're depressed. Maybe clinically."

"I'm working on the case, Mandy."

"*Alone? Without me?*"

"Of course not. I—"

"*You're forgetting* things, Touch! You're . . . distracted. You've—"

"Lost my edge? Look, I've maybe got a little midlife thing going and—"

"Bullshit! I want you to see a doctor."

"Mandy, I'm not—"

"And *I'm* not going to get my ass shot off in a firefight because you *forgot* to load your piece!"

His anger became fear. "Mandy . . . hold on . . . Okay, I've been a little down lately . . ."

"I want you to say you'll see someone! I want to hear you say it!"

"Honey, Noland is already looking for an excuse to bump my ass."

"And you're handing it to him."

She had answers for everything.

"Touch, what is it? Is it Liz? Are you seeing this Ransom woman? Is she screwing with your head? You don't need that shit, Touch."

"You're the one who suggested—"

"I thought it would do you some good! But if she's depressing you, if she's a nutcase like . . ."

"Like Liz?"

Amanda didn't say anything for a moment. "All right. You're right. I'm not your mother. So I'm going to stop covering your ass at the office. And I'm going to tell Steve Ditko and Sid Mathers to stop doing it too. Then I'm going to the department psych and suggest an evaluation."

Benson sighed. "No, you're not."

"I will, Touch. Damn it, this is my fault. I've seen it coming for months. I've been a shitty partner."

"You've been a great partner. I wish you'd marry me."

"I wish you'd—" *Mean it* she was going to say.

"Then you'd be stuck with an alcoholic," Benson said. Jesus. He'd said it. Didn't hurt as much as he'd imagined.

"Touch—shit, I have to go. Are you coming in?"

"On my way. And I *am* on the case. When I'm sure of a few things I'll tell you."

"What 'things?' What can't you tell your partner now?"

"Just give me a little while, Mandy. Trust me."

"I do. That's my problem." And she hung up.

16

Benson hooked out of Calabasas onto the Ventura Freeway heading south for The Glass House, the nickname for the Robbery-Homicide Division.

Located downtown at the Parker Center on North Los Angeles Street, the massive eight-story structure, built in 1955, was named after William H. Parker, the former police chief so instrumental in cracking down on L.A. crime in the 1940s. Benson shared its halls— and particularly its third level—with seventy-six other RHD detectives assigned to its seven sections—in Benson's and Amanda Blaine's case, the Homicide Special Section I, which handled serial killers, high-profile, and other homicides requiring extensive time. It also assisted other detectives and outside agencies in cases of mutual interest. Benson was thinking about the center's narrow underground parking spaces when his personal cellular (with newly installed batteries) went off.

The voice was tense. "Touch? It's Michelle."

Michelle? Had he given his cellular number to Michelle Ransom?

"I'm sorry to call like this. Are you very busy?"

"No, it's okay . . . How'd you get—"

"I phoned the department and asked for you. They put me through to Amanda Blaine. I guess I sounded stressed, so she gave me your number."

"You do sound stressed. Are you okay?"

"Yes. No. I . . . would you have time to talk?"

Christ, of all times. "Are you in Pasadena?"

"I'm at the museum. I'm not even sure what I'm doing here!"

"Take it easy. Which museum?"

"The one with the animals, the . . . fossils, you know."

"The *Page*? The tar pits on La Brea?"

"Yes. Can you come? I need to tell you something. *Now!*"

"Calm down. I'm on the 101, about thirty minutes from you. Stay there. There's a gift shop, I think, maybe a café. Sit down and have something to drink, but don't leave the museum, understand?"

A sigh of relief. "Thank you so much—"

"Don't leave the museum."

Benson left the 101 at Santa Monica Boulevard, hooked a left onto La Brea, then a right at Wilshire and he was there.

The La Brea Tar Pits are one of the few places in L.A. whose surrounding structures accommodate *them*. The swamps of bubbling tar, incredibly still active after millions of years, are carefully fenced-off from public and fauna alike, lest modern mammals fall victim to the sticky treachery the way their ancient ancestors did. A tourist attraction for decades, someone erected a statue of a struggling mastodon mired to the shoulders in the muck, its infant waving its trunk piteously from the safety of the shore. Benson could never figure out how they kept the big elephant from sinking.

Michelle Ransom, dressed to the nines in an expensive, tasteful Halston suit, clearly coming from her office, was staring at a glass display case of dire wolf skulls in the main foyer. Benson had visited here countless times to ruminate. The big animals got trapped in the tar, the wolves came to eat the big animals, became trapped themselves. There was a contemporary L.A. metaphor there somewhere.

Michelle turned at the sound of his approach.

She looked haggard, showing her true age for the first time, mascara slightly smeared, face wan. But still beautiful, Benson thought. Good bones. You had them or you didn't.

"Amiel. Sorry to sound so desperate. I haven't slept all night." She came into his arms, hugged him tight, cheek to his.

Benson held her until people began looking. Then he took her arm gently, found a bench. "Let's sit a second. Is Jana all right?"

Michelle jerked. "Why do you say *that*?"

Benson frowned. "No reason. What is it, Mikki?" He took her hand.

Michelle drew composing breath, closed her eyes a moment. "You're going to think I'm crazy. But I've *got* to talk to somebody!"

"Easy. Tell me." Though he thought he knew.

Michelle stared past him, hand to brow as if feeling for the memory. "I didn't tell you about it before, but the night of the reunion, I had a dream . . . you know, like the others." She turned to him, anticipating ridicule.

"I'm listening."

She looked at her hand. It was trembling. She seemed momentarily fascinated by it. Benson took it, covered it with his own.

"The same thing that always happens. Same dream. I see the girl. She's coming at me out of the fog. Or the mist. Or whatever it is."

"Go on."

Michelle shrugged. "That's it. It doesn't last long."

Her hand was freezing in his. "And this girl—she doesn't say anything?"

Michelle shook her head. "Nothing that makes any sense. It's more like a shriek. Like '*Hasten!*' "

"Hasten?"

She shrugged helplessly. "Got me. She always says it as she comes at me."

"Can I get you something? Coffee?"

She shook her head again. "I drank gallons waiting for you. I'm floating." But she didn't move from the bench.

Benson took both her hands, rubbed them between his. "Comes at you how?"

"How?"

"This girl. Is she threatening? How?"

She stared past him. "No. No . . . just . . . I don't know . . ."

"Sure you do. What's her body posture like?"

Michelle thought about it. "She just . . . she's floating . . . arms out . . ."

"But not threatening."

Michelle frowned, staring at space. "No . . . more, almost . . . imploring? Maybe. Yes."

"Asking for help?"

She nodded. "I think so." Still nodding, getting it for the first time. "Not 'hasten?' 'Help me?' She's asking for my help."

"What is it you suppose she wants?"

"I have no idea."

"And you can't see her face?"

"Her hair. Blondish. No face. I already told you that, remember?"

"No face as in *blank* face, or as in shadowed?"

Michelle frowned, eyes slitting. "Just . . . I don't know . . . indistinct."

"Could she be wrapped in something? Bandaged?" he asked, rembering the ME's nickname.

"I don't know. I *don't* know!" Michelle stared at him. "How could you know that?" she said, her usually deep, reflective voice turning shrill.

"Easy. Okay. What about her clothing?"

She shook her head. "I can't . . ."

"Her hair. Is it familiar in any way? A style or cut you've seen before?"

Concentrating, trying to see it, Michelle finally slumped. "I don't know. Just blond. Blond hair. Coming at me by the elephants."

"Elephants?"

She turned to him as if he should know. "The last time I dreamed it, it was *here*. The *elephants*. Outside. You've seen them."

"Here? At the tar pits?"

Benson's cellular went off and he actually started. "Excuse me." He thumbed a button. "Benson."

"Thank God you've got it working!" Amanda. Breathless. "Are you on your way from the valley?"

"What's going on?" Someone rushed past their bench, stepping on Benson's shoe, not stopping to apologize. He looked up. Other museum visitors were following the man eagerly toward the east window, a crowd forming.

"We just got a dispatch from the West Los Angeles Division. Some woman phoned in a DB from a restaurant on La Brea. Are you anywhere near Hollywood?"

"La Brea and what?"

"Curson, across the street from the Page Museum. The tar pits. Are you close?"

Benson was watching the crowd craning at the window. He could hear sirens now. Michelle, staring down at her hands, jerked up when she heard the siren wail.

"I'm close," Benson told the cellular.

"Good. See you there." Amanda rang off.

Benson held the cellular absently, staring at the crowd gathered at the window.

"What is it?" Michelle whispered. The sirens were louder.

Benson replaced the cellular with exaggerated calm. His heart was racing.

"They've *found* her, haven't they!"

"Someone phoned in a dead body near the museum. Michelle, listen. You need to talk to my people when they get here—"

"No!"

He reached for her hand but she jerked away. "Michelle, please. You can talk to Mandy if you want—"

But she was on her feet, pulling away from him. "I can't do that! Don't make me do that, Touch!"

He reached for her again, but she stepped back, nearly losing balance. "Michelle, we're talking about people's *lives* here."

"You want me to face a squad room and tell them that I dreamed a woman came out of the mist beside the tarpits? I'm a lawyer, Touch! What do you think that's going to do to my credibility?"

"What choice do you have?"

"I can bow out and chalk it up to an amazing and disturbing coincidence."

"Mikki, you're connected with this thing somehow, if only peripherally. You might be able to help prevent the next murder."

A black-and-white screamed up out front, followed by two more, strobes flashing, several unmarked cars joining them. Detectives.

Benson cursed the timing. "I have to go out there. Will you stay here, Michelle? Will you promise?"

She said nothing, looking at him steadily, unyielding.

"Just stay here, or in the café. I'll be right back." *Breaking procedure. Breaking it all over the place.*

On the back patio, Benson was greeted by Eddie Parker, the skinny, freckle-faced civilian photographer employed by the LAPD's crime lab. Impatient with youthful hubris, Eddie bounced on one heel, then the other, under a bushel of flaming hair, Nikon proffered, smiling expectantly at Benson.

"Damn, Eddie, you got here fast."

"In the area." He gave Benson a quick, funny look, then brightened again. "Sir—?"

"Okay, but just panoramic and establishing, no close-ups until the SID wagon gets here."

"Check!" Eddie was already in motion, bucking for the Pulitzer. Benson trailed, grinning; Eddie was *always* in the "area."

Benson came down stone steps as West Los Angeles Division Homicide detective supervisor Daniel Felps was coming up. There could be disgruntled attitude here; detectives from Benson's Special Section usually got called only under high-profile conditions or when an investigation crossed divisional boundaries within the LAPD. To many in L.A. law enforcement, Homicide Special detectives walked on water. Felps gave Benson a strange look but when Benson showed his shield, Felps didn't even glance at it, extending an accommodating handshake. Probably Felps had heard of Benson. Anyway, he seemed almost relieved. Both men knew the handshake symbolized the transfer of this investigation from the West L.A. Division to Homicide Special.

"Touch Benson."

"I know. Dan Felps, West L.A. Thought I was gonna get home for supper."

"Yeah. What have we got, Felps?"

They walked toward the east side of the fenced tar pits, the side street now looking like a parking lot for black-and-whites and detectives' vehicles. The inner block was in the process of being cordoned off by the standard yellow police tape, uniformed patrol officers posted around the perimeter. Before Felps could answer, he and Benson were approached by another patrol officer, Miguel Gonzales by nameplate. He stared at Benson, then handed him the crime-scene log to sign. Enduring a wedge of guilt, Benson checked his watch and signed in at 4:27 P.M.—a full twenty minutes *after* his arrival here. *Breaking more procedure.* He resisted an impulse to look back and see if Michelle was still standing inside the museum.

Felps knew little more than Amanda had already explained over the phone.

The body was on the street side of the hurricane fence, a few yards from the mother mastodon, nearly hidden by high weeds. Dishwater blond and pale, it could have been a grouping of sun-bleached rock. "Who found her? After the woman called, I mean."

"Tesser!" Felps motioned to a skinny rookie, who hustled over.

"Sir?"

"You found her?" Benson asked.

"Yes sir!" Tesser gave Benson a distracted look.

"Did you touch her, Tesser?"

"Only her eyes, sir!"

Benson groaned inwardly. The corpse was clearly rigored, swarming with flies, and now the crime scene had been tampered with. But first-arriving officers were allowed to assess a victim's death by touching the eyes, and Tesser was just doing his job. "All right, son, thanks."

Benson turned to Felps, but didn't have to say it. Felps nodded. "I'll keep my people away from her, Detective."

Benson slapped the other man's shoulder in thanks just as Felps's cell phone chirped. "Felps." He turned

toward Benson, nodded. "Right. I've got them here
right now. Hold on . . ."

Felps handed his cellular to Benson.

"Detective Benson."

"Detective, this is Commander Sam Connors, chief
of operations, West Bureau. Where do we stand on
an ID for the victim?"

"We stand fifteen feet away until my crime lab people get here," Benson assured him companionably.

"I understand, Detective. We all know this may be
one of yours. But I've just received some information
you may want to know about."

"Shoot."

"You know Giles Fowler, the *L.A. Times* guy?"

"Hotshot crime reporter."

"Right. Well, we just got a frantic, jumbled call from
Fowler's wife. Seems their teenage daughter, Kim, was
in the Wilshire-Fairfax area last night, maybe near the
tar pits. She hasn't shown up at home yet."

Great. Benson looked past Felps to see Amanda's
Accord pull to the curb. "Christ, Commander, it's four
in the afternoon. The parents are just now calling it
in?"

"The old man is out of town and the mother was
visiting with friends or some damn thing. The daughter's a rich-kid celebrity wanna-be, comes and goes as
she pleases. She was with friends last night, some mix-
up about who was staying over with whom. Anyway,
our people are sweeping the area, but if your DB is
her . . . well, Fowler's been anti-LAPD since the South
Central riots, and well, he's . . ."

"A prick."

"You said it, not me. So there you are. Sorry."

"Appreciate the warning, Commander. Just another lovely day in paradise."

"Ain't it grand? Good luck."

Benson handed Felps back his cellular, used the movement to glance over at the museum. He couldn't see Michelle through the window, but that didn't mean she wasn't still there.

Five minutes later the coroner's team arrived with Sid Mathers.

Five minutes after that, they knew all they needed to know. She was one of the Mummy Killer's, and she was Kim Fowler, daughter of newspaper celeb Giles Fowler.

Benson filled Amanda in on Commander Connors's call, casting another glance at the museum as he did. Amanda watched him distractedly until he was through talking, then took his arm and pulled him behind a tall acacia. She licked her thumb, stretched up, and rubbed hard at his cheek.

"Hey!"

"Hold still!" She rubbed until it burned, shaking his head. Then looked at her thumb. "This looks fresh. *Christ*, Touch."

Michelle's lipstick. He'd been conducting the crime-scene investigation with it on his cheek, getting those funny looks.

Amanda held up her red thumb, jaw set. "Michelle Ransom's color, by any chance? Is she here?"

Benson played dumb. Stupidly. "Where—?"

"Back there in the goddamn *museum* you keep glancing at! You were *with* her when I called, weren't you? And you brought her *here*, to a crime scene!"

"No. Not exactly . . ."

"What the hell does that mean? What the fuck are you doing during work hours, Touch?"

As if to underscore the accusation, Eddie Parker took that moment to blind Benson with his flash. "That's *enough* goddamn pictures, Eddie!" Benson barked too loudly. A couple of uniforms turned his way—Benson rarely raised his voice even in emergencies. Eddie slunk off like a kicked dog

"Nice," Amanda said. "Yell at the poor kid."

Benson willed himself calm. The museum pulled at his back.

"I have to take a leak," he mumbled finally, turning toward the building.

Amanda followed smartly. "I'll come along."

"Why?" Benson demanded, irritated.

Amanda shrugged. "Shake your dick?"

"Stop it, Mandy!"

"Or is that position filled?"

He whirled on her.

And she was waiting for him. "Have you been drinking?"

"Blow me."

She nodded icily. He preferred the fire to Amanda's ice.

"Thanks, Touch. I don't do sloppy seconds. Excuse me now. I gotta notify Fowler about his dead kid before the media does."

"Wait a second!"

She turned back to him.

"Look . . ." But he didn't know what to say. "I'll take care of notification."

Amanda watched him a moment, didn't say,

"Thanks for sparing me the shitty job," didn't say anything, just turned and marched back to the SID crew.

Benson almost went after her, turned, and hurried back to the museum instead. Trying not to run.

"All for nothing," he murmured out loud a minute later to the empty foyer.

A few patrons were still pressed to the east window, but Michelle Ransom was not among them.

He didn't bother to scan the parking lot for her car. She was gone.

17

Amanda Blaine, coffee and doughnuts in tow, came into the homicide suite in morning light and was hit with it from the first person she saw—Sal Peterson, slumped at his desk, simultaneously talking on the phone and screwing with some papers and deliberately avoiding eye contact with Amanda. "Captain wants to see you."

Peterson liked Amanda, and vice versa, and he always made eye contact, sometimes breast contact, but she didn't care in Sal's case because he was a good husband and father and men will be men. She had been to Sal's house, had dinner with his wife, Kaye, whom she also liked, helped put Band-Aids on their kid's scraped knees. Amanda felt a sting above her heart when Peterson didn't look up at her. She faltered, almost said something to him, but went on by his desk, then more quickly by her own desk—dropping the doughnuts, retaining the coffee, and straight to Captain Noland's office, where the nightmare began.

The traces of it were in the captain's face when he turned to her from staring solemnly out the window.

Noland pointed at the chair in front of his desk. Today even Noland didn't look at her breasts—a *really* bad sign.

Amanda sat. "What's up, Cap?"

"Your partner. Up to his ass in deep shit."

Amanda almost smiled, almost shrugged and said, *So what else is new?*

But the atmosphere in the captain's office was too serious for even that. And abruptly Amanda knew. "You've taken Touch off the case."

Noland nodded grimly. A little strange since everyone knew the captain had no love for her partner, had been, if anything, itching for an excuse to bump him from this case, even demote the well-liked Benson from RHD to another division. But Noland didn't seem happy at all at the moment. He appraised Amanda with genuine concern. "Have you seen him this morning?"

"No." And another spiky thrill found her heart. This was going to get worse. *"Why?"*

Noland assessed her a moment. "He fucked up, Detective. Fucked up good. The Giles Fowler thing—the *Times* reporter whose kid was killed."

"What about him?"

"It was never called in to the parents. No notification. Fowler had to hear his daughter was dead from one of his own staff on the paper."

Amanda blinked, collecting her thoughts. "But . . . wait. I was at the museum with Touch . . . Maybe I—"

"Don't try to cover for him, Detective. I already read your report. Benson was supposed to notify next of kin. He admitted it."

Amanda looked away a second, thinking, *Touch, damn it!*

"Fowler was here—in that chair—just before you came in. Yelling loud enough to be heard downstairs. Threatening a suit against the division."

"A *suit*! He can't do—"

"No, he can't. But he's got friends, important friends, and he can make us look damn fucking *incompetent* in the middle of a high-profile investigation. And he can do it in front of millions of rabid readers. Just what the RHD needs, another O.J. fuckup."

Amanda's mind was racing. "Listen, Captain, let me talk to Fowler. He owes me some favors from—"

Noland waved her off. "There's more." He handed her a piece of creased stationery from atop his cluttered desk. Amanda recognized the attorney's logo at the top immediately.

"Benson beat up some guy on the 101. Did he mention this to you?"

Amanda's heart was racing now. "No."

Noland actually winced, apparently disappointed Benson hadn't confided in her. He sat back wearily, rubbed at his forehead. "Beat him up pretty bad. Some Marine, ex-Marine, whatever. Unprovoked attack, he claims. Benson just went berserk, he claims."

"He *claims*!"

"Got himself a whole freeway of witnesses, Amanda."

Amanda kept reading from the attorney's stationery, the same line over and over. *"Please be advised*

*that, acting on behalf of our client, Ronald Short, the
law firm of Johnston, Baker and Gleason hereby
claims . . ."*

"His attorney's coming on like it's a slam dunk."
Noland grunted. "Says they'll settle for a million out
of court, knowing full well Benson probably can't raise
it, that his client can get three times that much from
a judge." Noland leaned forward again and said, *sotto
voce*, "Benson *doesn't* have those kind of resources,
does he?"

Amanda—staring into space—snapped toward him,
"Captain, I'm his *partner*, not his wife." But she softened. "No . . . I don't think he does."

Noland blew out breath, sat back heavily again.
"Two of the witnesses were cops."

Amanda's eyes lit. If other law-enforcement officers
were present, some of the blame might be deflected,
even if Touch was innocent. "They came forward?"

"They had little choice with half the goddamn drivers
in L.A. rubbernecking at them. Traffic was stalled—
roadwork—they had fucking ringside seats. Apparently
these two patrol cops roared up right toward the end of
the ruckus."

"They made statements?"

"Both officers heard Benson claim the Marine was
detaining an officer on duty."

Amanda felt a small wave of relief. "Then he'll be
defended by the City Attorney's Office. If judgment
goes to the plaintiff, the city taxpayers will pay, not
Touch."

"Won't that make the city happy?" Noland snorted
sarcastically.

Amanda knew what the captain was thinking: Rodney King. They'd burn Touch at the stake unless he was proven innocent. It would light up the media, maybe turn ugly. There could be riots. Fires. South Central all over again. It was a potential powder keg.

Noland grunted. "Might be better for Benson if he *was* off duty at the time."

Amanda's eyes jerked to him. Suddenly she knew why Noland was being so charitable concerning her partner. The prick was looking out for his own ass. And the Robbery-Homicide Division's.

"Well, *was* he?" she demanded impatiently.

Noland turned officious. "Hey! He's *your* goddamn partner, Detective!"

Amanda sat back. "I'm sorry. When did this so-called beating occur?"

"Wednesday afternoon. You had a dental appointment remember? I don't know where the fuck Benson was, do you?"

Amanda presented a poker face. "He told me he was seeing the chief ME."

"Well, he wasn't."

She couldn't not swallow. "What does Touch say?"

"He isn't saying anything."

"He's *refusing*?"

"Not refusing, not yet. Just not saying. Would you know why?"

Michelle Ransom's face flashed before Amanda's eyes. She said, "No."

Noland stared at her a moment, expressionless. If he didn't believe, her he wasn't registering it. After a moment he said, "Well, technically the beating did occur during Benson's shift, and *technically* he was working a case, a damn big case. Whether that constitutes 'in the line of duty' is a matter of how one interprets the book. We'll back him, of course. Go along assuming he was out doing his job. If the trial begins that way, it'll stay that way."

The captain regarded her with genuine perplexity. "Why would he do it? I know he's got some drinking problems, but punching out a civilian? He's arrogant, not stupid."

"I do know him, sir, and I don't believe Touch would hit a man without provocation. Legal provocation. I'd testify to that."

Noland grunted. "Wish that was all it took."

He stood, went back to staring wearily out his window. "He didn't even argue with me. Just stood up and walked out of my office this morning without a backward glance."

"This morning?"

"Right after Fowler slammed out."

"So Fowler also knows about—"

"Detective, half the fucking drivers on the 101 know about it."

"Oh. Yeah."

Noland turned from the smog. "He's your partner, Detective. Go find him. He hasn't been officially suspended yet. IAD hasn't come sniffing around. I'll talk to the AC, try to stall this out."

It all made sense.

Prick or not, covering his ass or not, Noland could only benefit if Touch stayed close to the case, especially if he was instrumental in solving it. A community's ire over a cop's procedural ethics might soften markedly after said cop helped remove a madman from the streets. It might not make him a hero, but it couldn't hurt.

"I've already phoned him at home."

"That doesn't mean he isn't there," Amanda told him.

"Go find him, Detective."

Amanda was already heading out the door.

She was pretty sure he'd gone home—even though he wasn't answering her cell phone calls from her car—and she was pretty sure he was drunk, probably very drunk.

Just to be sure she phoned—in transit—every bar she knew he frequented to double-check. Benson was at none of them.

He was indeed at home.

But sober. Sitting by himself on his bed with the lights off, blinds pulled and no bottle in sight, holding his service revolver in his hand.

Amanda knocked, waited, knocked . . . let herself in, looked in the living room, kitchen, then the bedroom. She stood in the bedroom doorway, knowing he'd heard her come in, aware he had not bothered to answer her calls. She looked down at the .38 Special in his hands. She spoke softly. "Hey . . ."

"Hey, Mandy."

She came into the room, leaned against a bureau. "What are we doing?"

He turned the weapon in his hand, appraising it. It shone blue under the small wedge of light from under the window shade. "We're shooting ourselves in the head because we're suspended from division."

She saw the cloth now, the bottle of cleaning solvent behind him. She nodded. "Good idea. Can I borrow it when you're through?"

He looked up now. "Use your own damn piece, that crappy plastic Glock of yours."

"Never jams, though."

He grunted. "Piece of plastic. Service weapons should be steel."

"You're antiquated."

Benson placed the .38 on the oil cloth, leaned back against the headboard, hands behind his head. "The word you're looking for is 'pastured.' Why is it I don't seem to give a shit?"

"Delayed reaction." She came and sat next to him on the bed, lifted one of his shoeless feet and began to massage it. "Had an interesting powwow with Noland."

"Toasting my demise?"

"You won't believe this—I didn't—but he's behind you in this thing. Really."

"Only if it's tried as a police case. If I'm found to have been 'off duty,' he'll pull back the life ring."

"I don't think so. He's thinking 'a cop is a cop in the eyes of a jury.' He may be right."

"He is right. He's still a prick."

Amanda sighed. "What is it with you two?"

Benson shrugged his elbows, gave her his other foot. "Probably something to do with your great legs. *Mph.* That feels great. I don't suppose you'd like to make love?"

She bent a toe back until he winced. "A mercy fuck?"

Benson grinned.

"A smile. That's better. So. Why didn't you tell me?"

Benson stretched, groaned. "The guy had a tire iron, Mandy."

Amanda's brow went up. "Well, then somebody *saw* that!"

"No one's coming forth. And the iron seems to have mysteriously disappeared. I think some in this town suspect us of police brutality, don't you?"

Amanda was visualizing the witness chair. "If this guy—this Marine—denies he used an iron on you he'll perjure himself."

"And get away with it unless the weapon turns up. And it would have by now. Exhibit A." He snorted, shook his head ruefully. "My ass is grass, my dear, and Lawrence Gleason is the lawnmower."

Gleason was the Marine's attorney, a diminutive black lawyer with bantamweight tenacity, famous for making big stinks and winning large settlements during the South Central riots. Gleason had built a career on cases like these, bending the truth, appealing to the black community's often justifiable biases. It would be a media circus.

"All those witnesses, Touch, somebody must have seen the tire iron."

"Not necessarily. I didn't see it myself until the last second. Guy was fast—clumsy, but fast. It all happened very quickly. It always does. I don't know where the damn iron sailed off to."

Amanda shrugged indifference, cheerleading. "So we'll just have to catch the Mummy Killer first."

Benson winked at her, smiled without conviction. "You bet." He went back to ruminating.

Amanda squeezed his leg. "Hey. Where are you?"

Benson laced his fingers atop his stomach, closed his eyes. "Well . . . maybe in love. A little."

She stopped rubbing his feet unconsciously. "Good. Good for you. I mean it."

"Don't stop that. I'm getting a hard-on."

She looked down at his socks, straightened one absently for him. "Was she with you? At the time of the fight?"

Benson opened one eye, smiled coyly. "If she was, she'd vouch for the tire iron, right? Only with an old high school sweetheart in the car, our noble Detective Benson wouldn't exactly be an on-duty cop, would he? Paradoxical, ain't it?"

"Was she? With you?"

"No. And I'm not sure she'd vouch for me even if she had been."

Amanda stopped massaging. "What do you mean?"

"Michelle Ransom does not like cops."

Amanda bent the toe again. "Quit fucking with me. Are you covering for her or something? Talk to me."

Benson stared at the ceiling.

Amanda crossed her arms. "You *are* covering for her. What the hell are you into, Touch?"

"Way fucking more than you want to know, sweetie."

She said nothing until she had his eyes. Hers said: *If I didn't want to know . . .*

Benson finished for her out loud. "You wouldn't be here. Yeah." He smiled warmly at her. "Why *are* you here, Mandy? I'm just this amazing pain in the ass to you, and yet you're always there. Why? And why don't I marry you?"

"You're in love with Michelle Ransom."

"Oh. Yeah. Why is that, do you suppose?"

Amanda rubbed his feet. "She reminds you of Liz?"

Benson drifted away.

She squeezed his foot. "Hey. There's nothing wrong with that. It's your life, Touch. *Yours.*"

He looked over at her, then looked back at the ceiling. "I wasn't with her at the museum. I mean, I was, but I didn't bring her there. She called me. We were there before the Fowler kid's body was found. Before you called."

"Michelle called you from the museum?" Amanda could see he was struggling.

"She knew about it, Mandy."

"Knew about what? The *body?* The Fowler girl?"

"She saw it"—he turned to look directly in her eyes; he smiled, lips flat and mirthless—"in a *dream*." He made big eyes, fluttered his hands, made a spooky *Ooooooooo* sound.

Amanda watched him a moment, then pursed her lips. "In a dream. Uh-huh."

"The other victims too. Saw them all. Every one the Mummy Killer did."

Amanda probed her inner cheek. "Came to her in *visions*, did they?"

"Dreams. Look, you don't know her. Mikki was always the most logical, sensible—"

"Touch—"

Benson pushed up, held up a hand. "But here's the thing—"

"Touch—"

"No, listen a second. Here's the really weird part. She has this dream about the Fowler kid *before* it made the papers. On the night of the reunion."

Amanda stared at him. Lost. *"Excuse me?"*

"No shit. She stood there in that museum and de-
tailed the goddamn murder to me. Body type, color,
and"—he held up a finger—"location. Want to explain
that one, Detective Blaine?"

"Yeah, your girlfriend watches too many *X Files*
episodes."

"I knew you'd love this. Guess what else? I spent
the afternoon playing golf with the Feebs. Found out
all about VICAP's psychic investigators and remote
seeing and all kinds of cool stuff like that. Did you
know that some psychics are even retired cops? I
mean think of the implications! Some might even be
Republicans!"

Amanda rolled her eyes. "Touch, are you—did you
really go to the FBI without—"

"Consulting Noland? Yes. It gets better. By law-
enforcement definition, Michelle Ransom is a bona
fide psychic. Dyed in the wool. The police *have* been
known to use them, you know."

Amanda couldn't tell if he was kidding anymore.
"The FBI *assured* you she was psychic?"

"Well, let's say she fits the profile."

She gave him a flat look. "You didn't tell them
her name."

He smiled.

"Jesus." Amanda sighed, shook her head. "Glad
you're smiling . . . Glad you're so fucking amused by
this. You know, in accordance with your oath, you're
bound as a law-enforcement officer to come forward
with information like that. It could save lives. So
what's with this Ransom broad? She's embarrassed by
her strange metaphysical abilities—that it?"

"Something like that."

"And what—she made you promise not to tell anyone while polishing your knob?" Amanda made an exasperated sound. "Christ, Touch, the parents of those victims don't care *who* you're screwing. You're a cop!"

Benson lay back again. "Not presently."

"That hasn't been decided! And in any case, there's a moral obligation here."

Benson watched her calmly. "So you're saying you *believe* she's psychic? Uh-oh! That what you're saying, Amanda?"

"Don't get cute. I hate it when you get that cute look."

He shrugged. "Gee, for a second there I thought you were on her side."

"I'm on the law's side. As I thought you were."

"Only now you think I'm a lovesick alcoholic incapable of professional decision making."

"I didn't say that."

"What do you say?"

She tossed his legs off her lap, stood up. "You have a drinking problem. I think you've been depressed continually since Lizzie's death, some days more than others. It may have affected your judgment of late."

"And?"

"And nothing." She stopped pacing, gave him a searching look. "You *want* to get suspended—is that it?"

Benson licked his lips. "How about a drink?"

"No, thanks. So Michelle won't talk to a cop, but she *will* to a civilian lover—is that where this is going, where you're headed with your life?" She threw up her hands. "Touch. Hey. You're gambling a brilliant career on a metaphysical supposition."

Benson looked down at his stocking toes, wiggled them. "Maybe I'm sick of my brilliant career."

"Yeah? Well, I'd love to chuck it all too. Honeymoon in Cancun, fuck my brains out for a week or two, but it don't work that way."

"Even if it saves lives?"

"Can you fuck and save lives at the same time?"

"Like you said, those grieving parents don't care who I'm screwing. Which I'm not, by the way."

Amanda paced back toward the bed. "Not what?"

"Screwing Ms. Ransom. I can't believe I'm telling you this. I must really trust you."

Amanda felt a knot of conflicted impatience and warmth. "She should see a doctor, your girlfriend."

"She won't."

"You've encouraged her?"

"She's afraid of being found certifiable. Like Liz." He looked up sharply. "Don't say it."

"What?"

"My penchant for attracting sicko women."

Amanda grunted. "Hey, you attracted me."

"Yeah, but you won't screw me either."

Amanda looked over at him, then looked away and changed the subject. "So what are we doing? Are you going to help me catch this asshole or what?"

"Buy me a drink?"

"Is that a yes?"

"Uh-uh."

Amanda sighed, grabbed her purse from atop the bureau. "Put your shoes on."

He didn't get off the bed.

Amanda put her fists on her hips in exasperation. "I'll *keep* my mouth shut about her, Touch. You know I will. For now, anyway."

Benson reached for his shoes.

18

"You never take notes," Michelle Ransom said off-handedly.

Dr. Otter—who was becoming more and more liberal with his smiles of late—granted her one now. Or half of one. Maybe it just took getting to know him, Michelle thought. Maybe even psychiatrists could be shy.

"I have an eidetic memory," Otter told her.

"I'll bet you think I don't know what that means."

"I'm sure you do. You're a very intelligent young woman."

Michelle's turn for half smiles. "Thanks for saying young. How do you feel about psychics?"

"Psychics? How do you feel about them?"

Here we go, Michelle thought. "I don't believe in them, Doctor. Your turn."

Otter tapped the eraser end of his pencil confidently. "I don't believe in them either."

"Why?"

He pushed out his lower lip. "I'm a pragmatist. Psychiatry may be an inexact science, but it's still a science, based on cause and effect. Psychics deal outside the boundaries of physics, and thus our ability to measure their claims conclusively."

"And dreams don't?"

"Not at all. Dreams are manifestations of the subconscious. The subconscious is clearly rooted in brain chemistry. Biology. Often cleverly disguised, but clearly diagnosable."

Wow! Pretty expansive for the retiring Dr. Otter. She had him on a roll. "What about the soul?"

Another small, whiskered smile from the doctor. "A question for your priest or rabbi, I'm afraid. Why do you ask?"

Michelle watched him a long moment. "No reason."

"Have you been thinking about psychics lately?"

"You mean *dreaming* of them? No. I still dream about the woman in the mist. You said once you don't watch TV or read the papers. Does that include the news?"

"For the most part, I'm afraid."

"You don't feel out of touch?"

Otter almost chuckled his confidence this time. Michelle admired confidence, but there was something arrogant about his. "Ms. Ransom, year in and year out, despite so-called advances in science and the arts, things don't really change very much. Not the basics. Including people. But let's get back to you."

"We don't seem to be getting anywhere with me."

"I wouldn't assume that."

"Then tell me why I shouldn't?" She knew impatience got her nowhere with him but couldn't help herself. "*Talk* to me, Doctor! You've been hearing these same damn dreams for months now. You've even put me under hypnosis. You must have something to say about my dreams!"

"What would you like to know?"

Michelle threw up her hands. "Shit! *Anything!*" She got up, folded her arms, began pacing. "I dream about a woman. Okay. What does it mean when people dream about a woman? And could you please not do that? It's distracting."

Otter looked down at his pencil, stopped tapping it, and dropped it in its cup. "All right. A woman can mean many things in a dream—"

"*Please!*"

"I was about to say, a woman in a woman's dream might connote a facet of herself she is not immediately identifying with. A woman might dream of a sister, or female children. These would represent herself. The characteristics of the dream woman—loving, angry, lazy, sexual, whatever—provide the clue to what part of the dreamer it's referring to. If she dreams of an older woman, this might be the dreamer's mother, her feelings about aging, or her sense of inherited wisdom. How old is the woman in your dream would you guess?"

Michelle thought about it. "Younger."

"Um-hm. Well, you may be dreaming of your younger self."

Michelle shook her head. "I'm not, though." She stopped pacing to look up. "I told you we weren't getting anywhere."

"But we are. Knowing what your dreams don't represent is a step toward finding what they do."

Michelle made an unconvinced sound, began pacing again. Next he'd be reminding her that patience was a virtue. "What about the mist?"

"Rather straightforward, isn't it? You already said you feel lost in your dreams. Mist or fog can represent confusion, indecision, the inability to see the real issues in yourself or your environment. Hence the expression *'Haven't the foggiest.'* "

"All sounds a little too pat, if you'll forgive me, Doctor."

"Never confuse indecision with truth, Michelle. They're often one and the same. The human mind excels at disguising the obvious. I'd be collecting unemployment if it didn't."

Michelle stared at the Persian rug.

"Let's take a rest from dreams for the moment. What else is going on in your life right now? Your relationship with the policeman, for instance."

"He's a detective and we don't have a relationship, at least not the way you mean it."

"Forgive me."

"A very smart detective in a very elite sector of the LAPD. The RHD. Do you know what that is?"

"Robbery-Homicide Division, I believe."

He loved to show off. Michelle gave him a jaundiced look. "I thought you didn't read the papers."

"Occasionally. Are you still seeing him, this detective—what was it?"

"Benson. Not at the moment, no."

"May I ask why?"

"No." After a moment she caught herself. "Is that significant, my not wishing to discuss it?"

"What do you think?"

She looked at the rug again. "We had a fight, sort of."

"Over what?"

"People have fights."

"Indeed they do. Are you in love with him?"

"I'm not comfortable with this." She sat down again, smiled tightly. "Which is why we should talk about it, right?"

"Perhaps. Perhaps we can sneak up on it. Tell me more about his job, what attracted you to him."

"I knew him in junior high school. We were best friends. Before he became a jock."

"And you were attracted to jocks?"

"I was attracted to this one. He was my dream fuck—excuse the language. Uh-oh, more dreams!"

"And what attracts you to him now, his job?"

Michelle shrugged. "I hadn't thought about it. Why do you ask that?"

Otter started to reach for his tapping pencil, remembered, stopped. "Detective work is somewhat glamorous, dangerous. They often keep late hours, see an unpleasant side of life, bring that home."

Michelle watched him. "Make lousy husbands—that it? I deliberately involve myself with men I won't be inclined to marry?"

"You said that, Michelle, not I."

"You implied it."

"No. You did the extrapolation."

"Right." *Smug prick.*

"On the other hand, perhaps he confides in you.

Finds in you someone other than a departmental mind he can share his thoughts with. Perhaps that endears him to you."

Well, he was right about that. "I suppose."

"Does he ever talk about cases he's worked on, cases he is working on? Michelle?"

She was conscious of gripping the chair arms. "He has, yes. And I'm really not comfortable . . . I really can't discuss that kind of thing with you, with anyone."

Otter held up his hands. "Fine. I understand."

"It has nothing to do with my neuroses."

"That's fine. Let's move on. What would you like to talk about?"

Michelle stared at the floor.

"Or you needn't talk at all, if you wish. You seem tense."

"Do I?" She was sick of this, sick of the whole slick psychiatric game. She wanted to go home to her mess of a house and her beautiful daughter and forget she ever met this slick-haired little rodent.

"A bit. Why, do you suppose?"

"You're the doctor." A hot bath would be nice. Some of that new green tea oil.

"What are you thinking about, Michelle? What's on your mind right now?"

"This rug." She tilted her head. "It's Persian, isn't it?"

"It is. I did some traveling years ago. It's genuine. Do you like it?"

Michelle pursed her lips; she didn't, particularly. "It's interesting. I wasn't sure . . . some of the design . . ."

"Yes?"

". . . looks almost Egyptian."

19

Benson almost didn't recognize the house this time.

He'd been looking for the *Gone with the Wind* whitewashed brick columns that graced the front of the Ransom home. When he finally found the curving, brick-inlaid drive, he found all that was left of the Southern-style columns: a crumbled pile heaped around the front steps. His first thought was: earthquake. But on closer inspection, the dismantling looked deliberately professional.

Michelle's daughter, Jana, opened the door a foot, peered out from shadow, cell phone to her ear, peanut butter sandwich in her other hand. The index finger had a missing fake nail. "Yes?"

Benson started to remind her who he was when Jana pointed the sandwich at him. "You're the policeman, right? 'Feelie' or something?" Mikki's husky voice, even behind the peanut butter slur.

"Touch."

"Right. Mr. Benson."

"Close enough."

She nodded blond tresses, motioned him in with the sandwich, turned, and walked away. She wore a man's Arrow shirt above long tanned legs.

Benson came inside, scraping white brick dust from his shoes on the entrance mat. There was more remodeling going on in the foyer.

He found Jana in the kitchen, phone against her shoulder, pouring a glass of milk from a plastic jug, nodding, muttering. The shirt was open in front, a bright orange two-piece under it.

When she saw Benson, Michelle's daughter hooked a kitchen chair with her toe, pulled it out and around from the wooden table for him. Benson sat, enveloped in the musky odor of her tanning oil.

Jana said, "No," into the phone, pointed at the liquor cabinet behind Benson, blue eyes inquiring. Benson shook his head.

Jana turned her back so Benson couldn't see. In a moment, she nodded and put the phone down on the counter. *Boyfriend,* he guessed.

"Sorry." She started to take a bite, then held the sandwich out to him. Benson shook his head and she sank white teeth into white bread.

"Me too. Didn't mean to interrupt you."

She shook the fine gold mane again, shifting the mouthful of peanut butter sandwich. "Just Jason." She frowned. "Did you meet Jason?"

"Briefly."

"Right." She took another bite, leaned against the counter, looked Benson up and down like someone appraising a used car. She was Michelle—except for the nose—and Jana had probably had hers done. Kids did it routinely nowadays—that and body piercing.

Jana chewed, watched him.

Benson watched back.

"You arrest serial killers and stuff, right?" She poured more milk up to the rim.

"When we find them."

"Yuck. Isn't that gross?" Gulping.

"Sometimes." Benson glanced around the wood-paneled kitchen. Lots of wood, all of it looking hand-fitted and snug, polished to such loving luster the light from the sink window seemed to penetrate the grain a millimeter. "Great house."

A thirst-quenched sigh from lovely Jana, and a little burp she didn't apologize for. Benson got the feeling she could fart without apology and get away with it. She was a stunner, but too blond and bright against so much dark, thoughtful detail. Out of time and out of place in this house.

"It's a Craftsman," she informed him. "The house. You know what that is?"

"A kind of style, right?"

She nodded, chewing. "*Really* old style. My mom bought it."

Benson didn't know what to say to that or to her sudden thoughtful expression so he said, "Well, she has good taste."

"You like it, huh?"

"The house? Very much. Warm."

Jana shrugged, gulped milk, glancing around the kitchen. "The architects were these two brothers named Greene. They worked here in Pasadena in the early 1900s. They're famous for turning these old California bungalows into works of art. I did a paper on it."

Benson nodded toward the patio pool. "Well, they certainly did that."

"Do you live in Pasadena?"

"The valley."

"Oh."

A small put-down, but a guileless one.

"Anyway"—around another huge mouthful— "these Greene brothers, they started this thing called the California Residential Style. They didn't exactly start it. They sort of, you know, took off from what was already there. Some people think they're the most perfect houses ever built."

"Yeah?"

She nodded. "They had this thing about *detail*. You know, *anal*. They'd look at a house, and the land around the house and try to, you know, make the house fit the land, instead of the other way around. So it was . . . what's the word . . . ?"

"Harmonious?"

"Right! So—*shit!*" She swiped spilled milk from her ample bosom. She shook her head. "From one udder to the next, right?" She clucked without embarrassment. "Just washed this damn shirt for him." She sighed, looked up at Benson. Squinted.

"Harmonious," he supplied.

"Right, so anyway, Craftsman homes are highly sought now. Right after my mom and stepdad got married, my stepdad started turning this architectural masterpiece into this . . . Southern mansion or whatever. Columns and carriage houses and stuff."

"That's interesting."

"Not to Mom it wasn't. He totally fucked up the house."

"Your mother didn't like it?"

Jana studied what was left of her sandwich, dropped it in the sink. "She went along at first, because, you know, I guess she loved him or whatever. Then one day I came home from school and she was standing in the backyard. He was having this thing built . . . this . . . those *round* things—you know, wood—you stand in them when it rains or whatever . . ."

"Gazebos."

"Right! Did you study architecture?"

"No."

"Anyway, so Mom's standing there just staring at this hideous gazebo. And then she looks at me and she says, 'Honey, we're turning a silk purse into a sow's ear.' "

Jana leaned back, lovely and long, elbows on the sink, as if waiting for his reaction. She kept the pose to see if Benson's eyes would drop to her breasts. When they didn't, she challenged, "So . . . are you guys serious, or what?"

"We've only just started seeing each other."

"But you dated in high school or whatever, right?"

"We knew each other then."

"Were you fucking?"

You need that potty mouth slapped, Benson thought. "Like bandits."

Jana Ransom showed him her perfect white teeth. "You're screwing with me, right?"

"Not if your mother's home, I'm not."

And that made her laugh aloud. She stopped with

the sexy slump and Benson smiled and they finally began to like each other.

"You're all right," she told Benson. "And cute."

"Too cute for you."

She laughed again. Not many people outflirted her. "Will you smoke some weed?" She took a short roach from her bikini cup.

"On duty."

"Right. Will you arrest me if I do?"

"Sure."

She grinned, scrounged a match from the counter, lit the joint, coughed once.

"Old pro."

"Fuck you," she laughed.

She propped her elbow on her other hand, making herself look older. She arched a playful brow. "So *are* you guys fucking?"

"Are you and Jason?"

Jana rolled her eyes. *"Touché."*

They watched each other a moment, eventually smiled again. She held up the roach. "Are you going to tell Mom about the dope?"

"Sure."

"I'll tell her you felt me up."

"Then I might as well feel you up."

She laughed again, harder, and colored a little. "You're okay, for an old guy." She turned and washed the butt down the sink. "I gotta get back to class. This is my lunch hour. Hang around if you want. She should be home in"—she glanced at the kitchen clock—"a little bit. Liquor's in the cupboard if you change your mind."

"She's shopping?"

For a moment it seemed as if Jana wasn't going to answer him. "Yeah . . . shopping."

She turned from the sink soberly, then smiled, started past Benson. She ruffled his head going by his chair. "Got a lot of hair. For an old guy."

Benson smoothed it back. "You're a very fresh kid."

Jana lingered a moment in the doorway. "Not really."

Benson swiveled toward her. "No, not really."

She smiled, but it faded. "She hides things, you know."

"Your mother?"

"From herself, mostly. Are you going to be good to her?"

"Of course."

Jana nodded. "You should know about that. She's very secretive. She does hide things."

"I'm a cop. I'll arrest her."

Jana wiggled fingers good-bye and left him there in the kitchen

Benson had hoped she'd laugh at his little joke, but she hadn't.

He sat there for ten more minutes by himself, eyes wandering occasionally to the liquor cabinet, but feet staying firmly on the floor. He didn't really want Michelle to come home to find an unexpected guest helping himself to her booze.

But after a while, it began to look as though Michelle wasn't going to come home anytime soon and the liquor cabinet began to pull at him.

Benson stared at the wood-paneled, Craftsman cupboards.

Finally he got up and got out of the kitchen. And did what any self-respecting cop would do when left alone in a strange house. He went snooping.

Within two minutes he found the stack of mail on the living room settee. The psychiatrist's bill was second from the bottom.

20

Each time she finished coupling with Charlie Grissom, Kurtzy did the same thing.

She lay quietly for a few minutes, listening to the ticking of his apartment's aged iron heater, the muffled rustling of the people upstairs—lay there damp and unmoving, his stickiness oozing from her, pooling the sheets—lay there until she heard the familiar soughing of Charlie's sleep, until the soreness between her legs was a pearly ache. Then she crept softly from the lumpy mattress, padded into the front hall and phoned Jason Richards.

It was usually around ten, just before she headed back to Dykstra Hall and her dorm bed. Sometimes Sue Thornquist was awake when Kurtzy came in, sometimes not, it didn't matter.

The first time she called it was only to hear the sound of his voice.

"Hello?" And a little of his breathing. "Hello?"

Always hanging up before he did. Always protecting herself from his rejection, even if it were unaware on his part.

One night, to her astonishment, before she hung up—the distant sound of Charlie's snoring in her ears—she had actually spoken into the receiver. "I love you."

It just popped out.

Kurtzy immediately slammed down the receiver, so loud she thought she must surely wake Charlie. She'd sat there by the phone, feeling her heart crashing against her chest.

Even she couldn't have predicted the long-term effect it would have.

The next time she made love to Charlie (he was a terrible lover—*huge* but inept, clumsy, uninspired, and quick to ejaculate, and always deeply involved in the Egyptian game of them being star-crossed gods), she thought about Jason—as she always did. Except this time she experienced a climax of an intensity over and above anything before.

And afterward, when she phoned Jason, she screwed up her courage enough to whisper, "I want to make love to you"—this time holding on to the line a terrified moment to the sound of Jason's breathing before hanging up. Throat dry. Legs weak.

It progressed from there.

"I want you to make love to me under the stars," she said next time. And stayed on the line, listening to Jason breathe, realizing he wasn't going to hang up until she did. Realizing she was actually *communicating* with him! It was the most intensely thrilling moment of her life.

"Hello?" was all Jason ever said. While Kurtzy controlled the other end of the conversation, as though Jason preferred it that way, was titillated by it that way.

And because he seemed to like it, even crave it, her voice, her tone, became ever more provocative. "I want to kiss your lips," she told him one night. "Kiss your chest . . . your sweet cock." Her voice quaking, ears burning in the darkness. Doing all these amazing things, *saying* all these incredible things. Realizing with a rush of near blinding clarity it wasn't Sue Thornquist at all, not her moody roommate whence she drew her strength, her courage. It was Jason Richards.

"I want you, sweet lover . . . I want you in me . . . everywhere . . ." The receiver trembling in her hand, her own breath echoing raspily back, shocking herself, thrilling herself, glorying in the throaty catch of his own breath in the receiver. Control. It was opium straight through her vitals.

It went on that way. Night after night. As though a deep inner lock had finally burst. *You've come so far, little Kurstin Mallon . . . You've come from so dark and distant a place to this, finally this . . . the sweeping, joyful landscape of a woman's true estate. You are loved. And it is a gift from the gods.*

She wanted nothing more on earth now than to please him, to bring him to the tremulous, dizzying brink, and over. With *her* mind, *her* voice!

A low groaning came from Jason's end, a sucking hiss . . . Then, finally, his first real words to her . . . sweetly, softly . . .

"Jana . . ."

Kurtzy slammed the receiver.
And screamed.

Charlie found her that way, sitting beside the phone,
naked in the dark, screaming, beating her fists against
the floor. She had stopped screaming by the time he
got her into a hot bath, but she would not uncoil
her fists.

He pleaded with her for nearly two hours, Kurtzy
lying there in the steaming water, eyes locked on
empty space, on some distant place beyond the faded
wallpaper. Charlie pleaded until he cried, laid his head
on the porcelain lip of the tub and sobbed and begged
his sweet Nephthys to come back to him. At mention
of her alter ego, Kurtzy finally turned to him. Her
eyes were so black with hatred, Charlie got down on
his naked knees and bowed before her tub.

Kurtzy lay as if in a coma.

A fantasy. A silly schoolgirl fantasy. That she had
stupidly allowed herself to believe in, get caught up
in. In the end, no more real than cold, laughing halls
of the university, the cold indifferent shoulders pushing past her to the next class.

And why? Because she had let herself believe. Because someone had showed her a little kindness,
shared her room with her. Because this man Charlie
had seen in her face, her eyes, only beauty, only trust.

Dear Charlie. Sweet Charlie.

And before she knew it, before her mind quite became her own again, she turned to him there in the
bath and told him all about it. Told him of Sue, and
Jason, and most of all the lovely Jana Ransom.

Jana Ransom. Her nemesis.

Because who else, really, could she tell it to? Who else could she trust never to repeat it? And it helped, the telling. Made her feel just a little less alone.

For his part, Charlie listened quietly.

So quietly that by the time she finished Kurtzy was sure he'd fallen asleep.

She was pretty done in herself by then. Could hardly make it to the street, back across the wide green quad to the dorm.

Charlie sat exactly still by the bath. Exactly still and in the same position, hours after Kurtzy had left. Stayed that way all night, and into the first pink streaks of dawn.

Jana Ransom.

Sworn enemy of his beloved goddess.

In the sunrise glow, Charlie's eyes burned bright as the great hunting hawk's.

21

Friday morning, having spent the entire night wide-awake, neither drinking nor sleeping but very much on edge, Benson called the department early. His supervisor, Lieutenant Scott, was usually there by eight. If he wasn't, Benson would say nothing to the duty officer, hang up, and try a few minutes later. This morning, Lieutenant Scott was there.

"Benson, Scotty. How bad is it?"

"Pretty goddamn bad, Touch. The captain was on the phone with the deputy chief last night, so the rumor goes. I think they're going to open a one point eighty-one on you and your partner." Scotty's usual officious manner was softer than normal; everyone in the squad room knew about the fracas on the 101 with the tire iron, and Benson's failure to call in the murder of the reporter's kid. If the deputy chief was opening a case against Benson, that meant an investigation. And even the elite Robbery-Homicide Division wasn't

immune to the all-powerful IAD. Cops policed the
citizenry, but the Internal Affairs Division policed the
cops. All cops. They were fucking omnipotent, or
thought they were.

Benson went livid. "Is Amanda in yet?"

"Haven't seen her."

"When she shows, get her the hell out of there,
Scotty! She hasn't a goddamn thing to do with any of
this and Noland knows it."

"She's your partner, Touch. She was with you at
the museum covering the Fowler kid's death."

"That was *my* goddamn responsibility! Amanda's
clean, and I don't want any fucking IAD suits ruining
her day!"

Under normal circumstances Benson would never
have addressed a superior in that tone. They both
knew it. Lieutenant Scott sighed. "All right. I'll send
her on an errand somewhere before Noland can get
to her. But if the suits want her, they'll get her eventually."

"Just keep them off her this morning, that's all."

There was a moment of silence on Lieutenant
Scott's end. "Have you got something, Touch?"

"I might. But I need time. Is Noland planning a
meeting with me and the Internal Affairs assholes at
his office?"

"I assume so. That's usually how it goes. I'm getting
all this secondhand. Listen, I'll be there for you,
Touch—"

"I know you will, Scotty, and I appreciate it. Just
keep Amanda from their meat hooks for a few hours.
I'll be in touch."

Benson hung up.

He looked down at himself. He hadn't changed clothes since yesterday, hadn't changed clothes or changed a single thought since the minute he'd left Michelle Ransom's house in Pasadena.

He actually jumped when his front doorbell rang.

He peered through the bedroom curtain at the front walk like a damn fugitive. It was Amanda. Thank God.

Benson pulled open the door without saying good morning and went to get his suit jacket.

"What—?"

"We have to talk, Mandy."

They took Benson's Mustang.

As they drove, he filled her in on the conversation with their supervisor, Lieutenant Scott.

"Noland, that prick!"

Benson waved her off. "It may not even be Noland. The deputy chief may have instigated the one point eighty-one. I don't know. Never mind that. Listen, Mandy. Get ready to hate me."

"I already hate you."

"I'm serious. I fucked up, sweetie, in the worst way. I fucked us both."

"Whoa, whoa, take it easy—"

"It's one thing to harbor information from your superiors. It's another to keep it from your partner."

"Are you talking about the psychic thing? You already told me—"

Benson shook his head, angry at himself. "I *finally* told you, after protecting Michelle Ransom instead of doing my job. I was over there yesterday. Michelle was out. Her daughter, Jana, let me in. We had a nice talk."

Amanda turned in the seat with that way she always had when her partner was about to drop a bomb.

"Jana had to get back to class. I hung around waiting for Michelle to get back from shopping. I got bored and started snooping. Interesting house. Ever heard of Craftsman architecture?"

"Yeah. Expensive. She rich?"

"I guess. Anyway, I found a stack of bills on the living room settee. One of them was from a Dr. James P. Otter. Guess what he does for a living?"

"Oh, shit."

"Yeah. We're headed for the shrink's office now. I would have nailed him yesterday afternoon, but he'd already left work. Besides, I want you along, I want this all very official and aboveboard, what with my suspension pending and this IAD shit."

Amanda couldn't hide her excitement. "You confronted the Ransom woman with this?"

"No. I phoned his office from Michelle's, got his machine telling me he'd closed shop for the day. I beat it over to his office anyway, thinking he might still be around, cleaning up. He wasn't."

Amanda closed her eyes. "You're not going to tell me you pulled a B and E."

"No. But I was tempted."

"Thank Christ. But I thought you said Michelle told you she wasn't *seeing* a psychiatrist. How screwed up is she?"

Benson made a wry sound. " 'She hides things.' That's what her daughter told me yesterday. I should have picked up on it right then, even before I found the bill. Actually, Michelle never really denied seeing a shrink. She just made it clear she wasn't comfortable with the idea."

"It's the same thing, Touch"

Benson shook his head wearily. "There's no way Mikki could ever kill anyone. You don't know her."

"*You* don't know her, Touch. Christ, she *knew* about the murders! She was dreaming the damn things."

Benson said nothing, just drove, eyes on the road.

Amanda watched him. "Don't come down too heavy on yourself. Okay, you were trying to protect a friend. But even the most broad-minded cop would have trouble with this clairvoyant, mind-reading stuff. We're on our way to the first tangible lead we've had, and I'm *still* having trouble with it."

Benson glanced at his partner. "Now you're protecting *me*, Mandy. The fact is, I had information that might have saved a life, and I didn't act on it."

"Touch, you *did* act on it. You went to see the feebs, found out that stuff about VICAP, about the use of psychics in government work."

"I could have found that out from Scotty. The RHD has used psychics."

"So? You didn't want to look like a fool in front of your superiors, who quite likely would have nixed the whole thing anyway. Quit beating yourself up. Credibility is everything for a cop, whether just or not. You were being reasonably prudent. There's nothing wrong in that."

"Yeah? Could you tell that to that *Times* reporter with the dead kid? I sure as hell didn't."

Amanda looked away a moment, then looked back. "You didn't have anything hard until you saw that psychiatrist bill."

"It doesn't take a rocket scientist to connect the dots. Michelle Ransom dreams a girl is going to die at such and such a location. She goes to her shrink and tells him about the dream! Two days later a girl turns up dead. Gee, I wonder who the real suspect is."

"Right. So where is this Dr. Otter?"

"Studio City."

"Michelle lives in Pasadena and she drives all the way to Studio City to see a shrink?"

Benson grunted. "I think she didn't want her colleagues at the law office to know."

"Jesus. Talk about an identity crisis."

Benson let it go. "Anyway, the bill by itself isn't evidence. All we've got is a shrink who's listened to a bunch of weird dreams. *Maybe.* If we really do have Hannibal Lecter here, we still need something more than circumstantial. Even if we locate transcript sessions with Michelle, even if he admits she's told him the dreams, we're still in la-la land. You can't convict a guy on overheard dreams. You can't even arrest him."

"He must have read about the killings. That's withholding evidence."

Benson grimaced. "And we charge him with what? Failure to do his civic duty? We have cause to question him—that's about it. If he's a shrink, he's smart enough to know about search warrants, probably studied enough law to shield himself. We're going to have to outsmart him. Oh . . . *shit.*"

Amanda followed his eyes to the rearview. She

turned around in the seat, spotted the black sedan behind them. "IAD?"

"I can smell those silk suits a mile away. We're fucked."

"Okay, calm down."

She'd no sooner said it than the red strobe lights flashed over them. Benson cursed, pulled to the curb. They were just two blocks from Otter's office.

"Keep your mouth shut, Mandy."

"Touch, I—"

"Just keep your damn mouth shut! You're clear in this thing. I'm not going to let those fucking apes pull you down with me." He gave her a withering look.

Someone rapped on Benson's window. He rolled it down, recognizing Daryl Sizemore from South Central days. His partner, the other IAD cop, Benson didn't know.

Benson said, "What's cookin', Daryl?"

Sizemore flipped open his badge case anyway. "Your captain would like a word with you, Benson."

Benson stayed cool. He'd never fully bought in to the movie clichés. The police hated the feebs, the feebs hated the IAD, the IAD hated everyone—all that crap. People were people. Shitty and not shitty. "My captain or the deputy chief?"

"Doesn't matter, dickhead," came a voice behind Sizemore's shoulder.

Sizemore was a big man under the silk suit—worked out—but his partner was even bigger. Razor cut, lantern jaw, superior attitude. Jesus, maybe the clichés were right.

Benson craned around Sizemore at the bigger man. He wasn't sure he could take him. But then, you never

really knew. "Don't think I've met your surly boyfriend, Daryl."

"Let's just keep this nice," Sizemore said, hands
folded in front of him. "Why don't you and your partner just follow us back to Parker Center?"

Benson held the smile. "My partner's off duty right
now. We were just going downtown for some coffee."

Sizemore's partner shouldered to the window,
squinting down at Amanda's skirt. "Coffee or blow
jobs, Benson?" He smirked at his partner. "Why don't
you have legs like that, Daryl?"

"Hey, asshole—" Amanda began but Benson put
out a hand to stop her. It landed on her thigh.

The bigger IAD cop grinned lasciviously. "Don't
mind us, Benson. Go for the pussy!"

Benson jerked back the hand reflexively—caught
himself, ignored the bait.

"Knock it off, okay, Neff?" Sizemore muttered.

Neff bent closer, elbowing his partner aside, eyes
traveling up Amanda's blouse. "Love to, Daryl. Love
to knock off a warm piece of that! We talking silicone
or the real thing here, Benson?"

Benson's hand moved for the handle, and Amanda
grabbed his arm. "Touch, don't fall for it!"

Hit an IAD cop. Yeah, that was all he'd need
right now.

Benson let go the handle. "I'll come with you. My
partner stays here," Benson told Sizemore.

Sizemore didn't look completely unsympathetic.
"They'll just send us after her again, Benson. Look,
if she's clean—"

"No, hey!" Neff pushed in again, grinning. "Detective Benson's right. You take him in. I'll stay here and

interview the partner. Little *private* investigation, huh, Detective Blaine?"

Amanda leaned across Benson, partly to keep him from going for the door again. "I'd *love* that, Neff. We could spend the whole interview searching for your dick!"

"Let's just stay loose," Sizemore tried weakly.

"I phone my lawyer first," Benson said to everyone.

"Fuck your lawyer, Benson," said Neff. "You and your big-titted partner are dead meat."

"Hey, asshole," Amanda spat, "ever hear of the Police Protective League? How'd you like my attorney shoving that IAD tin up your faggy silk ass!"

Neff laughed, low and dirty. "You hear that, Daryl? She takes it up her silky ass!"

Benson was out of the car.

"Touch, don't!"

Sizemore attempted a restraining hand but Benson shoved him aside easily. Too easily? "Okay, shit-for-brains, where do you want it?"

The big IAD cop smiled delight. "Got us a weight lifter here, Daryl!" He jacked his thumb toward the adjacent alley. "Step into my office, Mr. RHD!"

Sizemore tried one more time—"C'mon, you guys!"—but this time Neff pushed him away, and when Amanda started out of the car, Benson pointed threateningly. "Stay in the vehicle, Mandy, I mean it!"

"Now you behave yourself with the lady, Daryl!" Neff sniggered, eyes on Benson as they crossed the sidewalk.

Amanda yelled, "Don't be stupid, Touch!" but they were already cloaked in alley shadows.

It was ten degrees cooler in here out of the sun.
Maybe that was what took Benson down a notch, or
maybe the fact it suddenly didn't feel quite right. He
knew how guys walked when they were about to start
swinging, and the big IAD cop didn't walk that way.

Neff kept his eyes on Benson, kept backing up, pulling them deeper into alley shadows.

When he'd backed to his satisfaction—well out of
sight of the car—he reached under his jacket, still grinning. For one crazy instant Benson thought the cop
was going for his piece. Neff shook out a pack, took
a cigarette with his mouth. "What's your handicap,
Benson?"

Benson stood there, arms loose, legs tensed, still
waiting, confused.

Neff lit the cigarette, blew smoke. "From what I
hear, Tiger Woods's career is safe. Which is more than
we can say about yours."

"What the fuck do you want, Neff?"

Neff spit tobacco particle from his unfiltered Camel.
"We want Bill Campbell. Someone with self-control.
That leaves you out, Benson."

Benson leaned back on his heels. There would be
no fight. They were in here to be away from Amanda's
ears. "Fuck you."

Neff nodded. "I can do that. Cite you on a CUBO
and have the suspension papers ready for the chief to
sign by tomorrow morning."

"You can't do shit, Neff, without my attorney present. And not with any 'conduct unbecoming an officer'
bullshit. You started the harassing. And my partner's
a witness."

"So's mine."

Benson stuck his hands in his pockets. "Let's cut the crap. Who sent you, Noland or the deputy chief?"

"What were you doing on the golf course with Special Agent Campbell? Besides picking your nose in the rough?"

"You first."

Neff smiled like a tiger. "Okay. It was the chief."

That was a relief. At least Benson's own captain wasn't after his ass. A relief and a bit of a surprise. "Why?"

"Your turn. Quid pro quo."

"Fuck that shit. *Why?*"

Neff flicked ashes. "How the hell do I know? I run his errands. I don't wipe his ass."

"Just kiss it."

Neff smiled, let it go. He still thought Benson might have something. "Probably the chief's getting heat from the mayor. Elections coming up. Lot of voters read what that prima donna Fowler writes about the LAPD in the *Times*."

"I'm the sacrificial goat for a multitude of sins. That it?"

"Whatever. What about Campbell?"

"Why you dogging him?"

"That's our business."

Benson waited.

"You're a real asshole, Benson."

"*Really?* Gee, golly! No one's ever—I'm so *distressed!*"

Neff blew sour smoke. "Okay, okay. Graft. Maybe. Someone in his unit is dirty."

Benson shook his head. "You're chasing the wrong feeb. Campbell's a fucking saint. Ask around. I don't even know him and he took the afternoon to shoot golf with me. And you know how feebs feel about cops."

"Why the golf game?"

Benson thought about it. He had nothing to lose, and the truth might sound far-fetched enough to work. "You know about the Mummy Killer, I assume."

"Yeah, we stay up nights tapping into the RHD's frequency," Neff muttered sarcastically. "The whole fucking *town* knows about the Mummy Killer, Benson."

"Then you know we don't have jack. I was probing Campbell about the FBI's use of psychics."

Neff nearly laughed. "Jesus! You guys hurtin' *that* bad?"

Benson didn't even have to fake it. "Just about."

Neff watched him with diminishing interest. Finally he flicked the butt at the brick wall, where it exploded like a comet. "Oh, fuck it. It's no more crazy than this shit we got on Campbell. Looks like we're both going in circles, Detective."

"So. You issuing a ROD on me or not?"

Neff smirked. "If I wanted a relief-of-duty paper on you, Benson, it would already be signed by the chief and on its way up your ass. Get used to my handsome profile, though."

Which meant Benson was going to be tailed for a while, probably until the tire iron case came to trial. Maybe Noland had intervened on his behalf, maybe not. Neff wasn't going to say even if he knew.

"One more official question, Detective Benson, then we can get out of this pleasant-smelling alley."

"I'm listening."

"Your partner. Silicone or the real thing?"

Neff didn't expect an answer, but Benson gave him the one that would hurt most. "The real thing, Neff. Soft and heavy, and pink as ripe cherries under your tongue."

Neff groaned envy. "Lucky prick."

Benson grinned, heading for the car. "That's what I call it!"

He slid behind the wheel next to Amanda and watched the rearview until the IAD Caprice had pulled around and gone by.

"So?" Amanda asked. "Who won?"

"We did, for the moment. They're just following for now."

"That asshole goads you into an alley to tell you that?"

"They thought I might be dirty with Bill Campbell at the FBI. Didn't know if you were involved. I told them they were full of shit and I think they believed me. The deputy chief is having us dogged, not Noland, or so they say."

"At least there's that."

Benson turned to her earnestly. "No shit now, Mandy. What have you discussed with Noland?"

"What do you mean?"

"Have you recommended I see the department shrink?"

She hesitated.

"Don't bullshit me now. I know Scotty wants me evaluated. The truth, Mandy—I need it."

"I mentioned it once. Hell, *he* mentioned it. I didn't *recommend* it. You think I would without consulting you first? Jesus, Touch, thanks a lot."

"But the captain wouldn't be exactly surprised to

find I've started seeing a shrink, right? I'm sure Scotty wouldn't, hell, half the damn Homicide suite probably wouldn't. Place is worse than a coop of old hens."

Amanda finally caught up to where this was leading. She gave him a level look. "No, Touch."

"Why not?"

"Because your ass is in enough of a sling as it is. You walk into this Dr. Otter's office masquerading as a civilian and those IAD apes *will* have cause to bust your ass!"

"What masquerade? I'm a guy in a suit."

"And when Otter asks what you do for a living?"

"Civil servant."

"Oh, Christ. It's fucking entrapment, Touch."

"Not if I haven't seen that stack of bills at Michelle's house."

Amanda hesitated. "And haven't told me."

"And haven't told you."

She snorted. "Lot of 'haven'ts.' "

"Two isn't a lot. It's a couple."

She wasn't convinced. "Touch, look. Let's just interview the guy. If he gives us shit, we'll threaten to take him downtown. But let's give the guy the *chance* to spill. He's a high-profile suspect. It'll make the papers. We'll be doing our goddamn job. It's *something* in a week of *nothings*. Make an impact when Noland's threatening your suspension."

"Amanda, we go stomping in there with our shields and he isn't going to say shit. This is a doctor, not some dumb-ass street snitch. You know the kind of attorney a guy like that can afford. Otter will be on the street by the six o'clock news."

She was thinking about it.

"It's that, Mandy, or we wait till dark and do an illegal B and E with the Bobbsey Twins watching us through infrareds. I stroll in under daylight, on the other hand, and everything's clean, no matter who's watching. And you're out of the picture."

"Sort of clean."

Benson made a show of looking at his watch. Amanda made a show of acknowledging it. "Yeah, yeah, I know you're racing the clock. I also know you're cowboying this thing to beat the *Times* and the tire iron trial. Only if it blows up in your face, it's three strikes and you're out."

"It won't blow, I promise."

"He said, his dick in her mouth."

Benson grinned. "You Vassar girls are so provincial."

But she wasn't smiling. She was giving him that look all of a sudden.

"What?"

"You son of a bitch!" Amanda turned in the seat. "You're still protecting her."

Benson looked away.

"You're going to blow the collar on purpose to save that blond bitch! You never believed this psychic shit for a minute!"

"Mandy—"

"You're going down anyway—nothing to lose—and you're taking me down with you! You think I won't get nailed too, just because I wait in the fucking car?"

"It's not like that, Amanda."

"The hell it's not. Look at you. Your goddamn Motorola's turned off. Your cell phone's out of batteries half the fucking time. You're already *out* of here!" She shook her head in disgust.

"Mandy—"

"Don't 'Mandy' me! Where are you and Miss Glendale headed, Jamaica? She got that expensive Craftsman house up for sale—that it?"

"Mandy, listen—"

"Fuck you! Start acting like a cop instead of a lovesick—" Amanda reached out angrily and snapped on the Mustang's Motorola.

The dispatcher was right in the middle of a sentence. "—enson, turn on your police radio! Your red light is flashing. Detective Benson, do you copy?"

Amanda grabbed the handset. Benson jerked it away from her. "Yeah, Benson here."

"About time. You still on the force, Benson?"

"What have you got, Fred?"

"Something pretty garbled came in over the Pasadena frequency. They're having transmission problems. Possible B and E and homicide. Lost the address, but the victim's name is Ransom, Michelle. Don't you know somebody out there by that name?"

22

Benson called backup for his partner, and Amanda took the psychiatrist's office with a couple of patrol cops. Benson beat it to Pasadena.

Police tape and detective cars were there when he screeched up. Benson ducked under the tape, heart racing, and trotted up the familiar walk and debris-strewn stoop. There was bright blood sprinkled on the fallen Southern columns. A thin trail of it led him into the foyer that was crowded with uniforms and suits.

Benson flipped his badge case at the first plain-clothesman he saw. "Detective Benson, RHD. What have we got?"

The Pasadena detective was a robust black man with a shaved head and impeccable taste in suits. He glanced at Benson's badge with an unimpressed expression. " 'We,' paleface?"

"Is she dead?" Benson blurted, scanning the crowded front room.

"I didn't get any word about RHD involvement with this, Detective—Hey, you're the guy on the Mummy thing, right? Got some civil suit pending?"

"Look, I'm a friend of the family, goddamn it! Where is she?"

"Sorry. Detective Anderson, Pasadena Police." He pointed with a pencil. "Victim's mother is right over there. She's been asking for you."

Michelle was at one end of a beige divan, arms wrapped tight as though she were freezing, face drawn but in control, conversing with another detective beside her. She looked up gratefully when Benson approached, but did not get up and leap into his arms. Benson didn't know if this was to spare him embarrassment or if Michelle was just in shock.

He flashed his badge at the seated detective without looking at him. "Benson, RHD." He bent to Michelle. "Michelle, what happened?"

"They've taken Jana! Touch, they've taken *Jana!*"

Benson elbowed his way unapologetically between Michelle and the investigating detective, as though the Pasadena cop didn't exist. "Easy, Mikki. Who did?"

"I don't know! I just came in and—the *blood!*" Her pupils were dilated but her eyes weren't red-rimmed. She hadn't cried and needed to. Benson glanced at her fingertips. He whipped off his suit jacket, draped it around her huddled shoulders, and glared at the detective beside them. "Get her some bourbon."

The Pasadena cop gave him an affronted look. "She doesn't want any—"

"Get her some goddamn bourbon! It's in the kitchen!"

The Pasadena cop lowered his pad and pen slowly,

like he was about to say something, reconsidered when he saw the look in Benson's eyes. He got up and went for the kitchen.

Benson turned back to Michelle, who was trembling now despite the wrap. He pulled the lapels of his jacket together over her breasts, took her hands, and rubbed them briskly. He saw a female patrol cop by the door, jerked his head at her. She hurried over.

"You got a medevac team coming?"

"I don't know, sir."

Benson pulled the patrol cop closer by her sleeve, jerked the cellular off her belt, and tossed it at her. "Call one."

He turned back to Michelle, rubbed her arms through his jacket, tilted back her chin, and looked into her eyes. "Okay, Mikki, we're going to take care of it. You sit here with the officer now. I'll be right back, okay?"

Michelle nodded vaguely, staring into space. A spasm shook her spine.

Benson stood, turned sharply to the patrol cop. "Keep her warm."

She nodded, on the phone, and sat beside Michelle. Benson went searching for Anderson again.

He found him at the head of the stairs studying the trail of blood drops. Anderson straightened with a grunt, scanning the room. "Nice house. Craftsman, I think. Ever heard of them?"

"Yes. What have you got so far, Detective?"

Anderson walked him upstairs. He was loose and detached, almost bored. The way Benson *should* be. Anderson looked like a smart cop, a thorough one. Benson was grateful for the clearheaded presence. "Well,

I'm thinking kidnapping. Maybe somebody the victim knows. Lots of blood"—he indicated the carpeted stairs—"victim may be dead, maybe not. But she fought. Hard. Have a look at this."

They came into Jana's bedroom. Blood on the floor, the wall, the bed. An assistant ME in plastic gloves was using tweezers on the rumpled bedspread, dropping what Benson assumed was pubic hair into an evidence bag.

Detective Anderson swept an arm at the room. "Guy comes into her room, probably invited. No tampering on the downstairs doors."

"Front and back?"

Anderson nodded. "Lifted a couple good latents from the doorknob, but they could be anybody's. So, anyway . . . he comes in while Mamma's out, and he and the girl have a toke or two. Phil—"

Another medical tech, on his knees beside the bed, looked up, reached over, and put a bag in Anderson's outstretched hand. Anderson handed it to Benson, who held it up. It contained two partially smoked roaches.

Anderson watched him. "So they have a little smoke, then go to bed and make boom-boom. Smoke a little more afterward—afterglow—and, what? Get into an argument? Somebody's pissed. Boyfriend wants to try the dirt path or whatever. Girl says no way. It escalates. Somebody starts hitting. The guy hits hardest. Blood flies. Boyfriend panics—maybe she's unconscious, maybe dead. Drags her downstairs." Anderson indicated the red drag marks. "Puts her body—unconscious or dead—in his car, away he goes. Ten minutes later, Mom comes home."

Benson pictured Michelle coming through the door, finding this.

Anderson held up his palms, like it was cut and dried.

Benson glanced around the room. "Where's your tox man?"

Anderson motioned over one of the medical techs. "Barry Eisen, Detective Benson, RHD."

"Sent your blood off yet?" Benson asked him.

"No, sir, just getting ready to. It'll take a few days. We're pretty stacked at—"

"I want you to send a separate sample to Parker Center, the chief ME. Name's Mathers, Sid Mathers. Got that?"

The tech glanced at Anderson. Anderson nodded.

"Tell him Detective Benson says to rush it. And he's to call me with the results."

"Yes, sir."

When the tech left, Anderson gave Benson the up and down once. "Think this is one of yours?"

Benson was staring at the rug, thinking: goddamn deep pile, hard to lift a shoe print. He wished one of his own people were here. "Probably not. The Mummy Killer hasn't abducted one yet."

Anderson grunted. "Yet."

Benson mentioned nothing about Michelle's dreams. He wanted to get back downstairs to her. "Got anything else, Detective Anderson?"

"Yeah." Anderson walked over to Jana Ransom's bedroom desk, the one she'd probably done high school algebra at. There was a blue teddy bear with one eye atop it, a translucent blue Apple computer, a CD tower, books, a corkboard above the desk studded with color photos. School friends, family. Benson recognized Jason Richards among them.

Anderson picked a large evidence bag off the desk chair, tossed it to Benson. There was red, satin-looking material folded inside the plastic.

Benson turned it over in his hands.

"Look like a man's windbreaker to you?" Anderson asked. "Young guy's?"

Benson nodded. "Yeah, it does."

He looked back up at the corkboard, and the photo of Jason Richards grinning there.

By the time Benson arrived at Parker Center, the news was all over the third floor.

Benson felt a pulling feeling at his gut as he came through the doors. The feeling increased when his superior, Lieutenant Scott, hurried over. "Your Motorola broke, Benson?"

Scotty was angry but there was no edge to it.

"What's up, Lieutenant?" Benson asked him, already knowing.

"Captain wants to see you, pronto."

"The IAD goons in there?"

"Not anymore." There was genuine sadness in Scotty's eyes.

"Where's my partner?"

"In the hotbox with the psychiatrist. *And* his attorney."

"Fuck."

"Yeah. And not just *any* attorney. Dick Sheim, the Prince of Darkness. The shrink's closed up tighter'n a ninety-year-old whore. Amanda's done about all she can with him."

"And you've done about all you can for me with Noland, right, Scotty?"

The lieutenant looked away apologetically.

Benson slapped his shoulder and headed for Captain Noland's office.

Noland's venetian blinds were down—never a good sign. He was stealing a nip from his top drawer flask when Benson barged in. "Don't you ever fucking knock?"

"Can I have some of that?"

For a moment it looked like Noland was actually going to offer him the flask. Then he put it away quickly. "Sit."

"Why, am I staying?"

"Would you mind very fucking much obeying what may be my last official order to you?"

Benson sat. "It's not the shrink," he told Noland flatly.

"I'm going to need your badge and your piece," the captain told him.

Benson took them out, slapped them together, put them on Noland's desk. Noland put them in his desk drawer.

"I want that oiled and cleaned when I get it back."

"The City of Los Angeles officially suspends you from all further—"

"When did you get the word, Cap?"

Noland sighed. "Twenty minutes ago."

"Okay, look. It'll take the IAD at least twenty-four hours to fill out the papers and get them before the chief's desk. Let me stay on the case until then."

Noland glanced at the drawer as if contemplating another nip. "No can do. Besides, you just said it isn't

the shrink." He looked up hopefully. "You got something else?"

"The shrink's too smart. He'd know Michelle Ransom would be too much of a liability, that she might
eventually talk to us. And it's not the Richards kid
over in Pasadena either."

"Who the fuck are you talking about?"

"Jason Richards, the kidnapped girl's boyfriend. In
about thirty minutes a Pasadena detective named Anderson is going to figure that out. Richards's high
school windbreaker is there, and SID will mark the
kid positive as having had sex with the victim from
the pubic hair found on her sheets. But he didn't
take her."

"How do you know all this shit?"

"Let me stay on. Twenty-four hours."

"No. And I'm letting the shrink go. This psychic
stuff is bullshit."

"I agree, but there's a link."

Noland shook his head. "It's bullshit. Your Glendale poke dreamed them up *after* they were done."

It was pointless arguing with Noland; he was too far
behind the curve and they were wasting time.

"The Ransom girl is still alive. Let me stay on."

"You know where she is?" He waited. "That's what
I thought. You're off, Benson, suspended until further
notice. And if you fuck around I'll have you pushing
a pencil at an IAD desk or chasing down pimps at
the Hollywood Division."

But like Scotty, Noland's tone didn't have that
angry edge. Everyone knew Benson was still the best
shot, the only cop who'd come up with anything at all
on the Mummy, even if it wasn't quite adding up.

"Then this conference is over," Benson said and hit the door.

"When I *say* it's over!" Noland shouted, started to rise . . . then sat back down heavily.

"Screw it."

He looked askance at his top desk drawer. He licked his lips.

Benson joined Lieutenant Scott at the hotbox window.

Scotty was watching Otter and his attorney through the two-way glass. Amanda was inside, pacing before them, looking impotent.

Scotty glanced up at Benson, then went back to watching the two nattily attired gentlemen seated within the spartan room. "Prick."

He could have meant either: the perfectly calm Otter or the arrogant-looking Sheim. Benson didn't ask. "She's getting nowhere, right?"

Scotty nodded. "Smart shrink. Smart enough to co-operate fully, come downtown without an argument. And it probably cost him patient time."

"Got nothing to hide is what he's saying. Also it got everybody out of his office before someone could trip over a file."

"He keeps records of his patients' dreams. So what? Doesn't prove jack." Scott folded his arms. "Still . . . there's something . . ."

Benson turned to him. "What?"

Scotty's eyes narrowed. "Look at the smug prick. He's enjoying this inconvenience. Making himself look cool in front of the fumbling flatfoots or something. I don't know."

"You think he did them, Scotty?"

"No. You?"

"No, but you're right. He's getting a kick from our frustration."

Scott shook his head. "Otter. What the hell kind of name is that?"

"Looks like he just swallowed a mackerel."

The lieutenant laughed. Amanda came out of the little green room looking sour, spotted Benson, and pretended to brighten. "Ah, another sucker! Now it's a complete circle jerk."

Benson snorted. "S'matter, Mandy, can't outsmart that simple country lawyer?"

"Fucker knows the law. Every time I open my mouth, he cuts me off with some bullshit legalese you'd need a wall of law books to check him on. He's either a very good attorney or a very good bull-shitter."

"He's both," Scott muttered. "And we're not getting anywhere because we haven't got dick. I'm going to cut him loose before he threatens to file. And wins."

Amanda waited for an I-told-you-so look from her partner but didn't get one. "How's Michelle?" she asked him.

"I've got her over at St. Francis for observation. Freaked out when she found out I wanted her to go there, but she's okay. Oh"—Benson turned offhand-edly to the lieutenant—"the captain wants a word with you, Scotty."

If Scott had been about to ask Benson how it had gone for him in Noland's office, he put it off to go see what the captain wanted. When he was around the corner, Benson headed straight for the hotbox door.

"Touch?" Amanda started to follow but he waved her off.

Benson hustled in without shutting the door, looking at neither the lawyer, nor the psychiatrist. "Okay, gentlemen! You're free to go, Dr. Otter. Sorry we took up your time!"

There were empty cups and napkins on the table, while Benson began to tidy up like a duty officer, still ignoring the two men.

Attorney Sheim rose from his chair with a triumphant smile.

His back still to the two men, Benson added casually, "And I'm looking forward to the book, Doctor. You should make a fortune from all the notoriety once we nail this guy."

Otter, halfway up, hesitated, regained his chair. "Excuse me, Officer?"

"Detective. You are writing a book on the Mummy Killer phenomenon, right? Who's your publisher?"

"Little Brown," Otter said tonelessly.

His attorney moved in fast. "That will do, James! Let's get out of here. The place smells."

Otter started to get up again.

"Of course you may not be able to use her complete transcripts." Benson threw the trash in a corner wastebasket. "What I mean is, they might be edited once you get them back."

Otter stood this time, but didn't move from his chair. "Edited?"

"James, come on!" from the attorney.

Benson turned to Otter innocently. "Oh, we will sub-poena them, Doctor. We know the Ransom woman is somehow involved, just not the particulars yet."

Otter didn't move.

"My client doesn't have to answer another word, Detective."

Benson folded his arms calmly. "I haven't asked him a question."

Otter turned to his attorney. "Can they do that? Subpoena my records?"

"No," Sheim assured Otter firmly and took his arm.

Benson just chuckled.

Otter pulled away. "Do you think I killed those girls, Detective?"

Benson watched the psychiatrist's face. It was composed, without a hint of guilt. "Did you?"

"Most assuredly not."

Benson shrugged. "Well, we've got the numbers of your associates."

Sheim took his arm again but Otter yanked away angrily. "I share my client sessions with no one, Detective. It's against the law, as you should know."

Benson tossed his head, went back to collecting dirty cups. "Well, someone read your transcripts. At least that's how the *Times* will see it."

Sheim shouted and pointed in his best oratory style. "That's a *threat,* Detective!"

"Yeah? Which part?"

Otter held up a calming hand to his attorney. "It's all right, Dick. I don't even take notes. I record all my sessions." And before Sheim could protest again, he added quickly, "Go over them that weekend, then erase them. Completely. There is nothing incriminating in either my office or my home. In fact, I would happily have agreed to a search of same, if the officers had merely asked."

"James, please—"

"I have nothing to hide," Otter told his lawyer pointedly, then turned serenely to Benson. "I have nothing to hide."

The two men turned on their heels and walked from the room.

23

She thought that he wasn't smart, and that was her mistake.

They all thought he wasn't smart. Many who thought it were dead now.

Even the one here now, the pretty blond one with the chest, sobbing and wetting herself, even she thought he was stupid. Thought he wasn't clever, like Nephthys. Fine. If he was the stupid one, then why was he in control here in the little pine cabin with her tied to the wooden chair with the scarf tight around her pretty, bloody mouth?

He wasn't stupid. He knew the scarf—the gag—wasn't really necessary way out here, that no one could hear her screams. He knew that the other one had left it in place sheerly for the sake of cruelty.

She hated the pretty one. The one named Jana.

But she was not Nephthys. She was not his goddess. It was a lie. They all lied. All women lied. Just as his mother had said. *There will come many false prophets,* she had read to him, and it was true.

It was amazing. He could see it all so clearly now.

His mother was not Nephthys, and he had been wrong to put her to the sacred knife even though she'd begged him. Wrong to burn down the house, though that had, in fact, covered the evidence. Even at the cost of his face.

His mother was not Nephthys and had never claimed to be. *You will know her when she comes,* she had told him that rainy afternoon before the old black-and-white TV, watching *The Mummy's Ghost,* with Chaney. *I will always be with you, Charles,* she had told him. Holding him, kissing him, making his thing grow big, taking him to her bed. And she had been right.

He knew it the instant he heard her voice there in the doctor's office. She had come back to him. To guide him. Her wonderful, husky, seductive voice . . . clear, and soft, and yes, perhaps a little frightened. Frightened for him, Charlie. Frightened he wouldn't make the right choice no matter how many times her clear, calm voice directed him to the next one.

But she had never given up on him. And each time he put the next one to the blade, each time he opened up her heart and let her spirit free, watched while she writhed and died and did not come back to life—did not become his beloved Nephthys—Mother was always there with him. And always there the next time in the doctor's office, to speak softly to him, guide him to the next location, the next young girl. Never giving up until he found her.

He *thought* he had found her. In the one called Kurtzy. But she had proved false.

It made his heart hurt to think about it. He'd thought the journey was over. He did not enjoy the killing. But it had been another lie.

Kurtzy had never let him put her to the blade, and the blade was the only true way to free the spirit, to release the lovely goddess. The only proof.

It was his own fault. He had waited so long, wanted so much to believe. Wanted so much for the killing to stop. So much blood, so many earthbound lives. Was even a goddess worth it?

Yet he knew she was. As surely as he knew he had not yet found her, that she was still out there. That he would somehow, even with the threat of the police now, have to go back to the doctor's office and listen to his mother's voice. Listen to Mother, let her direct him to the next, and the next, and on and on for however long the Ancient Ones decreed it should take.

He was so weary.

It was so hard being a god.

He sat on the wooden floor against the cabin's rough-hewn wall and watched the pretty girl in the chair. Watched the golden hair hanging in her face. Listened to her whimpering.

He knew she had to pee again. Knew she didn't want it running down her leg again, dripping on the floor, humiliating her further.

Charlie didn't want it either. It smelled and he had to clean it up. He'd told the other girl that before she left for the groceries. And she'd turned angrily on him. "Just leave the bitch in the goddamn chair!" she'd ordered him. "And don't take off the gag. It'll help stanch the blood."

Ordered him.

Thinking that she was intimidating him.

But he was not intimidated. And he was not stupid. He was biding his time.

Because some lies could be good. Some lies could work for you. Some of her lies made sense. Leaving the apartment, for instance. Cleaning all traces of his presence and leaving it had been a smart thing, even if she had ordered it. And coming here to the little cabin in the woods had been smart too. He would be even more secluded than in the Hollywood apartment. So he had gone along.

Just as he had gone along with this whole silly ransom lie.

For it was a lie, he knew. She did not intend to give the pretty girl Jana back to her mother. She would take the mother's money, yes, then have him kill the girl.

Then leave him, leave him for a man like the one they called Jason. A mere man. Not a god like him!

The thought made him sick.

They were full of hate and lies and they were using him. All of them. Lying and using him. Fucking him and moaning about his big thing and using him, just as Mother had warned.

Which is why, in the end, he would kill them all. It was what his mother would have wanted. *Beware, Charles. They will use you. Tell you they love you, and use you. Only I will remain true.*

Oh, yes, he understood it all. He was smart too.

And he was all through taking orders, all through being used.

The pretty one was moaning again now under the tight scarf. Charlie pushed up from the hardwood floor, came to the girl, and ripped the gag away with one movement, causing the pretty head to jerk, the pretty eyes to open wide in terror. The pretty mouth to suck in grateful air. It stopped the whimpering. But only for a moment.

"Don't do that." See? He could give orders too.

She looked up at him with wet eyes. Her mouth had stopped bleeding where she'd been hit. "Please . . ."

"Don't make that noise. I don't like it. Don't whimper."

She stared at him. Her breath made a ragged sound. But she wouldn't stop the whimpering so he replaced the gag.

But felt a little bad about it. He stared down at her. With her makeup smeared away, she reminded him of the other, the pale one he had loved so truly. "Do you have to pee again?"

She nodded helplessly.

Charlie went around behind the chair and untied her. "I'm not going to clean it up again. But if you try to run, I'll kill you. I am Set, brother of Osiris, and Isis. Patron deity of all Lower Egypt."

But she could hardly stand, much less run.

He helped her outside to the little house with the wood seat, the wooden hole, and placed her on it and even turned his back when she looked at him. When the sound of her water splashing below ceased, he turned back to her and lifted her from the wooden seat. It stunk in there, and he pulled her back into the clean sunlight.

But back in the house, she still smelled. Even pretty ones can smell, he surmised.

So he took her underthings and dropped them into the rusty sink with the metal pump and ran cold water over them. He came back and hung them across a chair back, even though this was defying the other girl, even though she would scream at him and turn purple. He didn't care. He could scream too. And do far worse things than turn purple.

When he put the pretty girl back in the chair she began the mewling sounds again.

"I told you not to do that."

She looked up at him, golden hair stringy now in her face, and shook her tightly bound wrists.

He could see they were blue from the cruel ropes, that she could hardly lift them, and he thought about it, about the false goddess screaming at him, ordering him—and he loosened the ropes and told the pretty girl that if she moved from the chair he would kill her and take out her heart.

The pretty girl stayed in the chair.

24

Lieutenant Scott chewed Benson a new asshole when he came out of the hotbox.

Dr. Otter and his attorney were on their way out the door when both Scotty and Noland came around the corner and nailed Benson.

Noland could easily have had him arrested. Benson was technically suspended from the department and he had lured Scotty away from the hotbox so he could get in there, play his little mind game with Otter and his attorney, then illegally dismiss them.

Noland, already red-faced from one nip too many today, started to wade into Benson when Lieutenant Scott opened his mouth first. "You have been relieved of duty, Detective Benson," he growled, punching a finger in Benson's chest, "and you had neither the right nor the authority to let the doctor go." Benson took the chest jab without reacting; Scotty never behaved like this. Unless it was an act.

Noland tried to say something again, but again

Scotty cut him off, grabbing Benson's arm and shoving him toward the elevators. "Real hot cowboy, aren't you? Don't give a damn who you get in trouble as long as it makes you look good!" He was shouting so loud the whole division could hear—so loud Noland didn't get the chance or maybe feel the need to unload. When the elevator doors opened, Scotty shoved ·Benson inside and got on with him.

He let go of Benson's arm when the car started down.

"Thanks, Scotty."

"Don't thank me yet, boyo. I can bullshit past Noland but I doesn't carry much weight with the AC. And it doesn't look good for you. When's this tire iron caper go to court?"

"Couple of weeks."

"Jesus." Couple of weeks was too fast for L.A.'s usually ponderously slow judicial system. "They really got it in for you. Any idea who the judge will be?"

Benson shrugged. "They'll probably get Ricker. She'll eat my balls and shit them back at me."

"Christ, Touch."

"Don't worry about it, Scotty. I'm going to solve this case."

"With what?"

"I'll tell you when I'm sure."

The elevator doors opened and the lieutenant stayed on. "Hey, Touch—"

Benson turned, keeping the doors from closing with his hand. "Yeah?"

"I can't cover for you anymore, not now."

"I know that, Scotty. I'm not going to do anything to hurt you or Amanda."

Scott nodded, a little wistfully. "All right. Be careful for chrissake."

Benson shot him with a finger gun and the doors hissed shut.

On his way to the Pasadena Division, Benson called Detective Anderson, the cop who was heading up the Ransom kidnapping.

Anderson, like almost everyone else, didn't know Benson had been officially suspended yet, though news carried fast across division boundaries, especially ones concerning high-profile RHD cops like Benson. Even if he didn't know about the suspension, a lot of regular L.A. detectives hated the lofty RHD unit; Anderson could have told Benson to bugger off. Robbery-Homicide hadn't officially taken over the Jana Ransom kidnapping, and maybe never would. Benson was banking on Anderson's sympathies, since he told the Pasadena detective that he was a friend of the family.

Whether that was part of it, or whether Anderson was just one of those confident cops who didn't feel threatened by other divisions, he allowed Benson into the Pasadena holding cell without apparent resentment. Anderson was a smart cop—the wheel always comes around—and he might have need of a friend in the RHD someday.

The duty cop swung back the steel door and Benson entered Jason Richards's temporary new home. The Pasadena tank was better than some, but the stink of urine and vomit was still in the corridor amid the attendant cursing and delirium rambling. Not a pleasant place for a young kid.

He was curled up in one corner of the bunk, scared

for his own life. And probably for Jana's. Benson's heart went out to the kid. "Hey."

Jason Richards looked up at the half-familiar face with haunted eyes.

"How you doing, kid?"

"All right. Don't I know you?"

"Detective Benson, friend of Jana's mother. I was at the house that day when you two were upstairs banging." He didn't soften verbs; despite his sympathy for the kid, Benson wanted to let him know he was here on business.

The Richards kid was too distracted with fear to be embarrassed. "Do you know who took Jana?" he asked hopefully.

"Listen, Jason, I need you to be absolutely honest with me—can you do that? Now nothing you say to me is going to hurt you because I'm no longer a cop at the moment, but I need you to be truthful with me."

Jason hugged his knees. "They fired you?"

Benson smiled. "Something like that. Were you with Jana Ransom the day she was abducted? I already know you didn't take her, so tell me the truth now."

Jason looked down at the toes of his Nikes for a moment, then nodded above his kneecaps.

"Were you in her room at the house?"

Jason swallowed, nodded.

"Did you have sex with her?"

Nod.

"Did you wear a condom?"

Jason bit his lip. "No."

Benson sat at the other end of the bunk, studied the kid a moment. "Look at me, kid."

Jason looked up, eyes brimming. He'd probably convinced himself he was going to die.

"Tell me what happened."

Jason wiped at his nose, sniffed. "I was . . . we started fooling around, you know? Usually she just gets me off with her hands, or her, you know, her mouth. But that day—I don't know—she was hot or something. She wanted . . ."

"Some for herself."

"Yeah. She wanted me in her and she didn't have anything."

"Any condoms."

"Yeah. So we were horsing around and I guess I didn't have as much control as I thought, you know?"

"If memory serves." Benson sat back. "Jesus, kid, your timing was lousy."

The Richards boy hung his head, nodding. "I'm going to die, aren't I? They think I raped and killed her."

"Who says she's dead?"

But the jab had no effect. The poor kid was devastated. But not from committing murder.

"Jason, can you think of anyone, *anyone,* who might have had reason to do this? A jealous boy, maybe? Someone at school . . ."

Jason shook his head, chin atop his knees. "I've been thinking about it all morning. Everybody liked Jana. Everybody."

Not quite, Benson thought, rising from the bunk.

He slapped the kid's shoulder—"Hang in there"—and signaled the duty officer to let him out.

He phoned St. Francis from the Mustang, but they'd already released Michelle, sent her home with tranquilizers.

Benson pulled into her drive to find her down on

hands and knees on the front walk with a bucket and scrub brush. He got out of the car.

Michelle was rubbing furiously at the blood on the front stoop with the wide, soapy brush. She looked up once when his shadow fell across her, then went back to it with a vengeance. She was wearing a new dress, expensive heels, scuffing them obliviously.

"Michelle."

"It doesn't even come up with vinegar! How do you get it *up*?"

He bent, pulled a straggle of hair from her face gently. "Mikki. Stop. We'll get someone to do this later." It was the wrong thing to say. "Later" had taken on a whole new meaning in her life. Her child was missing.

But she finally sat back on her heels. She took a long breath and looked up at the bright blue sky. Her eyes looked even farther away than the few fleecy clouds. "Sometimes if you don't see something, it's almost like it didn't happen."

Benson didn't like the look. "Honey . . ."

Michelle Ransom looked down at the pink brush bristles in her hand, pulled debris from one the way a woman will pull a strand of hair from her comb. "This is the price of pride, Touch. This is the price of vanity. I thought you were beginning to like me . . . really like me, as a woman, not a twelve-year-old play-mate. And I thought that if you found out you'd stop liking me."

Benson squinted at her. "Found *out*? That you were seeing a psychiatrist? Why would it matter, Michelle? I have to see a shrink every time I shoot someone. It's the law. You want to know the truth, half the department thinks I need to see one now, shooting or not. Who *cares*?"

"*Believe* me, you don't have to tell me how stupid I've been. If I'd spoken up sooner . . . All those girls. And now Jana."

Benson took her shoulders, lifted her to her feet, took the brush from her hand. "Michelle, listen. I don't know about the other girls, but you can stop blaming yourself about Jana."

She looked up at him. "What do you mean? Touch, I've read the papers. All his victims were blond, bosomy, young girls. Just like the girl in my dreams."

A car *whooshed* by behind them, tires making a crisp sound in the street, half masking her last words. Benson urged her toward the door. "How about a drink? I'm off duty."

In the kitchen she sat across from him at the island counter.

"Blond and buxom," Benson told her over his bourbon, "but not beautiful like Jana. Plain, in fact. Every one of them. Otter didn't abduct Jana. And I don't think he killed the others."

"What are you saying? It has to be him! He's the only logical connection!"

"You aren't the only connection to your doctor, Michelle. He has other patients, friends, family, associates."

She shook her head. "If you're thinking someone read Otter's notes you can forget it. He didn't take notes during sessions. He just listens. Sits there and listens and says nothing. It's maddening."

"He also records them."

Michelle's mouth dropped. "How do you know?"

"He told me. I baited him, implied he was a money-grubbing prick intent on making a book deal over the Mummy case. He might be, for all I know. The point is, he spilled the beans about the recordings before his lawyer could stop him."

Michelle thought about it. "Then it has to be Otter himself."

"I don't think so. The mad cannibal doctor scenario is dramatic, and a tempting leap because of novels and movies, but frankly, Otter doesn't fit the profile. He may have associated your sessions with the murders, might be trying to make money on it, might even be gloating that the police can't do anything about it. Likes to think he's smarter than the bumbling LAPD, especially the elite RHD. But he didn't do the crimes. He's the key—somehow—but he didn't pull the trigger. Or wield the knife, in this case. And listen, I don't want to give you false hope—the truth is, most abductions end in tragedy—but I'm sure Otter didn't take Jana and I'm pretty sure she might still be alive."

False or not, hope shone in Michelle's eyes. "Who? *Where?*"

"Like I said, don't get your hopes up too high. We'll know where when we know who. And it has to be someone who's heard the tapes of those sessions. Maybe Otter shared them—though I don't think he's that stupid, and I'm not talking ethics here. Or maybe the tapes were stolen. Which also seems unlikely, unfortunately."

"Why?"

"Because he erases them after he's reviewed them."

"Isn't that illegal? Taping sessions without patient permission, I mean. Can't you get him on that?"

"It's probably illegal. But all the DA is going to do is slap his wrist, maybe fine him, guy with his standing. And anyway, I don't want to get him. He's thought this through, anticipated a possible investigation. I think he'd even like the police to think he's a suspect. Good for his book. And good for his pocketbook when we can't prove squat and he sues our asses. Otter's the kind of egoist who'd risk a fine or even a short jail sentence in exchange for spectacular publicity. He'll probably insist on playing himself in the movie. Arrogant prick. But he's not pathological. At least, I don't think so."

Michelle held her head in her hand a moment dizzily. "But . . . if he didn't take notes, didn't talk, and he erases the tapes . . . who could have heard them? Why is Otter a connection?"

Benson started to reach for her hand, stopped himself, and leaned back on his counter stool instead. "In the past several days I've made a lot of stupid mistakes, Michelle. Even behaved badly as a cop, maybe jeopardized the lives of some people. Part of the reason I did it was because I wanted to be close to you. My life has been pretty much a shit hole of late. I've been suffering depression, sometimes severe, even contemplated suicide. Then I saw you at the old gym that night."

Michelle made a wan smile.

"I wanted to be with you, Michelle. Close to you. Make love to you. I wanted to be in love again, alive again. Box up all the blood and death and loneliness and put it behind me for a while. I wanted to be stupid and irresponsible again. Like Jason and Jana."

"But we can't go back, Touch—"

"No, let me finish. I sat in this kitchen and watched your daughter flirt with me. And I flirted back. And it was great. Like flirting with you again. Sure, it was silly—middle-aged cop silly—a shrink would call it midlife crisis or some crap. But fuck it. It felt good. And it kept on feeling good every time I saw you. Even after you started doing what you didn't want to do, telling me about the dreams. The truth is, I probably would have dismissed the dreams, the whole psychic thing, if I hadn't been so involved with you. But I was, and I wanted to help, be there for you even though all the red flags were waving, the alarms ringing. Even if everyone else thought it was all voodoo bullshit. And the thing is, because I hung in there— maybe because I *wanted* to believe you—somewhere along the line I began to believe it myself. Or at least, I began to see there was some kind of connection. Something between the dreams and the killings. Something that was grounded in reality, even if I didn't understand completely what."

Michelle looked away. "You felt sorry for me."

Now Benson did take her hand. "No, I felt sorry for *me*. I know that's not very flattering, but it's what kept me dogging you, and—inadvertently at first—the case. When I found the bill from your shrink, everything leapt into focus. I finally had *something*. I know you can't understand what that means to a cop, but it was like a gift . . . a little like giving me part of my life back. I started getting caught up in your dreams, and my drinking, the depression, was kept at bay.

"Then when I found out about Otter, I was so ecstatic I didn't have time for the depression. Everyone around me told me I was acting like a lovesick maniac, and I never felt more rational in my life, hadn't seen things so clearly in years. I still do, Michelle."

Benson pointed to his nose. "This thing is working for me again. And when it works, really works, I always listen to it. Sometimes it's all I have. And it's telling me now that Otter is somehow connected to this thing, that he's the key if not the killer. And it's telling me that your daughter is still alive. It's just a feeling. That's all I have, and it wouldn't hold up in any court. But it's strong. And when it's this strong, I've learned to listen."

Benson reached for his glass. "Sorry. End of speech."

Michelle looked down at her own glass. "What are you going to do now?"

"Officially, nothing. I've been suspended."

"Touch!"

He shrugged. "Happens to all the best cops. It has nothing to do with you, not directly anyway. I pissed off a big league reporter at the *Times* and then . . . some guy's filed a civil suit against me for conduct unbecoming. It's bullshit, but the *Times* reporter will make another Rodney King out of it. I'll probably end up at the Toilet Table."

"The what?"

"Demoted to the Hollywood Division. They call it the Toilet Table."

"Why 'table?' "

"It's the way the squad room desks are all jammed together, all the divisions are called tables. Never mind, it isn't important."

"It's your job. Of course it's important."

"Getting Jana back is important, and catching this

asshole. Did I ever tell you that before I decided to become a cop I was thinking of being a writer? I didn't have the chops to be a good novelist, but I think I could have been a pretty decent crime reporter."

Benson took another pull from his glass. "And reporters sometimes catch bad guys too."

Michelle was staring at his glass.

He caught her eye, knew what she was thinking.

He reached for the bottle again anyway, poured them both another slug. "Don't worry about it," he told her. "Screw it. I'm *back*."

25

Ronald Short sat in his little Studio City rental drinking cheap Mexican beer and watching wrestling on his cheap black-and-white TV while roaches crawled over the cheap, faded wallpaper around him. And Ronald Short knew great happiness, great hope.

He was getting the fuck out of here. Finally. Everything was paying off.

And just when it looked like everything was going down the shitter.

He'd been out of work since he'd left the Marines on a Dishonorable. He was big and muscled and nasty-faced and had shit for education and nobody but construction companies would hire him. And construction was slowing in L.A.

Ronald had come all the way from Arkansas to enjoy the sunshine, put some tan on those big deltoids and 'ceps, scope out the bitches at the beach, enjoy the good life. And he'd wound up working part-time construction and living in this roach hole. It had made his very short temper all the shorter. Made him a fuse waiting to be lit. Made him even consider buying that gun at Costco, waiting the obligatory three weeks, and hitting that Chink-owned ReadyMart around the block. Anything to get the green to get out of this fucking smog and get back to familiar hills, and shitty winters and chicks who maybe weren't the knockouts on Sunset and Ventura, but who'd give you head without asking for pay. California sucked.

Or had.

Until he jumped that cop on the freeway.

Took a beating there—the beating of his life. Fucker was fast, knew his shit, not like those fat-bellied Arkansas troopers. And afterward, Ronald had gone to Brewsters to knock back a few and lick his wounds and think even more seriously about hitting the Chink store, maybe even blowing the fucking Chink bitch behind the counter away and not grieving about it, grabbing the cash from the till and getting the hell out of la-la land.

Funny the guys you can meet in bars. Sit right down next to in a bar. Start telling your troubles to. Ramble on while the guy in the dark suit just sits there listening (Ronald thought he might be a faggot at first), not even lifting his drink anymore, just listening until Ronald was all through. Then reaching out to shake hands and say the magic words. *I'm an attorney. And I think you've got a case here.*

Ronald Short didn't know jack about the law. And this guy in the dark suit didn't exactly look like F. Lee fucking Bailey, or that black guy—what was his name, the one that got O.J. off. But both he and Ronald knew about Rodney King. And the little attorney next to him on the bar stool knew a lot about police corruption in L.A. County. He explained to Ronald about political opportunism—whatever the fuck that was—and police ineptitude and kept calling the LAPD an understaffed paramilitary organization that used guerrilla tactics on private citizens. And even if Ronald only understood about half of what the little guy was saying, he knew that all of it was in his best interest, in both their best interests. That he had—by sheer accident and the same short temper that had gotten him ejected from the Marines—stumbled into a scheme that could set him up financially for life.

All in the flash of an instant. And all because he had *lost* the fight! First one he ever lost in his life. And more important, lost the tire iron. Lost and won at the same time. Won big, it was looking like. Funny how life can go.

Last week he didn't have enough to pay the phone bill. Now the goddamn thing was ringing off the hook. Reporters mostly. Some magazine people. Even a movie guy, once. The little attorney had told him to politely decline them all, bask in the light if he wanted, but keep his mouth shut until the trial. Look humble. Taken advantage of. Like just another innocent, caring citizen. And when the reporters phoned or knocked, thank them very nicely but decline to talk at this time without his attorney present, though he certainly appreciated their interest.

A reporter was knocking at his crummy little rental door right now.

Ronald grinned, knocking back the rest of the beer. He'd gotten to where he could tell just by the sound of the knock. He was learning. Learning fast in the Big City.

The blond in the doorway wasn't much of a looker. Not much better than the regular stuff he'd gotten back home. But she had big jugs, and no problem showing them off under the low-cut sweater. And she wasn't exactly a reporter. Not in the real sense. Just some kid from the local college trying to write something called a *thesis* and she'd been thinking of doing something on community violence anyway, and when she read about Ronald in the paper, especially the way that Fowler guy had painted the scene, well . . . she thought maybe Ronald wouldn't mind if she just asked him a couple of quick questions, helped her out with her school paper before, you know, before he became so famous she'd have to go through his agent and stuff. Did he know he was practically a celebrity? It would really mean a lot to her. Also, it had been a long hot drive over here, and she was dying of thirst.

So he let her in.

Not because he was going to tell her anything. The little attorney had already coached him on how to answer questions without really saying anything. The trick was to turn the question around so it became another question. Besides, he could tell from the way she acted it was all a ruse. She didn't give a damn about any school paper. What she wanted was to get laid by a celebrity, which Ronald was certainly becoming.

That was why he told her all he had was beer to drink, even though he had a whole case of Cokes back there. That was why he kept the beers coming even as he was evading everything she asked him about the

freeway beating, turning it around like his attorney
had told him, talking about crime in general, about
how a kid like her couldn't even feel safe in a class-
room anymore, and wasn't that a shame, but never
really saying squat about the incident.

All the while knowing from the look in her eyes
and the fact that she was hardly scribbling down anything in her spiral notebook that the real reason she
came here was to get poked, have it socked to her by
the celebrity Marine, then go brag about it to all her
school friends. She wasn't really his type but he felt
flattered anyway and spent several moments leaning
back on the couch, legs wide, bulge exposed, just so
the poor kid could get a good eyeful of what she was
going to miss.

He even gave her his autograph before she left.

Even walked her to her car and let her know she
could come back anytime. Even laughed when he saw
the helpless way she reacted when she found her right
rear had gone flat. How flustered she got getting the
trunk up, fumbling with the spare and jack.

The least he could do was help her change the damn
tire. And he could tell how grateful she was. Her eyes
had that liquid look of admiration and respect. If he
just wasn't so sure she was underage. . . .

Admiration. It turned her on. It turned them all on,
the stupid bitches, watching a real man go about his
business. His big, manly biceps lifting the spare to the
axle. His big, manly hands tightening down the lugs
with her tire iron.

26

The nightstand phone beside Amanda chirped above her husband's snoring and she snagged it blind. "Yeah."

"Wake you?"

"Almost. I was just thinking about you."

"Well, stop. I'm fine."

Not what I was thinking, she thought, but said: "What's up?"

"Feel like a little B and E?"

She glanced at the radium-faced clock beside the phone. "It's past midnight, Touch."

"And your point?"

Amanda sighed. "The psychiatrist's office, right?"

"That's my girl."

"Your girl is still with the task force . . . not to be unsympathetic."

"I just need you for lookout. You can stay out front in your car."

"And what do I do when the IAD assholes show up? Honk the horn?"

"The IAD is out of it. I'm officially suspended. Look I'll be in and out in five minutes."

She made him wait on the line for a moment. "I don't even want to know what you're looking for."

"Fine. You were never there."

"What *are* you looking for?"

"I have no fucking idea. Meet you on Sunset in twenty minutes."

"Give me twenty-five."

Benson gave her forty-five, drove by her Accord to make sure Amanda was there, then turned the corner and parked around the block from the psychiatrist's office. He pushed a Dumpster under one of three fire escapes in the rear of the office complex, climbed the steel ladder, testing windows until he found an unlocked one on the eighth floor. He pushed up, slid in, and stood in the lighted hallway, listening for the night watchman making his rounds. If Benson ran into one he'd have to fake it; he had no badge now. And if that didn't work . . . well, what more could they do to him?

No sounds of a night watchman. Maybe there wasn't one. Benson found the fire door and took the stairs quietly to Dr. Otter's floor.

No watchman here either. He used his credit card to open the doctor's office door. It was almost too easy. He locked the door behind him again but it was glass so he left the office lights off, using his penlight to look around. It was just an office.

After three minutes of this he checked his watch

and was starting toward the only other room in the office when he heard the sound outside in the hallway. Benson snapped off his penlight.

He waited in darkness in front of Dr. Otter's desk as footsteps approached the door. Footsteps and a clanking. Even before the sound of the key in the lock, Benson knew who it was.

The door opened with a wedge of light, more clanking, and then the light came on. The cleaning lady with her mop and bucket gasped but did not scream. Benson reached reflexively for his badge case before remembering. With no case, he simply held up a calming hand. "It's okay. I'm a cop, just leaving. Have you seen anything unusual around the building tonight?"

She was a portly Hispanic woman with a brown scarf in her black hair, brown work dress, brown thick-soled rubber work shoes. She calmed under Benson's officious tone. "Noh!" Thick accent, but she'd understood him. Thank God. His Spanish was pretty rusty.

He nodded and started toward the inner office door as if it were all routine. "We've had some break-ins in the neighborhood, just checking. You can go on about your work." He didn't look back at her. But he listened, and breathed a little easier at the sloshing of her mop.

The second room was a smaller, more personal office. Just a desk and chair and photos of the family, citations and diplomas on the walls, a small tennis trophy. Benson flicked the switch but the room remained black. There was no ceiling light, just a small lamp atop one side of the desk.

He glanced around quickly. Bank of filing cabinets, Goya print.

He walked to the desk, looked down at a green Apple computer, double-decker tray, cup of pencils, small Sony tape recorder, short row of hardcover books. He could see the spines from the outside light: *Mind Over Madder,* one of them read.

Benson reached down and opened the middle drawer of the desk. It was full of loose papers and spiral notebooks. He turned on the desk lamp to see better.

"—walking in a kind of mist . . ."

It was Michelle's voice.

Benson looked over the desktop quickly, spotted the little recorder. Turning on the lamp had activated it.

". . . I'm in Santa Monica . . . I can see the pier. I'm crossing the street when the blond girl comes out of the fog and approaches me. She makes me feel afraid . . ."

Benson heard a noise behind him and whirled to find the cleaning lady standing there in the doorway, openmouthed.

Benson switched off the lamp and the recording ceased. "Do you clean in here every night?" he asked the woman.

She shook her head. "These mi furs nigh."

Benson came toward her and she stepped back uncertainly. "Don't be afraid. You don't have a green card, do you?"

The woman bit her lip, eyes going moist. *"Please, Seen-yhour!"*

Benson held up the calming hand again. "Don't be afraid. I'm not from Immigration. I just need to ask you a couple of questions. It will be best if you tell the truth. *Comprende?"*

"Sí!"

"Please put the bucket down."

The woman looked at her hand as if just aware of the wash bucket and did as she was told.

"You say this is your first night on the job. Have you ever been in this office before?"

"Noh."

"Have you ever been on this floor before?"

"Noh. Ees my fur tie."

"Did the building people employ you?"

"Sí."

"When?"

"Las wee."

"What day?"

"Whas . . . too-dae. Yew gone half me fire?"

"No, don't worry about that. Do you know the person who worked this building before you? The previous custodian?"

She frowned. "I doh *compren*—"

"The janitor before you. Do you know his name?"

"Noh."

"What's your name?"

"Maria Sanchez."

Benson nodded. "Okay, Ms. Sanchez. Thank you. Just go about your work now. You're fine."

A few minutes later, tapes hidden in his coat, Benson walked right past the night watchman, asleep at his desk.

•

Benson opened the passenger door of Amanda's Accord and slid in.

"Hey," she started, "I thought we were incognito!"

"Fuck that. We got him!" He flipped her his notepad with the name and address he'd scribbled down minutes before in the personnel office. *"Drive!"*

Amanda put the car in gear, pulled from the curb into nearly empty early-morning streets. She picked up the notebook with one hand. " 'Charles Jones'? Who is he?"

"The goddman *night janitor*! Or was until last week. Jesus, how fucking stupid can I be? It's the obvious ones that go right by you." Benson began unfolding her L.A. street map, tracing a line with his finger. "Take a left here."

"I know how to get to Highland. How do you know it's this 'Jones' guy?"

"Because he was the only person besides Otter who had access to the good doctor's office, other than the current custodian and maybe a security guard."

Amanda glanced at him quickly. Benson was still tracing invisible lines on her street map. "What'd you find in there, Touch?"

"Otter's tapes. Michelle Ransom's voice, describing the scene of one of the crimes."

"Touch, Otter never denied he recorded his patients—"

"But he never erased Michelle's!"

She looked at him skeptically.

"Listen to me. It fits. Guy gets a job as custodian in Otter's building. Night job. All alone except for the sleepy watchman. Guy is making his rounds, doing his job, swabbing the halls, vacuuming the office floors with his building passkey. He comes to Otter's office, cleans the outer room, no problem. Goes to clean the inner office. Uh-oh, light won't come on, dark in there.

Can't see to clean. Sees a lamp on the office desk. Switches it on to clean. Voices come from out of the air."

Amanda glanced at her ex-partner again. "The air?"

"Out of the recorder on the desk. Otter's got it hooked to the lamp switch circuit so he can come in after a hard day, sit down, and turn them both on at once without wasting time. Maybe the janitor knows the voices are coming from the recorder. Maybe he doesn't see the recorder there under the papers and books—but whatever, he hears the voices. He hears Michelle Ransom's private sessions, her private dreams. Like I just did. And the dreams are always the same. She's walking in a fog, a mist, and she sees a blond woman approaching her . . . a woman whose face is hidden. Bingo! The guy is taking directions from her tapes, Mandy. Turn here."

"I *know* the way. Wait a minute, slow down. You're not making sense. The janitor hears the dreams about a girl with a hidden face, so he goes out into the streets and repeats the crime?"

Benson shook his head, street lamps briefly illuminating his excited face. "The tapes didn't say anything about the girls being murdered. All Michelle said is that she has this repeating dream about seeing a girl coming at her out of the mist, that the sight frightened her. But no murders. She always wakes up before the girl reaches her."

Amanda waited patiently at a light. "So what does that prove? Are we back to the psychic bullshit, or what?"

"Mandy, forget about the girls a second. They're all

random, because they don't matter. What matters is the locations. That's what we should have been concentrating on."

"What locations?"

Benson was squinting at her street map.

"What are you looking for? I said I know the way." Amanda craned to see—

—a blaring horn. She yanked the wheel, dodging around a big van, the driver's curse lingering in their slipstream.

"Jesus, Mandy, get us there alive, huh?"

"We are there."

Benson looked up as the car slowed, pulled to the curb. The two detectives sat looking out the side window a moment, then turned and looked at each other.

In a moment, they got out of her car and stood on the sidewalk near the Highland Avenue sign and regarded the empty field of blowing sage before them. No address.

Benson said, "Shit."

Amanda shook her head slowly. "Sure you copied down the right—"

"It's the right fucking address, Mandy." He pointed left down the block. "Two-thirteen Highland"—he pointed right—"two-fifteen Highland."

Amanda stared at the empty field. "But no two-fourteen in between. Son of a bitch lied on his job application. Maybe nuts, but not stupid."

Benson grimaced frustration. "Goddamn it, we *had* the bastard!"

"Still got his name," Amanda began.

Benson gave her a look.

She nodded. "Yeah. 'Jones' *is* a bit too cute. Christ,

didn't the personnel office bother to check on the guy?"

Benson blew weary breath, leaned against her car. "They didn't bother to check on a Hispanic woman without a green card, why bother with him? Cheap labor. Fucking racket."

Amanda sighed. "No phone number on his employment sheet, of course."

"Of course."

She folded her arms against the cool night. "Well, we can get a facial ID from his employment manager in the morning, that's something."

Benson didn't look encouraged. "It's only something if he looks like Bozo the clown. I wonder why the creep picked last Tuesday to quit? Jesus, we were just *days* away!"

"Maybe he left a tip with his employer about his next whereabouts."

"Mandy, he lied about his *first* whereabouts."

She grunted. "Well, we have to follow it up anyway."

"We who, paleface? I'm unemployed and you were never here tonight."

Amanda looked over at his profile in the feeble streetlight, night wind blowing a lock of his dark hair, making him look young, like a kid. It was times like this a woman put an arm around her man to comfort him, give support. But not her. All she could do was try to burn his profile into her retina. Save the memory for the next time with her husband.

"What were you looking for on my street map?"

Benson turned to her a second, hesitated—then pushed off and reached into her car, pulling out the

L.A. street map. He craned up at the street lamp a moment, moved to the Accord's trunk, and spread the map atop it under the crummy light, unfolding the ends. Amanda watched patiently.

Benson pointed to Silverlake, the scene of the first crime, with his left index, keeping the fingertip there. He located the second crime scene across the creases and fold marks with his other index, and kept his finger there. "Now find the Page Museum. Notice anything?"

Amanda stepped under the light, squinted down at the trunk. She began tracing a line with a red-lacquered nail between the two points of his fingertips, then to the museum. She stopped, looked up at him.

Benson nodded. "Yeah. Not so random, is it?"

She shrugged. "Proving—?"

Benson considered a moment, then refolded the map, handing it to her. "Just a theory." He looked around. "I'm hungry. Is there a Denny's around here?"

Amanda sighed, threw up her hands, rounding the fender to the driver's side. He wasn't going to tell her yet. Not until he was ready. "Isn't there always?"

Benson arrived back at his Valley home after three in the morning.

He had drunk too much coffee at Denny's with Amanda, but it didn't matter; he wouldn't have slept anyway. They had been so close. As Conan Doyle's famous detective had said: *The game was afoot again.*

Benson thought about it as he pulled into his driveway.

Suspended from the force.

Love life in a shambles.

Prospects for the future dim.

But he was closing on the killer. He could feel it in his gut. And it was all that mattered. Catching the maniac and getting Michelle's Ransom's daughter back. The rest of his life took a far back seat.

He sat in the garage for a moment listening to the Mustang's engine tick itself cool. That was it. That was why he never pushed for grade three detective. Would get himself busted down before he did. It was the hunt. When everything else in his life was a shit-storm, he still had the hunt.

He locked up the house as usual, contemplating lying in bed sleeplessly, staring into the dark, and running the case over in his mind. They almost *had* the fucker! Amanda would check with the building's personnel director in the morning but he didn't except much from it.

The creep works as a janitor for six straight months, cleaning up Otter's office, then suddenly splits. Why? The only answer was that, for some reason, he had broken the pattern. He'd taken a victim alive. Abducted her. And though Benson had no proof of this, he had reason enough to hope. Serial killers break rhythm occasionally, sometimes to deliberately throw off the cops, but this was more than that. This was showing someone you were doing the crime before you did the crime. It didn't fit. Didn't fit in the way that Jana's physical beauty didn't fit the other victims. It was her beauty that might, ironically, be her saving grace. The killer had other plans for her.

But what?

Ransom? It's what the department was thinking, and really the logical assumption.

But not in a serial killer case. No signature killer on record ever switched his MO from brutal murder to bargaining for money. They didn't care about money, even if they were stupid enough to risk exposure that way. They cared about sexual power and fantasy.

Unless . . .

. . . the killer knew the police were closing in.

That the cops had connected the dots to Otter's office, discovered the tapes of Michelle's sessions. And the killer had abducted her daughter in an attempt to throw them off. Turning it into a missing person's case. Time and manpower would be expended searching for a possible living victim. It was common knowledge the LAPD was underforced. Was the killer simply trying to take some of the heat off himself? If that was it, then in all likelihood he had already killed Jana Ransom and dumped her body somewhere . . . no, not dumped, hidden it. And well. The longer it took the cops to look, the longer they weren't looking for the killer.

Benson rolled it over.

His mind was forced to chalk it up as a possible. A real possible.

His gut didn't buy it.

This guy wasn't that calculating. In fact, he was even sloppy to a point. They probably would have had him by now if they could have traced the knife. No, the girl was alive. He could feel it. The Mummy Killer's brain didn't operate that way.

Benson got undressed, turned out the lights, poured himself a shot, sat back against the bed board with it.

A follower? A copycat?

The idea couldn't be dismissed. It was—unfortunately—not uncommon.

Except that followers acted like followers, copying the original killer's crimes, not inventing variations on them. That was the whole point.

But the idea of a second mind intrigued Benson. For one thing it helped explain the sudden departure in the killer's MO. Could the killer have joined forces with someone? This too was not unheard of. The Hillside Stranglers, et al.

He was still running it over when the familiar banging sounded from the front of the house. The screen door. He'd forgotten to lock it again.

Benson pushed up and padded through the darkened house. Not that a screen door would keep anyone out. Just force of habit from childhood. His mother calling from down the hall. *"Did you lock the screen door, Amiel?"*

Navigating by memory and dim streetlight, he found the front door in his underwear, pulled it back, and reached for the screen. Something was lying atop the aluminum weather strip between the screen and main door. A bomb.

Every detective in every city in the country had the identical thought when encountering a strange package at work or home. The damage inflicted on law enforcement minds by the Unabomber would linger for years to come.

Benson switched on the hall light and looked down again. Not a package exactly, not a box, just an arm's length of orange crepe paper wrapped around something.

Call the Bomb Squad.

But even in thinking it, he knew he wasn't going to. He did, however, move to the hall closet, retrieve his gloves from his winter jacket pockets—the heavy leather bomber jacket he'd spent ninety bucks on at the Discovery Store and used maybe twice in L.A.'s Mediterranean climate.

He pulled on the gloves and bent to the orange paper, rocking on his heels and studying it a moment. His mind formed a sudden, brilliant white-hot blast taking away his face and his future.

Who hated him at the moment? Nobody came quickly to mind: He was suspended, his enemies should be elated. Still . . .

He picked up the crepe paper package gingerly. It was heavier than it looked. But it didn't blow his hands off.

He carried it to the dining room table, switched on the lights, and carefully pulled back the bright orange paper. The single piece of folded paper spilled free. Standard typewriter paper folded in half. Benson opened it:

> *Thought this might be useful.*
> *—a friend*

Typed. Probably on a computer. Untraceable.

Benson unwrapped the rest of the bright, whispery paper.

He was glad now he'd elected to put on the gloves. They would prevent him from leaving his own prints.

The silvery metal tire iron shone dully at him under the dining room light.

27

Charlie bungled it.

Of course he did. He'd bungled things all his life, even his mother had told him so.

Not a good planner. *Charlie, you are not a good planner. And planning and detail provide the stepping-stones of life.*

And he supposed it was true. She had certainly done all the planning of his early life: cooking the meals, cleaning the little tract house in the Valley, working to feed them, helping with his homework (okay, *doing* his homework for him clear up through the eighth grade), picking the old movies they watched together on the old TV. His mother was great with the details. Which was why it was so devastating after the fire. After she was gone. On his own, Charlie wasn't a great planner.

But he'd thought he'd done a good job with the false goddess. Thought it quite reasonably through.

The idea was to hide the sacred knife under his pillow, wait for the rattling wheeze that always signaled her sleep, and give her to the Ancient Ones there in the dark. Quick and silent. An easy cleanup. If he had learned anything from her it was about cleanup.

But he should have left the pretty blond alone, shouldn't have loosened her ropes. Should have endured cleaning up her pee while the other one was out shopping. Because she was a great planner—had planned this whole ransom caper, taken care of all the details about leaving the apartment, dealing with the super, everything. And she had good eyes. Like the great hawk Ra. They didn't miss much. Like his mother's eyes, they caught all the little details. Even how the scarf gag had been moved on the pretty girl's mouth, even the way the ropes binding her to the chair had been retied.

"You moved her."

Three little words. But they'd been like sword strokes through his heart. Made him sick inside. All his previous bravado blew away like a candle flame. The way it used to when his mother addressed him. *Commanded him.*

Charlie denied it all, of course. Denied that he'd even gone near Jana Ransom. Which only compounded his mistakes. She might have let it go if he'd simply owned up. But she was maniacal about the details. What was the word? Anal. Had been from the moment she'd shown up at his apartment and first outlined the plan to him. Okay, not exactly outlined . . . more like *instructed.* Very convincingly. As convincing as Mother.

But he'd been on to her from the start. He'd gone along on purpose. Because even he could see that clearing out of the apartment was a good idea, that the cops were bound to get close sooner or later, even he could see the merits of this little nowhere cabin hidden out here in the woods. She had it all worked out. Right to the second. Every ticking detail. Thought she was so smart. Thought he was following along blindly the way he'd followed Mother. Thought he was stupid. He wasn't stupid.

Just afraid of her.

He should have left the Ransom girl alone, let her piss her pants. Because once she saw he'd touched her, once she figured out he'd moved her, she went ballistic. He'd messed with the details.

"I *told* you not to touch her!"

Yelling at first. Then screaming. Then throwing things. The newly bought bags of groceries mostly, one of the soup cans caroming off his forehead, drawing blood.

That was what had done it.

The soup can. That was her mistake.

They all made the same mistake, thinking just because they were good with the details, just because he occasionally bungled it, just because he was scared of them, that he didn't have a threshold, a breaking point. Thing of it was, Charlie didn't even know it himself.

Didn't know that without the drugs, without spiking their drinks, making them sleepy and helpless, he could hurt them.

Not until the soup can.

And her incessant screaming.

"Stupid *motherfucker*! You'll ruin *everything*!"

Standing there in the cabin, red-faced, hurling cans at him, tomatoes, beets, green beans. Then laughing at how ridiculous he looked. And right in front of the pretty Ransom girl, the only one of them who'd shown the least kindness toward him, had not asked him to put his thing in her, only just to be let free a moment so she could pee. Maybe that was it. Maybe it was the look he saw in the Ransom girl's swollen eyes above the tight, cutting gag. Not pity, really. Not pity for his waxy face and skinny frame and the way he just stood there dripping with potato salad and hamburger while the girl screamed and screamed until his ears rang. Not pity. Concern. Genuine concern.

Maybe that was when he reached his threshold, his breaking point.

She saw the way Jana looked at him, and whirled on her, turned her screaming wrath on the pretty girl. Started slapping the pretty face, slapping and hitting with such violent conviction it made Charlie think she was trying to slap the prettiness away, make the face like her own, lumpy and blemished and the waxy, tallow color of his.

She might have gone on slapping and kicking Jana like that all night. Charlie thought she really might, if he hadn't turned and walked slowly to the old, lumpy bed, taken the sacred blade from under the mattress, walked slowly back, and driven the blade into her slapping, jerking back.

Caught her right in midswing. Right before the beefy hand could deliver the next stinging blow.

Only he bungled it. Bad with the details.

The blade went deep, but mostly into fat. So that

she just said, "Ow!" at first, like it was a mild distraction, and almost went on hitting.

But she turned finally, hand still raised . . . turned and gave Charlie the funniest look, the strangest look. Then turned some more and even some more in this little circle that became a kind of half-hitch dance step, her arm still raised high for that next slap, her head, turning, craning back to see, figure out what it was sticking out of her back and starting to hurt now.

Charlie had to take hold of the sacred hilt and yank the blade out again and this time the girl didn't say "Ow!" This time she screamed.

Never stopped screaming, even after he put the blade in her front this time. And even that he bungled, didn't come anywhere near a vital spot, and the girl—still screaming—was running now, screaming blood from her fat lips, running—faster than he would have imagined—toward the door, arms wide and waving like she was trying to leave the ground, trying to fly out of the cabin. And lots of blood. A fine, constant spray of it that got in Charlie's eyes when he chased her, but didn't seem to slow the girl at all, didn't keep her from reaching the knob, flinging herself into the night, still screaming, the sound knocking across the dark hills.

Charlie chased her in the dark.

Nearly a quarter mile, he calculated later. Following the thud of her shoes on the damp leaves after the screams turned to gargles, then silence.

He came upon her still on her feet. She stood with her back to him, one hand against a dark maple, quiet, composed, like she was just getting her breath for the next sprint. He watched her a moment, then took hold of her shoulder and turned her around. She was light and airy, no fight left in her, no hatred or fear, just a sort of dull curiosity when she looked up. The girl opened her mouth slowly and fell at his feet.

He dragged her all the way up the hill to the cabin.

Left her in a sitting position, leaning against the woodpile. Then he laid her down and placed the cord of wood over her body. Like a small burial pyre. He could hear her under the wood, her heavy, raspy breathing. But she would go nowhere. Too much of the life blood had come out of her. She would stay there under the wood until the bugs found her.

He cleaned up the cabin pretty good, the way she'd made him clean up the apartment. He cleaned the cabin, but he could never clean up the woods, all those little twigs and leaves, the winding, spattery trail of them.

He'd have to leave the cabin now, go someplace else. And he didn't know where. Always a bad planner. Missed the details. Made another mess.

He'd have to be neater with the pretty girl.

28

"Mandy, it's Touch. What are you doing?"

"What am I doing? I'm sitting here across from your empty desk doing goddamn paperwork—mine *and* yours. What do you think I'm doing? Listen, I've got some good news. The personnel director at Otter's office building remembers this so-called Charles Jones clearly. The guy has a face like Silly Putty. Burn scars or something."

"No shit. That's a break."

"Yeah, finally."

"Listen, what are you doing for lunch?"

"Touch, I don't think it's a good idea us seeing each other before your civil trial—"

"There may not be a trial. I think I've got something."

"You found the Mummy's address!"

"No. I found a tire iron in my doorway."

"Jesus! Okay. All right. I'll meet you at—"

"I don't want you to meet me, Mandy. Here's what you're going to do. You know the Mulholland overpass on the 101? That's approximately where I beat up the Marine. I want you to pick up the iron there. Just driving along, minding your own business—glance out your window and there it is. It'll be just off the shoulder behind an old Bullocks box. Wear gloves, not LAPD issue plastic, regular dress gloves. Try to handle it by the forked end only. I want you to take it directly to Jerry Todd at SID. He owes me one. Make sure it gets to Todd. If he's not in, wait or come back."

"Touch, I—"

"You're not doing anything illegal, honey. A lot of people have been looking for this thing. You just saw an iron on the road, picked it up on a hunch, and took it to SID—nothing improper about that. Jerry has the Marine's latents right next to his hand. He'll phone you the second he gets a match from the iron."

"Touch, I'm your partner. Don't you think it's going to look—"

"I don't give a fuck how it looks. What's important is if it's legal. And it is. The Marine's attorney will try for collusion, but he can't do jack about the prints, if they're there. And if they are, the trial will never come to pass. Ronald Short's prints on that tire iron will put Noland, the assistant chief, and the entire LAPD behind me. There isn't a judge in L.A. County who'd want to go up against that. Mandy, I need you to do this. I know it's messy, but it's the only way."

"Any idea who sent you the iron?"

"No. And right now I don't care. Can you be at the overpass by noon? Mandy?"

"I heard you. I'll be there."

"Good. I don't want some yahoo tripping over that Bullocks box before you get there."

"What are you going to do?"

"Pay Otter another visit."

"Touch, is that wise? He could—"

"What? Get me suspended? I need to get to him now while I'm still off the force."

"Why? Otter won't know the Mummy's address."

"I'm not going to ask him about addresses."

Benson waited until off hours to approach Parker Center.

Nearly all RHD officers clocked in on a reliable eight-to-three shift. After police work a lot of them earned extra pay moonlighting as bodyguards, security officers, and other high-paying jobs the lower echelon cops couldn't get. RHD were the hotshots. A lot of them saw the job itself as a means to a better financial end.

Benson hung around outside the glass doors for a few minutes beside the memorial to officers killed in the line of duty, listening to the sprinkling fountain. There were lights in all the Center's windows, but that was just for show, the people were mostly gone; it was just that the LAPD didn't want anyone thinking the lights of justice weren't constantly burning.

He finally entered the building, and waved at one of the duty cops behind the desk. Before they could object, ask to see his badge, he smiled and told them he was just finishing up cleaning out his desk. The cops glanced at one another but no one tried to stop him.

Benson walked by the desk, stepping past the yellow line on the floor indicating directions to Internal Affairs for newcomers. He studied the line absently while waiting at the bank of elevators. He didn't really expect trouble from the IAD suits at this point, but it was impossible to know what the assistant chief was really up to. And technically, Benson didn't belong in this building.

But screw it. No one was going to arrest him. He was a friend of a friend of too many friends, someone who might need him for backup if he ever got back on the force. The worst they could do was throw him out of the building and slap his wrists.

He took the elevator to the third floor, walked by his old desk in Robbery-Homicide without looking at it, and straight to the rear of the room to the department's main computers.

He punched up the California Department of Justice information network and typed in the name James Otter, MD. As he expected, he got no hits. Otter was clean.

Clean but not untraceable. Benson punched up the FBI's NCIC files. He had to go through a regiment of permutations to reach it: software protection, background protection, encryption protection, on and on. And at that, he wasn't able to get into all of it—only the feebs could do that. But as a law-enforcement officer—official status or otherwise—he was privy to any information the FBI might have in assisting a crime. There was nothing about James P. Otter, MD, in the NCIC files.

Benson moved to another computer, and punched in NCAVC.

He'd already been through the VICAP section of
the National Center for the Analysis of Violent Crime
concerning the use of psychics with Special Agent Bill
Campbell. And Ditko, Peterson, Amanda, and others
from the Mummy task force had scoured it for leads.
But there had been few leads in this case, and no one
had been looking for a psychiatrist.

VICAP was basically a nationwide information center designed to collect, collate, and analyze crimes of
violence—specifically murder. That included solved or
unsolved homicides or attempts, particularly ones involving abduction, random crimes, as well as mo-
tiveless or sexually oriented crimes. Also missing
persons, where circumstances indicate the possibility
of foul play. Arrested or identified offenders are sub-
mitted from all over the country for comparison and
possible matching with unsolved cases in the Violent
Criminal Apprehension Program database. Once a serial murder suspect has been identified, VICAP can
assist law-enforcement agencies with relevant cases by
coordinating a multiagency investigative conference.
So far, they had been little help to the RHD in
tracking the Mummy Killer. But Benson wasn't after
that information tonight.

He went to the Sources and Information Section
and punched in Otter's name. He got a hit.

Otter had assisted VICAP directly on a number of
serial cases while practicing in New York in the eighties. He had also written two textbooks on the subject:
one for FBI special agent distribution and one for general distribution to college bookstores. So far, nothing
with a major publisher. But that was in the works,
Benson was sure. Otter was headed for the limelight,

and Michelle Ransom and the Mummy Killer were the ticket.

Benson shut down the computer and looked at his watch.

The only light on in the Otter home was the one in the doctor's study.

It was a walnut-paneled study, richly appointed with expensive, trendy furniture at once traditional and strikingly contemporary. A professional decorator might have discerned an excess of leather. Certainly it extended beyond the red desk chair and desktop, to the coffee table, lamps, and anything else in the study that could hold the rich texture of animal skin without quite crossing the boundaries of good taste. Otter was into leather.

At the moment—alone in his study, his wife and child in bed—he was dozing lightly, sitting at his desk, his head erect and his eyes slitted, a trick he'd learned through long hours of listening to boring clients.

There came an almost indiscernible metallic *click* behind the doctor's head.

It might have been the water heater turning on. Dr. Otter thought not. He smiled.

In a moment the anticipated pressure of cold steel touched his nape. "Good evening, Detective Benson, and how are you this fine fall eve?"

"Finer than you, you sick fuck."

Dr. Otter—unruffled if slightly wilted—tightened the sash of his robe with dignity, smoothed back his sleek otter hair, and closed the book before him, all in one fluid motion.

"Leaping to any number of grotesque, erroneous assumptions, are we, Detective? Or is it still 'detective?' Rumors of your recent defrocking abound."

Benson came around the oak desk, the automatic's nickel muzzle never leaving the doctor's skin, sliding around the nape, up the cheek, finally coming to rest in the middle of Otter's forehead. The doctor could see the weapon's glint above the bridge of his nose . . . and past that, Benson's knuckle curled behind the trigger guard, the detective's arm beyond that, wide shoulders, broad chest. The face was masked in shadow behind the lamp's glare.

"What assumptions would those be, Doctor?"

Dr. Otter sighed, seemingly indifferent to any embarrassment his compromised position might imply. He sat confidently in the chair again, the gun following him down. "First, that I am in some way linked to the Mummy killings. I am not. Nor can you prove such. Second, that because you are temporarily suspended from the police force, your reckless act of breaking and entering will somehow go without repercussion. Quite the contrary." He smiled satisfaction. "Under your present circumstances we hardly need add 'assault with a deadly weapon' to the above, though I'm confident my attorney will insist otherwise. May I get you something to drink before you leave us?"

Benson pressed the barrel forward; Otter made an impatient grimace. "Please, Detective, these theatrics."

"Did you hypnotize Michelle Ransom?"

"That is an area of privileged client-therapist information, not privy to law enforcement—"

"I'm not a cop, remember?" Benson shoved the barrel harder. "Did you put her under, you fatuous little turd?"

Otter's composure slipped a fraction. The officer had suffered recent emotional strain, might be on the edge of breaking. "I do not employ hypnosis, Detective, as a regular part of—"

Benson jammed the barrel down hard enough to press Otter back into the chair. "I'm not asking again. What did she tell you when you had her under?"

The officer's voice was as cold as the steel barrel. Best to cooperate at this point. Otter did have a wife and child, after all. *Buy time. Outsmart this Gestapo thug.* The doctor cleared his throat. "We had a few short sessions using the technique, I believe."

Benson pulled back the automatic, toed a chair over, and sat before the desk, the barrel still level with the doctor's head. "Now listen to me, asshole. You're a smart guy. Smart enough to know withholding evidence during a homicide investigation is punishable in the state of California by fine or imprisonment or both, the last of which can double in the case of a smart-guy professional like yourself." This was part bluff: Benson hopped even a smart doctor wasn't that smart.

It must have worked. Otter's upper lip held a light patina of sweat, even if his composure remained in tact. "My attorney will—"

"Drop your skinny shrink's ass when he finds you deliberately withheld pertinent information from the authorities. Now one more time—what did she tell you while you had her under? And don't bullshit me—

I studied hypnosis with the RHD when it was still part of the witness program."

Otter swallowed uncertainly. "About that drink . . ."

Benson spotted a half-filled bottle of Old Grand-Dad in a leather casing, snagged it from a nearby bookshelf, and slid it across the leather-topped desk. Otter licked his lips, pulled the cork, and drank without use of a glass.

He wiped his mouth with pale, delicate fingers. "Nothing terribly revealing, really. We talked mostly—"

"Tell one more lie and so help me Christ I'll pull this trigger. Michelle Ransom and the City of Los Angeles have suffered enough from your arrogance and stupidity." Benson thought a second, then added some birdseed. "Give me what I want, on the other hand, and I may see some departmental information comes your way."

Otter looked up at him.

"For your big bestseller. And you can wipe the look of shocked innocence off your face."

Otter swallowed, glanced at the bottle again. Benson shoved it at him but the doctor declined. He smoothed the cuffs of the silk robe for something to do with his hands, stalling. "She . . . apparently Miss Ransom worked as a paramedic with an ambulance crew while she attended medical school."

"Give me something I don't know."

Otter took a fluttering breath. "She . . . under hypnosis, it was revealed she may have encountered a slight trauma during her short period with the staff at the St. Francis Emergency facility."

"I already knew that, Otter. Try again."

Otter cleared his throat again. "There was a . . . singularly disturbing event during the second week of her tenure as junior paramedic. It took several sessions of intense therapy for me to break through her subconscious." He attempted to puff up again officiously. "These things can *only* be handled by a highly *skilled* professional, Detective—"

"I'll make a note of your diplomas in my report. Stick to the night in question."

Otter wiped quickly once at his upper lip. "Apparently it was no more than a routine ambulance call. Miss Ransom—Michelle—had been working with a staff of three other ambulance technicians covering the Silverlake district. A call came through involving a house fire at a duplex. Michelle's team arrived at the scene ahead of the police, and one paramedic short. Apparently someone on the staff was out sick that night. In any event, Michelle and the remaining team performed CPR on two of the four patients, one of which was DOA. The remaining three patients were stabilized, loaded on gurneys, and placed aboard the ambulance. One of them, a young blond woman, had apparently incurred severe cuts as well as terrible facial injuries in the fire. Her face was . . . well, anyway, Michelle treated it as a third-degree burn, swathed it in medicated bandages to prevent infection, employed an IV, then turned to help her partner with the other patients, who appeared to be in good to fair condition. That's all I know."

But it wasn't. Otter was padding the story with elaborate detail, putting off the most important part. The part that might indict him. Benson stood. "Fine, let's go downtown."

"What! I just— You can't do that!"

"I'm doing it." He reached behind his waist for his cuffs.

"Wait a minute!" Otter rubbed his mouth, finally reached for the bottle again, took a sip, then another, coughed—took one more. Placed the bottle back on the leather-topped desk, drew another careful breath. "The, uh, member of the medical team other than Michelle was new to the area, didn't know his way around Los Angeles. It was decided that Michelle would drive the ambulance. They left the scene with her at the wheel."

"No patrol cars had arrived yet?"

"Police? She didn't relate any, no."

No patrol cars. That meant no police escort to the hospital. "I'm still here."

Otter paused again to lick his lips. "They . . . Michelle drove to the hospital. St. Francis. The emergency staff took over immediately. That's all."

Benson sat back, lowering the gun. He stared at Otter. "She got lost, didn't she?"

Otter cleared his throat.

"Michelle lost her way getting to the hospital. *Answer* me!"

Otter jumped. "She . . . yes, she did."

"For how long?"

Otter sighed. "She didn't recall, exactly."

"But long enough. The patient died. The one with the bandages."

Otter said nothing.

"Didn't she?"

Otter nodded. "Apparently."

For the first time since his arrival at the psychiatrist's house, Benson allowed his eyes to drift away a moment in thought. "What's it called?"

Otter started, as though he'd gone away a moment himself. "Pardon me?"

"Michelle Ransom's disorder, what's the clinical name?"

"Why, just"—Otter waved a hand at the air—"simple hysteria, really. Mental block. In Freudian terms, the superego masks what the id knows. Quite treatable usually, once the root of the neurosis has been isolated and . . ." He trailed off when he saw the look in Benson's eyes.

"Once it's been isolated," Benson repeated levelly. "How long have you known, Doctor?"

Otter collected his silk robe about him. "I am a professional psychiatrist who has never once violated the Hippocratic oath! My standing within the medical community, including Hopkins, is above reproach! I have aided law-enforcement agencies like your own on numerous pro bono cases and—"

Benson waved him off, pocketing the automatic. "Save your merit badges for the jury. You fucked up, junior." He headed for the door.

Otter fought to regain the old decorum. "You entered these premises without a warrant or legal authority! I can—"

Otter was half out of his chair when Benson turned and stopped him cold with one look. Two different colored-eyes can do that.

Otter sank back. "All right, all right. It's possible I did use poor judgment in this—"

"Possible!"

"That I certainly used poor judgment in this instance. I am, however, aware of my shortcomings and am prepared to cooperate with the authorities, do whatever is necessary, Detective, to make amends for my actions. You are an intelligent man. A reasonable man. You are—"

"An asshole, like yourself, Otter. Is this going somewhere?"

Otter was through dispensing with confident facades. The delicate hands patted the top of the leather desk now as if to hold it down, as if anticipating someone taking it away, along with the rest of his expensive furniture and his license to practice. "I was about to say that I am willing to offer my services in any way you see fit in order to insure that this patient—that Miss Ransom—is given the best means medical attention can provide for a timely recovery. I think you would agree that, considering our mutual history, I would be the logical choice to ensure that means. I cannot do that if you take away my—"

"Your what, Doctor? Are you accusing me of threatening you in some way?"

"No, no! I'm merely saying that I am prepared to do anything necessary to help you and Ms. Ransom— to lend my services to this case in any way I . . . it . . . oh, Christ, *I did not kill those young women, Detective!*"

Benson wandered back to the desk. "So what are you saying, Otter? Exactly?"

"S-simply that I will do anything within my power to help you, in exchange for—"

"Are we talking some kind of bribe here?" He was way past having broken Otter, but Benson was enjoying too much watching him squirm.

"I never implied that! No, indeed! I wouldn't call a mutual cooperation bribing! It's just that, as you must know, I have important friends in the community, influential friends, who might be willing . . . that is . . . I know you are currently involved in some type of civil suit and—"

Benson motioned toward the desk phone. "Call him."

"Pardon me?"

"Call him now."

"Who? It's two o'clock in the morning, I—"

"The law never sleeps, James."

Otter blinked. But only once. He reached across the fine leather surface for the receiver and dialed his attorney's home. "Dick, James Otter. So sorry for the late hour . . ."

29

Judge Judy Ricker kept Benson, his lawyer, and Ronald Short and his lawyer waiting nearly twenty minutes in her own chambers.

When she finally came in, dressed in conservative suit and sensible heels, and chewing a Reuben sandwich, she didn't apologize. She never apologized. And she never forgot.

It was rumored she could remember the first names of every detective, every cop in the Sheriff's Department, their wives' names, and their kids'.

Her Honor Judy Ricker was a light-skinned black woman reared in Watts of the sixties in the worst kind of palm-lined poverty that area and time could dole out. Much of her early life had been spent on Spring Street across the way from the federal courthouse she now presided in. Her mother had been a hooker. She had never known her father. She recalled more about the County Criminal Courts building than she did her mother's tenement apartment; it was a second home. Nearly all her childhood friends were black or brown, and all of them were poor and played jacks in the crowded, smelly Criminal Courts hallway, and none of them knew better. Most of them never would.

Her mother's pimp had raped Judy when she was eleven. When she was eighteen, he was sent to Leavenworth for thirty to life, where he did a remarkable thing by sending her mother money. Her mother saved every dime for Judy's college. It changed her life. She graduated from law school at USC with honors, and spent the first three years working to successfully get the pimp out of prison. He came back to Watts, where both he and Judy's mother were shot to death in a drug-related killing just two weeks shy of the case that would have given Judy the money to buy her mother out of the L.A. slums. She never forgot the incident.

Judy stayed in L.A., worked her butt off, and became a respected, admired, and feared criminal lawyer. No bullshit, from black, white, Hispanic, or Eskimo. Every day on her way to work, she went out of her way to follow the same routine: cutting through the familiar, still-crowded halls of the old County Criminal Courts building she'd played in as a kid, on her way to the U.S. District Courthouse and her chambers. And she remembered.

She took her black robes from the closet beside her desk, stuck the Reuben in her mouth while buttoning up, nodded good afternoon at the four men seated across from the desk, and took her position behind it, still chewing her lunch. She sat before the wall of red-spined law books, looking from one face to the other while swallowing—a diminutive figure, radiating no-

nonsense power. "I have a two o'clock in courtroom six, and a bad attitude from this sandwich I am forced to eat from canceling a luncheon at The Ivy for this conference. This is a conference, gentlemen, not a trial nor a hearing. You will remember that, counselors. I will remind the clients once. I will not remind the counselors again. Is that clear?" It was.

She directed her attention to Benson. "Detective Amiel Benson, you are aware that the tenants of this case allow you the services of a lawyer from the City Attorney's Office?"

"I am, Your Honor."

"But you have elected to hire your own defense?"

"I have, Your Honor."

Judge Ricker glanced at Dr. Otter's attorney, the infamous Dick Sheim. She knew Benson and she knew Sheim and she knew they were oil and water. She had no idea what Benson was up to and she didn't care. It wasn't pertinent.

She slipped on half-rimmed glasses, opened a folder before her, glanced down at it a moment. She peered over the glasses at Ronald Short's attorney, a Mr. Gleason. Gleason was young, black, ambitious, and unscrupulous. He was an ambulance chaser, and everyone knew it, except his client, Ronald Short. "Mr. Gleason, you are aware that the defendant is a detective with the Los Angeles Sheriff's Department, and he claims that an implement, possibly of a nature evidentiary to these proceedings, has been recovered?" She glanced down at the folder. "Namely a bar of metal used to remove vehicle hubcaps and lug nuts, commonly called a tire iron?"

"Yes, Your Honor," Gleason said guardedly. Anyway, he knew it now. The exact details of this meeting, he wasn't sure of—only that Benson's attorney had requested it.

"And that Detective Benson intends to show proof that said tire iron belongs to your client, Ronald Short?"

Gleason hesitated . . . immediately regained his poker face. "Yes, Your Honor."

Judge Ricker turned to Benson's attorney, Dick Sheim, peering over her glasses. "Attorney Sheim, is your client prepared to make such a claim in a court of law?"

Sheim nodded confidently. But not as smugly as he might have with the prestigious Dr. Otter. Judge Ricker was known for her lack of tolerance with prima donnas. "Yes, we are, Your Honor."

"And do you further intend to prove that said iron was used with force and malice aforethought against your client, Detective Benson, during an incident on the Hollywood Freeway last month?"

"Yes, we do, Your Honor."

Judge Ricker nodded, removed her glasses, rubbed the bridge of her nose a moment, and flipped the folder shut.

She laced her fingers atop her desk in a slightly less formal gesture, as though proper procedure had been dealt with properly. She raised a speculative brow. "Well, gentlemen," she began, less officiously, "I feel a nasty little bugger of a stalemate coming on. And a very long, very costly trial just behind it." She poured herself a glass of water from a plastic pitcher on her desk. "Would anyone like a glass of water?"

No one did.

She popped a tablet in her mouth. "My doctor informs me I have a stage-one ulcer, the likes of which a lengthy trial could only exacerbate." She let that sink in for a moment. What might have looked like a slam dunk to Ronald Short's side was turning into something potentially messy. The judge replaced her glasses. "Does anyone have anything to add to the above?"

Benson looked at Short's lawyer. This was Gleason's moment, and everyone knew it.

Gleason could protest about the iron—more specifically how and where the iron was obtained—claiming it was a setup. This would certainly put Benson in an even more defensive light, and Benson might well be bluffing.

But Sheim and everyone else present (with the exception of Ronald Short) knew Benson had access to the police department's forensic labs, or at least might have a cohort who did. And that he might not be bluffing at all.

If Short's prints were really on that iron, it would shift everything. And Gleason had been checking into Short's past. Not exactly a rap sheet a jury would sympathize with. Also, Benson could have stuck with the City Attorney's lawyer, costing him nothing if he lost. Dick Sheim, however, did not come cheap. Unless, of course, that was part of the bluff. Definitely no longer a slam dunk.

More like poker. And Gleason's hand had been called.

"Mr. Gleason? Anything?"

And here was Judge Ricker asking for *his* response first. Not Benson's lawyer's, but *his*. Not good. Gleason suddenly had the creeping feeling Benson was very good at poker.

He thought another second, then caved. "Your Honor, my client wishes to withdraw the suit at this time."

"Hey, wait a minute!" Short started, flaming.

And Gleason grabbed his arm. "Shut up."

"This is not a trial, Mr. Gleason. Your client is free to speak if he wishes."

Short started to stand, turned angrily to Gleason, caught a withering look from his lawyer, and was actually smart enough to sit back down. He shook his head at the judge.

All eyes turned to Detective Benson. *Benson.* Not his attorney.

Benson had not chosen to countersue up to now. Presumably because he'd had little or no ammunition to back him up. He did now. Or claimed he did. And Sheim would go for the throat at a trial, get the biggest settlement he could. Of course, he'd try for that anyway if it went to court.

To keep within parlance, Judge Ricker addressed Benson's attorney. "Mr. Sheim, anything?"

"Your Honor"—and Sheim held it a moment, just as Benson had instructed him to, just the way he'd made that little ferret psychiatrist squirm—"we accept the plaintiff's wishes."

Ronald Short turned an outraged expression on his lawyer. Gleason didn't even grant him a return look. He was already picking up his faded leather attaché and raincoat, already contemplating his next case. If there was one.

Judge Ricker blew out grateful breath, looked up

at the black hands of the big wall clock, and stood. "In that case, gentlemen, I have a previous date in courtroom six. Good afternoon."

Sheim put out a congratulatory hand to Benson.

Benson swept by him without shaking it.

On the courthouse steps he called Amanda on his cellular. "Wanna get a drink?"

He'd called her at the Center, and he could hear her trying to conceal her elation from prying ears. "Touch! It's over? They withdrew?"

"Limp and deflated. Can you get free?"

"Yeah, sure. Where? Never mind. Which Denny's?"

"Your choice."

"C'mon, give! I want details!"

Benson smiled. "Over lunch."

"Fuck lunch. I want to know now! Tell me everything!"

"Jesus, Mandy, it wasn't that big a deal." But he couldn't stop smiling.

30

Benson watched his partner devour runny Grand Slam eggs at the Denny's on Olympic. He was spreading a Gousha Los Angeles City street map on the Formica tabletop between them. "How do you eat those things like that? Ever hear of salmonella?"

Amanda dipped a wedge of toast into congealed yolk. "Take me to Jerry's Deli next time. Did you read Fowler's column in this morning's *Times*?"

"Fuck him."

"Yeah, right. He didn't mention your coming trial once. In case you're interested."

"I'm not," Benson said curtly.

"He's never written anything about your failure to notify his family after the death of his kid, either."

"You must have missed it, sweetie. He mentioned it all right—how negligent the LAPD is these days."

"Yeah, but he's always writing that. He didn't use

your name . . . didn't even refer to the RHD, as I recall."

"Good for him," Benson told her dismissively, smoothing the map flat between them. He started to say something . . . paused, and gave her an appraising look. "Hey."

Amanda sipped coffee, looking at her food.

"Hey!"

She looked up at him now with irritation. "What!"

Benson sat back, forgetting the map for the moment. "You've been talking with him."

She frowned. "Who?"

" 'Who?' my ass. That prick Fowler. You've been covering for me."

"You're whacked." She nodded at the map. "What's this—?"

Benson's eyes remained on her. "Did you fuck him, or what?"

She looked up, and this time her eyes said, *Back off.* "How'd you like these nice runny eggs in your fat cop's face?"

Benson smiled at her. "You phoned his office at the *Times*, didn't you? Right after I called you from the courthouse. You gave him the lead for tonight's paper. All the details. He'll scoop the other papers in town over this thing."

"You're full of shit. What's with the map?" She looked down at it.

He didn't take his eyes off her, and they softened with emotion the longer he gazed at her. "You've been keeping him off my ass all the time." He shook his head with humiliation. "Mandy, I—"

Without looking up again she said, "If you start with that why-don't-I-marry-you routine again, so help me I'll leave you here. Now what's with the friggin' map. Have you got something on this asshole or what?"

Still smiling affection, Benson turned back to the map, pointing near the top under the green, geometric pattern of Griffith Park at the biue squiggle of the Silverlake reservoir. "In retrospect I should have figured this out sooner. I mean, the map tells the whole tale."

"What tale?"

"Remember that night we went looking for the Mummy's address, found that empty field? I put the map on the trunk of the car, asked you to trace the path between the three crime scenes."

"Yeah, so?"

"The path was leading somewhere—to St. Francis hospital. Look at the map. From the Silverlake house to Los Feliz, from Los Feliz to 5, the Golden State Freeway. From 5 over the Glendale Freeway to the 110, the Pasadena Freeway. From there it's a clear shot all the way past Slauson down to the hospital here near Hyde Park."

Benson sat back a moment. "Like I said, I knew there was some pattern to the locations, that they weren't random. Look back up near the Silverlake district. There are at least three perfectly good hospitals within a few miles of the area. If you were an ambulance driver on an emergency run, why would you waste time tearing all the way down here to St. Francis? More important, why would you use such a circuitous route in which to do it?"

Amanda looked up at him. "Uh . . . I'm lost, kid."

Benson nodded. "So was she."

"Who?"

"Michelle Ransom. She was a paramedic for a time, when she was in medical school, before she quit—told me so at the reunion dance, and Otter tipped me off to the rest. Twenty years ago she was answering a code three in the Silverlake area. April fifteenth, 1982, to be exact. A duplex fire. One DOA, two in fair condition, which she and her team loaded into their ambulance and stabilized. And a third patient, in critical. Victim's hair and clothing went up in flames and took most of her skin with them. Took away a good part of her face too. She was a stout, buxom young blond woman named Selma somebody. Michelle treated the victim's injuries like third-degree burns. She shoved an IV in the girl's arm and wrapped her face in medicated bandages to prevent infection."

Amanda blinked. "Oh, shit."

"Yeah. Anyway, everything was fine so far, proce-dure followed, patients secured and stabilized. Only one thing different from all previous calls Michelle had ridden with. Her team was short a member—out sick—and he was the regular driver. So Michelle took the wheel that night, and that's where everything began to go wrong."

Amanda sat back, hypnotized. "She wrecked the ambulance?"

"No. Might have been better if she had. At least someone could have found her then. No, she drove off, siren screaming, bubble flashing, right onto Los Feliz like we would have. Only she didn't turn right and head for the 5. She turned left and headed for the 101."

Amanda turned the map toward her, found the area. "Well . . . that's not so bad . . . a little out of the way, but she'd still hit the 110 connector here at the Music Center."

Benson nodded. "She would have. But I don't think she was heading for the 110 in the first place. I think she was heading for the hospital here off the Santa Monica Freeway near La Brea, Carson Medical Center. But she had two things going against her that night. For one, it was foggy. Very foggy. I checked records with L.A. Meteorological for the night of April fifteenth. Everything between Santa Monica and Redondo Beach was socked in with heavy fog. It stretched inland all the way to Alhambra and neighboring communities. Freakish, but it happens. That was her first problem."

Benson moved the map closer to his partner, indicated with his index. "Also, the 101 was blocked with roadwork from Sunset all the way to Beverly. Bumper to bumper. Imagine coming upon that with a critical patient when you already couldn't see the street signs."

"Jesus."

"I think, rather than try to use the shoulder and cut around the jam-up, Michelle elected to ditch the 101 on 2 and take the surface streets to Morgan Emergency on 170. Somewhere between the Farmer's Market and the Civic Center she got lost. From there, it became a nightmare. I'm sure she was on her radio begging frantically for directions, but even when the dispatcher gave her a street she couldn't make out most of the signs. And every sign she could see told her she was that much more lost."

"God . . ."

"I'm guessing that, in a frenzied attempt to get *somewhere*, she grabbed the first major artery she could find. That would be the 405 if she was headed west. Maybe she remembered St. Francis or maybe the dispatcher told her, but whatever, the only clear path she could see was the 405 to Inglewood. From there she exited onto Highway 42, passed La Brea again, and probably took Crenshaw on into St. Francis."

"By which time it was too late."

Benson nodded soberly. "The girl with the bandaged face was DOA at St. Francis Emergency."

"But it wasn't Michelle's *fault*! She did everything—"

"I'm sure she was assured that by the staff. Maybe she even tried to convince herself. But she never got over feeling responsible for it, blaming herself. She quit med school, completely forgot about her dreams of being a doctor. And over time, the guilt got too much to deal with. So she repressed it. Buried it. Until the esteemed Dr. Otter pulled it out of her subconscious through hypnosis."

"Otter hypnotized her?"

"Oh, yeah. Without telling her the results. I think he thought, if she started to remember the truth, she'd stop coming to see him. And once the Mummy killings started he knew he was on to something big, of national interest. That's why he kept the tapes of their sessions."

Amanda bent to the map again, tracing her finger between the first Mummy killing in Silverlake to each successive one. "So . . . in fact, the killings aren't really random at all. They just look that way because—"

"In her dreams, Michelle Ransom kept seeing a girl with a bandaged face coming at her through the mist, at every wrong turn she took, every street sign she could make out in the fog. The bandaged face, the wrong streets coalesced in her mind . . . and became the road map the Mummy Killer used twenty years later. Thanks to her psychiatrist recording them and leaving them on his desk player for his janitor to find."

Amanda shook her head. "How did you get Otter to admit he hypnotized her?"

"I put a gun to his head."

"Oh, Touch . . . Jesus." Her face fell. "Goddamn it, Sheim will have the whole case thrown out before it even reaches—"

"It was the only way to get him to admit what was on the tapes. I needed to nail that down. Time's running out. If we're going to find Jana Ransom's kidnapper we at least have to be looking for the right guy. Besides which, the esteemed Dr. Otter and I have an *understanding.* And prick or not, he still knows more about Michelle than any other professional. In fact, I'm probably going to advise she continue seeing him. I think she may be close to being free of this thing."

Amanda—aware she'd been leaning forward tensely—sat back in the booth. The waitress came by and asked if she wanted more coffee. When Amanda didn't answer, Touch nodded for her, the waitress poured and left again.

"We still don't have anything but a phantom address and a phony name. It's a big city, Touch."

"He's not in the city anymore. And he's not alone. Somewhere along the line, the killer's MO went south.

He's breaking all the rules, and not just to throw us off. He's changing the whole scenario. I'll bet you lunch he'll come to us."

"A ransom note?"

Benson nodded. "We'll be rubbing elbows with the feebs before the sun sets. I can already smell the stench." He gave her a sharp look. "In fact, I want you to approach Noland about contacting Bill Campbell at the FBI office. If we're going to have to deal with the feebs, I'd just as soon it be with someone who doesn't have an automatic hard-on for the RHD."

"Why don't you tell the captain yourself? With the tire iron thing over and Fowler off your neck, Noland will probably jump through hoops getting you back on the payroll. Make both himself *and* the AC look good again."

Benson reached for the check, and his wallet. "I'm not sure I want back on the force yet."

"Why not, for chrissake?"

He shook his head. "I don't know. Just a feeling. Maybe it'll pass."

But he was thinking about the tire iron.

31

The rain changed everything.

At first Charlie didn't understand exactly how—*always a bad planner, missed the details.* All he understood was that the storm was of torrential proportions, the wind and rain buffeted the little cabin like the hand of an enraged Ancient One. And that he could not possibly travel in it.

He moved about the uneven floor of the wooden house using everything he could find to put under the leaks as rainwater dripped steadily from the long neglected roof. Mostly all he had were empty cans of SpaghettiOs and they filled up pretty fast. It was just about all she brought from the little store down the mountain. That and soda pop. Coke. Regular. She'd open two cans of Coke at once, dump a can of the red, runny spaghetti stuff into the single pot they'd brought from his apartment, heat it on his electric burner, and eat it, sometimes right out of the pot. Sometimes three and four a night. And she'd throw the empty tin cans into a pile in the corner, soon forming a mountain, so the next can bounced off and rolled against the wall. It made Charlie sick.

But maybe now it wasn't such a bad thing, her downing all those cans of noodles and bright red sauce; at least he had plenty of containers to stick under all the leaks and there were *plenty* of leaks. He had to keep moving all the time, grab the one that filled first, replace it with an empty one, dump the filled one out the window, hurry on to the next, and start the whole thing over again. Grab, dump, replace, grab, dump, replace, grab, dump—

Oh, *why* was he thinking of her now anyway! She was *dead*, or dying, anyway, lying under the woodpile with water dripping on her from the heavens and her blood soaking into the rich brown soil. Maybe the damn rain would wash her clean, rid her of the stains of the lies she had told him.

Wash her clean.

Of course it would! And the leaves too!

Charlie hesitated at the window the next time he emptied a can. Under strobes of lightning he could see that the hill and brush beside the cabin was *moving* . . . a river of turbulent, muddy water, swirling leaves and pine nettles. Douglas firs. That was what caused all the nettles. They stuck in your heels if you went out barefoot. They were everywhere now, gathering against the lee of the trees in brown clumps, then breaking apart as the flood water carried them down the mountain . . . along with the blood. And all traces of the killing.

The mountain would be clean. And he would be free again.

The whimpering brought him from his reverie. It was the Ransom girl again, her shiny hair not so pretty now, a straggly, golden waterfall where the dripping caught her. Charlie sighed and trudged to the back of the wooden chair and pulled her from beneath the dripping ceiling and placed a can under it. Putting the cans around was bad enough, but constantly moving the girl. He really didn't know why he was bothering. He should just kill her. Except that he'd already cleaned the cabin. Kill her first, then clean the cabin— that was what he should have done. Not good with the details.

He stood there for a moment watching her. She hardly ever looked at him anymore, and she couldn't talk with the scarf in her mouth. All she did was whimper when the leaks hit her and make that sound when she had to go pee, and with her makeup all streaked like that and her attitude—a kind of dreamy acceptance, her eyes all empty-looking—she wasn't nearly as pretty anymore. He really should have had done with her long ago.

He moved back to the window and watched the rain. He liked to stare at his reflection in the pane. It warbled and stretched his already warbled and stretched face, and sometimes, when the rain ran just right, he could almost remember himself handsome again. His hair dark and thick, not like the orange wig. He used to stand in front of the long door mirror in the old house and look at himself after his bath and he knew he was as handsome as the boys on TV and in the magazines, the ones the girls were always kissing. Mother had caught him staring at himself once, embarrassed him. But she'd come up behind and put her warm hands on his small shoulders and turned his head back to his reflection and told him it was all right. He was beautiful. There was no point in denying it. He was beautiful all over. That was the first night she had taken him into her bed.

She had danced for him first. Dressed in the Egyptian costume she'd sewed together by hand (well, some of it she'd bought at Kreskie's on Halloween) and he had sat on the big green sofa and watched her prance and swoop with nothing but the flickering blue light from the TV illuminating her. That was the first night she'd told him who she really was, what her mission here on Earth was. Sung to him while she dipped and swayed and ran glistening sweat before the blue light. Then took him in her arms and carried him to the nuptial bed and held him, stroked him, kissed him, and did other things with her mouth until he was ready, then told him where to put his sacred blade. How tightly she'd clung to him, especially near the end. *"Oh . . . oh, you're reaching my very heart!"* It had frightened him how tightly she'd clung, so that he never wanted to do it again. But they had. Regularly after that first time. Usually right after supper, or after *Shock Theatre* on TV, especially if they showed a Karloff film. He'd see that look in her eyes, that sleepy *wanting*. And she'd dance for him or sometimes not even bother, just pull him impatiently into the bedroom and over her. *"Now!"* she'd plead. *"Now kill me with it . . . Now drive it deep, deep into my heart!"* And afterward the bath, always the bath, washing every inch of him, every telltale sign from prying eyes at school. *"The gods have their little secrets, Charles,"* she'd croon behind him in the water, crooning and softly soaping.

Thunder vibrated through the old cabin walls.

But more softly this time, and farther away. Charlie looked out the window to see the storm moving away on legs of lightning.

Now was the time. Bury the body while the earth was still soft and runny. It would be easy in the mud. He could use his hands if he had to, but he wasn't stupid, he'd find a broken stick from the storm, or maybe something in the trunk of the girl's car.

Jana was whimpering again. Not much water dripping on her. She must have to pee again. Well, let her. Let her pee her pants this time. He was getting out of here. Getting away from it all. Starting over in some small town where there weren't so many newspapers and police and shoving, crowding people.

It was all so clear now. He should have realized he hadn't heard The Voice once since he'd come to the cabin. Not once since he'd left the city. Only in the doctor's office, cleaning up, emptying the trash, dusting. Only there. He should have figured it out sooner.

The Voice wasn't real.

It was a hoax. A phony. Just like his mother when he put the true blade to her. She hadn't come back any more than any of the others had. They never would. The Old Ones had lied.

He was just an ugly little man running from the past.

Well, he was through running. He would stop running as surely as the storm had stopped. He'd get in the dead girl's car and drive and drive until all the rubber wore off the wheels if that's what it took to find a warm, safe place. Then he'd run no more.

He was tired. Of the killing most of all.

First, though, he had to bury the body. Then come back and take care of the pretty one.

Until then, she could just pee her pants.

32

From the day he'd found the crepe-wrapped tire iron behind his front screen door, Benson had followed the same routine on every day thereafter: driven into his garage, hit the automatic door button, walked through the house, opened the front door, and looked down. Hoping.

He did the same thing this afternoon. And this afternoon he was rewarded. An unmarked envelope lay atop the aluminum threshold. He picked it up, threw it on the bar, mixed himself a drink, took one swallow, and opened the envelope. A single piece of paper was folded inside, with a single, computer-typed line:

> *Your place, five p.m.*
> *—a friend*

He looked at his watch: 4:18.
He turned on the living room TV, found *Headline*

News Network, and sat watching it for the next ten minutes, nursing his drink.

At four-thirty, he switched it over to KTLA for the news hour. The Mummy Killer was still the top story. Benson had seen himself on TV before, but it always gave him a jolt. He knew women thought him attractive. To himself, he always looked haggard and somewhat nonplussed. And older.

Tonight all they had was file footage from other cases. But the story was the Mummy Killer's. And the token blond anchor who had just moments before been chuckling with her partner over a cat up a tree story looked theatrically serious now. She didn't read the prompter particularly well, but she had great teeth and a full rack. "Stan, tonight *L.A. Times* crime reporter Giles Fowler's nightly report is disclosing that Robbery-Homicide Detective Amiel Benson, recently suspended from the force, has apparently won a victory in the upcoming civil trial concerning his part in an alleged episode of police brutality on the 101 last month."

The TV anchor quoted most of the detail Fowler had already printed. In fact, Fowler was probably the one who called the station. You scratch my back, I'll scratch yours. But Fowler had got there with the news first. In the flash of a moment, Benson had been exonerated. The anchor went on to say that, in Fowler's opinion, Benson had been the prime motivator for whatever progress had been made on the Mummy Killer case thus far. No, more than merely exonerated; he was practically a hero. Thanks to Amanda.

When Benson's phone rang he half expected it to be Captain Noland welcoming him back to the fold.

"Benson."

"Did you get my note?"

A woman's voice. Young. Benson reached across the end table beside the sofa and switched on the micro recorder, the suctioned microphone already attached to the back of the handset's earpiece. "Which one?" he asked casually.

"I know you got the first one. I watch TV too. Now here's the way it's going to be. I'm going to ask some questions, you're going to answer. If you answer correctly, I may have some information for you. If you lie to me, I hang up."

Confident. Aggressive. But a touch of uncertainty there, maybe even fear, that carried even over the phone line. "I'm listening," Benson replied in an even tone.

"First of all, this *is* Detective Touch Benson with the Robbery-Homicide Division—am I correct?"

Knew his nickname. Done research on him. "I am."

"Good. You're young-looking for your age, Detective, at least on TV."

"How young do you look?"

The phone went dead.

Benson winced, hung up the receiver.

He shut off the recorder, made a note of the time on a pad beside the phone, and kept his eyes on his watch until the phone rang again, five minutes later. He made another quick note before picking it up again. In fact, he let it ring three times. "Benson."

"One more like that and I hang up for good."

"Sorry. What can I do for you?"

"Plenty, I should think. Considering all I've done for you."

"I'm listening."

"Good. Keep it that way and you'll make detective three."

Done her homework. Smart. Benson allowed himself a wedge of excitement.

"First off, Jason Richards is innocent. He had nothing to do with the kidnapping."

Benson thought about saying, *What kidnapping?* But she was way ahead of that. Instead he took a gamble on being hung up on again. "Tell me something I don't already know."

Silence on the other end. She hadn't expected that one. But she hadn't hung up either.

Benson decided to push it. "You still there?"

"I'm here. You know he's innocent?"

"I know it. The Los Angeles Sheriff's Department doesn't agree. And they're short on suspects. He'll probably go down."

"No!"

Benson waited in silence. She'd made her first mistake, shown vulnerability, shown she had some kind of stake in this. It was leverage for his side. Some, anyway.

Benson waited. She was thinking the same thing he'd just been thinking. Vulnerable. But not stupid. *Be careful . . .*

After a time he ventured, "Hello?"

"I can see this was a mistake. You're just another stupid cop."

Losing her. "Not at the moment I'm not."

"They'll drop the suspension."

"Takes time. Paperwork."

"How much time?"

Time to show strength. Appear cooperative, but not acquiescent. "Maybe as long as it takes to convict Jason Richards."

If she thought he was lying—which he was—she didn't tell him. Her fear for the Richards kid was overriding everything else.

"I . . . can prove he didn't have anything to do with it."

"Forensics seems to be proving otherwise," Benson lied again.

"He screwed her. He didn't take her. He wouldn't hurt her! What the hell's the matter with you people? Don't you ever consider motive?"

Benson kept his voice even, routine. "We consider what we've got. Facts. In the eyes of the law he's a suspect. The only suspect at the moment."

He let that sink in. Could almost feel her anxiety through the wires.

He decided to take another gamble. "If you're as smart as you seem to be, then you must know the police have had just about zero on the Mummy case up to now. To be frank, they're clutching at straws. Nobody likes to look like a fool, the LAPD least of all. They look bad, the mayor looks bad. Mayor looks bad, the governor . . . You get the picture." All of this was true if not entirely pertinent in this instance. Unless she was a young woman studying law, she probably wouldn't know that. Probably.

"Jason didn't do it. And they'll know that soon enough."

"Why is that?"

"Because it's a ransom case now, and if you keep

pretending you don't already know, I'll hang up for good!"

Benson thought fast. "I never said I hadn't considered it. I've considered everything, so has the LAPD. But one thing you learn in this business is that nothing's for sure."

"What's that supposed to mean?"

"Well, suppose it is a ransom. Suppose it does start out that way. A lot of would-be kidnappers have started the crime, gotten cold feet halfway through, and dropped it. Usually before the ransom note is sent. Without the note, it's not technically a ransom, just a kidnapping."

"*Just* a kidnapping? Think I don't know about the Lindbergh Law? Kidnapping is a guaranteed trip to the gas chamber!"

"You're wrong."

"Bullshit!"

"It's only an automatic first degree if the victim or anyone else is harmed as a direct result of the crime."

"You're lying!"

"Look it up."

Silence from the girl's end.

Benson waited, mind racing. Who was she? Friend of the Richards kid? Michelle's kid? Both? She was scared, but she had something. He could feel it. *Play the line. Don't lose her. May not get another chance.*

"Hello?"

"I'm here. And I'm at a phone booth, not a private line, so if you're tracing this, fuck you. I'm hanging up before the requisite three minutes."

"All right."

Another pause. "I saved your butt."

"Did you?"

"You know I did. Now it's your turn. Get Jason Richards out of jail."

"I've been trying to."

Another long pause. "And?"

"I need help. The best way to clear Jason is to get the Ransom girl back." He regretted it immediately. If she was going to get scared off—hang up again—now was when she'd do it. But goddamn it, he was running out of time.

She didn't hang up. "Suppose I told you who took her."

He waited.

"Did you hear me?"

"Go on."

"Suppose I told you! Could we work a deal?"

"What . . . sort of deal?"

He waited, eyes jammed tight. So close now. Don't envision the line going dead. Envision it, and it will happen.

He glanced at his watch. The micro recorder made a whispering sound.

"Suppose . . . I knew the—"

Say it. *Say it!*

"—the guy who took her. Would that implicate me?"

"Just knowing him? Not by itself, no."

"I don't believe you."

"Fine. It's your life. But you can believe this. If the LAPD doesn't get something solid to the contrary, Jason Richards is the man who's going to trial. He's *admitted* to being there, for chrissake."

It worked. "He didn't do it! He's an innocent. Didn't you talk to him? You really think he's the type to do something like that?"

"I already told you my personal take on Jason. But it isn't up to me. Look, I appreciate your concern, but I've really got a lot to do tonight. The best way to clear the Richards kid is to find Jana Ransom, and I've got to get busy doing that. I can see you're upset, probably a friend or something, but you're not helping anyone's cause right now. If you have something to report, I'd be glad to give you the number of the desk sergeant who can—"

"His name is Charlie Grissom."

Benson held his breath. Charlie Crissom, Charles Jones—he'd bet they were one and the same. "Yes?"

"He's the one you've been looking for."

"Is he an acquaintance of yours?"

"I know who he is—that's all you get. But he's not the one who took Jana. At least not alone."

"Who did?"

"I want a deal."

"All right."

"A guarantee."

"The police will do everything they—"

"I don't want the police! Why do you think I called you? You're off the force! You wouldn't be committing a crime, not as a cop, anyway. Why do you think I sent—did you that favor? Now are you going to help me out or not?"

"I'm trying to."

"I want a guarantee I won't be implicated."

"I can make that guarantee, from what I've heard so far. But so far it hasn't been much help. We already know about Grissom. We just haven't been able to find him yet."

"You know about Grissom?"

"Yes."

"What's he look like?"

He had her. "Like a lump of wax. He was a late-night janitor until a few days ago. Then he split. I shouldn't actually be telling you this . . . I mean, I'm taking you at your word here, trusting you."

She didn't bark back. And she owed him one now. He let her think about it another few seconds. "So if you don't know where he is, I'm afraid you're really not—"

"I know who he's with."

An accomplice. Benson slumped with relief, felt a wave of vindication . . . if not complete elation. "And are you going to share that information with me?"

"If I do, you'll find out who I am."

"Why is that?"

"Trust me."

"I am."

"Here's what we're going to do. I'm going to tell you where I am. You're going to get your redhead partner to pick me up. Call her right now. Instruct her to tell the department she got the call from me, that I gave myself up. That leaves you in the clear."

Just like the tire iron, Benson thought.

"Your partner will take me to the station. Turn me over to the duty officer. After that, I'll ask to see you. You are the only one I will talk to. I'm a smart girl and I want a cop who's on the case—like that. Your superior or whoever will see it's done."

Benson could picture Noland hurrying the paperwork through.

"When that's done, I'll talk. But only after they let Jason go on bail and only if they cut me a deal, a plea bargain or whatever. That's it. Have we got a plan?"

Benson's mind raced. It was hard keeping up with this little bitch. "I'll have to speak with my—"

"Your partner will do anything you ask her to. Do we have a deal? Yes or no."

"All right. Where are you?"

"One more thing. When your partner picks me up— puts on the cuffs, drives me downtown—one more thing—"

"She forgets to read you your Miranda."

A wry snort on the other end. "I knew you were the right guy. Why haven't they made you captain?"

"She won't do that."

"Make her."

"It could get her suspended, maybe worse."

"And catching Jana Ransom's kidnapper will get her unsuspended, just like you."

"I won't ask her to do that."

"You have five minutes to think about it. Five minutes for the chance to save Jana Ransom, get good with the department, and let Jason go. That's it."

"Listen—"

"Five minutes."

"Wait a second—"

The line went dead.

33

Kurtzy hung up the phone.

Stood there in the Dykstra Hall corridor staring at the black pay phone receiver for a moment.

Trapped. She still felt it, even with the plan in motion. Powerless now. Not in control. And Kurtzy Mallon had had too much of being out of control lately.

Ever since she had hit Charlie Grissom's apartment door running, panic distorting her delicate pink face. *"Charlie!"* she had yelled.

The door banged against the wall, taking a scab of white paint with it. She started across the living room carpet in a frenzy. She froze. It was empty. The apartment was cleaned out. Vacated. *Scrubbed* down.

Kurtzy had thrown back her head to scream again but caught herself. She began to pace in tight circles on the living room floor where the rug and little table used to be, the statue of Anubis. She shook uncontrollably despite herself.

She looked up at the wall where the doorknob had taken the scrap of white paint. White. It had been sepia-colored before . . . and decorated with carefully labored over hieroglyphics.

Gone. Every trace of evidence, of Charlie Grissom. Gone. For one wild moment she even imagined she'd gotten the wrong apartment. But she hadn't.

She put her hands to her temples, pressing hard, trying to *force* the logic of it inside her brain. He'd painted the apartment, covering his tracks, then taken the Ransom girl—abducted her—then disappeared. To *where?*

And *why?*

Kurtzy had never said anything to him about going to Jana Ransom's house! She could hardly remember what she'd said about Jana, except that she hated her—but that was enough, wasn't it, knowing Charlie? His insane belief in her Egyptian divinity? What if it hadn't been a game to him, if he truly believed he was immortal, if Jana was the enemy—

What had he done with her?

Just kidnaped her, run off with her? Would Charlie have killed her with that crazy ceremonial knife of his? There was blood all over the Ransom house bedroom, the newspaper said so. He *must* have killed her. Killed her and . . .

What?

Dumped her somewhere?

It still wasn't adding up. Charlie didn't respond to this world, didn't truly live in it. Charlie thought he was a god, searching for his goddess. Someone else might have been that clever, that thorough, but not . . .

. . . someone else . . .

Kurtzy sucked in breath so quickly it hurt her teeth.

She had stood in the living room of Charlie Grissom's empty apartment, stood there amid the blank, white walls, and suddenly understood it all.

Who had painted the walls, who had helped him move, who had convinced him she was his true goddess, his real Nephthys?

And the reality of it almost made her scream again. The floor seemed to rush up at her . . . She actually put her hands out, expecting to hit it. But nothing happened. Nothing but the black growing hole of emptiness spreading from her center.

The dream had become a nightmare, a horror story, the life she had only recently believed possible a hideous mockery. Because it wasn't just she and Charlie anymore. There was a third party, another witness. And it wasn't about jealousy anymore. It was about pure unadulterated hatred.

Miss Glendale rich bitch. I hate her.

Kurtzy could almost see Sue Thornquist's sneering face in the soft amber lighting of His Pants.

So now, with the phone call to Detective Benson, Kurtzy had taken another step in her plan.

She couldn't think of any other way to help Jason. Her roommate had been gone for three days now. And sooner or later that phony note she'd left in their room and at the front desk about being called away on a *family matter* wouldn't hold. Sue could never come back here. And when the cops came around, asking questions, digging, Kurtzy would say nothing. Sue was counting on that. A ransom note would come. She would get her daydream fortune. Jana Ransom

would die and so would Jason. And so would *Kurtzy*
if she ever opened her mouth.

Sue had it all worked out. Like a game of chess.
The only way to beat your opponent was with a dou-
ble check. But Kurtzy would lay down her life for
Jason, if need be. She hadn't counted on that.

She walked back to their room, closed the door behind her, and stood with her back pressed to it, eyes
closed, trying to find solace in a cleansing breath.

She'd done the best she could for Jason. What else
could she do? It was still no guarantee he was out of
danger. Just as the arrival of a ransom note was no
guarantee of his innocence. He'd still be under suspicion as an accomplice. Even if he didn't burn, he could
be tied up in court and prison forever. Jesus, had Sue
planned *that* too? Was she more clever than Kurtzy
had thought? It seemed impossible. Still . . .

Her fists smashed reflexively against the door. And
she pushed away, face in her hands, letting the an-
guished moan escape her throat, letting the tears
start. Jason!

She was nearly to her bed when she tripped over
something, nearly fell. She looked down. More of
Sue's crap strewn across the dorm room floor.

She stooped in sudden frenzy, gathering up the
books and papers and combs and other things in her
trembling arms, flinging them across the room at her
roommate's disheveled bed.

That was part of the plan too, *right*, Sue? Leave the room
in a mess! Like you were called away on emergency.

Yeah. Sure. Only don't say what emergency, don't
say *where*.

There had to be a better way. It wasn't too late.
Something could still be done, something she hadn't
thought of. Sue Thornquist wasn't *that* bright. No one
had a brain like Kurstin. She just needed to start using
it again. Sue would have screwed this up somewhere
along the line. The cop was right—the answer was in
getting Jana Ransom back.

Kurtzy sat on the edge of her neatly made bed a
moment. *Think!*

It was there. Somewhere it was there: some fatal
flaw in Sue, some Achilles's heel. She just had to take
time to see it, to think about it . . .

Sue was there now, lying on her rumpled bed, arms
folded behind her head, smiling at Kurtzy, gloating.
*Got you, didn't I, bitch? And you paved the way. You
and your psycho lover with the waxy face and big john-
son. Thought you were going to ditch me for good . . .
but I got back at you and that rich bitch Jana Ransom.
Me! Sue Thornquist! The white-trash kid who never
had a dime in her life. Who never had a future. Well,
I got one now, Kurtzy baby! I got one now!*

Kurtzy screamed, a strangled sound that ended in a
kind of growl. She picked up one of her roommate's
textbooks from the debris-strewn rug, prepared to hurl
it at the wall—

. . . hesitated.

Lowered the book slowly. . . . *white-trash kid who
never had anything* . . .

Kurtzy dropped the book, looked back at Sue's
rumpled bed. Her roommate was still there, only Kurtzy was beside her, listening patiently while Sue un-
loaded about her crummy, white-trash youth, her
lousy parents, how they left her nothing . . . nothing

but a one-room cabin in the San Gabriel Mountains . . .

"Shit!"

Kurtzy, galvanized, grabbed the fat L.A. phone book under her nightstand, began whipping through the pages with one hand, reaching for her cellular with the other.

"Bronson Realty, may I help you?"

Kurtzy put on her best middle-aged voice. "Yes, this is Mrs. Smith in Palm Springs. I'm . . . To tell the truth I'm not even sure I have the correct real estate company."

"Well, let's see if we can help you, Mrs. Smith. Were you looking for a home?"

"Actually it's more of a lodge, a small cabin. My husband's birthday is coming up and, well, he always wanted a little place in the woods, you understand."

"In the woods?"

"The thing is, we're friends of the Thornquists, Mazie and Bill? Had a little girl Sue? Been years. But they had the cutest little cabin up in the San Gabriel mountains. Phil—that's my husband—Phil and I used to spend the best summers there. Anyway, we haven't heard from the Thornquists in years, but the last I knew Mazie was talking about selling the little place. It would be so perfect for my husband. Thing is, I'm not sure who the Thornquists had it listed with and—"

"Mrs. Smith, I'm afraid Bronson Realty only deals in area estates. Now if—"

Kurtzy hung up.

She drew a red line through Bronson Realty in the yellow pages, inched her finger down the column to the next firm, punched the cell phone, one eye on the dorm room clock. It had been ten minutes since she'd told that cop Benson she'd call back in five.

"Good morning, Carlson Realty, may I help you?"

"Yes, this is Mrs. Smith in Palm Springs. I'm . . . To tell you the truth I'm not even sure I have the correct real estate company."

"I see. Well, how can Carlson be of service, Mrs. Smith?"

34

"My," Amanda told the receiver, pacing before her desk at the homicide table, "confident little thing."

Benson grunted. "And smart. Anyway, that's where we stand."

"Fine. When she calls here, I'll go pick her up. Damn! We've finally got something, Touch!"

Benson sighed into the mouthpiece. "Pick her up and what, Mandy?"

"Bring her in. Isn't that what she wanted?"

"Not all she wanted."

Amanda made an impatient sound. Her blood was up. "So I forget to read her her Miranda. So I left my card in my other purse. It happens."

"Not to you, it doesn't. And she's right. A judge will throw it out."

"Touch, she's giving us the Mummy! Who cares if—"

"*Says* she's giving us. And only *after* we let the

Richards kid go. At which point you will be guilty not only of failure to read a citizen her rights, but of false arrest. She needs the Miranda thing for a back door, and you're going to take the fall."

"It's her word against mine. And yours. I'm willing to take the chance."

"I'm not. And I won't let you. Christ, this is getting worse than fucking Watergate!"

"Touch—"

"And in any case, she hasn't called back. Five minutes, she said. It's been over ten."

"Well, hang up, then—"

"I'm at home, Mandy. Call waiting. I'll hear anyone trying to beep through. Hold on a sec. I want you to listen to something . . ."

Amanda waited, tapping her foot, checking her watch again after only a few seconds. She could hear a high-pitched sound in the earpiece, an ascending squeak. A tape rewinding.

"It's a small recorder, and the sound is for shit, but see if you can hear another voice behind the caller's. Ready?"

"Go."

Benson played a portion of the tape.

"I saved your butt."

"Did you?"

"You know I did. Now it's your turn. Get Jason Richards out of jail."

"I've been trying to."

[Long pause.]

"And?"

"I need help. The best way to clear Jason—"

Benson turned off the tape. "Did you hear it? Right after I say, *'I've been trying to.'* There's a pause. Sounds like someone talking in the background for a second."

"I heard, but barely. Play it again. Can you amplify that thing?"

"Not much, it's just a Radio Shack recorder."

Benson rewound, played it again. "Well?"

Amanda paced. "It's a girl's voice. Echo-y. Enclosed."

"Yeah, no traffic noise. The caller told me she was using a pay phone."

"An indoor pay phone. Gee, that narrows it down."

"Listen again." Benson held the recorder against the headset, replayed the section of tape.

"Plaza . . ." Amanda murmured, "something about a plaza. 'I'm bowling over at the *something* plaza *something'?*"

"A bowling plaza—is that it?"

Amanda shook her head. "They don't call bowling alleys 'plazas,' Touch."

"What do they call them?"

"I don't know . . . bowling *centers* or something. Christ, I don't bowl. Don't you bowl?"

"Since when?"

"Play it again."

He did. Amanda listened carefully over the caller's voice. There was a conversation behind it, in the background, echoing off walls . . . a hallway or corridor . . .

Amanda clucked thoughtfully. " 'I'm . . . *going* over to the *something* plaza *something'* . . ."

Benson picked it up. " 'I'm going over to the 'nerve' plaza *later*'?"

"That's it! She said, 'later'! She's going over to the *'something* plaza later.' 'Nerve'? Sounds more like *'naive.'* Have you got a yellow pages?"

"Already looking. Shopping plazas . . . shopping centers, uh . . . we got Neiman Marcus . . . Nordstrom . . . Nichols'. . . . damn. That's it for the Ns in the greater L.A. area."

Amanda sighed exasperation. "Maybe she's outside L.A."

"Well if she is, we're screwed."

Amanda licked her fingers, flipping hastily through the department's phone book. "She sounds like she's in a hall somewhere, passing by your caller, her voice fading as she goes by."

"Yeah. You looking too?"

"Yes . . . nothing . . . no shopping plazas that sound like 'nerve.' What the hell kind of plaza would be called that anyway? Oh, hell, Touch, bring the damn tape in. We'll have the techs analyze it, bring up the background voice and—"

"Amanda."

"What? Oh. Shit. I forgot what else is on the tape. Little mention of a gift. Can't exactly pass that tape around, can we?"

"Not exactly." Benson ground his teeth. "Goddamn it! I fucked myself!"

Amanda rubbed her temples. "Hold on a second." She put the receiver to her chest, turned to the other desks lined in the three rows that made up the Homicide Special bullpen, and hailed the other detectives loudly. "Anybody here know of a shopping center in L.A. called 'the Nerve Plaza' or 'the Nive Plaza'—something like that?"

A couple of detectives looked up from computers. Nobody said anything.

Amanda grimaced. "*Anybody?* Peterson, your wife shop at the Nerve Plaza maybe?"

Peterson, holding on a line of his own, shook his head.

Harve Boland five desks down looked up wearily from a sheath of paperwork, used the excuse to remove his glasses, rub the bridge of his nose. "Who wants to know?"

Amanda shrugged. "Some girl."

Boland replaced the glasses. "My daughter stays at DeNeve Plaza on campus."

"Campus? What campus?"

"UCLA."

Amanda blinked.

"Touch? Bolland says his kid stays in a dorm called DeNeve Plaza at UCLA." She was already seated, pecking rapidly at her keyboard, fingers anxious, making mistakes. "*Damn it!*"

"What?"

"Nothing, typo . . . hold on, I'm bring up UCLA dorms . . . shit, what do they call the damn things now?"

"Try 'housing' or 'residence.' "

"Here we go . . . student housing . . . DeNeve Plaza Housing Project. New. Regents approved financing in May 1997, blah, blah . . . 1,258 student bed spaces, blah, blah . . . Christ, the thing is enormous."

"Find a map. We need an area map." It was hard to contain the excitement in his voice.

"Looking, looking . . . okay . . . On-Campus Housing Map . . . Sproul Hall . . . Hedrick Hall . . . Dykstra

Hall . . . Rieber—here's DeNeve Plaza! Looks like
it's between Gayley Boulevard and Charles E. Young
Drive. An enormous complex of buildings."

Benson paced. " *'I'm going over to DeNeve Plaza
later,'* the voice said. 'Over' could mean the same as
'close.' What's the closest building to *DeNeve Plaza*
on the map?"

"Dykstra Hall, right behind it. Christ, Touch, it says,
capacity 842, 271 double rooms and 100 triple rooms.
And our girl may not even live there, may just be
using the phone there."

"She lives there. Listen, call the dean and— No,
screw that. Get over there yourself. You're closest.
Check with the admissions office or whatever it's
called, find out what students are out sick or on leave.
Our caller could be talking about a roommate. See if
there's a pay phone on every floor or just some. Talk
to any student you see, find out who might be close
to Jason Richards or Jana Ransom. I'll call Michelle
from here and see if Jana ever mentioned anyone at
Dykstra Hall."

Amanda already had her purse. "On my way."

"Michelle, it's Touch."

"Touch! I'm so glad you called."

"Is everything all right?"

"Yes, fine . . . as fine as things can be. Have you . . .
do you—?"

"Nothing solid yet, but we may be close. I need to
ask you a couple of things about Jana. Are you up
to it?"

"Of course."

"At school, did she always stay at home, or did she ever live on campus, a sorority or resident housing?"

"Only at home. Why?"

"But she must have known girls in sororities and dorms."

"Yes, I suppose. What—"

"Think now. This is important. Did she ever mention a campus dormitory named Dykstra Hall? Think before you answer, honey."

"I'm . . . I don't know, she may have. Touch, I really can't remember."

"What about DeNeve Plaza, does that ring a bell?"

"DeNeve . . . no, no, I'm sorry."

"Okay, it's okay. Just a shot. We'll take care of it. How are you? Really."

A sigh over the wire. "I wish you were here."

"Me too. But I can do Jana more good where I am. Do you still have the sedatives? I don't like the idea of your being alone in that big house."

"I'm all right. I don't want the damn sedatives. I don't want anything from a doctor ever again. I just want my daughter back. God, Touch . . . how could I have been so—"

"Never mind, now. This is not your fault, Michelle."

"But it is! My daughter's life is in danger because I was too stupidly prideful to—I should have told you from the start I was seeing a psychiatrist. All those *girls*!"

"Michelle, listen to me. Don't play that game. Don't buy into that. Start a guilt spiral now and you'll never climb out of it, believe me, I know. You need to be strong now, for Jana. You need to believe we'll get her back. *Think* it will happen."

"Touch, I know what you're doing—"

"No, you don't. Listen, I've done a lot of research in the area of psychics over the past few days, and I'm convinced there's something to it. I don't pretend to know how it works, but they all say the same thing. We all—each of us—has some psychic ability. We're born with it. It's just another kind of energy, nothing mystical about it. Call it karma, call it God, whatever you like. But it's susceptible, Michelle, to negative energy, bad thoughts if you will. Start dwelling on guilt and self-pity and you'll wall it off. I don't care how ethereal it sounds. Now Jana's out there, and she's alive, and she needs you. And you can be there for her, Michelle, just by believing, just by thinking that she's coming home, that she'll be with you again. And the more you think that, concentrate on that, the quicker it will happen."

"Touch . . . do you really believe that, or are you just—"

"I really believe it, honey. Absolutely. And I need you to believe it too. There's shit out there in the cosmos none of us understand. But we can tap into it. Use it. Concentrate all your energy on her, Michelle. Believe she's alive and thinking of you. And she'll hear you. She will. And it will give her hope."

"All right. Thank you."

"And listen, I know how you feel about Otter now. But the truth is, creepy as the guy may be, I think he was actually helping you. You've gone a long way with him. He knows your history better than anyone. I think you should consider seeing him again."

"But I—"

"I've had a talk with him, Michelle. I think you'll

find our friend Otter both cooperative and useful. Anyway, think about it."

"All right."

"I'll be in touch. Call if you need anything, I'm at home."

"Thank you. Bless you. I believe you."

Benson hung up. Almost believing it himself.

He punched in Parker Center.

"Lieutenant Scott."

"Scotty, it's Touch—"

"Touch! Listen, I heard about the hearing with Judge Judy!"

"It wasn't a hearing, Scotty."

"Whatever. I talked to Noland, and he's going to lift the suspension just as soon as he hears from the AC. But it's a slam dunk—"

"That's great, Scotty. Listen, I think I may have our boy."

Benson heard the rustle of paper on the other end. "Go."

"I need someone to use the department computer, get into the NCIC files for me."

"What have you got?"

"Grissom, G-R-I-S-S-O-M. Charles. See if you get a hit from Quantico. I'm at home."

"Grissom. Got it."

35

The campus could be seen from Sunset Boulevard, but the big stone marker engraved UCLA, flanked the road, and opened the way up the mountain to the sprawling university above.

Amanda took Sunset to Charles E. Young Drive and from there hooked around the horseshoe curve past Drake Stadium and on into DeNeve Drive at the western edge of the campus.

DeNeve Plaza was indeed enormous. A huge, imposing, newly built cluster of buildings, comprised of four distinct residential structures for students—thirty of which had single-student status and private baths—an 850-seat dining room, a commissary and bakery, two computer labs, a 3,800-square-foot meeting room, a 430-seat lecture auditorium, an informal student recreation/entertainment room, a formal study area, and several beautifully manicured and landscaped plaza areas surrounding the site.

In marked contrast, outdated Dykstra Hall hunkered forlornly in the shadows behind the newly built usurper, as if anticipating the wrecking ball. Amanda found parking in the sweeping lot between the old dorm and L-shaped Tom Bradley International Hall.

She showed her badge at the front desk, got her information, and called Benson on her cell phone from the elevator to the fifth floor. "Hey, it's me. Our friend call back?"

"She's not calling back. Are you at the school?"

"Yes, in Dykstra, and we're in luck. Only three students out of town today, the first two of which have been accounted for. I'm on my way to the third now. How's Michelle?"

"Holding up. I've got Scotty running the NCIC for Grissom."

"Good. Call Harry Selten, get him to run everything in CAPS. And check with the DMV in case Grissom drives."

"I already checked DMV. Zilch."

"Have Selten check the HITMAN database for you."

"Why?"

"*Why?* The Homicide Information Tracking Management Automated Network, Touch. It—"

"I know what the acronym stands for, Mandy. Why Harry Selten?"

"Just . . . why not?"

"Never mind. I get it."

Amanda sighed. "Noland hasn't officially partnered me with him yet, Touch. Selten just dropped by my desk to see if he could help out after you left."

"I'll bet he did."

"For chrissake, not the office macho bullshit *now*, huh? I'm right in front of the kid's door. Call you back." Amanda thumbed off the cellular and rapped on the dorm door.

She waited a few seconds, then opened it with the passkey she'd acquired from the downstairs desk. The room was a mess, especially the far end; the bed looked like it had never been made.

Amanda came in, stepping around books, wastepaper, and paraphernalia. Messy but not atypical of young girls' dorm rooms. She pulled the index card from her pocket and checked the names again. Sue Thornquist was the one out of town. *A family matter,* the note had said.

Amanda wandered into the bathroom, an equal disaster area. Panty hose across the shower rod, hair dryer in the sink—what could be seen of the sink— floor sticky, littered with debris. Still, she'd seen worse. Remembered worse from her own university days.

She came out, glanced around, giving the room a final sweep. Nothing here. The other girl must be in class. Amanda was wondering if she should stick around when her eyes fell on the nearer bed's headboard. It contained a built-in bookcase.

She stepped closer. Mostly nonfiction. Medical books, maybe one of the roommates—Amanda checked the name again: Kurstin Mallon—was premed.

Amanda bent closer, tilted her head to read the spines, both hardcover and paperback: *A History of Serial Killers* by James Dourghty, PhD; *Tracking the*

Hillside Strangler; Ted Bundy: Inside the Fractured Mind; The Signature Killer in Our Midst.

"Jesus."

She sat down on the bed, unclipped her cellular, dialed the Registrar's Office.

"Miss Wilson, Registrar's Office."

"This is Detective Blaine with the Los Angeles Sheriff's Department. I need to check on the whereabouts of a student. You have some kind of enrollment schedule on computer I take it?"

"Do you have the student's name?"

"Mallon, Kurstin, A."

"One moment."

Amanda waited. Her attention kept being drawn to a lump on the floor beside her, something half hidden beneath a twist of bedsheet and wads of discarded, college-ruled paper. She bent, brushed aside the wads, pulled back the sheet, and picked up an opened yellow pages. On the right hand side, under the heading *Real Estate Agencies* she noted a series of red ink lines drawn through the first list of company names.

"I show Miss Mallon has a two o'clock course in Ancient History with Professor Ivers."

"Where would that be? Never mind. Can I contact Professor Ivers by phone?"

"Is this an emergency?"

"Yes."

"One moment."

Amanda put down the phone book, began walking the room again, moving through the debris with the toe of her shoe, bending, brushing wastepaper aside, searching.

"Professor Ivers can be reached in class at 555-9423."

Amanda thanked her and dialed the number.

"Professor Ivers."

"Sorry to interrupt your class, Professor. This is Detective Blaine with the Los Angeles Sheriff's Department. Is Kurstin Mallon in class today?"

Pause. "Kurtz? Uh, no, as a matter of fact. She didn't come in today."

"I see. Would you know why?"

"Me? No. No, I wouldn't . . . She, uh . . . she's normally quite prompt. May I ask what this involves?"

"It's a police matter. Would you take down my number please, and call immediately if Kurstin comes in?"

"Of course. What is this in reference to, if that's not classified information."

The professor sounded nervous, Amanda noted. "It is, Professor. Here's my number . . ."

She gave him the number and rang off.

She swept through the rest of the room, through the closets, then back into the bathroom, checking the medicine cabinet. Aspirin. Diet pills. Some were prescription.

The last thing she did was check under the beds. Nothing.

She stood, exasperated. Turned to the night table beside her and chewed her lip. It looked heavy. She shrugged to herself, gripped the edges of the bulky table, and levered it aside, grunting with the effort. She peered behind it. The cellular was there amid a pile of debris, crushed cigarette packs and an empty tampon box. Maybe the phone had been deliberately hidden there, maybe just carelessly tossed and fallen behind. Amanda bent and retrieved it.

She sat on the bed again, reached for the phone book, traced her finger down the agency names to the first one that hadn't been red-lined: Covina Real Estate.

She picked up the retrieved cellular—held her breath a second—and dialed the number for Covina Real Estate.

"Covina Real Estate, Miss Lane. May I help you?" An elderly voice, a granny voice.

"This is Detective Blaine with the LAPD on official police business. I need to check on a call made to your offices within the last hour. How many operators do you employ at Covina, Miss Lane?"

"Why, oh . . . normally three. But Trudy and Jeanette are at lunch right now. Is someone hurt? Is *Trudy* all right? It's her *boyfriend*, isn't it? I warned her about—"

"It's not about Trudy. You're the only one in the office taking calls, is that right, Miss Lane?"

"Why, yes. We keep someone here during lunch breaks. It was my turn at rotation. Tomorrow it will be Jeanette's turn, then—"

"Does the company keep any kind of records of incoming business calls?"

Pause. "Records? Why, uh, that depends. If there's an actual transaction, or if a client seems genuinely interested in a property, we may keep them on file."

"Do you recall how many calls you've taken within the last hour?"

"Let's see . . . why, two I think. One was a Mr. Lopez. He's looking at one of our properties in Covina. Lovely place—"

"And the other one?"

"Let me think . . . uh . . . it was a woman, I believe . . . what was she asking about? . . ."

"Take your time, Miss Lane, this may be very important."

"It was . . . ah! A Mrs. Smith! I knew it was a common name like Jones or Smith. You know, you hear so *many* names in this business, it's hard to—"

"Mrs. Smith. And what was she inquiring about, do you recall?"

"Yes, I remember now. she wanted to know about one of our older properties, something we've had listed for years, way back before I came to work for the company. I had to look it up. The reason I remember is, it wasn't in the computer. Thought I'd never find it. A little cabin. Up in the San Gabriel Mountains, I think. A kind of hunting lodge. I have it here, though, in the index file . . . Yes, here we are. Where are my glasses?"

Amanda switched the cellular to her other ear.

"Let me see now. . . . yes . . . one-room cabin, handcrafted, lovely mountain view, terrific getaway—"

"Do you have the name of the client the property is listed with?"

"The client? Uh . . . yes, here it is . . . Thornquist . . . Mazie and John. There's a number, but it's crossed out. The card indicates the couple is deceased, oh, dear."

"Does the card say who the property is held with now?"

"Yes, the property is held with the First National Bank now."

"Under whose name?"

"Uh . . . well, it says Thornquist."

"Does it give a first name?"

"Susan."

Amanda slapped the phone book shut. "Miss Lane, you are a dream. May I have the address of the property, please?"

"Surely. But, my goodness, it's way up in the mountains! Do you have a map, dear?"

Amanda called Benson from her car.

"Touch. Any word from our girl?"

"No, she's long gone. But NCIC has a rap on Grissom. A short one from L.A. Sheriff's Department. It's dated 1982. Grissom was eleven years old, held on suspicion of second degree murder and arson. Case Number 41 dash 7882. His mother's home. She died in the flames. Case unresolved, Grissom released to the custody of his uncle and aunt. Nothing after that. But it's our boy. You can see the burn scars in the police photo."

"Listen, I may have our caller. I found a yellow pages in the Dykstra dorm opened to the real estate section, several businesses checked off in red ink. Traced a call to a Covina Real Estate Agency, from one of the girls' cellulars."

"She left her cellular in the dorm?"

"It was either deliberately hidden or just tossed and she forgot about it. Kids do that."

"Or she was in a rush to get out of there."

"Yeah. Now the cabin is listed under the Thornquist

girl's name. Susan or Sue. She's the one who left the *'away on a family matter'* note with the front desk. That was several days ago, and she hasn't checked back into the dorm since. Her roommate, a Kurstin Mallon, is listed as in attendance, but she cut her Ancient History class today, which, according to her teacher, is a rare thing. Both girls are listed with the DMV. The Thornquist girl's parents are deceased. She lived with her in aunt in Arcadia before college. The Mallon girl lived with her aunt in Downey. I talked with her. She says Kurstin is at school as far as she knows."

"And the Thornquist girl?"

"Same thing. The aunt hasn't heard from her in weeks. And she's the only living relative Sue Thornquist has."

"Which takes care of *'a family matter.'*"

"Right. So which one of the roommates called you?"

Benson thought about it. "Kurstin Mallon. She phoned the real estate office because she didn't know the address of the Thornquist cabin. Smart kid."

"Which puts Sue Thornquist with Charlie. And hopefully, Jana Ransom."

"Hopefully. Call Scotty, Amanda. Get a SWAT team up there."

"Touch, listen. The cabin is way up in the San Gabriels off the old 2 Highway, clear past the Mount Wilson Observatory. They used to call it the Angeles Crest Highway. The cabin's somewhere between that and La Cienega, way the hell out in north bunnyfuck."

"And—?"

"I'm already to the Foothill Freeway, just a few miles from the 2, way ahead of any SWAT team."

"Mandy—"

"Touch, the only way that SWAT can beat me is with choppers, and the Mummy will hear those from five miles away out there in the quiet boonies. That's *if* choppers can even find a place to set down in that wilderness. But you know damn well the AC will give those arrogant pricks the chance to try, charge in like the fucking cavalry. Now the nearest sheriff's office is in La Canada-Flintridge, and even that is miles from the cabin. Anyway, I don't think we want a bunch of local deputies with squirrel rifles stomping around up there, right?"

"Fuck this, Mandy. It sounds too much like Ruby Ridge!"

"I'm trying to *prevent* a Ruby Ridge! And this is a serial nut, an abductor, not some barricaded citizen's-right yahoo defending family and creed."

"San Gabriel's way out of even RHD boundaries. I don't even know who the fuck boundaries those are."

"Touch, the Mallon girl calls you, right? Puts herself in deliberate jeopardy with the police. Then she doesn't call back, suddenly lights out for the mountains—so fast she forgets to take her cell phone. She must believe things are getting hairy up there. Do you really want me to turn around?"

Benson still didn't like it. His partner wouldn't be up there by herself now if he hadn't screwed up. But he had to concede her point.

"All right. But I'm leaving right now. Put your Motorola on the 206 freek and stay in contact with me. Got that?"

There was no reply. Some static.

"Amanda, do you copy?"

No answer. *"Amanda!"*

She was already in the mountains. Beyond reach.

36

It was harder work than he would have imagined.

The rain had helped some—the top layer of soil was soft mud—but the rain had come and gone quickly, the ground beneath the mud was hard and full of rocks. And he knew he had to dig deep, because Sue Thornquist was not small, not a petite girl.

Charlie broke three tree limbs trying to use them as shovels to dig a hole deep enough to bury her. And through all of it had to endure her incessant moaning from beneath the wood. Still alive. How could it be possible? It gave him the shakes, making him afraid of her all over again, as if she possessed some super-natural power after all.

He sat down on the damp earth beside the shallow grave and let the latest piece of stick fall from his hands. This was no good. This would take forever. And even after that he'd have to find a way to get her into the hole. What if she fought him again. What if the moans were more of her faking? She was an expert at faking, an artist. And why bother anyway? Nobody ever came up here. If someone eventually did, she'd be long dead.

But he knew some things about the police. He wasn't stupid. He knew about dental records and things like that. He had been with the Thornquist girl, at the apartment in L.A., and the Thornquist girl knew the pale one, the other phony one, Kurtzy. And the police had ways of tracing. He knew that much. Maybe not so good with the little details, but he knew that much.

He was so tired. He needed sleep. And there was still the pretty girl in the cabin to deal with. Another killing. And he was sick of them. Sick to death of them. Still, it had to be done. Somewhere in his logy mind he knew this was the safest way, had learned that covering his trail was the way to do it, had learned that from the Thornquist girl. You couldn't help making mistakes. But you could cover them.

He stood wearily, picked up the digging stick again.

He could go back in the cabin, kill the Ransom girl, get a few hours' sleep in the hard cabin bed, then come back and finish . . .

But the bed smelled of mildew and the cabin was a bad memory now, another thing he needed to put behind him. And he wanted it over with, all of it, now.

He thought about Sue Thornquist. He could knock out her teeth. That would take care of the dental records. He thought about it a weary moment.

No. They had other ways of detecting. Skull fragments. And if they found her before she decayed, fingerprints. And he didn't have the energy to cut off all the fingers, bury them separately, that would only mean more digging and he was sick to his soul with digging.

You need a real shovel.

I know that, he thought, *but I already looked in the cabin and there wasn't one.*

He trudged to the shallow hole, jammed the stick in, tossed out a few more handfuls of dirt. His back was a twitching nerve of pain. He already knew he couldn't possibly do this. Not in one day. He'd fall asleep on his feet doing this . . .

He groaned. Right out loud. No one to hear him way out here. Certainly not the gods, the Old Ones, the Ancient Ones. They were a lie. His whole life was a lie. He wished now he'd have died in the fire. That would have made all of it so much simpler. The fire would have erased everything . . .

He stopped digging, straightened with a wince.

He looked back at the cabin. The trees hid it but he knew it was there. And like the trees, it was made entirely of wood. And it would burn . . .

Relief swept through him like warm milk. The kind mother used to give him before bedtime.

All so simple. Why hadn't he thought of it before? Not good with details.

Oh, yeah? Maybe better than she thought.

He dropped the stupid stick. They could burn together, the dark girl and the pretty one. So simple.

Charlie staggered ahead, brassy shafts of sunlight lancing the trees now, chasing the chill from the ground in clouds of steam. It was going to be a nice day.

*   *   *

When Charlie opened his eyes he was on his back, looking into the sun.

And that hurt, so he had to look away, but only by moving his eyes . . . his neck was too weary to move his head.

Had he fainted? From hunger? Thirst?

He couldn't remember. Everything was hazy.

His swimming vision came to rest on a red-tailed hawk hunkered in the branches of a nearby oak. His exhausted mind merged the bird with the sun so that it became Re, sun god of Heliopolis, deity of the Fifth Dynasty, creator of men.

Charlie lay there peacefully a moment, resting contentedly from his heavy burden in the warm rays of the sun god. *Isn't this fine,* he thought. *Re has come to enfold me in his wings and carry me away to the underworld. My journey here on Earth must be over.*

But gradually the blood rushed back to his brain and he realized he was still on the earth, on his back in fact, and it was damp and even a little chilly and the hawk was only a hawk; he had collapsed from exhaustion trying to bury the dark girl and he had yet to set the cabin ablaze and drive away from here in her car. And the thought made him tired all over again.

He almost closed his eyes again and surrendered to sleep . . . but the ground was cold, and hard with rocks, and sleep was not the way, not yet.

He pushed to his knees, felt an eddy of vertigo, waited patiently for it to pass, then got to his unsteady legs.

He dragged the dark girl by one arm through the

cabin door and let her flop on the wood floor, receiv-
ing a single grunt. He had to go to his knees again to
get his breath and stop the spinning room.

How could he ever have thought her a goddess? He
must have been mad. Thoth, god of wisdom, must
have departed him, leaving the big-eared donkey-
faced Seth to laugh at him.

The pretty girl, still tied to her wooden chair—still
tied after all these hours—was slumped forward when
he looked, blond hair cascading forward over her
breasts, head so low her neck looked broken. Charlie
thought she was dead until he trudged over dizzily
and took a handful of golden tresses and lifted her
chin, at which point her eyes flew open and filled with
bright fear as she saw the dark girl draped on the
floor.

Still alive. It was too bad. He didn't relish the idea
of burning her alive, and he was just too tired to use
the sacred blade again . . . even if he could find it.

He did find it though, tripped over it, nearly falling,
regained his footing, and picked up the knife from the
wooden floor and stuck it in the back of his belt.

It was as if the world was rushing past him and he
couldn't hold on to it. If he kept still long enough it
would rush past completely and he would be alone in
an empty void, more empty than the burning desert
Horus had cast him into.

He stumbled a weaving path to the cardboard box
in the little kitchen area and found two chocolate
doughnuts left in their smaller box—one had a fly on
it—but Charlie made himself eat them both and made
himself drink some of the orange stuff in the plastic

jug the dark one hadn't had a chance to open yet. It was warm and too sweet but he sat down at the rickety old table and felt a little better in a few minutes.

Then he got up and walked to the mantel and got down the matchbox and stood there looking at it curiously for a time. He suddenly realized that even with the cardboard and wastepaper and twigs outside for kindling, he had no assurance the little cabin would catch and spread enough to burn down; it was still wet from last night's downpour.

He had to take the box of matches to the rickety table and sit down again and think about that for a while. Where was Thoth, the god of wisdom, now when he needed him? Then he remembered that Thoth and Seth and all the others were lies . . . fables someone had told him long ago that held no truth of fact and that his journey had been a false journey and the real one was still ahead of him and difficult and he'd better figure out something about the fire and get on with it.

It came to him in a flash, like a gift.

There was gasoline in the dark girl's car. And a copper tube on the old stove. Now all he had to do was find a bucket or container to hold the gas he would siphon from the car through the tube. The gas, then the tube, then the container. He had to sit a minute blinking and think about the correct order. Gas first, then tube . . .

He looked around and saw the plastic jug still on the table and he stared at it for a time knowing it was important before his mind put it together.

He took the plastic jug from the table, poured the rest of the awful orange stuff in the rusted sink, tore the copper tubing from the old stove, and trudged past the pretty girl to the door, not looking at her this time, vowing not to look in her eyes ever again until it was over.

When he tasted the gasoline in his mouth he gagged, then threw up most of the doughnuts and juice on the rear tire, hunched there on his hands and knees, hot forehead against the cool fender of the dark girl's car, wanting to die.

But it passed and he struggled up and lugged the jug into the house. Starting with the kitchen, he began splashing the gasoline over everything, across the table, the floor, and the dark girl, craning his head so the stinging fumes would not make him gag again.

When he came in front of the pretty girl he forgot his rule and looked into her eyes and the look made him hesitate with the jug before he threw the smelly liquid on her. The jug was heavy anyway, so he used the excuse to set it down for a moment and rest. There were tears in the girl's eyes. "I'm sorry for this," he told her, but she couldn't answer, of course, with the scarf in her mouth, only squeeze out more tears and make that piteous muffled sound.

Charlie watched her, the petrol smell inside the little cabin making him dizzy again, or maybe he was just dizzy again all by himself. "Why did she hate you so?" he asked the girl, trying to stop the room from spinning again.

She watched him, a thin line of mucus running from her nose into the scarf.

Abruptly aware that the dark girl was not here to yell at him—that in fact because of him soon she would never yell at anyone again—Charlie reached out and pulled down the scarf, and wiped the snot out of the pretty girl's face, which was pretty again now with her full mouth exposed. He brushed some of the golden, fine-spun strands from her eyes. "Why did she hate you so?"

The girl made a croaking sound and licked her lips, and when no moisture came, Charlie realized she must have said, *"Water,"* but the water was clear outside by the pump and he didn't have the strength to go out there and fetch her some.

He followed her eyes to the box on the table, which reeked of gasoline but still contained an unopened can of Coke, and he went and got that for her and stared at the top for a moment trying to remember how to open the aluminum tab; then he remembered and got it open and held the rim to her dry lips and she swallowed a little and coughed but seemed to want more so he gave it to her and was astounded that she drank the entire can even though it must have been warm and the can smelled of gasoline like everything else.

"Did you do something to her? Is that why she hated you so much?"

The girl swallowed and when she licked her lips this time they stayed moist. "I knew what she was," she choked out.

Charlie staggered back, dropping the can of Coke and nearly passing out again.

The Voice!

He stood watching her a long moment, legs vibrating, heart hitting his chest so hard it hurt, then trembling all over which at first frightened him, then made him angry so that he came charging before her again and stuck his face in hers and demanded, "Who *are* you?"

And the pretty girl with the golden hair lifted her lovely blue eyes and told him, "I am Nephthys, sister of Isis."

And Charlie howled.

Stumbled away again and threw back his head and howled so long and high with his remaining strength, the cabin's log and plaster walls rang with it.

37

Kurtzy almost didn't stop.

Charlie she wasn't as worried about. He might give her some initial resistance, depending on how much Sue Thornquist had poisoned his fragile mind, but he'd come around after Kurtzy soothed him like a child.

Sue was not, at heart, any more courageous than she was cunning. That she had managed to pull off this stunt at all—gotten this far with Charlie without mishap—was a miracle in itself. Engaging Charlie, maintaining and handling his volatile sensibilities, was like handing a child a pistol, then entrusting him with the ammunition box. She could see this now.

These were the images Kurtzy pondered as she drove past the dusty little gun shop just outside La Canada-Flintridge. She gave the little shop a cursory glance and continued on. Then slowed the Caprice thoughtfully, hesitated more thoughtfully at the second of the little town's two hanging stoplights.

In a moment, she turned the car around and drove back down the dusty western street. Charlie and Thornquist were a bad mix. And Kurtzy herself had already painted a potently antagonistic portrait of poor Jana Ransom for Charlie's squirming brain.

The owner of the gun shop was a sober, sly-looking man in his fifties. He sported a black, old west mustache and a no-nonsense demeanor. He looked used to dealing with underage kids trying to illegally purchase .22 pistols and deer rifles. His eyes, dark like his mustache, said *not much gets past me.*

But he was walking out the front door of the gun shop, headed for Walker's Café up the street—one of whose waitresses he'd painstakingly groomed the mustache for—as Kurtzy was walking in. He gave her a lingering look in the doorway, but didn't stop.

The freckled boy she faced in the owner's stead appraised her from behind the counter with inflated self-importance.

Fourteen going on twenty. Mostly he appraised her full, pink cotton blouse, the top two buttons of which Kurtzy had unfastened before leaving the car—something she wouldn't have dreamed of doing just weeks before.

She gave him her best smile, moving so the blouse jiggled. He was roadkill.

She leaned over the polished wood counter to enhance the view of her cleavage, let the fragrance of her shampoo enfold him a moment, then pointed past

a skinny shoulder at the armada of blue-steel and wal-
nut stocks behind him. "Is that a pistol or an automatic?" she asked with guileless, girlish naïveté.

The freckled boy laughed and shook his sandy head
with patient amusement.

"Shoot, lady," he told her breasts.

And they both laughed at that.

Charlie had to sit outside on the ground awhile
under the sun and think about it.

And not just because of the sickening fumes filling
the little cabin. Not because the ugly angry moans of
the dark girl had driven him out. Because his world
had shifted so many times off its unpredictable axis,
he no longer knew for sure which world he was in,
much less who he was. Or what his purpose was now.

He'd really given it all up, he really had. The gods
had proven themselves false, leading him to one un-
worthy bride after another. Then the one called Kurtz
came along and changed all that. And then the dark
one named Sue had changed it again, come up with a
plan to kidnap the pretty one, the one both girls hated
each for different reasons. And now the pretty one
tied to the chair was changing it all around again by
claiming to be Nephthys.

It was dizzying. He *wanted* to believe. To cling to
the old ways, his only stable anchor. But he was so
tired. And what he wanted most was to just clear it
all up once and for all and get on with whatever was
left of his life. He wished he hadn't thrown up the
doughnuts.

Maybe he should just drive away.

But what if the beautiful golden girl was telling the

truth? If she was, it vindicated everything. And *The Voice*! Her voice. It *was* the same voice. The one that had commanded him from the very first there in the little doctor's office, a voice so like his mother's that he was sure she had come to him again! How could that be merely coincidence?

He must have been directed here for a reason, a purpose.

And then he had it.

He pushed up suddenly and strode willfully back into the cabin and took up the jug and splashed gasoline in the girl's face. She cried out and he could tell some of it got in her eyes.

"You *lie*! You heard me talking with the other one, the dark one—*Sue*! You just overheard us talking and you're lying because you don't want to die!" And Charlie pulled the matches from his pocket and struck one.

The pretty girl shook her head. "I am Nephthys, sister of Isis." Her voice was steady and clear . . . and it *was* The Voice.

Charlie hesitated. "Prove it! Who am I?"

The pretty girl's eyes ran with stinging tears from the gasoline. Charlie whipped out the match, reached down, and wiped roughly at her eyes with the scarf about her neck. "Who am I?"

"You are Set, patron deity of Lower Egypt, brother of Osiris, and my rightful husband."

Charlie straightened up.

It was a trick. She was lying. They all lied. "You're lying."

"No."

Charlie walked back outside and sat in the sun. It

was sinking, he noticed absently. He would have to get going or he would be driving in the dark in an unfamiliar car.

But how could she know so much if she were lying?

There was a simple way, of course, to find out. Bind her in the sacred cloth, plunge the sacred blade into her breast. If she did not die, she was indeed his sister and wife, Nephthys reincarnate.

He came back inside the cabin. He began pacing before the pretty girl.

"Who is my son?"

The golden girl regarded him calmly. "Anubis, of course."

Charlie paced.

"Who did I murder?"

"Your brother."

Charlie paced.

"Who is my sworn enemy?"

"Your nephew, Horus."

"And what did he do?"

"You attempted to kill him. He survived, and grew up to avenge his father by establishing his rule over all Egypt, castrating you and casting you out into the burning desert for all time."

Charlie stopped pacing. "Go on."

"In the Nineteenth Dynasty there began a resurgence of respect for you. You were seen as a great god once again, a god of benevolence who restrained the forces of the desert and protected mother Egypt from foreigners. You have walked the Earth as many mortals, until now. You are Set, the mighty, and I am your one true bride, Nephthys."

Charlie held the match. "One last question then.

Where is The Temple?" He chuckled inside. Stupid was he? He knew he had her this time.

The pretty girl blinked. "The . . . what?"

Charlie chuckled aloud now. "The Sacred Temple. Here in America. In California. Where is it?"

The pretty girl's mouth opened. But nothing came out.

"False prophet," Charlie proclaimed and held out the match. "Death to all false prophets."

"Put out the match, Charlie. Now."

The voice caught him off guard so he nearly dropped the match. He jumped a little and the flame went out. Charlie turned to the door.

Kurtzy stood there in the handmade wooden frame, backlit with the setting sun. She held a shiny silver gun in her hand. It was pointed at him.

"Untie her, Set. Now. Obey your wife, Nephthys. Before she blows your fucking nuts off."

38

Amanda got lost a total of five times.

Finding the old 2 Highway was a snap and she recognized La Canada-Flintridge with no trouble because it was actually a town. Of sorts.

After that, though, it became a series of rural route numbers, some of which were actually marked, some of whose signs had fallen over in the chaparral and rock, and some of which no longer existed.

She was looking for Lonesome Pine Road, which supposedly led past the little cabin in the woods.

What she got were signs indicating a succession of San Gabriel Mountain recreation areas. Commodore Switzer Recreation Area; Vogel Flats Recreation Area; Valley Forge Recreation Area; a sign and road that led to Mt. Wilson Observatory; then Devore Recreation Area; Spruce Grove Recreation Area; Charlton-Chilao Recreation Area; Lower Chi-

lao Recreation Area; Upper Chilao Recreation
Area . . .

Someone was doing some serious recreationing.

But nowhere could she find Lonesome Pine Road.

She did however, on a dusty little cow path nearly
hidden by towering pines and massive slabs of rock,
find a little woodland grocery store where she stopped
off to get her bearings and take a desperately
needed pee.

When she came out of the single bathroom with the
dirty toilet and the photo of Miss January on the wall,
she bought a Clark bar from the proprietor, a wan
little man with pure white hair and mustache, and
spotless white apron. Amanda attacked the candy bar
greedily, having missed both lunch and breakfast, and
asked the little old man if he might have an area map.
The little old man was singularly intent on sweeping
up behind the counter, too intent to even look at her.

"Ain't no maps of this area, lady. This here's the
woods."

Amanda told the little man that she could see that,
and purchased a Coke to wash down the stale Clark
bar. The little old man was still sweeping, over by the
dry goods now.

"Got a map of San Bernardino here if that would
be of use. It ain't new, though."

"Thank you, no."

He finally looked up, gave her a resigned face, as if
he'd tried to unload the map before. "Up from L.A.,
are we?"

"How did you know?"

"Can tell. Lost, are we?"

"Something like that."

"Ever been to Disneyland?"

"Yes. Would you happen to know where a Lonesome Pine Road is around here?"

The little man looked her up and down once, turned to the store window—frowned, and wiped dirt from it with his apron—then looked beyond the pane at her car parked in the rock-strewn lot before the store. "That your vehicle?"

"Yes, it is."

"Well, it's sittin' on Lonesome Pine Road."

Amanda swallowed the last of her Coke. "I'm looking for a hunting lodge, a little log cabin really, off this road. Do you know of it?"

The little old man grunted, shook his head.

"What's the matter?"

"Lady, ain't been a soul up to that cabin in years. Now here you are the third woman who's asked after it this week. What's goin' on up there? A hens convention?"

It was dusk before she reached the "road" (two tire tracks) leading past the little cabin. She would never have seen that without the light dancing through the trees.

At first Amanda thought it was a bonfire, and its movement an illusion due to her moving car. Then she saw that the fire was moving independently, erratically, and—to her horror—had legs.

Amanda slammed on the brakes and leapt from the Accord.

The burning figure raced toward her downhill, arms

trailing yellow tendrils, its rapid movement only fanning the flames higher.

Now that she was out of the car, Amanda could detect the terrible screaming. Like no sound she'd ever heard before, amplified all the more hideously by the silent forest. The figure left a little trail of smaller flames behind it.

Twenty feet from her the fireball swerved left and headed blindly toward the trees. Amanda caught a glimpse of pink, open mouth engulfed in orange, a tuft of singed hair—

"Jana—?"

She chased the blazing thing into the trees, not even remembering to draw her gun. The figure ran headlong into a wide oak, bounced in a shower of sparks, and lay flopping and thrashing, kicking at the air like a cartoon.

Amanda ran up, breathless, thinking, *Roll her over the ground, smother the flames, fire needs oxygen,* but she couldn't get closer than five feet before the terrible heat drove her back.

The thing would not stop shrieking.

Amanda stood helplessly with the Glock. *Get a blanket! Throw dirt on it!*

But she had no blanket in the Accord, and the ground was hard and rocky.

Why doesn't it die? Amanda kept thinking. But it would not die, would not stop kicking and shrieking and the shrieking seemed to fill Amanda's world, drive everything else out until she was shrieking back, *"Stop it! Stop it!"* and Touch ran up beside her and said, *You stop it, Mandy. You have to stop it . . .*

Amanda pointed the Glock and pulled the trigger twice.

The blessed silence of the forest rushed back.

Amanda stood quietly, breathing hard, breathing burnt flesh, and she heard a funny *mewling* sound that she thought must be Touch . . . but Touch wasn't there when she looked and so the sound must have come from her. She started toward the black smoking thing, finally remembering to lower the gun. And the *mewling* came again, this time from up the mountain.

Amanda ran toward it, wiping tears from her eyes.

The cabin was a red glow in the dying light, encased in an amber pulse with a white-hot core. There was the occasional crash and hiss of fallen timber, a quick plume of sparks.

Billowing black smoke rose to blacker night sky. Amanda followed it with her eyes and could already see a million, million stars in the early evening heavens, the sight so breathtaking it was distracting. Not since she was a little girl . . .

The source of the *mewling* was curled against a leaning aspen, nearly as black as the first figure, but not, Amanda could see on close inspection, from burns but from smoke.

"Jana—?"

The girl looked up at her with vacant eyes. A newborn's eyes. She could see now that it wasn't Jana— only a plain blond who resembled her.

"You're okay now, Kurstin. You're not hurt. Where's Charlie? Is he in the cabin, with Sue Thornquist?"

The girl crawled into Amanda's arms, hacked a phlegmy cough.

Amanda held her a moment, but the girl pushed away, eyes bright with sudden awareness. "He's gone . . . He's *gone*! . . . He took her!"

Amanda stroked her hair. "Where? Where did he take her, Kurstin?"

The baby eyes looked up into hers pleadingly. "I tried to save her! I bought a gun!"

"Shhh, that's over now. Where did Charlie take Jana?"

"He took her! In the other girl's car!"

"Sue Thornquist?"

Kurstin nodded, choking.

39

Benson kept fiddling with the Motorola during the entire trip.

He ran from one end of the frequency dial to the other, thinking that—up here in the iron-ore-filled mountains—Amanda might have tried any number of frequencies to keep in touch with him. He got a lot of static for his trouble.

On a narrow mountain road, pushing the Mustang to sixty on an uphill grade, he thought he heard a faint something from the radio, just as the explosive blaring of a horn drowned it out.

He looked up—

—jinked the wheel hard, tires screaming, narrowly missing the dented front fender of a rusty-red antique pickup bearing down on him. The pale-faced driver yelled something at him in the *whooshing* darkness.

First vehicle he'd encountered in twenty minutes and he had to be screwing with the damn radio. But after he got the Mustang back in lane and straightened out again, he began screwing with it some more.

"—you copy *static* . . . is Detective Amanda Blai—*static*—ou copy?"

Benson yanked up the handset. "Amanda? It's Touch!"

"Thank God. Where the hell have you been?"

"It's the mountains. Filled with iron ore, they squelch the signal. Where are you?"

"At the cabin. I've got Kurstin Mallon. She's okay. Some bad burns, but she'll live. Sue Thornquist is dead. Where the hell are you?"

"Floundering along in the twilight. What burns? Did he torture her?"

"No. There was fire, the cabin."

"What about Grissom?"

"Kurstin says he got out with Jana. He must have taken the Thornquist girl's car, an old blue Ford Pinto. He had to take a back way out of here somehow, or I'd have seen him coming in. He's gotta be driving through the goddamn trees. There're no other roads. But he'll have to circle back. It's the only way to get to the 2 Highway."

"I'm just off the 2 now, some road called Millstone Cutoff."

"No, no! Get off that. It's the wrong way. I was there. Cut back to the 2. You're about twenty minutes from us. Charlie didn't leave here more than ten minutes ago. Get back on the 2 and you'll run right into him!"

Benson was already turning the Mustang around on the narrow mountain road, heart in his throat. *Don't look down . . .*

"Jana's okay?"

"She was alive when she left here. The cabin's history."

"Did Kurstin say where he was taking her?"

"Someplace he called The Temple, wherever the hell that is."

"Shit!"

"Just keep your eyes peeled and you'll run right into him. Blue Ford Pinto, around 1979. I tried to get the tags from DMV but you can't reach shit up here."

"All right, I'm on it."

Ten minutes later, Benson detected an orange glow on the southern horizon that looked like another sunset. The cabin.

His radio burped.

"Yeah?"

"Touch, it's Amanda. I'm at a little grocery down the mountain from the cabin. The owner, a little old man, has been shot. There's a blue Pinto parked out front."

"Goddamn it! Is the guy dead?"

"No, but I can't bring him around. He's got a real phone here. I got through to the DMV—the Pinto is Sue Thornquist's, all right. It's out of gas. I think Charlie took the old man's—the grocery owner's— vehicle."

"Have you got a make on the old man's car?"

"No, nothing. And I can't find the guy's wallet. I've got the L.A. DMV tracing it to this address, but without tags . . ."

"What about Parker Center, you get through?"

"Yeah, we've got five deputies from the Pasadena table converging on Michelle's house as we speak."

"Good girl. Do you want me to come in?"

"No, we're okay. Ambulance and fire-fighting equipment from La Canada-Flintridge are on their way. I found some stuff to put on Kurstin's burns. She's doing fine."

"What about you, you sound rattled."

"I'm . . . okay. Couple of police choppers are on the way. Kristin and I'll take one back to the city. I'll get a deputy to drive my car back down the mountain."

"Then I'm heading back to town. Charlie must have passed me and I missed him. Maybe I can catch up."

Amanda's tone shifted slightly. "Touch. Take it easy. Don't get yourself killed on those hairpin mountain turns in the dark."

"See you in the city." Benson replaced the handset. He turned, stepped hard on the gas.

40

Michelle had hardly responded when he told her the news about Jana. Not that he'd expected a response, really. What was she supposed to say: *Touch, you blew it again. A maniac is driving around L.A. with my daughter?*

He drove east on Sunset to La Brea, turned left and headed up to Hollywood Boulevard, turned right heading east toward the Mann Chinese Theatre, formerly Grauman's Chinese. Benson glanced out his side window as he always did when approaching the imposing structure; it just seemed to draw you in. Even at this late hour there were a couple of tourists out front putting their shoes in the stars' footprints. He'd done it once himself. Clark Gable's. Benson had been surprised to find his own shoe size bigger. People were smaller in those days.

He passed a patrol car going the other way. Out looking for Jana? Maybe, but the city was short on manpower of late. Probably just a couple of cops out of the Hollywood Division making their rounds.

His cellular vibrated. "Benson."

"Touch, it's Amanda. Kurstin's been thinking about some things Charlie said during the—well, here, I'll let her tell it—"

"Hello?"

"How you holding up?"

"Fine. Have you found Jana yet?"

"We're closing in, Kurstin. Have you got something for me?"

"I don't know. I was thinking about some of the stuff he said to me."

"Okay, shoot, anything, even if it doesn't sound important."

"We played this kind of game. He would call me *Nephthys* and he would say he was *Set*."

"Set? Like the Egyptian names?"

"Yes. Sue was in my Ancient History class, so was Jana, and so was Jason Richards. Does that help?"

"It might. Anything else?"

"Are they going to let Jason go?"

"Yes. Tell me about the game. Who was Nephthys?"

"The goddess of women. She was the sister of Isis."

"Go on."

"Anyway, when I got there I heard Jana pretending that she was Nephthys, and Charlie kept accusing her, you know, testing her, like he didn't quite believe she was really who she claimed to be."

"Nephthys."

"Right."

"Did he buy it? The act?"

"He started to. He kept asking her all these questions about Upper Egypt, the Nineteenth Dynasty, stuff like that. We're right in the middle of that stuff in Ivers's course, so she could ad lib pretty well—at least she answered all his questions. I think she really had him going there for a while before I came in. But he finally asked a question she couldn't answer. Even I couldn't have answered it."

"What question?"

"Something about a temple. Where is the temple, something like that. I didn't know which temple he meant. There are dozens of them in—Wait a second . . ."

"What? What is it, Kurstin?"

"I remember now. He said, 'Where is the temple in America?' That's what threw me. I didn't have a clue what he was talking about."

"But this temple, he didn't say where it was?"

"No. I'm sorry."

"Don't be sorry. You've been a big help. Anything else?"

"No . . . not that I can think of right now."

"Okay, would you put Detective Blaine on again, please?"

Benson heard the muffled sound of a receiver changing hands.

"Anything?"

"Mandy, what have we got here in L.A. that looks like a temple, possibly an Egyptian temple?"

A pause while she thought about it. "I don't know, right offhand. Want me to call the Center, see what we've got in the city files under 'Architecture?' "

No answer.

"Touch?"

Benson pressed the Mustang's brake, slowed.

"Touch?"

"Hold on a sec, Mandy."

He put the car in reverse, backed up twenty feet. He stopped parallel to a rusty-colored truck canted against the curb. It had a dented fender. Rust red. Red like a match.

He had a sudden vision of a red truck bearing down on him on a narrow mountain road . . . a quick glimpse of the pasty-faced driver behind the wheel . . .

"Touch?"

"Hold on."

Benson jumped from his car, hustled around to the rear of the truck, squinted under feeble street light at the vehicle's tags. The numbers were preceded by the letters: SG.

"San Gabriel."

Benson looked beyond the truck to the sidewalk. Just another series of Hollywood Boulevard street fronts. Then he saw the alley.

Only it wasn't an alley. It was a lengthy stone corridor, a new-looking walkway the color of sandstone, down the center of which rose a double line of towering palms. Benson hurried closer.

At the far end of a richly ornamented walkway, a colonnade of ancient-style columns and stone walls led the way to three new-looking ticket windows.

Grauman's Egyptian, the Deco letters announced near the movie temple's roof.

41

Benson walked up the stone corridor, drawing the automatic.

If not for the empty storefronts along the east side of the courtyard he might as well have been in ancient Egypt. The detail was incredible.

He remembered reading now of the theater's restoration, but he hadn't had time to come take a look for himself. He'd really missed something. Somebody'd knocked himself out, gotten it right. Maybe it was just the night, the soft entourage lights, but there was a solemn power about the place. It was, for all the world, like walking through a newly excavated Egyptian temple.

At the end of the forecourt—at least 150 feet, Benson gauged—he moved past a series of massive, four-foot-wide columns that towered into the night sky. Within the portico beyond were three ornamented ticket windows, now dark. Looming against the west wall, a twice-life-sized Egyptian figure of a dog-headed man guarded the doors to the lobby. A huge stone pharaoh's head watched Benson balefully from a ten-foot pillar as he tested the lobby doors. Locked.

But he knew Charlie was in there. And he wasn't alone.

Benson spoke quietly into his cellular. "Amanda, it's me. I've got our boy. Maybe Jana too."

"Jesus! How'd you find them?"

"Never mind, now. Listen carefully. I'm at the entrance to the Egyptian Theatre on Hollywood. The one they restored to look like a temple? The grocery store owner's truck is at the curb with San Gabriel plates. Charlie is inside the theater—I'm sure of it—but the place is locked tight."

"How'd he get in without setting off an alarm?"

"I think he must have gone in with the last show crowd, with a gun or knife in Jana's back. They sat through the feature and waited until the place cleared out, maybe hid in the rest rooms or whatever. Now here's what I want you to do—"

"Get a SWAT—"

"*No!* I'm not waiting for goddamn backup! This ass-hole has slipped by us how many times now? I'm taking him *now,* myself."

"Touch—"

"Shut up. I need you to stay by the phone. There's a Wallis Security sticker on one of the box office windows. Put in a prank break-in call at the theater. You're a security officer. You've got it under control, but you need them to cut off the alarms. Give me five minutes."

"You'll spook Charlie—"

"Maybe not if you get them to cut off after just a few seconds. There's no other way. Do it."

He didn't wait for her to protest again.

Benson shoved the cellular in his jacket, withdrew a penlight and stuck it in his mouth. He pulled his picks from his other pocket and went to work on the nearest lobby door. He slid the pick and pressure wrench into the lock, felt the pins give, and pushed open the door. The alarms rang immediately.

Benson shut the door quickly, stepped into the foyer shadow, gun drawn, and waited, breathing fast.

In twenty seconds the alarms went off again abruptly. *Good girl.*

Benson waited for the echo to die . . . listening for movement. There was none. He pushed out of the shadow, heading for the concession stand.

The lobby was surprisingly small, located between the street and the real wall of the auditorium. Even in the dark, Benson could make out the elaborate decorative ceiling paintings, all oriental or Egyptian motif. If it wasn't the original, it had been lovingly restored.

The auditorium itself was enormous, the kind of true golden-age movie palace that put a modern-day multiplex to shame. The first thing that caught his eye was the ceiling—a magnificent, low-relief sunburst design—exploding shards of brass and gold arrowing into midnight blue, spanning nearly wall to wall. Almost enough to make you believe the glory days were making a comeback.

Benson hesitated on the rich carpet, gun at port. Though deeply shadowed, the tiers of seats in the main auditorium were still faintly lit from translucent Deco fixtures on both walls. Safety lights. Walking down the center aisle toward the huge curving screen, he might be a dark silhouette, but he would still be exposed. Charlie could be hiding in the balcony or in any of the numerous boxes above. It would be like shooting fish in a barrel.

That was when he saw the movement on the stage below the screen.

On first glance, it had looked like part of the ornamentation. Now Benson could see that the pale, reedy nude with the upraised arms was alive. And that one of the upraised fists clutched a dagger. It was Charlie.

Waxen face thrown back, chin jutting toward the explosive sun design enveloping the ceiling high above, he might have been a pale statue, a god.

Benson's throat tightened. There was a second nude form at the killer's feet. Jana, supine and unmoving, golden hair cascading over the lip of the stage. Blood scalloped her breasts, her white ribs. *Too late.*

Benson felt an emotional constriction around his heart. It actually sent a lance of pain through his chest. No matter how inured you get to it, there's always something . . . something to remind you you're human. No matter what proceeded from here, he would, for the rest of his life, feel like a failure.

His brain felt bifurcated, caught in an emotional conflict between listing all the things he'd done wrong—should have done differently—and his duty now as a professional cop.

Benson pushed all the thoughts away, lifted the automatic, and sighted down carefully. Charlie Grissom's chest was open and exposed, a clean shot.

But a distant one. Benson thought about it, lowered his weapon, and came quietly down the carpeted aisle.

He never took his eyes off Charlie, who did not once move, not a muscle. Pale, naked, back arched, arms raised high, he looked like he was in trance. Praying to one of his ancient gods? Benson reached the halfway mark, and stopped again. Still not a slam-dunk shot with a handheld weapon. But he wasn't going to miss. He knew he wasn't going to miss.

Just before he spread his legs and braced again, Benson noticed something. The blade of the knife in Charlie's fist. It was clean. No blood.

He glanced down at Jana's sprawled figure again. And this time, from this range, he detected the shallow rise of her chest.

Gun leveled in both hands, eyes narrowed on Charlie's naked chest, Benson began walking slowly down the carpeted aisle again. Deliberate, measured steps. Soundless.

When he was within thirty feet of the stage—weapon still leveled—he spoke. As calmly, as evenly as he could.

"Charlie? That's it. It's all over. Put the knife down." Still walking, still aiming, not wavering, inching closer, target growing larger.

At first the killer made no movement. Maybe he really was in a trance. Maybe he was beyond hearing. Then Charlie lowered his head and looked directly into Benson's eyes.

"I've been praying."

Benson stayed in step, gun before him, unwavering. "Sure you have."

Charlie looked back at the ceiling, at the sunburst. "For an hour. I've been praying for guidance. But they don't hear me anymore. No one does."

Twenty feet.

"I hear you, Charlie. I'm here . . . and I hear you. Put down the knife."

Charlie lowered his hands now, looked down at the beautiful jeweled knife absently. "Do you believe in God?"

Benson kept coming. "Yes, Charlie. Yes, I do. And he wouldn't like this."

Charlie dropped to his knees, still clutching the knife, looked down at the pale form beneath him. Benson's finger tightened on the trigger, didn't squeeze.

"Which one?"

Fifteen feet.

"There's only one, Charlie. Put down the knife now and we'll talk about it. You don't want to hurt anyone. Not anymore."

Charlie tilted his head, so his next words might have been directed at Benson or the woman under him, or both. "Is your god a man or a woman?"

He looked up at Benson. The lambent theater lights erased many of the scars from the waxy face, made the man with the knife look like a child. "Is it a man or a woman?"

"I really don't know, Charlie. Do you think it matters much, in the end?"

Ten feet.

Charlie seemed to smile then, but it might have been the light. "No. No, I don't. I think we're all the same thing, really. Half man, half woman. In a way . . . in a way we're really just marrying ourselves, don't you think?"

A clear shot now. An easy shot. Even a rookie . . .

"Tell you what, Charlie. You drop that knife and I'll sit up there with you and tell you my whole personal take on the issue. How about it?"

Charlie looked up at him again. "Talk?"

"Sure. Just you and me. What do you say?"

Charlie nodded. "Okay. I'd like that. I don't talk with guys much. Mostly just women. I'd like that." He dropped the knife. "Are you going to shoot me?"

"No. Of course not. Why don't you back up, grab your clothes on the floor behind you there, and I'll come up."

Charlie looked back down at Jana. Her eyes were closed. But she was breathing.

He looked up at Benson again, eyes glistening. "The truth is, there is no one for me."

"Take it easy, Charlie."

"I've done bad things."

"You've been mixed up. We're going to get help for you. You don't have to be afraid. No one's going to hurt you."

"I couldn't stand prison. I spent my whole childhood in a prison. I couldn't stand that."

"No, not a prison, Charlie. Someplace where people will look after you, take care of you."

"A hospital?"

"If you want to call it that. All right if I climb up there now?"

"I didn't hurt her. She doesn't belong to me. She's alive, you see, and I'm already dead." He bent, scooped his arms beneath Jana's small back, and lifted. Halfway to his feet with her, the top of Charlie's head disappeared. Benson heard the distant shot an instant later, then a fine warm mist in his face. Charlie went over backward, Jana spilling forward over the lip. Benson caught her head before it hit the floor, the impact driving him to his back.

Lights began coming on . . . a predetermined, chronological order.

In a moment, the auditorium was bright as day. Benson heard shouting, the hurried tramp of feet. He swept hair from Jana's face, slapped her left cheek lightly. "Hey . . ."

He took off his coat as the running feet came closer, draped it over her. When he looked up again, her eyes were open. "Hi," he said.

Benson pushed the marksman with the scope and rifle aside and knelt beside the splayed, naked form.

Most of Charlie's cranial vault was missing, shards of bone stuck to what was left of his brain, yet amazingly his eyes were focused and blinking. There was surprisingly little blood. Charlie's mouth opened when he saw Benson.

Benson leaned close.

"Don't send me to prison."

"Take it easy, Charlie."

Charlie blinked. "Is my mother here?"

"She'll be here in a minute. Take it easy."

Charlie's eyes looked far away. " *'It is my son who causes my name to live upon this stela'* . . ."

Benson looked up as pant legs began to gather around, throwing things into shadow.

When he looked down again, Charlie was dead.

Benson came to the edge of the stage, searched the front row.

Jana was in one of the theater seats with a blanket

around her, Amanda beside her, arguing with a para-medic. "She doesn't *need* to go to the fucking emer-gency! She needs to go home to her mother!"

Amanda glanced up and saw Benson, said some-thing quickly to Jana, then came over and looked up. "Touch."

"She okay?"

"Yes, fine. It's just a scratch." Her eyes jerked to the stage beyond him, the crowd around Charlie. "Touch, I'm sorry. I instructed them not to fire. I'm going to report the sharpshooter—"

Benson shook his head wearily. "Forget it." He gave her a limp smile. "It wasn't Charlie you were worried about."

She gave him a limp smile back.

Benson rubbed absently at his arm. He'd bruised it in catching Jana. He tilted back his head and gazed up at the faraway, ornamented ceiling. With all the harsh lighting the sunburst lost most of its glory. The whole place looked much more like merely a movie theater. Not a temple at all.

42

Everybody who was anybody on the third floor was there at the Mummy task force meeting. Plus a few from down the hall who just wanted to look in.

Benson sat at his old desk again, ass-deep in backed-up paperwork, Amanda beside him. Everyone else on the force sat loose and relaxed behind their desks, some of them smiling at Benson, some just waiting for Captain Noland to come into the suite. Everybody knew he would, and everybody was waiting with their congratulations before he did.

Noland finally came in, carrying a sheath of papers like it was just another workday, trying to act like it was business as usual and the busy Robbery-Homicide Division hadn't time to sit around and rest on their laurels; there were still plenty of unsolved cases out there, still plenty of nuts to track down. And always the mountain of paperwork.

Noland stopped in front of Steve Ditko's desk and

cleared his throat and waited for everyone to look at
him before he realized that everyone already was.

"Okay. First off, I want to thank all of you for an
exemplary job on a very tough case. I can't think of
a time in my tenure with the department when we've
gone after higher stakes with fewer leads. You are all
to be commended for that.

"Before we get further into that, I want to take
a moment to welcome Detective Benson back into
the—"

And before he could even finish, the applause hit
like a crack of spring thunder. All the members of
the task force—except for Benson—were on their feet,
pounding their hands together, some whistling, some
cheering. Benson looked up once and smiled, then
went back to his paperwork. Amanda, also standing,
punched him hard in the arm, and Benson finally
threw his pencil down and sat back in his chair and
basked in the applause for a moment.

Noland held up his hand after a few moments to
quiet the room but no one looked at him, much less
stopped applauding. He put his hand up three more
times before the clapping finally trailed off.

"All right. I think we're all justifiably proud of Detective Benson's contribution to this effort and the
kind of opposition he's faced getting it done."

Amanda beamed down at her partner. She was
radiant.

"Some of that opposition came from my camp,"
Noland concluded.

Benson jerked up. He hadn't expected that one. No
one had.

He looked over at Noland, who cleared his throat

and began pacing immediately, all business again. *Son of a bitch,* Benson thought, amazed.

"Detective Ditko has some follow-up material on the Mummy Killer, I believe. Steve?"

Ditko referred to a printout on his desk. "I've collated a psychological profile from both the Parker Center Division and a team of doctors at USC. What we have here is basically a corrupted childhood. Charles Grissom was reared in a childhood environment almost entirely insular. No siblings, no father, and a mother who—though we have little profile information on her—was apparently extremely delusional, if not borderline psychotic. We know she sexually abused her son from an early age. We know he attended William Stout grade school in Glendale, but only sporadically after the third grade. The rest of the time he was either at home alone with only the TV for company, or with his mother in the evenings, usually at the local drive-in, usually watching horror movies. His mother, Theodora Grissom, worked days at the Natural History Museum in L.A. She was a curator in the west wing, the Ancient Egypt collection. We've traced the knife the Mummy had on him at the theater on Hollywood to the museum. There were originally two on display there, one iron, one gold. Charlie's mother swiped the gold one. It's at least three thousand years old, believed to be used in the burial ceremonies of the kings. The only other known knife of its kind is from the Tutankhamen collection in Chicago. Talk about a weapon with a blade ratio impossible to trace. SID almost went nuts over this one. Peterson has some more on Charlie's profile."

Peterson shuffled papers at his desk. "Well, not a

lot more. As Dick said, this kid led a loner's life. What seems to be absent in his background is the early brutalizing or killing of small animals usually associated with signature cases. In several respects, Charlie broke the rule. Without a patient alive to turn over to the profilers, we may never know exactly which slot he fit into. There's no question that he was a serial killer. What we're not sure of—and may never know—is exactly what kind. We do know that, from very early on, he began to confuse reality with the movies he was subjected to on the TV and at the small town's single indoor theater. By the way, anybody care to make a guess at what that little theater down the block from his house in Glendale was named?"

Nobody said anything.

"The Temple," Benson offered.

Everybody turned to him.

Peterson grunted. "You dig that up, Touch?"

"Just a guess."

Peterson nodded, went back to his papers. "Good guess. Anyway, the little theater was practically a second home to Charlie from what we can glean. He attended every Saturday matinee horror show from the age of six to the age of eleven. It was on his eleventh birthday that the fire occurred. But get this. The Sheriff's Department was never entirely satisfied with their conclusions as to who actually started the fire that burned down the Grissom home. We do know that only Charlie and his mother were in the house at the time, but there's no proof Charlie started the fire; it could have been the mother.

"In any case, Charlie went to live with his relatives in the Midwest after that. And shortly after that he disappeared for a number of years. Nobody knows where—the aunt and uncle are dead—and no one knows why he ended up back in L.A. We don't even know if there were other killings before the Silverlake girl, and we probably never will. Charlie's the one who could have told us, and Charlie is no more. That's about all I've got."

There was a general murmer of conversation in the suite, mostly between partners, and Noland had to stand up and raise his hand again.

"Okay, people! You can have your wives and husbands congratulate you in bed tonight on your brilliance. Right now, let's turn to other business . . ."

"Benson."

"Touch, it's Sid Mathers, your favorite ME."

"Yeah, what's up?"

"Are you at your desk at the homicide table?"

"Yeah, why?"

"Is your partner there?"

Benson glanced over at Amanda, who was filling out paperwork, munching a glazed doughnut. "Yeah, right here."

There was a pause on the other end of the line. "Listen, Touch . . . I'm standing here in front of Sue Thornquist's remains, just started the preliminary cut. I . . . uh . . . I've shut off the overhead mike."

"What's up, Sid?"

At mention of the ME's first name, Amanda looked up at Benson from her desk.

"I've, uh . . . I've got two .38-caliber entrance wounds in the victim's chest. Hard to see on initial inspection—she's pretty black, pretty crisp. But, the thing is, well, so far it's looking like the slugs killed her before the fire did, if you get my drift."

"Yeah. Yeah, I get it." Benson turned his back toward Amanda, began doodling on his scratch pad. "So what do you think?"

Mathers cleared his throat on the other end. "Well, I mean, did Amanda report this to you or . . . anyone?"

Benson could feel his partner's eyes on his back. "No . . . not at this time."

"I see."

Benson cleared his throat. "So . . ."

"She's right next to you, right? You can't talk?"

"Yes, that would be correct."

"Right. So, like I said, I haven't actually cut down to the slugs yet, don't even know if they are from a Glock. Haven't put anything in my report yet, is what I'm saying."

"Yes, I understand, uh-huh."

"So the thing is, *technically* speaking, there would be an inquiry of some kind if this *were* to go on my report."

"I understand. My question is, how necessary is that? In relation to the case itself, I mean."

"Well, if you're asking if the victim would have died from the burns anyway, then the answer is an unqualified yes. The slugs just spared her the pain."

"Which would have been considerable."

"Yes. Absolutely. I'd testify to that of course, but . . . well, you know how these things can go . . . from a strictly legal standpoint and all . . . it could get messy, go on her—on the shooter's record— possibly . . ."

"Yes," Benson told the mouthpiece, "I understand."

"Did I ever tell you, couple of years ago, my assistant here, cutting into a stiff—a hooker, I think—my assistant here, he actually—get this—he actually *lost* the goddamn slugs. Misplaced them or something. Can you imagine that? Pretty sloppy work, huh?"

"Yeah, pretty bad, I guess."

"Those things happen, of course. We're all human. I never did report it. Never told anyone. Not until now. If you follow me."

"Yeah. Yeah, I do."

"Right. So I guess that's about it, Touch."

"Right. Sounds good to me."

"Fine. See you then."

Benson hung up, went back to his paperwork.

"Was that the ME?" Amanda asked cautiously.

Benson shuffled papers, not looking up. "Yeah. That boy they found last week in Inglewood, the drive-by. It looks like a Saturday Night Special, all right."

"I thought we already knew that," Amanda told his profile.

Benson nodded. "Yeah." He shook his head. "That Mathers. Needs a vacation. Getting forgetful . . ."

43

Before her Grand Slam order came at the Denny's on Western, Amanda excused herself and stood. "I'm going to the ladies' room so you can call her."

Benson, waiting for poached eggs and toast, grabbed at her and missed. "Hey! Who says I'm—I didn't say anything about calling *anyone*!"

Amanda waved at the air without looking back.

When she was out of sight, Benson sat brooding a moment. Finally said, "Screw it," plucked out his cellular, and dialed quickly.

"Hello?"

"Michelle?"

"No, this is Jana."

"Oh, hi, sweetie. It's Touch Benson. You sound so much like your mom. How are you?"

"I'm good."

"That's good. That's great. How's Jason?"

"Jason? Oh, I don't know, really. Haven't seen him

for a while. We broke up. I think he's started dating someone else. Kurstin Mallon, I heard."

"Kurstin? Really?"

"Yeah."

"Ah. Well. I'm sorry."

"No big deal. I'm seeing a great guy now. I'll bet you want to talk to Mom. *Mommmmmmm!*"

Benson winced at the receiver.

"Hello, Touch."

"Hi. Just called to see how you're feeling."

"I'm fine. Fine. You?"

"Me, I'm fine."

"Good."

Benson cleared his throat. "I just . . . I don't know. I was just sitting here thinking about you. Thinking, you know, if I hadn't—"

"Touch, please! Shall I recite the catalog of mistakes that *I've* made when you're through? I think it's a little late for regrets, don't you? I'm just glad to be alive, to have Jana back. It's all I think about right now. I don't have time for lies and regrets. I just want to spend time with my little girl right now, you know?"

"Of course."

"And to thank you. For everything."

Benson didn't know what to say.

"And to tell you that . . . that I hope—in a while, after a while—you'll call me sometime. I'd like to be friends again. Best friends. What do you think?"

Benson looked up. Amanda was coming out of the ladies' room.

"I think yes. Listen, I have to run. You know what it's like."

"I know."

"Just wanted to check in."

"Thank you. Bless you."

" 'Bye . . . Hey! Who's the fastest runner you know?"

He could feel her smile through the receiver.

"Michelle Ransom."

"Bet your bippy," he told her.

Amanda slid back into the booth just as their orders came.

She picked up her fork and attacked the runny eggs voraciously. "Mmm. This is great. I missed breakfast again. *Yummy!*" She paused to sip coffee. "So how is she?"

Benson, startled, started to ask, *Who—?*

Sighed instead. Shook his head, let it go. Plunged into his own poached cup.

Amanda watched him, chewing. Smiling her wry smile.

Benson finally looked up. "*What?* What are you *looking* at!"

She nodded, still grinning, pointed with her fork. "Egg on your face . . ."

ONYX

BORIS STARLING
Messiah

"The killer's good...The best I've ever seen."

The first victim was found hanging from a rope. The second, beaten to death in
a pool of blood. The third, decapitated. Their backgrounds were as strikingly
different as the methods of their murders. But one chilling detail links all three
crimes. The local police had enough evidence to believe they were witnessing
a rare—and disturbing—

phenomenon: the making of a serial killer...

"He'll kill again."

Investigator Red Metcalfe has made national headlines with his uncanny gift
for tracking killers. Getting inside their heads. Feeling what they feel. He's
interviewed the most notorious serial killers in the world. He knows what
makes them tick. *But not this time.*

"Pray."

❑ 0-451-40900-0 / $6.99

Also Available:

STORM   ❑ 0-451-20190-6/$6.99